The Faces
of
Inanna

Robert G. Makin

Printed version ISBN: 978-0-9887553-9-0

This is a work of fiction. Any resemblance between contemporary characters herein and actual persons is purely coincidental.

The information contained in this book is intended to inspire, educate and affirm. The author and publisher shall have neither liability nor responsibility to any person or entity with respect to any loss or damage caused or alleged to be caused, directly or indirectly by information contained in this book.

Layout and interior design by Jonni Anderson:
        jonnianderson.com, starwatchcreations.com

Cover art by Briana Serna. brianaserna.blogspot.com

Sons of Aaron Publishing

Palm Coast, Florida

Acknowledgments

The people who made it possible for me to write *The Faces of Inanna* are the ones who most impacted my thinking and my attitudes at that time. Kathy Landers' encouragement stands out in the attitude department. Lectures by Illustrious Eugene Sayers, 33°, of the Valley of Jacksonville provided me with jaw-dropping revelations that fueled and excited my imagination. In me, he found an ear that hears. I had recently read Zecharia Sitchin's extremely well-documented Earth Chronicles that filled in historic blank spots I had been trying to fill for decades. It was Sitchin's perspectives that gave me the character of Inanna.

A special thank you to Jonni Anderson for her help in book design, formatting and cover graphics.

This section would not be complete without mentioning Good Ole Hazel who broadsided my car at a stop light and took me out of work for a month, giving me the time I actually needed to write this book. She was a friend, all things considered, however unwanted and unlooked for. If she had been looking, Faces of Inanna might never have been written.

This book is dedicated to Joyce

Contents

The Faces
of
Inanna

Robert G. Makin

Foreward

Inspiration for this book was drawn from many sources. The most important of those is the Essene Community as described by Flavius Josephus in his History of Israel, Modern Freemasonry and Zecharia Sitchin's works, The Earth Chronicles.

It is my belief that the rituals and teachings of Freemasonry have passed through many conduits over the millennia and that Essenism was one of the pieces of that conduit. The knowledge of the beginnings of Freemasonry have long since gone out of the memories of men. Its earliest clear message or shout of "hello" to the modern Fraternity came with the moving of Cleopatra's Needle in 1877 funded by Sir William James Erasmus Wilson. The Obelisk had been buried in the sands of Egypt for 2,000 years. (That's 22 B.C.) When the Obelisk was unearthed, beneath it they found the classic, symbolic tools of a Master Mason. These were not functional tools, but tools fashioned in stone as though they were ornamental or symbolic of the real tools. This was reported in the newsletter of the Grand Lodge of Israel in the 1980s. A copy of the newsletter was handed to me by Illustrious Max Kaplan 33°, who was then the Grand Liaison of the Grand Lodge of Florida to the Grand Lodge of Israel. This shout of "hello" also shouts of a fully formed, operational fraternity existing at that time. Coupled with Sitchin's descriptions of ceremonies very similar to modern ceremonies of Freemasonry in ancient Egypt and Sumer, thousands of years earlier, it hints of Masonic origins that are mind-blowingly ancient.

Sitchin speaks of "Watchers." The Essenes were known as "Watchers." Free Masons today, if they do nothing else, certainly watch. In Faces of Inanna, I only hint that the modern day Essene Fraternity is Freemasonry. The rituals described smack of Freemasonry but are not truly so. If such a fraternity, associated with Freemasonry, exists today, I am not aware of it.

Sitchin goes on to speak of the gods of Sumer being real, very long-lived, flesh and blood beings. I won't go into Sitchin's rationale in this space, except to say that his rendering of the Cuneiform scripts of Sumer claimed the gods aged one year for every 3,600 Earth years. If that's true, then Inanna is still very young and possibly still among us, with much of her family. Her domain was called Aratta and there, it is said, she lived on the twin peaked Mount Mashu.

I like to write fiction that could be true. This story of Inanna and the modern day Fraternity could be true. As an afterthought to that, here are two spooky anecdotes.

The day I put the last period on the last sentence on the last page of Faces of Inanna, I took myself downtown for a celebratory lunch. I had a neighbor at that time, a beautiful young woman who turned my head hard enough to give me neck cramps when I saw her. She used to walk past my place on the way to the beach from time to time. We would wave at each other. That was the extent of our friendship. When I reached the restaurant, there she was. She was alone and I was alone so we joined each for lunch. There, I learned her name was Ester. I later realized that Ester is a derivative of Ishtar, a name later used for Inanna. It was a wonderful lunch with a sweet lady. Strangely, I never saw Ester again. I mused that Inanna came and had lunch with me to celebrate the completion of the book. She was certainly beautiful enough that if she had told me she was Inanna, I might have believed her.

Sometime later, I did an exhaustive edit of the manuscript to prepare it for publication as an eBook. When I finished the work, I headed out in my car on some errand and got behind another car with a license plate that read "INANNA." Is that spooky or not?

RGM 2013

Chapter 1: Belili

Date: Autumn, 62,800 years (18 Sars)
before the beginning of the Christian era
The Mountains of the Sinai Peninsula

The god Enlil watched Belili approaching the sanctuary of his garden in the form of a large bird. He waited in comfort, snuggled on a reclining chair under the shade of a large awning. A light breeze was stirring the trees and foliage nearby. It saddened him that the changing climate would make this area a barren desert in only another SAR or two. It saddened him too that his time in this place would soon be over. Eduru, *meaning "home in the faraway"* had been a place of joy for him. There were many wonderful memories he would be taking home with him but it was his memories of Belili that came to him now.

Her innovative teaching methods for their young earned her recognition as far away as Nibiru. She performed as guardian of the most unlikely creatures, Humbaba the Bull among them. He smiled at the reports he received of her training of this most remarkable creature whose job was to protect the giant Cedars. A most beautiful woman, *when she chooses to be* - he smiled at that thought. His respect and almost suspenseful trust in Belili resulted from the impossible tasks she completed with success. She had never failed him. He assigned her projects no one could be expected to carry out, fully expecting failure, but that is one thing he never received from Belili; not Belili.

The bird glided close enough now for him to distinguish the shape of a large Owl. He admired the graceful beauty of its flight, its wings turned up slightly at the tips feeling their path through the sky. They manipulated the air gently, as would highly sensitive fingers exhibiting great skill on a musical instrument. As it drew very close, it spun slightly to slow its flight then dropped gently onto the stone wall bordering Enlil's personal gardens. From the wall, it hopped back into the air and glided gracefully to his feet.

Enlil waited while the great owl swelled in size. Its form drifted before his eyes into the image of a beautiful, ageless woman. She was wearing black lace, complete with a shawl and vale. Her long, black hair hung over her shoulders and down her back. Enlil always had difficulty distinguishing between where her luxurious hair ended and the lace of her gown began. It was an optical illusion that she deliberately presented to him then laughed at him, as she was doing now, while he tried to focus his eyes on her image.

"Belili," he said, his pleasure at seeing her again, obvious in his voice. "Thank you for coming. Won't you have a seat, a glass of wine perhaps?"

"The Great god Enlil honors me too much," she replied, her full, blue eyes dancing with delight. "I heard your thoughts calling me. I am here."

Seated together in Enlil's enormous garden, sipping sweet wine, Enlil began:

"As you know my time in this place is nearing its end. Today I looked into the past and I saw that we have done much, but those we leave here have yet as much to do as those who came before them. I have looked into the future. In that interest, we have begun a Brotherhood of men to be Netzorim, *meaning "Watchers."* They will watch over our work and see that our plans for the growth of the mind and spirit of humans are fulfilled." Enlil placed his glass on a stand beside him and smiled at Belili.

"Will any of us remain?" she asked.

"Eventually, all of our kind will return home," he said. "I have a favor to ask of you."

"Ask and it shall be done, if I am able," replied Belili.

"At this time, there is a stone being carved to be a throne for Inanna, the newly born daughter of Nanna and Ningal. I have taken a piece of it and formed it into a MU. I want you to take this amulet and hold it for me. One day, a human will come into being. He will affiliate with this organization of men we have formed, The Watchers, and in time he will have need of it. When this day comes, I will show him to you. He will fly to the western underworld to meet you. Give him the amulet and when he has no longer need of it, return it to the throne of Inanna. Will you do this for me?"

"I am honored that you would place this trust in me, my Lord. I will certainly do it."

"The wait will be long," Enlil continued. "His time will not come to us for almost eighteen SARS; more than 60,000 revolutions of this planet. Then I will show him to you..." In that time, I think you will be as glad for his help as he will be glad for yours.

α β

Modern Day

The flight out of Miami ended at San Juan Puerto Rico where Johnny changed planes. The next flight ended at Caracas in Venezuela. The continuous racket between Puerto Rico and Venezuela prevented his catching any sleep in route. People chattered loudly. Children played in the aisles, as they might in a mountain bus running between villages. The airplane rattled, keeping Johnny on edge.

He tried to doze but his mind kept returning to the enigma, his puzzle, annoying, nagging. In some ancient past life initiation he had supposedly been dubbed Hjet, the eighth Hebrew letter, meaning 'a fence.' He was supposed to remember - from the past life no less - what that meant. *I'm not sure I even believe in reincarnation. The things I saw in the initiations were amazing. I must have been hallucinating. People don't vanish. Well, I didn't believe in auras either, till I started seeing them myself.* But the fraternity was real. The initiations were in fact astonishing *and I did have some amazing mental images coming through. Could it be past life remembrances or just superstitious crap implanted in my mind by suggestion?*

Nevertheless, here he was high in the sky, south bound and for where, he really didn't know. "You must go to Arrata," he was told. "It's such a secret mission that not even you can be told about it. You'll find out what you have to do in time. We don't even know. You will know when it's time."

The Agudoss, much like its ancient ancestor, was a huge, ultrasecret fraternity composed in the present day of nearly three million members, world wide, but as in the past, divided into manageable enclaves of twentytwo. Each of the twenty-two members represented a single letter of the Hebrew Aleph-Bet and subsequently the mystical significance of that letter. Dr. Prill, Johnny's teacher, had been Zayin or Seven, in his particular enclave. "Zayin" means "a weapon," and in the high mysticism, it represents the weapon, that protects the innermost spiritual secrets from the profane. Prill's task was to protect the secret hiding place of the "Temple Treasures," until the time comes for them to be found. It was evidently such an important task, that Prill had to reincarnate to fulfill his ongoing obligation. Johnny, according to the modern day brethren, was a member of the same Aleph-Bet or enclave as Prill, in those ancient times. Prill was known then as Harai, and Johnny in this past life, represented the letter Hjet or Eight.

As the story goes, when Hjet appeared before Adonai to receive his name and duties he was told Hjet means 'a fence.' It is the fence standing between good and evil, dividing man's higher qualities from his lesser qualities, standing as the eternal and mystical Neshemah. Hjet is the allegorical Shekinah, the result of the balanced positive and negative energies of Chocma and Binah.

It boggles the mind, thought Johnny.

"The ancients believed man to have three souls," he was told. "They are the divine breath or spark, the animal soul which animates the body and gives it its drives, and the personality, ever caught between the animal tendency toward chaos and the divinely imparted knowledge of good and evil. You, Hjet, are the fence," the Aleph told Johnny, "which stands in the center, barring the evil from contaminating the good and equally barring the ever divine from preventing the animal acts necessary for survival. It is the responsibility of Hjet to maintain man's balance between the flesh which he is and the divine which he will become."

Every time Johnny reviewed the words in his mind, they made him feel intellectually dizzy. *What mumbo-jumbo,* he would think to himself, then the memory of his witnessing an actual ascension would shake him out of his doubts. What he had seen was an initiation in itself, life changing, an awakening, *but to what?* Johnny demanded of himself. *I'm supposed to remember some important task I promised to do two millennia ago when I can't even remember what I had for breakfast yesterday. Oh yeah. It was grapefruit.*

When he told his new fraternity brothers that his initiation had not reminded him of his destined, or past life obligation, there was a soft murmuring resulting in his being shunted off to a monastery in southern New Mexico where he was trained, "re-training," they called it. In time he had been set up teaching other new initiates some of the minor spiritual skills; how to see and manipulate aural energy, healing, how to control one's own aura using visualization exercises like making the form of an Ankh out of one's own aural energy.

Finally, after several years he was summoned to a special interview to be conducted at a convention that meets every ten years in the high desert near Antonitos Colorado. This was the Enclave of the Alephs, a sort of international organization of the fraternity's leaders. At this private session, he was directed to travel to Arrata and await further instructions.

"Where is Arrata?" asked Johnny.

"We aren't exactly sure," replied Rupert DeLaney, the delegate, a chubby, red-faced man with large, kind eyes. His frustration with the matter was evident in his fidgeting and evasive manner. "This direction came from the top. All we know is that it's in a remote area of the South Pacific, somewhere not too far, three hundred miles or so from Easter Island, we think."

"You think that's where it is? What's there? What's at Arrata? I've never heard of the place."

"Neither have I," replied DeLaney. "Knowledge of it has been kept from us by the First Aleph and the First Enclave. It's apparently a project, that has been going on for quite some time, but we are instructed to not question. It has been given to us that having too much knowledge of the First Enclave's agenda, in this matter, would be self defeating."

"So," said Johnny. "I am to be sent to a place, no one knows the exact location of, to complete a task of which no one knows the exact nature. Am I getting this right?"

The delegate smiled at Johnny's frustrated humor, straightened his shirt and said, "That's about the size of it. We are guided to tell you to keep in mind that you are Hjet, the number Eight of a very ancient and respected Enclave. Yours is one of the hardest of the tasks accepted by your Enclave. It may take you longer to complete yours than the others have taken, but you will be watched over. You cannot be guided, but it is the opinion of the First Aleph who resides on the next level of existence, that your own nature will be a good enough guide."

"Wait a minute," said Johnny, incredulously. "Are you telling me that these instructions came to you from some other dimension? What do you mean by the next level of existence? Isn't that a bit unusual?"

"Generally speaking, the First Enclave rarely interferes or offers specific guidance in this way. We, the other Alephs and I, find this very unusual. Yes. Will you go?"

"When will I be able to come back?"

"We don't know."

"Will I be able to come back?"

"We don't know."

CB   BD

Johnny was tired, a stranger in a strange land at 35,000 feet, where no one spoke any language he knew. Why couldn't I have studied Spanish? He kept asking himself. I can't even order a cup of coffee.

Just then a pretty flight attendant with long black hair, laughing dark eyes and a very well fitting uniform stopped next to his seat and asked, "¿quiere usted un poco café?" She had a coffeepot in her hand and was pulling a cart with cups on it. As she asked the question she lifted the coffeepot and raised her eyebrows in a questioning expression. The smile never faltered.

"Uh. Yeah. Thanks," said Johnny. Surprised by the blank look on her face he realized she didn't understand his words any better than he did hers. He nodded his head 'yes' emphatically and she poured a cup for him. What a cup it was, too, not much bigger than a jigger glass and with enough caffeine that he could feel the first sip hit the tips of his fingers and toes. *I wonder if her name is Mashu? They said Arrata has twin peeks,* he thought, chuckling. To his delight the flight attendant smiled at him again, with him, then winked as she pushed her cart to the next passenger. Then his attitude turned more serious. *They told me to leave all personal identification behind, that I would be known only as DeMuzzi. Why is that necessary - for meditation and study? What have they got up their sleeves? Why such a remote spot. Unbelievable! It's not on any of the maps. I checked. And they told me not to tell anyone where I was going - only to say I was going to Easter Island.*

He had taken the vow of obedience. Ha Agudoss (The Fraternity) was paying his passage. He loved traveling and had never been to Easter Island or the South Pacific. He was not complaining, just mystified and apprehensive.

The flight from Caracas to Lima Peru was worse. There was no coffee. It was a red eye flight but Johnny still couldn't sleep. The noise of people chattering, children playing and crying, kept him awake and even a bit fearful. At one point, he thought he even heard a chicken clucking. *Somebody has a chicken on the airplane?* By the time he arrived in Santiago Chile he had been in the air and in airports for more than thirty- six hours. Tarek was supposed to meet his arriving flight in Santiago. Good old Tarek wasn't there so he collected his luggage, what there was of it, one suit case, and wandered off till he found an airport shop bearing a sign which said in large flashing letters, "Restaurante." *Well. That wasn't hard. They just spelled it a little differently.*

El Restaurante was a surprise to him. Unlike the airport coffee shops he had been in elsewhere, this one had saw dust on the floor, no seats at the bar and a Cucaracha band playing a lively knee-slapper in one corner. His image in the mirror behind the bar startled him too. His dark hair and reddish beard were mussed. His beard looked as though he had fallen asleep sometime during the last flight; it was all mushed over to one side like he'd been sleeping on it. He tried not to notice that some of the red in his beard had turned gray sometime in the last seven years, since his initiation into Ha Agudoss. He smiled to himself. *Who would ever have thought I'd get so caught up in this? Is it a cult? It certainly is. It certainly is, but what an important one!*

ଓ ଚ

In one corner of the dining room, two Watchers waited for Johnny to come back from the restroom. They were not men nor women but androgynous, ascended, light beings, members of the Great White Brotherhood, who those of Ha Agudoss referred to as the Council of the Twenty-Four Elders, the First Enclave.

"I still think it's wrong to use him in this way," said the one called Chaim.

"He volunteered," said the other.

"Yes he volunteered, but that was a very long time ago and this personality knows nothing of the agreement," said Chaim.

"Still. He volunteered. He knew what he was getting himself into."

"He has no idea what he's getting himself into."

"He does on a higher level."

"A level he can't relate to in his present physical form. We're using him, as these physical beings call it today, as "canon fodder.""

"We agreed, Chaim, that if things got too bad he could come home. We also arranged for him to have the amulet. That's much farther than we have ever gone before to protect an agent. He'll be safe enough."

"Does he know of the agreement? No. Is anyone going to tell him? No. We dare not convey the information to anyone on his level of existence. Look at Belili waiting for him. It's his first pit fall. Not even she knows what's really happening. Does she have the amulet?"

"Enlil saw him coming, thanks to us. He thought he knew the threat Hjet represents, and the promise. Belili is here to use him, to protect Enlil's plan, but not even Belili knows all the twists and turns in this plot. Not even Enlil knew, nor EA who Enlil maneuvered into setting this ball rolling. Belili will protect him, thinking she is protecting Enlil's plan."

"Some protection. She'll protect him till he's in the very tiger's den. Then what?" muttered Chaim.

"'Then what' is why he is the chosen one for this task. Here he comes. Let's watch."

ଓ ଚ

In the restroom, Johnny tried to comb the snarls out of his beard. After washing his face and freshening up, he returned to the dining room and took a seat at a table. From the pictures on the menu, he determined that he could get some scrambled eggs if he wanted, and sausages; *huevos y salchichas*, he laughed to himself again. It looks like I'm going to learn Spanish whether I want to or not. In accordance with the old rubric of the tribe, he ordered a fruit salad [*ensalada de fruta*], the only living fare on the menu and bottled water [*una botella de agua*]. *Don't need Montezuma's revenge just yet.*

He took a bite, a section of grapefruit. He closed his eyes and felt the life of the fruit dancing on his tongue, entering his own life. *The life in my food nourishes my own life. The joy in the fruit fulfills my own joy.* He smiled and chewed slowly. The vegetarian life style of Ha Agudoss was a specialized one based on a simple idea. The life in the food we eat nourishes our lives. If there is no life in the food, there is no nourishment. Johnny's was a diet of living food.

He could feel the energy of someone's attention coming from his left. He stopped chewing. Turning his head slightly, he opened his eyes to meet the gaze of an elderly lady. She had long, snowy white hair covered by a black, lace veil hanging down over a black, lace dress. Her face was long and flat with tanned wrinkled skin looking as though it had seen too much sun for too many years. Her eyes were very striking, big, round, amazingly blue and smiling at Johnny Lewis with an expression of interested surprise. *So there you are!* He could feel her thinking.

Johnny met her gaze for a moment, taking in her wrinkled ankle length dress and sandals. As he watched, her lips parted slightly in a smile. *She looks just like the good witch from that old Wizard of Oz storybook I had as a kid,* Johnny thought; surprised to see the old lady still had her teeth. As these thoughts occurred to him, he watched in amazement, as her smile widened into a grin and her eyebrows shot straight up as though he had spoken the words instead of thinking them. She started chuckling and as she did, she motioned with her hand for Johnny to come to her, saying through her chuckling, "Venga aqui, Gringo. Llendas consigo sus frutas," she added, motioning to his fruit salad.

Johnny rose to his feet, not sure what to do. *She wants me to come and sit with her?* He thought.

"Si. Si," she said. Then she added in carefully articulated English and a look of distracted concentration, "Join me. Siete se, aqui," again motioning to a chair at her table.

"That could make you sick," she said as he sat down at her table, indicating Johnny's fruit. "But you will get over it," she added smiling, nodding her head in assurance and suddenly sitting back into her chair.

"So you speak English?" Johny wondered aloud.

"I am very good with human languages," her answer startled him.

"Who are you," asked Johnny emphasizing each word and shaking his head slightly in disbelief.

"You may call me Leelee," she said, her eyes sweeping the room suspiciously then returning to smile into Johnny's. "It's what my friends used to call me. It's short for Belili. Do you know that name?" She leaned toward Johnny with a look of intense interest, which turned to a smile as Johnny shook his head and answered.

"No. I've never heard that name."

The old woman sat back suddenly against her chair as she had before and laughed aloud. "I'm not surprised. It is a very old name." She lowered her head like a conspirator, and gazing up at him said, "I think you have heard my name before, but it has been a very long time, you, who is to be called, DeMuzzi."

"How do you know that about me, Leelee? No one has been told what I am to be called."

"Belili knows many things," with her eyebrows rising, again indicating that Johnny should be surprised if not amazed. And Johnny was amazed. "She does not know all. Only the great god, Enlil knows all, but he tells Belili things sometimes, just as he told me to meet you here and lend you a charm."

Johnny was still listening but he was beginning to think. *Enlil? Who is Enlil? This is just what I need, a religious nut for a dinner companion.*

"I am not surprised that you disbelieve what I have told you. I should mention maybe, that if you told others about where you have been and what you have been doing, would they believe you? What about making the Ankh? Did you tell anyone about learning to make the Ankh? They would laugh and say you were a new age freak. Am I wrong? Am I wrong?"

Johnny sat back from his salad and folded his arms, determined to still his mind so she wouldn't see anything else. Then he leaned into the table again, propping his elbows on the table and his chin on his fist, a look of puzzlement. "What do you want?"

Using the energy of his own aura to form the shape of the Ankh was one of the early spiritual exercises of the fraternity. It required good focus, practice at meditation, and was the first step in learning to leave written messages visible only to those with eyes trained to see.

The old woman leaned back again into her chair, folded her arms, cocked her head and looked directly into his eyes. First, I want you to believe what I am telling you. How can I gain your confidence?"

Who is this woman? Johnny wondered. *She looks like an old Indian woman from the mountains around here but her Spanish has vanished. She still has the accent, but the accent doesn't even sound Spanish. It sounds more middle-eastern than western European. There's obviously more to her than being an old Indian woman. How does she know about the Ankh exercise? How does she know I am to be called DeMuzzi?* Johnny removed his chin from his fist and leaned further toward the old woman. "Make the Ankh for me. If you can make the Ankh, then I'll believe you." He sat back and folded his arms across his chest again, watching.

She too sat back. She laughed at him again. "Nothing could be easier, DeMuzzi. Watch."

Belili extended her left palm. Johnny watched as the energy around her hand began to glow brighter than the rest of her aura. The energy focused at her left palm. Then the column of light began to rise from her hand, three feet into the air. The cross bar of the Ankh formed a little brighter than the column. "Since I am here as a woman, it is right that the part of the Ankh representing the female should be brighter. Do you not agree?" The Ankh stopped growing while she waited for his answer.

Johnny was astonished. When he focused to make the Ankh, any conversation would destroy his focus and the Ankh would vanish. But here was this old woman talking about the technical design details of the symbol even as she focused her aura on the job. "If you want it that way, that's fine." Johnny continued to watch in growing amazement as the column of light from the woman's hand completed the formation with the circle at the top, representing the Deity.

"So is this construction satisfactory?" she asked.

Johnny nodded his head not sure what to say. "If you think this is something, watch this," said the old woman. She slapped her hands together and brought them apart with both palms facing upwards. The Ankh in her left hand divided and now there were two Ankhs, one rising above each hand. Maintaining both Ankhs, she leaned forward slightly and said thoughtfully, "Hm. Let's call the one in this hand - indicating her left hand - Chocmah, shall we? And the one in this hand -indicating her right hand- Binah. Does that work for you, DeMuzzi?" her voice was growing forceful, almost commanding, almost irritating. "Then let's call the third one Shekinah."

Her hands parted to provide space and suddenly a much larger Ankh appeared between the other two with its base at the floor level and the top nearly touching the ceiling. Johnny wondered if he should be alarmed and glanced around to see if her show was drawing attention from others in the room. None were watching, at least none whom Johnny could see. When he returned his attention, all three representations of the Ankh were gone and the old woman was sitting benignly in her chair looking like a tired old woman in black with her arms folded across her chest and a wry smile on her face.

Johnny's astonishment was obvious. He just stared at her to see what else she was going to do. "Don't be so surprised, DeMuzzi. There has been more in heaven and on Earth than you will ever learn. Your life is a snap of the fingers compared to all the time that has passed. This planet's lifetime is a sneeze compared to the lives of other places. The secrets of Malchesidek (the ancient founder of Johnny's fraternity) were learned by him from others. Don't be so surprised that others know them."

"Alright," said Johnny. "I no longer think you're a religious nut. I will consider very carefully and seriously whatever it is you want to tell me. You said a god told you to meet me here. What else did he tell you?"

"The great god Enlil, eighteen Sars past, told me you would be here on this night, at this time. He said you are only a man, yet you would fly here. It was hard for me to believe this, but here I am and now I understand. Men use machines to fly, just as Enlil used a machine. He was ancient then. He said his time would end before mine. This is to be part of my last effort on his behalf."

"Enlil?? Never heard of him."

"Shhh," Fingers before the lips. "Such statements can be dangerous. It is true that Enlil has ascended, but there is no way to know what powers he may still have or if he's listening. It would not be wise to offend him or any of the other gods. They can be very, uh, vindictive."

"Aaaaa. What was he god of anyway? The ancients had a god for everything. And you're telling me you knew some of them? Hah. You may be old, but you're not that old."

The old woman was on her feet, annoyed. "Enlil said I would find that you had been educated beyond your wisdom. He was right, of course. Still I have not given you the charm I have held for you."

"And that would be...?"

The old woman sat down again. Fishing around in a cloth sack that served as a purse, she came up with a thin gold chain. Dangling from the chain was a blue stone in the shape of an obelisk, framed in gold. "When Enlil gave me this, the symbol had little significance. I did not recognize it until much later when the symbol actually came into use. He called it a "MU," because of its shape, but he said you would call it an "Obelisk." He said this would please you. What is important is the stone itself. It is called Lapis Lazuli and it is important that you pronounce it correctly. Say it now - [law peace - laws yul lee]. The accent is equal on all syllables." She handed the stone to Johnny and he received it.

"It is the stone sacred to Inanna, daughter of Nanna. Keep it against your skin at all times. It fosters integrity and will protect you from invasive powers. He told me to tell you no more than that. I don't know why Enlil would be interested in any mortal living so long after his departure, nor do I care why he was interested. Just tell me you will do as I have asked?"

"Okay," said Johnny. "I'll wear it until I have a good reason not to. How's that?"

"That will be fine. Adios, DeMuzzi."

The old woman rose and walked to the door of the airport café, turned left and headed for the exterior door of the building. Johnny walked to the door of the café to watch her leave. As she exited the airport's main building, Johnny realized he had not said 'thank you.' It somehow seemed important so he hurried after her.

Just outside the main terminal, Johnny looked around. She was no where to be seen. It was still dark outside. Just as he was about to return to the café, he noticed a mouse scurrying across the parking lot in front of him. As he watched it, a great owl swooped from the sky from his left, snatched the mouse from the ground and climbed back into the sky, screeching. Johnny turned to watch it disappearing to his right. *There is something significant about that,* he thought. *Is it from Homer?*

His thoughts were interrupted by, "Hey Johnny. It's great to see you. Sorry I'm late, man!! Traffic was unbelievable."

It was Tarek.

Chapter 2: Red Sky in Morning. . .

"Four hours on and four hours off, makes a man's brain grow hazy and soft," Oscar "Chip" Evans yawned to himself. He brushed his dark brown, overgrown hair out of his eyes and adjusted his Greek fisherman's cap, a blue one, to match the sea. It was first light, that last hour of the night, before the sunrise drives the flying fish back under the ocean's surface. In another hour or so, Joyce would come aloft from her bunk in the aft stateroom to stand her shift. "Four hours on and four hours off, hates a good sex life... So how do I finish the rhyme on that one?" He chuckled to himself. It was then he noticed the red hue of the clouds ahead, to the east and another rhyme started repeating itself in his head. *Red sky at night, sailor's delight. Red Sky in morning, sailor takes warning.* "So now what," he said, half aloud. Fear began to drive the haziness of boredom out of his mind. The 'Red Sky' rhyme caused him to recall the face of Bob Lipscom, who taught Chip to sail, reciting old English sayings of the sea.

"Herring sky, herring sky,
Not long wet, not long dry."

Chip looked overhead. Sure enough, the broken pattern of fish scales appeared in a high altitude cloud formation. That first time under sail in Tom & Elaine's sixteen foot open day-sailor under a full force Florida northeaster was nothing compared to a south seas blow, two thousand miles out. With a red sky in morning and the herring scale cloud formation, according to Lipscom's weather wisdom, that's what they could expect later that day. But they still had some time to prepare.

Oscar "Chip" Evans at six feet tall, two hundred twenty five pounds, a former United States Marine feared no man, but ninety foot seas in the middle of the Pacific Ocean could get his full attention. The old Salts who hung out at the wharves of the South Seas islands derisively called sixty footers, yachtsman's seas, but Chip recalled Joshua Slocum's mention of a one hundred foot sea that nearly swamped Slocum on his famous circumnavigation and actually did swamp several merchantmen in the area. Granted, MOON DAUGHTER, Chip's and Joyce's forty foot, center cockpit, ketch was much heavier than Slocum's yawl, SPRAY. MOON DAUGHTER had already weathered some very respectable storms but he and Joyce had not much enjoyed these storms.

Chip worked his way aft from the bow, his favorite perch when at sea, moving his lifeline clips as he went.   Lifelines were one of the secrets of surviving long crossings. It's too easy for a sailor to be swept overboard while the rest of the crew sleeps. With the helm under automatic pilot a boat can sail away much faster than any one can swim, leaving the 'man overboard' in its wake.

The barometer indicated thirty inches of mercury and had not moved in the last four hours since he checked it. The course heading was steady at ninety-two degrees. The weather vane style, self-steering mechanism they bought back at the Ortega River, at the homeport near Jacksonville Florida proved awkward to learn to use but it was a dependable spare hand. They were five days out of Pitcairn, east bound for Easter Island, the next 'shore leave' as they had been calling their island visits. They waited three weeks at Pitcairn for the wind to shift to the west as it does in October, the spring of the Southern Hemisphere.

MOON DAUGHTER stood under full sail with a fifteen knot quartering breeze from the starboard side. She rode, heeling slightly to port as Chip studied the boat's instruments. Suddenly the salon righted itself then rolled slightly to starboard. The wind had shifted. It was time to reduce sail. He moved aft toward the main hatch, pausing at the hanging locker for a life vest. *No point in being brave with weather on the way,* he mumbled to himself. The thought was interrupted by a shriek from above.

The wind shift woke Joyce who came aloft and found him gone. When he emerged from the main salon she was darting her eyes wildly astern, searching for him, her own lifeline snapped to the aft hatch cleat. She calmed visibly when she saw him - big sigh of relief. One of their greatest fears was that of someone being lost at sea while the other slept. As a result, the lifelines were inspected visibly during each watch, frayed lines being replaced immediately. When on deck at sea, they were religiously in use.

The wind had shifted north, putting MOON DAUGHTER on an

awkward port reach. Joyce disconnected the self-steering vane and manually took the helm, bringing the ketch back to a course heading of ninety-two degrees while Chip adjusted the sails, tying double reefs into both the main and mizzen sails. Then he worked his way forward. Lowering and stowing the big Genoa, he left the reefed main, mizzen and jib aloft to drive the boat. He went below again to check the barometer. No change, yet.

When he got back to the cockpit, he found Joyce had reset the self-steering vane for the ninety two-degree course heading and was reclining in the helmsman's seat, snapped between two lifelines. The rising sun now crested the horizon.

"Best to keep a weather eye lifted," Joyce quoted Joshua Slocum as she put on her ever ready sun glasses and added the Canadian, "Aye? (long A)" with one raised eyebrow in a smirk.

"Aye Aye, Mam," quipped Chip with a grin as he passed her to aft in search of the drogue and the attachment lines. I may be over-reacting to get out the sea anchor so soon but if we have any serious weather, I'd rather have it in reach than stowed in the lazarette.

When the seas get too strong, small boats head down wind with a storm sail hoisted from the forward shroud and a drogue or sea anchor trailed aft. The storm sail keeps the boat headed down wind with the seas coming from astern. The drogue holds the boat's stern back, preventing the boat from broaching or surfing down the wave, getting its nose stuck in the trough and having its stern pushed over by the following sea. Pitch-poling end over end like that has caused many a boat to break up at sea.

"Are we safe, Captain Rehab," smirked Joyce has he rejoined her in the cockpit.

Joyce was rereading Melville's whale of a tale and to stave off any more Moby Dick puns, he leaned in close to her and said, "Kiss me. Please. Just kiss me."

He watched her short curly black hair, wild from the wind, framing laughing Sicilian-brown eyes which she revealed more fully by slightly pulling her sunglasses down her long nose and peering at him over the frame. She then raised her fist in front of her face from which popped up her index finger which she touched lightly to her lips then to Chip's nose. "Don't you think you'd better check the barometer again? Make sure everything is tied down below? And while you're at it, a cup of coffee would be nice. And maybe one of your famous omelets?"

"Aye, Aye, Mam, if we still have any eggs that have survived." The custom had evolved during their eighteen month (so far) journey that the last duty of the watch officer was to prepare a meal for the one coming on duty. The transition seemed to work for both of them. After four hours on deck, the routine of cooking in the main salon then eating prepared them for a few hours of sleep before coming back for another turn on watch. So far from land and out of the shipping channels, it didn't seem so important that the watch person spend every minute on deck. Checking the horizon every five or ten minutes seemed adequate in daylight so Joyce joined him in the salon, poking her head aloft every few minutes.

Their two-year honeymoon was planned for a leisurely circumnavigation, with as much good weather sailing as possible. They left Jacksonville April 1 for Ireland, pausing at Bermuda and the Azores. After touring much of Great Britain, they touched shore numerous times in Western Europe and the northern Mediterranean. Planned stops included Italy and Sicily, then back through the Pillars of Hercules with stops at the Canary Islands, Cape Verde and the friendlier countries of western Africa, rounding the Cape of Good Hope, repeating much of Slocum's voyage but traveling in the opposite direction. Slocum had rounded Cape Horn "the wrong way," from east to west against the currents and weather. In the Pacific, they diverted from Slocum's path to visit Pitcairn and Easter Islands. The plan was to skip Cape Horn and head for the Panama Canal after visiting Easter Island. "The trip of a lifetime should be taken when one is young," said Oscar Evans Sr., Chip's father who backed them for the voyage. "Just please be careful."

Chip slept for a few hours while Joyce, literally lashed to the helmsman's chair, continued reading Moby Dick, as the clouds gathered. They were both devoted sailors. They had met as opposing team members in The America's Cup four years earlier.

The storm didn't break until halfway through Chips next watch. The barometer had been falling steadily. By the time it reached twenty-nine inches, Chip had the main and mizzen sails completely lowered, wrapped and lashed around their booms. The jib and self-steering vane had been lowered and stowed. The storm sail was aloft. With so little sail their speed wasn't much affected because the wind had freshened to nearly thirty knots and MOON DAUGHTER was racing downwind on a heading of one hundred five degrees, held back by the large sea anchor cleated by heavy nylon tethers to both sides of the stern.

Joyce emerged from the aft stateroom with a worried look on her face. "How bad is this going to be," she asked.

"Not bad. It may last a day or two at most, but with any luck, it'll pass in a few hours.

"The seas behind us look to be nearly twenty feet," she remarked.

Chip looked astern, again. The drogue was holding MOON DAUGH-

TER against the following seas. Each one broke over the stern, but since MOON DAUGHTER had a cockpit in the center of the boat, between the masts, the cockpit was still dry. "I hope they don't get any higher, but they could. We'll be okay. Don't worry. In fact, the storm sail and drogue are probably an over reaction. If the wind holds at this speed, we could still be under jib and reefed mizzen and making very good time."

Joyce had both lifelines snapped to separate cleats in the cockpit. She was staring at the mountains of white tipped water racing at them from behind. Her hair was blowing straight back. Her jaw was set and she was beginning to grind her teeth together, a habit she had long been trying to break. Both were wearing life vests, "Personal Floatation Devices," the United States Coast Guard called them.

Chip went below to check the barometer again. "No change," he called out through the open hatch. After a quick check to make sure there was nothing unsecured which could go flying around inside the main salon if the going got rougher, he rejoined Joyce in the center cockpit.

"Let's see," she said, philosophically trying to regain her calm, "if we're in the Southern Hemisphere, which we are, and if this is a hurricane, which it isn't, then the storm should rotate clockwise instead of counter-clockwise like it does in Florida, right?"

"That's what they say," said Chip.

"Okay. In the Northern Hemisphere, in a hurricane, they say to find the eye, face the wind and the eye is on the right. Right? Right. So, in the Southern Hemisphere where the storms blow backwards, if we face the wind, the eye of the storm should be on the left. Right?" She looked at him for validation."

"That seems right to me," said Chip.

Joyce turned to face the wind coming from two hundred eighty five degrees -- west, west by northwest. "If this were a hurricane then, the storm would be coming from about a hundred ninety five degrees, right?" asked Joyce, pointing in a generally southern direction."

"Your logic is flawless, Captain, we are not in grave danger," Chip fractured a quote from Mr. Spock to Captain Kirk. "The storm approached us from the East. That's where it got cloudy, this morning, first. It's not a hurricane."

Joyce glanced at the sky to the east, about fifteen points off the port bow. Then she turned slightly to look at the sky dead ahead, and froze, briefly. "Look at those clouds ahead, Chip. Isn't that strange?"

Chip had been checking the lifelines for fraying. He paused and followed her gaze. The sky ahead was darker than anywhere else. "It looks like the worst of it will pass us. It seems to be moving south." He went back to inspecting the lifelines.

"But look at the shapes the clouds are forming. It's eerie. Doesn't that look like two huge eyes looking at us?"

Chip glanced up again and saw the cloud shapes, but before he could remark, the rain started falling, almost sideways from astern, followed by the first bolt of lightning. The wind freshened again and was now closer to forty knots. The seas were breaking over the stern and almost washing into the cockpit. The following seas were lifting MOON DAUGHTER's stern so high that they both had to hang on to keep from falling forward. Chip could see down into the clearness of the wave's troughs as though from an airplane, *and four thousand feet of water beneath us,* he thought, but banished that thought. *The last thing I need to feel right now is fear.* Adding a third lifeline, he began working his way astern to check the drogue lines. Joyce could see what he was doing and moved to stop him since that's where the seas were breaking over the boat's deck. "We need those lines to the sea anchor to be holding," he shouted over the roar of the wind. "I'll be careful. Just keep us running downwind."

When he finally returned to the cockpit, he was dripping with salt water. "Nice that it's not cold," he shouted to her. Joyce didn't like the electrical display in the clouds and though she was still at the helm, she had tears on her cheeks.

"Look at the clouds now," she shouted at him. "Ahead, I mean."

A face had taken full shape to the southeast, with a clear nose, smiling mouth and very intense eyes. "So what do you think it is, for Pete's sake, Neptune?"

"It's just clouds."

She glanced at him briefly with a look of fear in her eyes. Then she returned her gaze to the eastern sky. The face appeared to be fading with sunlight and blue sky on the edge of the distant horizon. Chip was relieved to see it, but before he could comment, a stroke of lightning hit the mizzenmast. As it did, the mizzen halyard fell smoking to the deck. The powerful bolt then arched, striking one of the deck stanchions before grounding itself in the sea.

"Oh my God," Joyce muttered. She let go of the helm and grabbed Chip in a 'just-hold-me' plea. Chip was startled. His first concern was keeping the boat from broaching on the next sea, but it appeared to be well enough balanced between the drogue and the storm sail that it held its course. Joyce seemed to realize the danger as quickly as Chip did. She released him and clutched the wheel, checking the wind and course heading.

The wind now seemed to be veering back to its earlier, more south-erly direction. The seas were lower, back to maybe thirty feet. MOON DAUGHTER was back to her earlier dance, lifting her stern over the fol-lowing seas and riding them as they moved under her toward the east. "It's your watch," said Joyce. "Why don't you go below and get into some dry clothes since the rain's stopped. Then I'll fix us something to eat before I go to bed."

"Four hours already?" he groaned. "No rest for the wicked I guess."

When Chip returned to the cockpit, the wind had backed to just un-der twenty five knots. Joyce was shivering at the helm but before she would go below to change and cook, she pointed again to the sky in the east. "Is that weird or is that weird?" she asked.

Chip turned to face the east. MOON DAUGHTER was now back on her course of ninety-two degrees, east. The edge of the storm clouds had come closer but beyond them, the sky was not blue. It was brown-ish, as though he was seeing it through a bronze colored camera filter. Chip checked his wristwatch. "It's about three fifteen, local time," he said. "Too early for sunset. I wonder what's making the sky that color."

The wind was continuing to calm, so he lashed the helm briefly while he broke out the self-steering vane again and set it in its chocks. Then he went forward to lower the storm sail and raise the jib. After bringing in the drogue and stowing it back in the lazarette he hoisted the main sail, putting off accepting that he had to climb the mizzen mast in these rolling seas to replace the burned, mizzen halyards.

As he returned to the cockpit to contemplate this act, Joyce emerged from the main salon with a frightened look on her face. "What's wrong?" he asked.

"That lightning strike fried the GPS. I think it also fried the radio. Looks like we're back to dead reckoning our course with a sextant and compass. I hope it didn't de-magnify the compass or something. It has been a while since I used a sextant. Think you're up to it?"

"Well, if we get a moon tonight or we can see some of the stars we'll be able to see if we're off course. We'll also be able to re-magnify the compass. Nothing to worry about. Do you still have that horseshoe magnet you stowed in your luggage? We'll need that if we have to re-magnify the compass. If worse comes to worst, we can always use it for a compass." He attempted a reassuring grin, but his own fears were equal to hers. Neither of them had used a sextant since the boating safety course where they learned how celestial navigation was done. "At least we have a sextant. And we have all those tables we can use to fix our position with the moon. We'll make Easter Island in five or six days. Even if we miss it, it'll be pretty hard to miss the Americas. All we have to do is keep sailing east."

Several hours later Joyce popped open the hatch to the aft stateroom and put her head through it. "It's dark," she said. "What happened to the wind? It feels like we're floating on a lake all of a sudden."

"The wind died down about an hour ago, and it's dark because it's night."

"All right, smart aleck. What's for breakfast? Where are we, anyway? Were you able to get a reading?"

"Check out the sky. It's pitch black. There isn't a star in sight and moonrise isn't for a few more hours, not that it's going to make any difference if we can't see it. We have a solid cloud cover."

"I don't think I've ever seen the ocean this calm. There's no wind at all."

"A nice change from a few hours ago," quipped Chip. "Before I go below to get your breakfast, how about minding the helm while I climb up the mizzen mast and install the new halyard?"

ℭ ℬ

Three more watches changed. Chip was back on deck, six days out of Pitcairn and one day with no wind. He rested on the bow of the boat, his favorite sea perch, staring alternately at the mirror smooth sea and at the bronze colored, solid ceiling of clouds overhead. The big Genoa was bundled at his feet, ready to be hoisted to catch the least breath of air. The jib, main and mizzen sails were fully displayed, hanging limp from their masts and shrouds. With the electronic navigation system not working, no way to get a shot at the sun or the moon with the sextant, Chip only knew they were somewhere in the vast South Pacific Ocean, probably about half way between Pitcairn and Easter Islands. Joyce was awake. He could hear her moving around in the silence of the calm.

"So where are we?" she wanted to know.

"If the charts are right and if we're where I think we are, we have a bit of a northerly current. For all practical purposes, we're adrift till the wind comes back. My guess is we're probably just a bit north of due west of Easter Island by maybe eight or nine hundred miles. When the wind comes back, and if we can get a shot at the sun, we should be able to raise Easter Island in about five days."

"Are you sure we're drifting north?" she asked.

"No."

"Water, water everywhere and yet the boards did shrink..."

"Sorry," said Chip with a chuckle. "This boat's fiberglass and we have an osmosis salt water reclamation system. We aren't going to run out of water."

"I know the old boats with the tall masts needed a lot more wind than MOON DAUGHTER," mused Joyce. We can run on the slightest puff, so what could becalm the Cutty Sark would have us doing about six knots. This can't last."

"You're right, there," said Chip. "But this sure is a nice reprieve from yesterday. Isn't it?"

Chapter 3: A Rapanui Storm

Tarek had the window seat with Johnny beside him straining to look over his shoulder at the azure sea below. The Lan Chile airliner was a DC 767, jammed to the gills with tourists. The weekly flight to Papeete stopping at Easter Island usually was, in October, the beginning of summer.

Tarek was quiet. Everyone was, as the pilot announced in Spanish, then in English, "We are beginning our descent to Mataveri Airport on Easter Island. In the Spanish announcement, he called it 'Isla de Pascua.'" In both tongues he said it was also called Rapanui, meaning, "island toward the rising sun" and in the ancient tongues of Polynesia, it was called, "Te-Pito-Te-Henua," meaning "The Navel of the World."

"If you can see out of the portside windows you will see a unique weather phenomenon in the distance. For lack of a better term, we call it a Rapanui Storm. This phenomenon exists no where else in the world. It's characterized by bronze colored clouds punctuated by lightning bolts. The natives of Te-Pito-Te-Henua have in their legends, dreadful stories about this phenomenon. They say it's caused by the Moon Goddess Hina. In the old days, that is to say, prior to the eighteenth century, when the phenomenon occurred, the islanders would make human sacrifices to Hina, then eat the flesh of those who had been sacrificed.

"Today when they see it occurring, they no longer make human sacrifices but they still say 'Hina wants a sacrifice.' No one wants to be that sacrifice so everyone stays away from the sea until it goes away. No fishing boats go out. No one surfs or swims. None can say if the stories have any merit, but the Chilean and Rapanui Governments report that no one who has sailed into a Rapanui Storm has ever returned to tell what's there.

Johnny could feel the Lapis Lazuli amulet hanging around his neck and the stone against his chest. It somehow felt warmer than it had. He put his hand on it to verify that it had actually grown warmer and when he felt it, he wasn't sure. *Maybe I should show this to Tarek and see what he thinks of it. Who was that old woman last night? What a weird experience!*

"In a few moments," the pilot continued, "we will be turning to the left for our final approach. After we complete the turn, the Rapanui Storm will be on the other side of the airplane so passengers on the starboard side will be able to see it. Needless to say, we will not be flying anywhere near the Storm. We estimate its location to be about one hundred miles to the southwest and reaching far to the west and south beyond that point. The only reason we can even see it is our altitude and the altitudes of the clouds it contains.

"Please fasten your seat belts. Extinguish all smoking materials until after exiting the plane. Thank you for flying Lan Chile."

Tarek turned to try to see through the windows on the other side of the plane. He met Johnny's eyes for a moment. Johnny could see the wariness appearing briefly only to be covered with the ever-present smile. Johnny had guessed at Tarek's age many times without asking it and without conclusion. His guess was that Tarek was somewhere between forty and sixty-five. There was a hint of gray in his closely cut hair. Laugh lines framed his eyes, but his vigorous life style probably contributed to minimizing the appearance of age, as well maintaining his athletic appearance. Tarek liked to play tennis daily. "That's the only thing that keeps me trim," he had said almost every morning since they had been together.

If Johnny had known Tarek less well, he would have guessed his age to be closer to forty five than sixty five but for those serious moments when Tarek would look at him for that miniscule passage of a microsecond, before answering some question. It was an expression one might expect to see in the eyes of a well traveled grandfather who had seen the passage of wars, famine and pestilence, who had seen the deaths of friends and the births of grandchildren. The look communicated understanding of the answer to Johnny's question but the inability to communicate it, remorse for that inability and the determination to try anyway.

Their attention was drawn to a murmur arising ahead of them on the aircraft. Three of the passengers, apparently Easter Islanders on their way home had begun a low chant, "Heen-aah. Heen-aah."

The voices were low and reverent, soon joined by the voices of two more. Their appearance was that of Polynesian Islanders, the tanned skin, dark hair, the high set cheekbones and the eyes. If their faces and complexions had not revealed their island origins, their clothing and tattoos would have. The person who apparently started the chanting had pierced ears with heavy ornaments hanging from them.

"There aren't many left of the Island's old religion," said Tarek to Johnny at low breath. "Only a handful. And it seems that they still fear this moon goddess, 'Hina.'"

Johnny made an expression of disdain, rubbed his nose and asked, "Where do all these screwy pagan cults come from anyway?   They're everywhere. People worship moon gods, sun gods, weather gods, gods of this and gods of that. The Nordics believed in Aeser gods created by Ice Giants. Some Polynesians think the Earth rides on the back of a huge turtle, so they worship turtles. Then there's all this confusion of gods. The Druids were said to have worshiped a Bull god. But there may have been some confusion there, with the god Mithras who the Roman soldiers worshiped. He was represented as a bull. The Druids even named their Bull god, Mithras, didn't they?"

"I don't know. The Bull idea probably came from the Gilgamesh legend where he and Inkidu killed Humbaba the Terrible, with the help of the Bull of Heaven belonging to the god Anu. Humbaba the Bull was the protector of the forests of cedar, "continued Tarek. "It's endless and I usually get it confused."

"So. Is Mithras a later name for Anu's pet, the Bull of Heaven?" asked Johnny with a grin.

"Could be," said Tarek. "I'm more concerned with this Hina at the moment. You know what havoc people can reek with misdirected faith."

C8 80

Johnny flashed back in his memory to his first sessions with his teachers with Ha Agudoss, The Fraternity and his arguments.

"Faith is the creative motor," said Seth, the Elder. Seth looked like an insurance salesman with his constant smile, good grooming, a gold pen in his shirt pocket and the tie loose around his buttoned down collar. "Passion or desire is the fuel. The more fuel the better the motor works."

"If that were true," Johnny rebutted, "everyone would win the state lottery. Why don't they?"

Seth Johnson leaned back in his chair with an exasperated sigh. "The answer to your question is more advanced than your level. After you memorize and become proficient in this degree, you will advance to future degrees where some of these questions will be addressed. In the meantime, let me try." He put his hands behind his head and stretched. Johnny could hear his back crackling as he did so.

"How many people do you suppose, desire and believe that they will win the state lottery?"

Johnny furrowed his eyebrows and glanced out the window where snow was lightly falling. "I don't know," he answered. "Probably millions."

"Probably millions," echoed Seth in confirmation. "They put out an enormous amount of energy, but its conflicting energy. It's chaotic energy. Each person produces a little bit. Together, the power is unfathomable. All pitted against each other, it's a yearning self contradicting miasma of the impossible."

"Yet someone always wins," said Johnny.

"Not always. Much of the time it rolls over to make a bigger pot the next week. Let's look at something easier, something on a smaller scale. Group prayer is often the cause of miraculous healing. Take the case of my friend Ann who has cancer. She gets sicker and sicker, goes to the hospital and THEN everyone starts praying for her. Ann gets better and comes home. Everyone stops praying she'll get well, so she gets sick again, goes back to the hospital and everyone in her congregation starts praying again. Ann recovers enough to go home, and starts getting sick. Ann has been expected to die of cancer within the next few weeks, six times so far over a period of fourteen years."

"But prayer is a different subject. It's the power of God that helps Ann recover. Isn't it?"

"No," said Seth. "It's the power of faith, focused by several people at the same time. Do you see why misdirected faith can be so dangerous?"

"How can faith in God be misdirected," asked Johnny.

"It's not the faith in God that is so dangerous. It's the faith that God or a god will bring about some evil. But it's not the god that does the evil. It's the faith of the believer. In the case of Ann, the creative force of the believers brings about her healing. When more of them believe she will die instead of recover, then she will die."

He took a sip of coffee and glanced around the room at the other students.

"Her own faith is a pivotal part of that process. Her own faith is what brings the sickness back. Her faith in the power of her prayer group to influence Divine interference is what saves her, combined with the faith of those who are praying for her. So you see, it's not God who is healing her exactly, but faith. It works just as well when the believer places his or her faith in a negative goal or result, like the bad luck from walking under ladders. That is misdirecting faith. Do you see now why it can be dangerous?"

CB &O

Tarek interrupted Johnny's reverie with, "Take a look out the window. The plane is finished turning and on its final approach for the runway. You can just barely see the storm in the distance. It doesn't look like much from here, but keep in mind, that's where we're going."

Johnny leaned past Tarek to look through the small round porthole on the side of the airplane. In the distance, he could see the towering bronze colored clouds. "The Elders told me Arrata is there, an island no one knows about and no one returns from. When they said it, I thought they were speaking metaphorically. How do they even know there is an island? I don't think I want to be known back home as the man who never returned."

"Never is long time," answered Tarek with a smile, "and the 'Man Who Never Returned' lived in Boston. "I've accompanied fifteen of our people this far, over the years. This time I'll be going along. I have often wondered about Arrata. Now I am going to find out. It can't be that bad a place. Some of our people have been there for decades."

"Decades?"

"It could be worse. This is a semi-tropical paradise. Lunch grows on the nearest tree. Its climate must be something like that on Easter Island, just a little cooler. It's a bit further from the equator."

CB &O

The next day on a guided tour of Easter Island:

The young, effervescent, tour guide spoke English well enough to relate the stories of Easter Island's beginnings as a home for humans to Anglos. Her long black hair blew in the wind as she talked. "The first settlers of the island, we think, came from the Marquesas Islands to the west around 400 C.E. A loyal subject, Hau Maka, of the abdicated island king, Hotu Matua was searching for a new home for his king. In a dream he was led to a new island located, according to Alfred Metraux's Ethnology of Easter Island, 'In the dim twilight of the rising sun.'

"When Hau Maka awoke he told Hotu Matua how to get to the new land. He said:

i lunga   (Travel southeast, windward.)
e tau   (It stands out)
e revareva roa   (as a permanent projection)

i roto i te raa   (In the midst of the sun.)

Johnny interrupted the guide with, "would you mind repeating that last line, with the translation?"

"Of course," said the guide. "i roto i te ra a, which is interpreted "In the midst of the sun - probably the rising sun.""

"' Raa' means 'sun' then, in old Polynesian? Is that right?"

"Yes," said the guide grinning. "Are you wondering why ancient Polynesian has such a remarkable shared word with the Egyptian name for the Sun god Ra? We wonder about that too. We're hoping that someday someone will make a study of the two languages. It is after all, from the similarity of the language of Easter Island that people think our ancestors came from the Marquesas - similar language. No one really knows where the people of the Marquesas came from."

Another of the tour group made an interjection. He was an elderly man wearing a golf cap, dark sunglasses and a brightly colored, print shirt stretching its buttons over his stomach. "Genesis Chapter eleven, verse eight, after the languages were confused at the building of the tower of Babel, it says, 'So the Lord scattered them abroad from there, over the face of all the Earth.' It's beautiful how the ancient writings seem more true to me as I age. Did you know that the Hopi Indian language of Arizona has numerous shared words with some of the tribes of Afghanistan? It's uncanny."

ɔჳ ɛᴐ

At sea in route to Arrata:

Johnny hung on for dear life in a pitching and rolling, twenty-four foot, Diesel powered, fishing boat named SEA TROLLOP. The craft was made of aluminum with a small cabin, on a course heading of two hundred forty degrees, southwest, making about eight knots. "I don't like this," said Johnny. "Neither of us has any experience at sea, navigating, or driving a boat."

"Just remember, oh faint heart. It will be done to you according to your faith. So get your faith in gear and quit worrying."

"It's too bad we had to buy a boat. And if we had to buy one, that we couldn't get a nicer one," remarked Johnny.

"To use once and throw away? The fraternity was willing to spend more, but it really wasn't necessary."

"The boat is a bit small." Johnny glanced around. "What worries me more is that." He pointed at the bronze colored clouds ahead.

"We'll be alright. This boat has no electronics, even in the engine. It's an old Diesel engine."

"Why should that have anything to do with anything?" Johnny took off his hat, ran his fingers through is hair. "Do you think we'll have much rain with it or wind? If we get much wind, it'll swamp this bath tub you're calling a boat."

Tarek locked down the wheel and turned to face Johnny. "Listen DeMuzzi, and don't forget your name is now Muzzi or DeMuzzi. If you want to worry about something, worry about what happened to Easter Island. For a long time, it's been under the influence of the evil we're going to fight. It may even have been the influence bringing Polynesians to this area in the first place. Think about it.

"The old seer Hau Maka had a dream or a weird astral projection or something in which he learned of this uninhabited island, twenty five hundred miles away. Were there other uninhabited islands closer? Absolutely. Why Rapanui, 'in the dim twilight of sunrise,' upwind and so far? And look at what happened to the people who immigrated there in 400 A.D. Rapanui has been a curse to the descendants of the old King Hotu Matua and his brothers.

"When they arrived it was a pristine paradise. In a matter of a thousand years, they managed to deforest the island. In their mad statue building competition they destroyed the trees they used to make ocean-going canoes, so guess what - no more fishing. They were reduced to eating chickens and the rats they brought with them from Hiva, where ever that is. Then the white man came, bringing the curse of small pox, diphtheria, syphilis, and when the diseases failed to wipe them out, Europeans from the Americas started raiding the island for slaves. The population was decimated from thousands to a few hundred in a matter of three hundred years from the time the island was discovered by Jacob Roggeveen, the Dutch sea captain, on Easter Sunday in 1722.

"On no other island in the Pacific Ocean has such devastation occurred - only here. They had wars between short people and tall people. They had such difficulty finding food, after the ecological catastrophe that they eventually resorted to cannibalism. I know that humans have their prejudices, but short corpulent people and tall thin people having a war over their body shapes is a bit much, even for primitives.

"So ask yourself this question and stop worrying about the boat. Why did this happen here? Why Easter Island? Why not Papeete? Why not Pitcairn? Why here?"

"Do you know?" asked Johnny.

"No, but I've seen enough that I finally volunteered to come to try to help. That's how most of the people you will meet at Arrata came to be there. You're different. You were specifically sent to Arrata. You didn't volunteer. You've been given a different name, a very ancient name no one uses any more. Do you know who DeMuzzi was?"

"No," answered Johnny, slightly alarmed at the intensity of Tarek's monologue.

"I don't even know why this matters," said Tarek, turning back to check the course heading and make an adjustment to the helm. "I've been instructed to not tell you, not even a hint. This is maddening. No one I'm aware of knows why you were chosen for this.   We've never dealt in secrecy among our own before. This makes no sense to me. What do you know? Any clues?"

"None," said Johnny. "Let me fill you in a little about where I've been and maybe we can figure it out. You already know I'm from Pennsylvania and my theological background. Did you know I was with Prill when he... I'm not sure I should tell you about that. That's also supposed to be a secret."

"I know about Prill's disappearance but not why or how," answered Tarek. "How did he disappear?"

"He ascended, right before my very eyes. One moment he was there and the next moment he was a ball of light fading into the darkness."

Tarek smiled and said in a dreamy sort of way, "you actually saw it happen? I've heard about it all my life and hope to ascend one day myself, but I've never actually seen anyone do it."

"It was pretty amazing."

The boat was now passing under the bronze cloud cover. The wind stopped and the seas began to abate. "This is pretty amazing too," said Johnny. "Some storm. It's almost a dead calm."

"So tell me about Prill. Had he just completed some goal or other, some life fulfilling task? I heard he was a member of some ancient Aleph-Bayt and had to reincarnate to complete his mission. Is that true?"

"I believe it's true," said Johnny. "He was Harai, Zayin in his Aleph-Bayt."

"And what is your designation," asked Tarek.

"That's the strangest thing," answered Johnny. "They didn't give me a designation. I entered the lodge as a sojourner. When Prill ascended, he handed me this silver Ankh and told me that I am Hjet, the number eight, a successor of sorts. A fence. I believe he meant I'm a member of the same Aleph-Bayt in which he was a member so long ago and I'm next in line to fulfill some predestined task. The Ankh is like a baton and it's my turn to carry it. If so, I have no idea what I am to be a fence between, what I am to divide from what. A fence divides, keeps something out or something in. The Ankh seems to represent some sort of Baton, like a runner in a relay race hands off to the next runner. I really don't know the answers to these questions, yet. I hope I find out some-day. What do you think?"

Tarek was silent for a few moments, staring at the bronze colored clouds overhead and scanning the horizon for any sign of land. "I don't know why I keep looking for land," he said. "On this course heading and speed we shouldn't be able to see anything till tomorrow after-noon." He turned to look back at Johnny again, lounging in one of the fishing chairs. "My designation is Lamed, the Goad. My responsibility is teaching. Teaching is a style of enabling a person to expand from what they are to what they can be. I don't know why I'm with you. I'm not from some ancient Aleph-Bayt; I'm from Jerusalem in the State of Israel. My father was a Palestinian, my mother a Jew. My father was a member of Ha Agudoss and introduced me to it when I was very young. It would appear, for the time being, that it's you who I am to enable, but to do what, I have yet to learn.

"You, DeMuzzi, should go into the cabin and try to sleep so you can stay awake to steer later. We can take turns during the night. It'll be dark soon. I'll wake you at midnight. You watch for a couple of hours then wake me. Okay?"

Johnny gave a troubled look aloft at the bronze colored clouds now seeming to bear down on him. In the distance, far ahead of the small fishing boat, the clouds seemed to be swirling into odd shapes. *It looks like there may be wind ahead*, he thought to himself. *Maybe I should have told Tarek about helping Prill conceal the Ark of the Covenant at Masada. If we're never going back, what could telling him about it hurt?*

The boat was no longer rolling as much as before the wind died down so being inside the small cabin was not as disorienting as it would be in steeper seas. The previous owner's body odor hung in the air. Johnny looked around for a way to open one of the portholes to air it out some-what. *The smell of these Diesel fumes will make me sick if the smell of the former owner doesn't do it first.* After opening one porthole on ei-ther side of the boat, he went back on deck to give it a chance to air out.

The sky had grown darker in the few minutes he was below. Tarek still stood at the wheel. *Is it getting darker because it's getting lat-er,* Johnny thought to himself, *or is it some other force at work here?* "So." He said to Tarek a bit fearfully. "What in the world is a Rapanui Storm? I can almost hear those guys on the airplane, yesterday, chant-ing 'Hina, Hina.' Do you think there's anything to it?"

"No," answered Tarek. "But look at the clouds above us and ahead now. There seems to be a lot of turbulence up there, but it's still calm here, below."

"I keep getting this feeling of oppression, like a dark cloud forming in my mind. Do you feel it or is it just me?"

"Yes, " said Tarek. "I feel it too. I think we must be getting within its range. All I know about Arrata is that we have brothers there, standing off some evil. It sounds all too mythical to me, like so much fiction. I'm not superstitious, so I think it's just because we're so far at sea in a small boat going into unknown dangers. No one really knows what's going on with the Island of Arrata. It's just as the pilot said yesterday. No one has ever come back. Our only communication has been in meditation and from the Ascended Brotherhood and they won't tell us anything, except that this is very important. We will no doubt find out why, and soon."

"What did you think of that tourist's comment yesterday. Remember the guy who quoted Genesis chapter eleven?"

"Yes," answered Tarek. "I also noted that he made no mention of verse seven. It's common for Bible scholars to ignore the enigmatic. Verse seven says 'Come, let us go down and there confuse their language, that they may not understand one another's speech.' Did you catch that? 'Let US...?' Who do you suppose God was talking to? They try to tell us that the use of the word 'US' in this context is the use of the 'Royal We.' What throws a fly in that ointment is the fact that the paralleling older version of the same story from the land of Sumer actually does have other gods present, and tells the same story but in much more detail. The Genesis version seems to be a summary of the other, and that makes sense if you take into consideration that Abraham was born in Sumer and at the right time to have been acquainted with the older version of the story."

"I don't think I like where you're going with this," said Johnny. "I think I'll go below and get some sleep."

Chapter 4: Beached

Chip and Joyce had never before heard of a Rapanui Storm. The Lan Chile Captain noted it and flew far to the north, off his assigned flight plan to avoid it. Chip didn't see or know about the airplane. He was on his back with a flashlight in MOON DAUGHTER's engine compartment, glaring at the small black box he used to affectionately referred to as the engine's brain. "I can't find anything wrong with it," he called out to Joyce through the open hatch leading to the main salon, "unless it's the computer."

"You've checked and cleaned the spark plugs. You've checked to see that it's getting gasoline. What else could be wrong?" asked Joyce through the open hatch.

"I think that lightning strike may have fried the engine's brain. These high tech engines need the computer to do anything. That's one thing we don't have a back up for." Chip began sliding feet first out of the engine compartment hatch, talking as he came. "We have no engine, no wind, no global positioning system and a solid cloud cover that keeps us from being able to see any heavenly bodies. We don't know where we are and we don't know for sure which way the ocean currents are going. We may as well lean back, fish a little and wait for this to blow over, what ever it is."

"It's almost noon," said Joyce. "At least that's what my wrist watch says, but it's a wind up wrist watch. Everything electronic has stopped working. But even with the sun high over head, the clouds are too thick to see exactly where it is. They just seem to keep getting thicker and the sky darker. Everything has this sick brown overcast to it. Even the ocean is bronze."

"I guess this is why they call sea voyages adventuresome," he chuckled. "The only thing you can really be sure of is the unexpected. We'll be okay. We have the osmosis filter and plenty of food. Fishing hasn't been too bad. The barometer's holding steady at twenty-nine inches. That's a bit low for my pleasure, but there doesn't seem to be anything happening, so why worry? We can last as long as it takes, as long as we don't bump into any sea monsters or fall off the edge of the world."

"What's that noise?" asked Joyce in a hushed voice. "Do you hear it?"

Chip listened a moment to a loud, deep throated gushing noise coming from nearby. He climbed the companionway ladder and entered MOON DAUGHTER's cockpit with Joyce close behind him to watch a pod of whales passing close to the boat. As they watched, the closest one rolled to one side lifting a huge ventral fin slightly out of the glassy water, an enormous eye rolling above the surface, looking them over. Apparently satisfied, it righted itself. The eye and fin disappeared. The whale then blew a fountain of mist about fifteen feet into the air, took a deep breath and submerged. The mist from its exhalation drifted down over the couple.

Joyce gasped, "Gawd!! That thing's breath smells worse than yours," and climbed back down the companionway ladder, laughing.

Chip watched the pod of whales lazily passing on both sides of the boat. They seemed to recognize that MOON DAUGHTER posed no threat. Their passage was relaxed with several immature members of the pod, frolicking and splashing as they went. He leaned over the hatch door, wondering why Joyce had not stayed aloft with him to watch the show. "I wish we felt as at home out here as they do," he called down the hatch. Alarmed at no answer, he climbed back down the ladder to find Joyce in the forward stateroom, seated on the V-birth, crying.

He sat down beside her and put an arm around her shoulders, pulling her to him. The V-birth felt damp. The ever-present mildew was gaining ground. He could see signs of its reappearance under the starboard porthole. "Are you okay?" he asked gently.

"What I need's someone to hold me not some fool to ask me why," she misquoted the Smither song.

"I know," he said, "I wish we were at Tarpon Springs at a Smither concert, too. When we get home, we'll catch him as soon as he comes back. I promise."

"Don't practice your psychology shit on me," she snapped, pushing him away. "Ask me the little question instead of the big one. Would I like to start therapy on Monday or would Friday be better, instead of do I want to start some expensive therapy. You're promising that we'll go to a Smither concert instead of that we'll get home. Have you checked the bilge pump lately? The batteries are dead and the pump isn't pumping. In a few more hours we'll be ankle deep in the main salon." She walked out of the forward stateroom, took a seat in the main salon beside the bilge hatch and began hand pumping the lever to clear the lower bilge.

Chip followed her and lifted the hand hatch. The water level was much higher than normal, the bilge pump completely submerged and silent. "Not a problem. We have a perfectly good hand pump, but before I get it out, I'm going to tighten the bushing box so the leaking will slow down a bit. We are in no danger."

"Says you," she snapped. "The boat's slowly sinking."

He took a seat beside her again, and began to put his arms around her. She pushed him off and said, "How about get to it sailor. I don't like getting my feet wet."

He stood and watched her glance at him, fearful and angry. He leaned over, kissed her cheek and said, "Don't worry, Sweety. It'll be all right. I'll get to it right away."

Aloft, he opened the port locker and pulled out the photoelectric cells, two, one foot square black panels. After connecting them to the batteries he entered the port hatch and began loosening the access panel to the bushing box and propeller shaft. The bushing box is an ingeniously simple contraption in which greasy ropes are wrapped around the propeller shaft inside a short metal tube. By tightening one end of the tube, the ropes are squeezed tighter around the propeller shaft, preventing water from entering the belly of the boat through the propeller shaft housing.

While Chip was sweating at the bushing box, Joyce came aloft, mostly for the comfort of his closeness and was watching the horizon. When he emerged from his task, she said dreamily, "Chip. Look; way over there. Does that look like a dark spot in the distance? Do you think that might be an island?"

Chip closed the locker hatch. After glancing in the direction Joyce indicated, he opened the lazarette and pulled out a binocular case. He handed the binoculars to Joyce, saying grimly, "Take a look."

Joyce started jumping up and down saying, "It is. It is. Do you think we can get close enough to it to anchor? Maybe there are people there. Maybe they can tell us where we are and what this weird weather stuff is." She handed the binoculars to Chip and moved toward the bow of the boat for a better look.

Chip followed her before lifting the glass to his eyes. "It looks like an island, but if it is why haven't we seen any birds? Usually if there's land so close there would be birds."

"Who cares about birds?" she demanded. "There are trees. And it's big. There might be people there."

"For all we know, if there are people there, they could be cannibals. And if we're within five hundred miles of where we're supposed to be there is no island anywhere around here." He handed the binoculars back to Joyce and returned to retrieve the hand pump.

"I guess we must not be where we're supposed to be," she said to him. "And there are people there. I can see smoke."

"Is it a cooking fire or a rescue signal?" he laughed. "Maybe someone's marooned there. I don't know whether to try to get to it or try to avoid it and if we decide to try to get to it, how that can be done? The water is too deep for kedging. The engine won't do it and that little auxiliary outboard doesn't run either. It's too far to row. We can't sail. So if the tide doesn't take us there, then that's not where we're going."

"You mean, we're going to have sit here on this boat and watch that nice little island drift past?"

"Yes. Or we'll sit here helplessly while we run aground on it. The water may be shallow enough when we get closer that we can anchor off shore and row in with the skiff."

"Do you think there's a reef?" asked Joyce, quietly.

"Probably," he answered. "Most of the islands around here have coral reefs and its reef could reach miles out to sea. We could run aground on the reef and still be too far out to get ashore. Depending on how steep the descent of the land is at the reef, we might not even be able to anchor far enough off."

"So what are you doing Captain Rehab? Trying to do a Robert Ringer on me; maintaining a positive attitude through negativity?"

"I'm 'looking out for number one,' and two. I'm two. We're one."

"Look Chip. Over the island, the sky appears to be blue. The bronze clouds end there."

"It looks like it's just a break in the clouds. Beyond the island it looks like the sky is still bronze."

"Maybe so," she answered, "but maybe while we're in that break in the clouds there'll be enough wind for steerage."

Chip glanced wearily at the sails, hanging like so much limp laundry for the last few days, damp from the salt air. *There isn't even a hint of air movement from whatever current is carrying us along,* he thought to himself. *The air must be moving at exactly the same speed and direction as the current. That is too weird. Usually when there is absolutely no wind like this, the movement of the boat on the ocean current at least provides enough strength for steering or to maintain a weak reach. But not this time. We are totally dead in the water, drifting toward unknown shoals, unknown inhabitants. Is it danger or rescue?*

"The island seems to be getting closer," said Joyce with the same trepidation Chip was feeling.

"One of us should stand by the helm, just in case we get some breeze," said Chip. "We should also both be wearing our life vests in case we hit the reef unexpectedly and get tossed over the side."

"Well. That's a nice thought," she smirked. "I think I liked your positive attitude veiled in negativity better. Now you sound totally negative. We'll get past the island somehow, or be able to anchor near it."

"Let's hope."

They took turns standing by the helm, both remaining in the cockpit watching the approaching island and the depth gauge reading in the thousands of feet. Six hundred feet of anchor line was dangling in the water off the bow with a large Danforth attached to the end, just in case the bottom came up unexpectedly before the boat reached the land.

"It's amazing how fast we're coming up on it," Joyce said in a hushed voice.

"There must be a pretty fast current," he answered. "And a pretty good breeze following it. If the current turns to pass the island, we should have enough wind for steerage. We seem to be closer to the western end than the eastern end of the island. If the current shifts to pass the island, my guess is it'll shift to the west. We need to get the boat facing west so if it's too close, we won't have to turn before we can get under way to pass the island safely. And speaking of directions like that, I'm assuming the island is stationary. That gives us a fix on the direction of drift at least. It looks like we're drifting in a southeasterly direction."

"So how are you going to turn the boat?" asked Joyce. "We haven't had steerage in days."

"Help me untie the dinghy. I'll tie it off to the bow and row it around so MOON DAUGHTER is facing west. And while I'm at it, I'll keep rowing and may be able to tow us far enough to miss the island completely. With any luck we'll be able to anchor off the western end then row ashore."

"Let's get started. All I can see at this end of the island is rock cliffs with surf at the bottom. We don't want to go in there."

Working together, they released the lashing securing the skiff on the bow of MOON DAUGHTER. Then using the main boom, they lowered it over the side and Chip climbed in. A heavy line was secured from the stern of the skiff to the bow of the ketch, and Chip began to row with all his strength. Joyce remained on the bow of MOON DAUGHTER, checking on stern wake from time to time and reporting Chip's progress.

Gradually, Chip began to feel the sea moving beneath him in gentle swells, barely noticeable at first. After a short time, Joyce noticed the movement. "The bottom must be coming up," she called out. "The depth gauge is now reading just over a thousand feet. Is that enough to start the swells? Jeez, closer in the surf must be pretty fierce if we're getting this much swell with this much depth."

Chip was sweating at the oars. His hands were blistering from the unaccustomed work. He had rowed before, but never for his life. "How do we stand to the island?" he called to Joyce.

"I can't tell if we've moved enough or not," she called back. "Keep rowing. The current's bound to shift soon and we ought to be able to get underway and sail around it."

Suddenly MOON DAUGHTER stopped and began quickly shifting to face northwest, placing the stern of the boat toward the cliffs. Chip's skiff, tied from his stern to MOON DAUGHTER's bow was dragged along side facing astern. Now the current was obvious, pushing against the skiff's aft end and holding it tightly from any maneuvers Chip tried to make. They could both hear a sickening scraping noise as the ketch dragged its anchor over the sheer volcanic rock below, rising from the ocean's floor toward what? That question was quickly answered. The sound of the surf breaking over the reef was getting louder.

"Quick," called Chip. "See if you can get her head pointed either way and we can beat out of this." As he talked, he climbed on board, leaving the skiff dangling by its stern lines and he tried to haul in MOON DAUGHTER's anchor.

"She's in irons," Joyce desperately cried out. "I can't get her to point off the wind. The sails won't fill!!"

Chip wrapped the anchor line around a winch and began putting his back into it to untie the boat from the bottom so they could sail off. Failing, he grabbed a fire ax from its fixture on the gunwale and cut the anchor line. "Hard to starboard," he cried out. "The anchor that was holding us into the wind is cut."

Joyce gave the wheel a spin to the right. That should have turned the backing ketch to a westward heading, but as soon as the anchor line gave way they began drifting again with no wind. The sails fell limp again and MOON DAUGHTER resumed her aft-ward course toward the island.

They turned to look astern and could see where the swells were breaking over a submerged reef. "It's too shallow for us," said Joyce.

"But maybe not for the dinghy. We still have a few minutes. The dinghy's drifted off a bit. I'll pull her in. Grab the survival kits. We're going to need everything we can get off this boat."

"Are we going to lose MOON DAUGHTER?" asked Joyce timorously.

"Maybe not. Hurry."

In just a few minutes, they were both in the dinghy with the stern lines cast off. Chip thought he had found a break in the surf and started rowing in that direction. MOON DAUGHTER continued drifting stern first toward the unforgiving coral reef. They watched sick with horror as she struck, crushing her rudder blade, pausing for a moment then turning to face the east as the current dragged her sideways over the rock barrier. The ketch heeled over as though under a strong port wind. They could hear the scraping and crunching of the hull over rocks, louder than the sound of the surf. She heeled so far over that the main and mizzen sails both touched the water before she completed her passage.

"Look," said Joyce. "She's righting herself."

"Yes," Chip grunted over his work at the oars, "but look how low she rides in the water."

At that moment, the skiff shot through the opening and entered the protected bay provided by the reef.

"We may be able to get more stuff off of her if the water isn't too deep," muttered Joyce.

"Let's get to shore. We can wait till she comes to rest, if she's going to. Getting aboard now could be dangerous. She could sink beneath us in seconds, or lay over on her side trapping us below. Look. There's a sandy area over there."

"Look," said Joyce. "Someone is on top of the cliff, waving at us."

With relief, Chip looked up from his rowing. The figure seemed to be that of a young woman in a light blue sarong. He waved back and the figure gestured toward the beach where they were headed, and vanished.

"Well, at least there are other people here," he said.

 C3 &O

The beach consisted of course, brown sand, but the slope to the water was very gentle. Beyond the high tide mark was a dense forest. "Those palms look like they're more than eighty feet tall," remarked Chip. "And the vegetation is really thick. I bet there's plenty of fruit here. I suppose there are worse places to be marooned."

"I'd appreciate it if you avoided using that word again. It sounds so final."

"We probably won't be here any longer than it takes to make a phone call and wait for the mail boat or something like that," said Chip.

"I liked it better when you were being negative. It's awful about

MOON DAUGHTER. I loved that boat."

"Me too," said Chip. "This is what insurance is for. When we get home we'll get another one just like her, but I've had about enough of world cruising. How 'bout you?"

"It sure is nice to have a blue sky again, and to feel some breeze on my face."

"I agree, but look. The sky is still bronze all around the island. This is like an island in the sky as well as on the sea."

"It's an island in despair," said Joyce. "In any case, it looks like our rescuer has arrived."

They had dragged the skiff as far up the sloping beach as they could then secured its bowline to a tree, not knowing the tides. As they finished unloading the survival kits, the woman they had seen on the cliff appeared from the forest beyond with two men behind her. The blue sarong was wrapped tightly around a slim body of what appeared to be a woman of about thirty years. Her waist length black hair moved slightly in the breeze. Her skin was darker than most Polynesians, but lighter than most Africans. Her eyes were most striking, wide, full and very dark brown. Her sand-covered feet were bare with the second toe, longer than the first.

"My gawd," said Joyce softly so only Chip could hear. "She looks just like Queen Nefertiti. And she has my toes," with a low giggle.

"Thank you," the woman spoke with a deep toned, alto voice and a charming smile. "I know you meant that as a compliment, but I never liked Nefertiti. She was a religious fanatic. She had to be removed, with her husband. She was very beautiful. Call me Anna. You have landed on the Island of Arrata, my home. You are my welcome guests."

Her accent isn't Polynesian, thought Chip. *It's more Arabic or Middle Eastern, some sort of Semitic language. I wonder where she's from."*

"These two gentlemen with me are Jorge and Alphonso. They will deliver your things to my home where you are free to stay while you are among us." As she mentioned Jorge and Alphonso, she turned her gaze toward them in a gesture of affection under which both men glowed with satisfaction.

Jorge was a middle-aged man with dark hair, blazing black eyes, three days growth of beard, cut-off jeans and a Spanish accent. Alphonso was taller, thinner and younger, with a longer face and a scar along his right jaw. Both men were barefoot and seemed to be in awe of Anna, *and for good reason,* thought Chip. *She's a real beauty. I wonder how long they've been here.*

Jorge and Alphonso pulled the dinghy farther up the beach to a point above the high tide mark. Chip, ever distrustful of strangers caught them exchanging secretive glances. He watched surreptitiously, wondering if they would steal anything from the survival kits. *Hell*, he thought, *they can have the survival kits. Anna will get us home. We won't need them.*

"Come with me, now, if you like," said Anna. "You would probably like to rest and maybe bathe. You've been through quite an ordeal. Alphonso and Jorge will be along soon."

As she spoke, Chip felt soothed. He glanced at Joyce to see if she was as comfortable with this arrangement as he felt. She had started to follow Anna along the path through the forest. Chip joined in without so much as a glance over his shoulder. The loss of MOON DAUGHTER and their harrowing escape seemed almost forgotten for the moment. The charm of their new hostess and the relative safety they felt around them was enough for the time being. Anna talked as they hiked up the path. She seemed to move without effort, although both Chip and Joyce were beginning to sweat with what was becoming a strenuous climb up a steep hillside.

"I love Arrata," said Anna.

It's as though she's purring, thought Chip. *Her words are indistinct, but I understand everything she says.* Then he stopped thinking as he watched the lithe form ahead of them on the path; the slender muscles of her legs could be seen to move under the tight fitting sarong. He forgot for a moment that Joyce was there until he felt her hand slip into his. It broke the spell, temporarily. He leaned into Joyce and whispered, "I love you."

"I know," she answered.

Anna continued, "It contains two mountains, both of volcanic origin, like Mount Mashu where I once lived. Its vegetation is magnificent. There are no annoying insects, no rodents and no snakes. Every kind of fruit imaginable grows here. It's like the Garden of Eden."

"You saw the Garden of Eden?" asked Joyce with a coy smile?

Anna glanced around and Chip again felt that strong charm that made his knees feel wobbly. "My father planted it, or one much like it," she said, with such a broad grin that Chip and Joyce took it for joking.

"Well at least I can say," Anna went on, "that the Garden of Eden couldn't have been more beautiful or better supplied with food than this island is. I'm sure you will see what I mean. The water is sweet, too. It comes from the rain, flows down the mountain sides into small lakes and pools so pure that I'm sure no water on this planet could match it for sweetness, especially in these days when the industry of the LULUs pollutes everything."

"LULUs?" echoed Chip. "What's a LULU?"

Anna stopped and turned to face them briefly with a wide smile and a look in her eyes that seemed to reveal a slip of sorts. Then her smile widened into a grin and she said, "That's what I call people who do not live on Arrata with me." She continued walking, talking over her shoulder. "They are a slave race, created to serve the gods. Today they are still slaves, slaves to money, slaves to sex, slaves to television, slaves to drugs, slaves to religion."

"Mankind is free," disagreed Joyce. "We have free will."

"Yes, but that freedom of will is limited by your knowledge of your choices." said Anna. "Without full knowledge of your choices, your freedom is very limited. Yes the LULUs are free, they are free to enslave themselves to anything they wish, and they do so with great ingenuity. The LULUs don't seem to be happy if they lack a god who will enslave them. Most of the gods have left, so they create replacements of every kind. Every year there are new gods. Some have even made themselves gods and worship their own imagined purity of race or ability to collect expensive goods, or they worship their own intellect, thinking it makes them somehow a cut above the other enslaved LULUs. The truth is they are just slaves. They are programmed to be slaves, to need a god, something to serve. They will always be slaves, until they become like the gods knowing the full range of their choices and existence, the truth of their origins, how to attain true joy and satisfy true hatred."

With the word, "hatred," Anna cast a look over her shoulder that just about froze Chip in his steps. But then her expression changed back to the charming smile and she continued walking. Chip and Joyce were both sweating freely now with the exertion of the climb.

"I suppose I am very opinionated. I apologize if my ranting has become oppressive. My home is just around the next bend in the path," said Anna. "There you will find the most refreshing bath and food. I'm so sorry for the climb. I must be used to it, myself. I go down to the beach every day."

Chip could hear Jorge and Alphonso coming behind them and for a moment felt a stab of alarm, the same alarm he had felt earlier. *Who are these men? Who is this woman?* He had never before heard of Arrata or heard such ideas as espoused by this beautiful Anna of the hypnotic eyes. But as his thoughts of worry and distrust deepened, they rounded the last bend of the path and there before them stood the house of which Anna had been talking.

Chapter 5: The Monastery on Arrata

SEA TROLLOP was tied up to a short pier thrown together out of palm scraps. Johnny hesitated to step out of the boat onto this shaky looking contrivance, but the ethereal looking elderly gentleman offering his hand to steady him seemed to provide enough reassurance. Tarek was right behind him. Two men clothed in what seemed to Johnny to be scraps of cast off material leaped onto SEA TROLLOP and began unloading her cargo of luggage onto the makeshift pier.

"My name is Lucias," said the tall old man. "I am assuming that you are Tarek and DeMuzzi?" His graying beard brushed against his chest as he nodded politely. His blue eyes sparkling with cheer seemed to look straight through Johnny into everywhere and everything Johnny had ever been.

Johnny was a bit jolted by being referred to by this strange name. Tarek had been trying to get him used to it on the short voyage from Easter Island, but he still wasn't at home with it. *Back home, my friends call me Jack,* he almost said aloud, but caught himself.

"And this is Cardac," said Lucias, indicating a portly middle aged man. "Yakoll and Eshet," Lucias said indicating the men unloading the boat, "will bring your things to the lodge. Cardac will take charge of the boat. It's been a long time since we had a real boat with a function-ing engine," he added with a smile. "We might even be able to scavenge some Diesel fuel from time to time."

"SEA TROLLOP," read Cardac from the writing on the side of the boat. "Does that mean the sea had its way with her?" he asked with a smile, "or that she had her way with the sea. It seems she came out on top," he grinned, "with her engine purring. And a good thing too or you wouldn't be here."

Johnny grinned back and replied, "She gave us a good ride, sir." Tarek chortled and Lucias raised an eyebrow with a tolerant smile. Yakoll and Eshet were talking animatedly and joking in what Johnny later learned was Arabic.

Johnny's take on Cardac was, *Now here is a man with secrets. What bulging eyes. And he looks quite strong. I wonder where the clothes come from. Those jeans look like Levi's. I guess he could have brought them with him. This Lucias is striking. He looks like a medieval alchemist right out of "Fantasia." I wonder what his story is.*

"Come with me," said Lucias, heading up the pier toward shore. "I'll show you around a bit. I know you must be tired, but there's plenty of time for resting. I'm eager to show the place off. We so seldom get new arrivals."

With a quick glance around Johnny took in some of the scenery. The beach, if it could be called that was mostly volcanic rock, solid rivers of black reaching to the water's edge interspersed with black sand and pearly, white sea shells. The harbor was in the lee of the island, protected by the coral reef so there was very little surf. The water was crystal blue. He could see fish and various bottom dwellers as clearly as though he had a glass on the water. Beyond the beach were tall trees concealing the interior of the land. Many tall palms were visible with hundreds of species of shrubs, none of which he recognized.

Lucias led them into a trail barely visible from the pier. Someone had lined it with seashells and swept it clean. Flowers and cultivated ground cover were beyond the seashells. The soft pungent soil provided an attractive footpath into the forest. It seemed they had taken only a few steps when they came into a wide clearing with a high, terraced hillside. Each terrace was cultivated with various crops. Men of all ages and descriptions and a few women were working at tilling, weeding and harvesting. The path became a stone pavement leading to a long stairway, also of stone. Some of the steps were carved into the volcanic rock of what Johnny could now see was a mountain rising in the distance. Far above them appeared to be a large complex of buildings, all constructed of cut volcanic rock with some intermixing of what he took for native stone. Johnny wasn't sure if it was granite or cement, at this distance.

"That must be one of the two mountains we saw from the sea," Johnny said to Tarek.

Lucias answered, "Some say there is only one mountain and it has two peaks. Others that there are two mountains. The truth is there are volcanic vents at the tops of both and the eruptions ran together to form one large base for both. We think there was some uplifting here before the volcanoes because there is some natural rock that isn't pumice. Most of the island though, is from the volcanoes. Whether there is one mountain or two is an ongoing controversy. It gives us something to talk about. We don't have much contact with the outside world."

"Is this what they call Mount Mashu?" asked Johnny.

"Oh. So you've heard of that already," chuckled Lucias as they climbed the stone stairway. "Those of us who maintain there is only one mountain call it that. The others simply refer to them as the Eastern Peak and the Western Peak. You can't see The Western Peak from here. To see it you must climb higher. There's a path behind the Cloisters that will take you high enough for a clear view, if you're interested."

"What is the shimmering I seem to be seeing beyond the visible mountain?" asked Tarek.

Johnny looked where Tarek indicated. He could see now that the sky appeared to be slightly out of focus beyond the top of the mountain. He rubbed his eyes and looked again. The fuzzy focus was still there. "I see it too," he said. "That's as strange as the Rapanui Storm. What is it? And for that matter, what causes the Rapanui Storm?"

It's not surprising that you have a lot of questions," Answered Lucias. "All will become clear in time."

They reached the top terrace where they found a patio laid out neatly with home made lawn furniture of bamboo lashed together with some native fiber. Lucias sat down in one of the chairs. "Take a seat and rest a bit. I climb that hill every day, but I think it's starting to wear on me more than it used to. I'll tell you this, my new friends, growing old is not a gentle venture."

Tarek and Johnny chuckled politely as they realized they were puffing from the climb much harder than Lucias. As Johnny turned to take his seat, he almost gasped at the panoramic view of the sea to the east, north and south. The Rapanui Storm had cleared, leaving a bright blue sky dotted with clouds hurrying along on their world tour. Sea birds wheeled and turned far below, diving into the sea for a fish and climbing back into the air, watching for another and diving again. Johnny found their dance almost hypnotic.

"Quite a view, eh?" asked Lucias.

"Sure is," Tarek and Johnny answered almost in unison.

"I've been here so long I sometimes take the view for granted," said Lucias. His face turned serious and Johnny could see the wrinkles in his skin, of cares and worries. Lucias' brow furrowed as he turned to face them.

"When Captain Roggeveen returned to Holland after discovering many places and things on his long voyage, he reported strange findings on the Island he named Easter Island. He wrote of the statues, but also he wrote of the desolation he found there. The men of Ha Agudoss found this interesting but paid little attention to it until after Captain Cook's visit there in 1774. Cook found it even more desolate than Roggeveen reported. It seems that it declined in that fifty years between the two visits. He wrote there were no quadrupeds except rats. There were no trees to speak of, no fish, hardly any land birds and the only sea birds were Men of War Birds, Noddies and Egg birds.

"This was found to be strange, so Ha Agudoss provided for some of our people to come to Easter Island to investigate. They knew that other islands in the South Pacific were usually plush, green, virtual paradises. They wanted to find out what happened to Rapanui.

"In those days, our headquarters was in Ireland. When our explorers returned to Ireland they reported that there appeared to be a powerful source of negative energy emanating from somewhere to the south and their conclusion was that this was the cause of the devastation on Rapanui.

"Many of our younger men, being bored with the monastic life style in Ireland, wanted to go on an adventure and this crusade to identify and end the evil influence in this area of the South Pacific seemed to be perfect. It was debated for decades. Finally, some of those young men rose to positions of leadership in the Fraternity. Now they felt they were too old to go, but the younger men, the newer initiates, still wanted to investigate.

"When the expedition departed, there were thirty of our people on board the ship. It was a harrowing journey around Cape Horn - no Panama Canal in those days. The voyage took months. Many of our people died on the journey. Only nineteen arrived and when they did, they were greeted with one of these Rapanui Storms, as you called it. They were ship wrecked on this end of the island.

"Accounts of that experience are conflicting. Generally, it came down to us that this group of nineteen was strong enough in joint meditation to sort of polarize the negative energy, stabilizing an area on the eastern side of the island, where we are now.

"How ever they managed, it must have been quite a battle, judging from the ongoing fight we continue to wage. We've managed to learn that there are people over there, but none of them ever come here, and those of our group who have ventured to the western side of the island," he paused for effect, "never returned."

Some men dressed in loose fitting cotton wraps came out to bring tea on trays that they placed on a low table in the center of the group. "Thanks fella's," Lucias said to them, then "have some tea gentlemen."

Johnny sipped green tea as he watched the sea birds below. Some were still fishing, while some were tiny white specks floating on the ocean's aquamarine surface. Suddenly a flock of seagulls that must have been resting on the beach to the southwest took to the air. *I wonder what alarmed them*, he thought quietly. *Maybe I'll get a chance to walk down there later. Exploring this place is going to be fun.*

"What do you think is going on?" Tarek asked Lucias. "What does it feel like to you?"

"It's hard to think about such things when there is such beauty all around us. Our life style is idyllic. Do you see those large leafed plants at the edge of the lowest terrace, there?" He pointed. "Those are banana trees." He smiled widely, "When I lived in Switzerland, our bananas came from thousands of miles away. Now I need only walk outside and pluck one. Then, I need only to turn and face the other way to be reminded of the danger we're all in. There is still a serpent in paradise, my friends, a serpent that I think wants to consume all of us. What do I think is going on?" he returned to Tarek's question.

"Those in meditation have reported that the power increases shortly after each ship wrecks on the western side of the island. It remains stronger for a while, weeks or sometimes months, then recedes again. We know that the strange weather phenomenon you called the Rapanui Storm brings the shipwrecks. There was another yesterday, a small one apparently, not much power was drawn from it, at least not yet. We suspect that the source of this evil is very old, maybe even ancient, but we haven't been able to identify what it is. When the power increases, the shimmering you can see in the distance comes closer to us. It constantly tries to overwhelm us. Many of our people fear that it will someday succeed."

"Where do we fit into this, asked Johnny," putting his cup on the table. He leaned into his chair and glanced at Tarek whose face showed concern equal to his.

Tarek drained his cup and said, "I suppose there is a group in constant meditation to hold this off, whatever it is. We're probably expected to add our strength to that group, by meditation. Is that the idea, Lucias?"

"It was told to me in silence that you were coming. We had hoped for more than two, but the two of you is what they sent. We will add you to the rotation. Perhaps you have special abilities not yet apparent to me that will come to our aid in some way. I fear that the brothers on the mainland may not understand the danger that this situation represents. Our greatest fear is that an ocean liner or some other large ship will wreck on the western side of the island with thousands of people on board. It seems that the more people who wind up over there, the stronger the power gets. Come, let me show you the rest of the complex."

Johnny was fascinated with the construction of the complex. Each section was connected by at least a covered walkway, cloisters, they were called. The size of the complex alone was mind boggling. The large exposed area where they had tea with Lucias was imposing enough when seen from a distance, but that was a small section concealing rather than revealing the true living area cut into the very rock of the mountain side. Caves formed from volcanic vents riddled the area. These were incorporated with sections cut out for rooms or cells for sleeping.

The first room Lucias took them to see was a large auditorium where Johnny counted six rows with ten people in each row, in deep meditation. Lucias indicated with a finger to his lips that any conversation could disturb some of those at work. The walls of the auditorium were shear rock with torches set in the walls for dim lighting. Most of those in meditation were seated on mats placed on the floor. Some had chairs that appeared to be comfortable, while others, seemed to prefer a reclining position. *The form that works best is the one to use,* Johnny mused. *Talk about a sedate life style! There won't be any movies in this place, no newspapers, no football games, no baseball. It's going to take me a while to get used to this, and they say there is no way to leave! So, this is a lifetime commitment.*

The next area Lucias showed them was another large area cut out of the rock, but much better lighted than the first. Johnny noted windows cut through the rock to the outside, allowing sunlight to enter. *That window design is really clever,* considered Johnny. *When it rains, the water follows those channels and runs into floor scuppers. They must drain outside somewhere.*

"This is the refectory," Lucias said. "As you know, in our monasteries only one meal is served each day, and the food is in the Essene tradition, a live, vegetarian repast, but in this case, we have groups on four schedules so we serve meals every six hours, more or less. I say more or less, because we have no clocks here. We serve at first light, the first hour after darkness falls, high twelve and low or noon and midnight."

"How cold does it get here in the winter," Tarek asked.

"Good question," remarked Lucias. "The weather gets pretty cool sometimes and that means we need warm clothing from time to time. We have no coal here or fuel except for the wood from the trees outside. We try to cut no more than we can replace by growing new trees, keeping a cycle going. Last year, one of the brothers found a bog lower down in the forest. In the bog he discovered peat, so we have some peat to burn also, but mostly we use that in the gardens. Follow me."

Lucias led them through winding passageways leading up hill for the most part. Johnny completely lost his sense of direction and was surprised when at the end of a passage, he found sunlight and a grassy meadow. "Look down there," Lucias pointed.

"At what?" asked Johnny, noticing that the shimmering barrier was much nearer now. They were between the eastern and western peaks.

"Sheep," answered Tarek with a wide grin. "Is there also a loom?"

"Several looms," answered Lucias. "I'll show them to you tomorrow. Something else I want you to see while we're up here is that." Lucias turned grim as he pointed at the wall of the shimmering, toward the west. "It has moved a little closer since yesterday. Someday, I hope I can learn what affects it. We know it's the divider between them and us, but what 'them' represents, I have no idea.

"Over the years, we have sent emissaries hoping to negotiate, or at least to learn what it is we're fighting. We have sent some of our best people over there, thinking they could defend themselves, but none have ever returned. It's been a long time since we sent anyone. Now, I think it's a tragic loss and pointless. Whatever it is doesn't want to talk to us."

"Is it my imagination," asked Johnny, "or does its texture appear to change. I mean. It looks almost like the surface of a lake or some water body. For a while it appeared to be smooth, or calm, but now it looks like water with the wind blowing over it. It's agitated and sort of undulating."

"That's how it looks when it's growing stronger. I expect we won't be able to hold it at that distance much longer. I think we can stop it. We usually can."

"Usually?" repeated Johnny. "That doesn't sound very good. Do you mean that it can't always be stopped? Sometimes it overwhelms this side of the island?"

"I've been here just over forty three years," said Lucias. In those years, it has over run us twice. When it does, and it could well happen again, everyone goes to work, not just the sixty or so who are meditating at any one time, but all of us. The last time it took all of us to drive it back."

"What was it like when this happened?" asked Tarek. "Any unusual sensations or feelings?"

Lucias lowered his eyes for a moment, remembering. "It was like some powerful intelligence looking us over, trying to decide what to do about us. I seemed to feel it asking, 'Who are you? Why are you here? What do you want from me? Go away.' It's really ironic, in a sense. We came here, all of us, with the idealistic intention of defeating it, driving it into the sea, but all we've managed to do is survive here and hold it off. Before we can even think about defeating it, we must first understand it. In that, we have failed, so far."

"There's always tomorrow," said Johnny.

A white robed figure appeared on the edge of the meadow from the forest. Seeing them, it first hesitated, then realizing it had been seen, it continued to approach. "Ah," said Lucias. "It is Lee Moy, a very special brother. For his private meditations, he goes to an herb garden he privately cultivates in the forest. I know he does this only because of the wonderful herbs that sometimes appear in our food, and no one else goes into the forest like this. Most are afraid."

As Lee Moy approached he kept is eyes averted, watching his footsteps over the uneven ground. When he was close enough, Lucia said to him, "Lee Moy, my brother, allow me to introduce..."

"Tarek and DeMuzzi," Lee Moy finished Lucias' sentence. "I am glad to see you arrived safely. I watched over your voyage. If you will excuse me..." and he was gone down the passage.

"Abrupt?" asked Johnny, thinking, *deep voice, extremely slim, long nose. What strange eyes.*

"Preoccupied," answered Lucias. "He is very powerful. We're fortunate to have him on our side."

"Is he an American Indian?" asked Tarek with interest.

"He claims to be Anasazi," answered Lucias. "That in itself is amazing since the Anasazi disappeared a long time ago. What happened to them is a great mystery in the Southwest USA. If you ask him that question, he'll say, 'nothing happened to them. Here I am. We are called Hopi now, and Pueblo, and Navajo, among other things.' He appears to have made a study of ancient tongues. He can read Cuneiform and Egyptian glyphs, for whatever good that skill will do him here. He says it's almost the same as the Anasazi languages. What can I say?" Lucias grinned. "He believes it. I find it doubtful, myself."

Lucias led them back through the labyrinth of passageways to the main entrance where they had had tea earlier. Johnny was beginning to recognize caves they had been through before and was starting to get a feel for the layout of the compound.

"There are several hours left in the day," he said. "Why not wonder around and get to know the place. Smell the air. Taste the water. You may even want to go for a swim. There's a lake higher up that we use for swimming and washing. I'll look for you at prayer - last hour of the night, on the main terrace. After that, we'll get you assigned with tasks and on to the meditation schedule. I recommend those bananas." And he was off with a smile toward the interior of the complex.

ങ ഌ

Johnny went to the cell Lucias had shown him, that was to be his. He liked his stone cell because it had an opening he could see through to the sea. *An ocean view,* he thought to himself. *I love it.*

He had made a similar remark to Lucias, who retorted, "You may change your mind when the weather turns next fall, but you can cover the opening and that will break the wind, at least. Glad you like it. That's rare." Then he laughed.

Johnny looked out of his window now. It faced south and he could just make out the spot on the beach where the birds were alarmed earlier. *I think I'm going to see if I can get to that spot,* and he started out.

Outside he found a path leading to the edge of the highest cultivated terrace. Following it, he learned that at the end of the terrace the path headed down the hillside through the forest. It wasn't a prettied up path like the one from the pier, but a regular footpath through the trees. He walked quietly trying not to alarm any of the wild creatures he might find along the way and was rewarded by seeing some bright colored parrots and some other birds he couldn't identify. The vegetation was spectacular with many large leafed plants, flowering in the heavy shade of the rain forest.

Finally, the path had descended all the way to the sea. When he reached it, he turned right and walked along the sand with only his bare feet in the water until he came to a rock promontory, volcanic of course. He put his shoes back on and carefully climbed the rock, hoping to continue his walk on the beach on the other side of this old lava flow. When he reached the top, he was alarmed to see a head bobbing in the water just beyond.

It was a young woman, wearing nothing, but with her body mostly concealed by the very clear water. With the mixed emotion of wanting to not embarrass her, and not wanting to stop watching, he froze and backed a little down the rock so only his eyes were above the rim. *She has very unusual eyes,* he thought. Her long, black hair floated in the water behind her as she swam toward shore. As the bottom rose toward the island, she stopped swimming and stood up to her waist to walk the rest of the way toward her clothing which Johnny saw laying in the sand a little further up the beach from him.

That was too much for Johnny. His foot slipped and he fell off the promontory onto the sand, about ten feet below.

Inanna must have heard him fall because when he did, she turned, looking in that direction and smiled.

Chapter 6: The Power of Inanna

Chip rolled over and opened his eyes, thankful to give up the nightmare he had been having all night long of losing MOON DAUGHTER. Each dream was a little different. In one, they were aboard and dashed onto the rocks with the ketch. In another, the lifeboat was also dashed on the rocks. In yet another, an angel descended from the sky and guided the lifeboat through the rocks while the ketch foundered on shoals. Each dream was equally horrible because in each one, MOON DAUGHTER was lost and they were both marooned on an unknown island in an unknown sea.

In that first moment of disorientation that occurs on waking in a strange place for the first time, Chip became immediately frightened because the room was stationary instead of rolling with the seas and the wind. He and Joyce had been sleeping aboard for so long that the room fixed on solid ground was disturbing. Then he remembered and became frightened all over again. *Where are we really?* He thought to himself. *What is this place? Who is that woman? How did she acquire such a property? She surely didn't build these buildings, herself and there doesn't appear to be any other civilization on the island with the technology or machinery to do it, much less a team of architects.*

MOON DAUGHTER was lost. They were on an uncharted island called Arrata. He turned quickly and was relieved to find Joyce lying beside him, softly snoring. *She would be so embarrassed, if she knew how she snored,* he chuckled to himself. *But it's not very loud and it's such a nice reminder that she's close to me. I missed her snoring on the boat because we seldom slept at the same time.*

The bed they were in could hardly be called a bed. It was more of a mat on the floor, with a mattress stuffed with something soft, maybe grasses. The room at first impression looked like a vision out of old Mexico, stucco walls, one window with no glass or screen and the sounds of birds chattering. From his place on the mat, he could see one large leaf of a plant hanging from above the window and beyond it the side of a mountain. He stood up to see better, waking Joyce who stopped snoring, groaned, and rolled over onto her back.

"Is it my watch yet?" she mumbled. Then looking around in surprise, "Where are we? Oh. I remember. What dreams!!"

"You too?" muttered Chip, standing beside the window. "Take a look," he said pointing outside.

Chip was reviewing in his mind the site he had seen the night before when they arrived at what one of the other 'guests' had referred to as the 'palace complex.' When they rounded the last turn in the path, they had been confronted with a sprawling collection of attached buildings with stucco walls and mostly flat roofs. "Looks Mexican," Chip had remarked.

"I'm calling it my Spanish Colonial Period," Anna had laughed.

The wings appeared to house numerous rooms, constructed to look a little like individual bungalows, most of which were inhabited by either shipwrecked sailors like themselves or native peoples, Polynesians. Some were working on the spacious grounds maintaining several gardens of varying sizes. Each garden appeared to be specialized in one type or family of plants or flowers. All the gardens were connected by a labyrinth of paths paved in faded blue tile with a large fountain in the center of the maze.

The main building had a two-story cathedral ceiling with clerestory windows up top, housing a large ballroom with a dais at the far end of the room facing double doors at the entrance. On the dais stood a large magnificently carved chair, Anna referred to in a joking manner as her throne. The 'throne' was set up to a table with settings for nine. The eight preferred guests who sat at Anna's table for dinner last night were Chip and Joyce, two other American couples and two fisherman who owned and ran a charter boat which was docked nearby. The two couples, Al and Teri Johns, James and Rosemary Albert-Smithson had chartered the boat for fishing off of Easter Island. Numerous others were seated at tables on the main floor. All served themselves from a large banquet table at the north end of the room. Anna was served, while she leaned back in her throne of what she called Lapis Lazuli [law-peace law-zyulee].

Chip had never before seen this kind of stone. It was translucent blue with what appeared to be flecks of gold or maybe iron pyrite visible below the surface. "That thing must be worth a fortune," Chip remarked.

"I know," answered Anna. "I've had it for a very long time. My father had it made for me. The rock itself is regarded as semi-precious. Pieces this big are rare. There are only three known sources in the world, Chile, Colorado and Afghanistan. In Colorado they grind it up, remove the beautiful interior decorations and call it Lazurite. The best quality is from the Afghanistan mine, not a very friendly place, these days. That's where this piece is from, in fact."

"It looks like it must weigh several tons," remarked James Smithson. "It must be very difficult to move." Smithson was from Maitland Florida. Chip thought he looked about sixty years old, thin and fidgety. A typical 'A' Type personality, Smithson's driving questions about their departure from the island seemed aimed at pinning Anna down on when the mail boat would arrive, which she had referred to from time to time. Anna was obviously avoiding the question and when she finally became frustrated with him, Chip witnessed an amazing thing.

Anna stretched her hand across the table placing it on Smithson's shoulder. He stopped talking, in itself an amazing thing. His face, which had been growing red with his urgent questioning, calmed remarkably. His intense eyes grew soft and he said to Anna, "You are so beautiful, and so good. How could I ever mistrust someone like you."

Smithson's wife, Rosemary was a short woman with sandy shoulder length hair, full lips, gray eyes, about fifty years and a Dallas accent. At his remark, she looked like she had been slapped. Her face distorted in anger and she was about to retort when Anna looked directly at her and said in a most unique, almost commanding tone of voice, "It'll be alright, Rosey. He means nothing by it."

Smithson's face changed again from worshipful veneration to one of apologetic dispute. "But I mean..."

Anna interrupted him with, "I know Jimmy. I know. It's okay. I understand."

Rosemary looked disturbed but temporarily pacified. Chip smiled inwardly. He was thinking of the scolding, Smithson was likely to get from his wife, when they were alone again, later. He glanced at Joyce who met his eye with a warning glint, but she squeezed his hand under the table.

Al Johns was a big man, six foot three, probably sixty-five or better, and around 250 pounds. His male pattern baldness had resulted in severe sunburn earlier and his wife Teri spread a salve on it twice during dinner much to his embarrassment. Big Al was an obvious executive type, with that quiet aura of command about him. When he spoke, even James Smithson shut up and listened. *I bet Smithson works for him,* Chip thought. *I wonder what business they're in.*

Big Al cleared his throat in announcement of a coming statement. He ceremoniously took a sip from his water glass and said with a meaningful look at Smithson, "Easter Island can't be very far from here. Have you tried raising the marine patrol with the short wave radio I saw on the boat?" The question was directed to Jorge and Alphonso.

The fishing party had been lucky enough to drift over the reef without mishap, apparently on a higher tide with a shallower draft than MOON DAUGHTER's. It was anchored in the bay with a non-functional engine and dead batteries. Jorge and Alphonso spent all their daylight hours trying to get it running. Jorge repeated Big Al's question to Alphonso in Spanish then answered, in English. "We have tried to do this but either the radio is not working or it is not strong enough to reach Rapanui. Tomorrow I intend to rewire the antenna. Maybe something broke when we came over the reef."

Σ Ȣ ȣ

Chip was snapped back to the present by the sound of a loud bell apparently calling people to their jobs in the gardens. Morning had come and he was peering out of the window with Joyce, surveying the limitations of their sanctuary. In the grounds outside the window, he could see people going to work, with shovels, rakes, hoes and other gardening implements slung over shoulders or pulled along in carts. There were sea birds in the distance to the south and west and the mountain rising sharply to the right, beyond the 'palace complex.'

"We could be marooned in worse places, you know," she whispered in his ear.

"Maybe so, but look at this " he whispered back, indicating the window. All the people who had been heading for the gardens had stopped at the sound of the bell and turned to face the main building. Chip and Joyce both turned to see what they were looking at. They saw nothing at first, but then the double doors opened. Even from the side where Chip and Joyce were located in their bungalow room, they could see a bright blue light emanating from within. Then Anna emerged clothed in a blue sarong covering her whole body, except for her feet. "Does she seem to you to be glowing?" Chip asked Joyce.

"I think it's just the sunlight on her sarong," said Joyce. "She couldn't be glowing."

"But the sun is still behind the mountain," said Chip. "She's in shadow."

"Well it seems like there's a light coming from inside the ballroom. Maybe that's what makes her look like that."

Anna seemed taller this morning, her light almost filling the porch of the ballroom. The gardeners all fell to their knees. Anna watched them in approval, then suddenly, as though she felt them watching her, turned to look directly at Chip and Joyce, who almost as quickly, ducked out of her line of sight.

Joyce plopped back down on the sleeping mat, arms folded, legs crossed, a frightened look on her face and said, "I don't think I like this very much."

Chip stayed by the window, keeping as much of himself out of sight as possible but watching around the corner of the window frame, with one eye. Anna seemed to have focused her attention in the distance, on the charter boat anchored in the protection of the coral reef. One of the Chilean fishermen, Chip couldn't see at this distance which one it was, had climbed to the top of the charter boat's communication mast and was working on one of the antennas. The Rapanui Storm had passed and they had managed to get the engines started. Chip could see exhaust rising from the rear of the boat, a thirty six-foot sports fisherman possibly an old Hatteras design.

"Joyce. Come look. They got the engine started on that charter boat. The storm passed. Maybe it was some sort of electro-magnetic field or something that made everything electronic, screwy. Anyway, the storm is passed and they got their engine started. Maybe they can take us to Easter Island and we can get home from there."

Joyce rose quickly to look out the window again. Anna was still standing on the porch of the main building, shaded by the extended roof overhang. As they watched, the boat turned and began very slowly maneuvering toward the pier. The man on the communications mast called out something to the one in the wheelhouse and as he did, Anna raised one hand. Her fingers were balled into a fist except for the index and middle fingers that she pointed at the fishing yacht. Suddenly a bolt of blue lightning shot from her hand to the boat. There was a rippling effect in the air forming a corridor from Inanna to the boat's communications mast. The water between the shore and the boat rippled violently as though a large school of fish had suddenly darted away. The man on the communications mast fell to the deck.

Then she extended both hands toward the kneeling garden workers, palms open, facing them. There she stood for almost a full minute with her eyes closed as though experiencing some sort of ecstasy. As she did this, two of the garden workers collapsed, but none of the others turned to look much less ran to help.

Anna then opened her eyes, lowered her hands, smiled and returned indoors.

"We gotta' get the hell outa' Dodge, big guy," said Joyce softly. "I don't know what that was that we just saw and I never want to find out. In fact, I don't even want to remember it. We just need to really focus on leaving." She headed for the small anteroom Anna had showed them the night before, which contained bathroom facilities.

Chip went outside and headed for the pier to find out what had happened to the man on the boat. He was about half way there when he saw Big Al's wife, Teri and Jimmy Smithson headed in the same direction. "What's going on here?" Chip asked the two as they neared the pier at the same time. "This is some pretty strange stuff."

"You can say that agin,'" retorted Teri Johns, her Texas twang more in evidence than ever. Teri was of slight build, five feet tall, too much makeup, an ever-present cigarette, and sweeping applied eyebrows giving her a look of constant astonishment.

"We been here more 'n three damned weeks an' they been tryin' ta' fix that damned boat. Wouldn't ya' know it, as soon as they git it started that damned vixen bitch in there zaps one of 'em and now look. The damn boat's jist driftin' agin.' We ain't never gonna' git outa' here."

"Let's take a look and see if he's alright," said Jimmy Smithson, "and which one it is."

As they approached the pier, Jorge came out of the wheel house, glanced at his cousin Alphonso laying on the deck and before checking any closer dropped the anchor off the bow to keep the boat safe. Then he kneeled by his cousin, just out of sight, concealed by the gunwales of the boat. The boat was almost fifty yards away, too far for them to hear anything from the boat except the loudest noises.

Chip noticed an old woman emerging from the forest from the path he and Joyce had followed the night before, from the beach. She was wearing a long black gown, that even from this distance, Chip could recognize as lace. Over her flowing white hair, she was wearing a black veil and she was making her way in their direction.

"Who's that?" Chip directed his question to either Jimmy or Teri.

Teri answered. "I donno' who the hell she is," snapped Teri, clearly threatened by all that had happened here this morning. She stood solidly with feet slightly apart in an almost martial arts stance except for the crossed arms. "We seen'er around a couple a' times. Could be that bitch's Mama fer all I know."

"It's clear," said Jimmy, "that we need to focus everything we have on leaving this island."

"That's fer damn sure," added Teri.

At that moment, Jorge's face appeared above the gunwale of the Hatteras. "Muerto," he called out to them. "Alphonso es muerto." He followed this statement with adequate vulgarities in Spanish to make Teri flush.

"That foul mouthed son of a cold taco," retorted Teri. I'm gonna' slap that boy silly when he gits back in here. No man has a right ta' talk that way. He says his cousin's dayed. He says he's leavin' this island even if he has to swim back to Chile. That boy's given ta' exaggeration. Chile muss' be more n' two thousand miles from here."

The old woman whose approach Chip had been watching was finally within ear shot. She continued closer to them without speaking. Finally, she addressed them, "Good Morning Meester Smithson, Meesus Johns, and another stranger. ¿Como se llama? [How is he called?] she directed the question to Teri.

"He's called Mister Chip Evans, Mam," replied Teri. "An' a good mornin' to y'all too. Mr. Chip, this here's Leelee. She's been real nice ta' us. What brings y'all out sa' early, Miss Leelee? Didja' all see what happened to that poor boy on the boat, there, Mam?"

Chip could see that the doors had opened to the main building again. The blue glow was more apparent to him, now, than earlier because he could see directly into the building. The light was coming from two sources. The throne of Lapis Lazuli was one source but the brighter of the two was the woman standing in the center of the doorway. Anna was glaring at them. Without adieu, she began walking down the steps of the front terrace and heading toward them. When she appeared, the gardeners again dropped their implements and kneeled toward her, heads and eyes lowered.

Leelee spoke to them softly, in confidential tones, Spanish accent gone. "If you want to survive this experience, treat her with great respect."

Chip watched Leelee's face in amazement as she spoke. The deeply wrinkled skin revealed age greater than he thought he had ever seen. The burning spirit he could see shining in her eyes belied the wizened complexion. She smiled when she finished, winked at him and said, "Take care of that wife of yours, Meester Chip." As she spoke the smile faded, her face turning deadly serious enough to frighten Chip.

What does she know that she's not telling? Chip's thoughts shouted to him. *She looks older than God, wiser than a Judge and weirder than Halloween. Who is this old woman?*

As Anna passed among the Polynesian gardeners, a low chant arose among them, "Heena. Heena. Heena." Leelee began to walk back toward the path to the beach, slowly, deliberately.

Does she live down there somewhere? Where did she come from? Where's she going? Chip wondered.

Anna was nearing them, now. As she did, the chant grew a bit louder until Anna raised both hands and shouted "Silence." The chant stopped.

"Good morning, pretty lady," said Jimmy with a smile. The others were still too cowed by recent events to say anything.

Anna looked preoccupied, and watched Leelee as she disappeared into the forest. "Be gone old bird," Anna called after her with annoyance.

"Who is that?" asked Chip.

Anna's attention returned to the three. "She's a guardian of mine, a nuisance, if you ask me." Her eyes flashed in that way Chip found so hypnotic, glancing at Leelee's retreating figure and then back to Chip.

When Anna looks directly into my eyes, he thought, *it feels jolting, as though with her glance she can touch my very insides, see every part of me, my thoughts, my fears and desires. Gawd! To possess such a woman!!*

"She's supposed to be a tutor, of sorts, but the only thing I've learned from her in recent millennia is Spanish." When she said the word 'Spanish', it was with disdain and a soft snort. She turned to look at the yacht. Jorge was climbing into the dinghy to row ashore, confidant that the boat was adequately anchored. He had already lowered Alphonso's body into the dinghy, as they were talking with Belili. He untied the dinghy from the yacht. As he began to row toward the pier, they could see tears on his cheeks.

Chip noticed that the gardeners were still kneeling but had changed the direction they were facing as Anna walked from the main building toward the pier. The chanting had stopped, but Chip could still feel the pulse of it in the air around him. Heena Heena. "What were they chanting?" he asked Anna.

She looked at him briefly before answering as though considering what to say. "They think I'm their Moon goddess, Hina. When they asked my name for the very first time, I made the mistake of telling the full truth. My real name is Inanna. When I said that, all the fools heard is the first two syllables, Ina. Then they had to form it around the sounds of their own tongue, so it came out Heena. 'Anna' is the last part of my real name and it seems to fit the tongues of modern languages better than bits and pieces of Inanna. So, I am Inanna. If you want to call me that, I will not object. If you want to call me Anna, that's okay too. Just please don't call me Heena. If you do that, I will think you are food."

"Yer jist kiddin' right?" asked Teri. "I mean, fer gawd's sake. You don't really eat them islanders do ya?' I mean, I mean..."

Inanna cut her off with a look. Teri stopped talking, but seemed as though she was still trying to talk. Her eyes grew bigger with the effort, but after a few seconds she stopped trying, and displayed a look of angry frustration.

During this exchange, Chip noticed, the expression on Jorge's face had converted to one of angry determination. The dinghy he was rowing had changed directions and was headed out to sea. Inanna noticed about the same time as Chip. She glared after him, speaking softly, Chip thought, *to the three of us? Or is she just thinking out loud?* "See how the current carries him back to us? He'll never make it beyond the reef with the wind and current pushing him toward shore."

To Chip's horror, he noticed that the blue sky overhead had begun to cloud over with bronze colors and swirling shapes. The water lost its blue brilliance and began to reflect the color of the bronze sky. The dinghy Jorge was trying to row out to sea was being quickly swept back toward the pier, with the Chilean fisherman, struggling with all his strength on the oars. Finally, one of the oars snapped leaving him holding only the handle. In frustration and fear, he turned to watch the boat's progress as it was swept back to the beach beside the pier.

As Jorge drifted back toward the beach with the broken oar in his hand, Inanna continued her monologue. "No one can leave here. Not me. Not you. Not him. Not her. This is our eternal home, Arrata, my domain. The wind imprisons me. The sea imprisons me. The wind imprisons you. The sea imprisons you."

Belili appeared at the edge of the forest again, as though she had been waiting just out of sight. Chip heard her call out to them, "I can leave." Then with audible chuckling, she vanished again into the forest. Her voice seemed to break Inanna's focus, annoyance appearing on her face. The bronze of the sky began to fade back to blue as Jorge's boat touched the beach. Inanna broke off her stare at Jorge and turned angry attention toward the path where Belili disappeared. Without a word, Inanna walked off toward the forest. The gardeners resumed their chant as she vanished down the path.

"Heena. Heena," the voices resumed their chanting. When she was out of sight, they became silent again and resumed their work in the gardens.

Jimmy opened the conversation. "I wonder what hold she has over these people? They can't possibly believe she's a god. I certainly can't. Maybe she has them drugged in some way."

"Drugs ud' do it," Teri volunteered, again able to speak.

"What did she do to you?" asked Chip.

"I donno," said Teri. "I don think she done nothin.' She's jist sa' damn mean that when she looked right at me like that I froze right up. What I'd like ta' know is what she up an' done to Alphonso and Jorge. Looks ta' me like that Alphonso's sorta' all dried up, like.

"She might be usin' drugs on them people," Teri continued. "Ma siyister had a boyfrien' who was on nat stuff and she had total control over 'im when e' was high. 'Course, he was a gentle drunk. Some fella's when they git on that stuff git mean, but not ole Bubba.'"

"I think there's more to it than drugs," said Jimmy.

"I think so too," Chip answered. "She's intensely hypnotic. Have you noticed that, Mr. Smithson?"

"Oh, call me James. Please," Jimmy answered. "Yes I have noticed that she's quite charismatic. You might even refer to it as hypnotic, but I'm not willing to go that far."

"You'd go all the way if she wanted you to an' you know it," said Teri. "So why you holden' back from 'hypnotic?'"

"All right," said Jimmy. "I'll admit she's hypnotic. How do you react to her, Teri does she seem hypnotic to you too?"

"Well you seen how she shut me right up," Teri responded. "She's hypnotic alright, but I bet she's hypnotic in a different way for me than for you men, me bein' a woman and all. Jimmy's right." Jimmy winced visibly. "We need ta' git off this island right smart, but tryin' ta' row ta' Chile ain't the answer, if ya' ask me."

"Now we at least know the source of the Rapanui Storm. She somehow does it," said Jimmy.

"That had to a' been a coincidence," objected Teri. "Nobody can do stuff like that. The current was there yesterday. It was there last week. It's always gonna' be there. She didn't do nothin' but stand there and grumble, while the current pushed him back."

"But what did she do to Alphonso?" Chip asked generally, half to himself, disbelieving what he had seen.

Chapter 7: The Power of Lust

Life at the monastery was an easy adjustment for Johnny, except for the nagging thoughts of Inanna's naked body emerging from the surf - yesterday. *I thought I was rid of those urges,* he thought to himself in disgust. *Okay, so I'm only thirty-five years old. The older men say it never completely leaves us. But 'rising above Nefesh and the incredible Yentzer which drives man to destruction is only a meditation away,* he remembered the words of his first Nazerean teacher, Seth Johnson. "Nefesh is the animal soul eternally struggling against Ruach, the divine spark which creates us. Yentzer is the drive of that animal soul within all mankind toward chaos and our own undoing." The litany was his opening meditation ritual.

Johnny was seated on his sleeping mat, in his stone cell, legs crossed, eyes closed, entering his morning meditation. The last hour of the night, the time for morning prayers was fast approaching. *I have to shake the dreams of last night,* he thought urgently, but his discomfort prevented him from centering as he had hoped and before he had managed to enter The Silence, he heard the first sounds of voices on the terrace.

First light was just beginning to lighten the eastern horizon but only the glimmer of the last stars and the moon aided his night vision in finding the entrance to his cell. He had no artificial lights, yet. Many were hurrying toward the meeting place. No one spoke. There was only the voice of the sentinels calling the brotherhood to prayers.

The main terrace sheltered by a generous overhang of the roof, faced just north of southeast. Men were seated cross-legged on the tile floor and on chairs, facing east. Johnny knew that this was not nearly all of the members of the cloister because at least sixty of them were in the chapel in deep meditation. For the moment, he had managed to get the woman out of his mind and again felt the elation of oneness with his brotherhood as the words of the ancients' filled his ears.

"My brother Gimel?" asked Lucias now addressed as Aleph. "What is the hour?"

"The last hour of the night, when the light touches the horizon but the sun has not yet risen."

"What is the purpose of this gathering?" Aleph asked.

"To open the day," Gimel replied, "and to conduct such business as shall come regularly before us."

"The orb of day is driving away the darkness," intoned the Aleph, "and the intellectual and spiritual light we seek is upon us."

"How do we open the day?" asked Aleph.

"By welcoming the orb of enlightenment which is about to crest our horizon and praying that, like that light, true enlightenment may arise out of the darkness under which mankind dwells, bringing the light and joy of a New Day."

The voices of all the company joined in the chanting, prayers, and thanksgiving as the sun crested the horizon. Morning had arrived at Arrata. The first seagulls were whirling in the sky down below. Due drops were visible on the orchids growing along the edge of the terrace. He could see a couple of Noddies pecking for seeds in one of the higher terraces and hear the call of some tropical bird in the forest. The brothers of the Arrata enclaves were rising to their daily tasks of gardening, weaving, meditating; surviving on Arrata, but the warm glow on Johnny's cheeks from his dreams of Inanna's image, remained.

A slight man of about forty with thin brown hair, long, clean shaven face, pointed chin and a Rhode Island accent tapped him on the shoulder and said, "I'm Caleb. Lucias asked me to watch over you till you get yourself situated."

"Glad to meet you, Brother Caleb," said Johnny. "What do I do today? When do I join those meditating?"

Caleb glanced at Lucias' back disappearing into the shadows of the building. He turned back to Johnny and said, "Lucias suggested trying the evening shift, six to midnight, if that's okay with you? Want to start tonight?"

"That'll be fine," answered Johnny. "What about a work assignment?"

"Well," Caleb started thoughtfully. "How about give it some thought for today. What specialties or skills do you have that you think would be best for you to use here?"

Johnny laughed and said, "Real Estate, Life Insurance and Theology. Which do you think will serve the best here?"

Caleb smiled. "You might start out by preparing a Highest and Best Use Analysis for this piece of land we call home, after we defeat our opponent from the other side of the island. I served my turn in real estate too. What do you think?"

Johnny glanced around in mock gravity and retorted, "Condominiums. What else? And a golf course between the two peaks with the nineteenth hole right here on the top terrace."

Caleb laughed and said, "And before you know it we'll have toxic run-off from insecticides and fertilizer, just like back home in the States, besides, there's already a Co-op here, of sorts. And you know, you may be right. DDT isn't illegal here, yet.

"For now," he turned serious again. "Why don't you just wander around and get to know the place. Many of the jobs we have to do here are quite relaxing, like minding the sheep or weaving. And just because you choose one thing now, doesn't mean you have to do that for the rest of your life."

"Sounds good to me," said Johnny, thinking of another trip to the beach.

"At which of the four meals shall I tell Cook to expect you?"

"Oh, let's say, the noon meal. How's that?"

"Noon it is," said Caleb. "That would put you on the morning schedule. That is to say, you'd be working at your assigned task from morning prayers to meal time, rest, meditate or pursue some hobby from meal time to six, then join the Sleeping Warriors, as we like to call them, from six o'clock in the evening till midnight. That may cut your sleep short, but if you wish you can nap in the afternoon."

"Is there some sort of map or written layout of the grounds I can see, somewhere? This place is pretty complex," said Johnny.

"Not really. If you get turned around, just ask someone. You'll learn your way around pretty quickly, I'm sure. If you want to find me later or if you have any questions, I'll be in the Refectory. I'm helping Cook for the time being."

"That's a pretty quaint name," remarked Johnny, "considering that we don't eat any cooked food; only raw and natural."

"Cook thought so too," said Caleb. "I don't know how he got the name, but he didn't object, and it seemed to stick to him. It could be his real name, for all I know."

Johnny watched Caleb disappearing into the interior of the building, deciding to learn as much about the agricultural program of the

terraces as he could. Much of the food raised on Arrata by the Fraternity was originally imported as seeds or seedlings, but most of it was
native to the island, he learned. Each terrace was devoted to a plant
family with various types of underground products such as yams and
sweet potatoes grown in the same areas, beans and legumes on another
set, gourds on two terraces of their own, certain fruits, including a native grape, on yet other terraces. Johnny's footsteps led him gradually
down the south side of the slope. He did not realize until he was near
the bottom that he had unconsciously placed himself as near as possible
to the path leading into the forest.

It's insidious, isn't it? He demanded of himself, his cheeks once
again feeling warmer than they should. *I'm never going back there,* he
vowed vehemently to himself, all the while knowing that it was just a
matter of time.

When he had finished his tour of the terraces, receiving explana-
tions from the workers as he went, the call sounded above for the noon
meal. Most of the workers dropped their implements wherever they
stood and began climbing the slope, while others came out of the building and headed for the gardens, to replace them. Those going for their
daily bread, after the meal would rest and prepare themselves for the
evening's meditation against the unknown evil of the west. Those re-
placing them in the gardens would dine at last light, then prepare for
meditation from Midnight till first light, and so following.

When Johnny came to live at his first Essene Monastery, he was
shocked that they eat only one meal per day. "Doesn't that leave you
hungry almost all the time?" he asked.

As he seated himself in Arrata's Refectory and the bowls and plates
were distributed, he closed his eyes and recalled the answer he then
received, now using it as part of the opening meditation for the ritual
ceremony of nourishment.

*Our sanctuary is paved with the black and white tiles, symbolizing
the intermixture of good with evil as we find it to be in life, white, then
black then white then black, a balance of nature. So it is we teach the
flesh that contains us. We experience hunger, then satisfaction, then
hunger then satisfaction. This lesson constantly enjoins us to remember that just as life is so intermixed, we must be ever vigilant of the fact
that evil can be contained in good and good can be contained in evil.
The daily fasting sharpens the spirit's awareness, enabling it to see
the good in all things, and the evil. It enables us to learn to encourage
the good, discouraging the evil, and to rise above the currents of both
which so affect humanity.*

Johnny opened his eyes to find in front of him a large bowl of living greens, sprouted legumes, and grains, chopped nuts and a few slices of a butternut gourd. With his fingers, he lifted a few pieces to his lips, closed his eyes again and remembered the liturgy of eating.

Father! God Almighty, El Shadai, of the deserts and mountains, EEHEEA of the sky and the sea, God of my fathers and theirs: Forgive my conceits about my work. Help me recognize my mortal condition and forgive my hopes for my fellow man, and my belief that, through my own effort, I can make a difference. How kind you are, Great God, to provide me with the nourishment I am about to receive. I beg You, Lord, to bless these creatures of yours, whose lives I must consume to nourish my own life.

"No meat?" he remembered demanding of his teacher. "Nothing cooked? Why that?"

Johnny chewed, feeling the life of the plants, springing free to join his own life, as he remembered the answer. *It is the life in the food we eat that nourishes our own lives. If the food has no life, there is no real nourishment.*

After the meal, seated on the terrace again, overlooking the sea, he realized he had six hours free and made the conscious decision to return to the beach. *She probably won't be there, he rationalized, and it's such a pretty spot. Maybe I'll go for a swim myself.* He headed off down the prim rose path, so to speak, through the forest of orchids, bananas, palms, hauhau and toromiro trees. He had learned their names that very morning. One was good for making rope. The other was used for carving and firewood, if and *when the Essenes ever needed a fire.*

He glanced at his feet briefly. The sandals were chafing slightly on the downgrade. He smiled and said to his feet, *lead us not into temptation, please.* Then focusing back on his downward progress, he likened it in his mind to moral digression. *Why can't I just forget about it? Nothing's going to happen and I don't even know who she is. How far west is that corner of beach, anyway? Is it beyond the wall? Lucias said others lived over there. Maybe she's one of them and can tell me what's going on?* He tripped over an irregular place in the ground and almost fell. The moment of uncertain balance sobered him, reminding him of his present moral imbalance. He stopped walking.

What am I doing? I'm just going to tempt myself into something I'm afraid I'll regret. I am Hjet, a Fence. I'm supposed to be the divider between the good and the evil, not a seeker of wild experience. The voice of the teacher came back to his memory yet again, reminding him, *as Hjet, a Fence dividing good from evil, you are in a very tenuous position because implied in that division is the fact that you must conceptually polarize your own good and evil. Within all of us, we are a mixture, just as the black and white pavement teaches us. Just as the daily fasting reminds us. As Hjet, before you can function in your true capacity, you must subdue your own nature. You must know what it is within you which is good and what is within you that is not good. This knowledge will be the first real step forward you can take toward your life's goal, toward fulfilling the nature of and actually being Hjet.*

This was Johnny's final rationalization. His cheeks glowing warm already, he headed on down the path to the beach. *Why fight it? This is apparently a test I have to pass and I can't pass it if I don't take the test.* Television chatter from his past echoed almost arrogantly, "If you don't play, you can't win." *This isn't the Florida Lotto,* Johnny answered himself. *Maybe that's a warning. The chance of winning the state lottery is around fourteen million to one. Maybe those are my odds of passing this test?*

The sand on the beach gleamed in the sunlight, washed and moist from the receding tide. A fiddler crab darted away as he left the forest. It paused about fifteen feet away, regarding him with distrust, raising its bigger claw and lowering it in the ritual challenge of fiddler crabs everywhere. *Must be a male,* Johnny thought. *Females have claws the same size, and they don't challenge anything invading their territory. They only hide.* "Hey big guy," Johnny spoke to it. "Don't hurt me now. I'll leave your ladies alone, I promise. Well. At least most of them." He could see the ancient lava flow ahead of him, the one he climbed the day before. As he approached it, he was as annoyed as he was amused that his heart was pounding. The beach showed no sign of where he had fallen the day before.

Carefully, he began climbing the lava flow again, trying to be as quiet as possible. When he reached the top and peered over it to the beach beyond, he felt a sharp mixture of relief and disappointment. She wasn't there. Breathing a sigh of disgust at himself, his heart still pounding, he stood on top of the lava flow, and jumped down on the western side of it. He was, as yet, unaware that he had crossed the border lying between the eastern side of the island and the western side.

Johnny looked around cautiously, listening for any sounds that might not belong there. The beach looked the same as on the other side of the lava flow except that the rocks were behind him instead of in front. The sand displayed the same tracks as were left by the fiddler crab he had just seen. When he jumped down, the flock of gulls who seemed to like this section of beach took off, screeching. Looking at the inviting surf, Johnny took off his shirt, then his sandals and trousers. The water was neither warm nor cold, but just right. The sun was slightly past its middle mark in the heavens. *I can spare an hour. I haven't had a swim in the ocean since I left Florida.*

He waded out to waist depth and lowered himself into the water. The wind was apparently from the north and he was on the south side of the island, so the surf was very gentle, doubly so for the protection afforded by the coral reef. *I wonder what kind of fish are in here,* he thought to himself and was trying to see them through the clear water when he heard her clearing her throat.

He turned to see who was there, suddenly very aware that everything he had worn, except for the necklace of Lapis Lazuli, was lying on the beach at her feet. Inanna was still wearing the blue sarong. Her waist length black hair fluttered slightly in the breeze and Johnny became aware that her most prominent feature was her eyes, not to deny that several other features were also very prominent. Her eyes were wide, dark and intensely focused on him. In the flash of a microsecond, the expression changed from one of annoyance to surprise, then to deeper annoyance. "How dare you invade my territories," he thought he heard her say. Her arms were crossed defensively and she seemed bigger than life.

He could feel a warmth creep over his entire, naked body that struck him as more than a reasonable physical response to his awkward situation. *The best offense is a good defense,* he thought to himself, then *did I get that right? Or is it the best defense is a good offense?* "Come on in. The water's fine," he called out to her, amazed at his own boldness. Now she'll leave, he was sure.

Inanna regarded him for a moment with shock, then distrust. Johnny thought he could feel the air shimmering around him. Startled, he broke off looking at her to see if the sensation was visible. It was, but it faded almost immediately. He looked back at her to see that she had uncrossed her arms. She was now standing erect, looking into the sky, arms at her sides, slightly elevated, palms facing him. He couldn't hear what she was saying, but as she spoke, the water rippled violently all around him as though a large school of very small fish had all broken the surface at the same time, darting away. Startled, Johnny stood up, still concealed by the water to just above the waist. Realizing suddenly how clear that water was, he lowered himself to his neck again, blushing.

Inanna crossed her arms again, and leaning forward slightly said, "I see that the cloistered sleepers have yet another profligate. What are you?" she demanded with annoyance.

Johnny had been trying to figure out her age. There wasn't so much as a trace of growing old in this figure, or in the face. The sophistication signaled that she was no teenager, the defiance, that she was probably older than 25. The mixture of the defiance with so much uncertainty now in her eyes left Johnny believing that she was in her thirties, like him. "Maybe not a profligate," he answered. "I just like to swim in the ocean and this is a very nice beach." He pushed off, with an easy breast stroke, challenging her over his shoulder, "are you going to join me or not? A little company would be a nice change." He stopped swimming while still neck deep in the shallow water, turned to watch for her answer.

"Turn your back while I undress." Her tone contained a challenge of its own. Johnny turned to face the sea and waited. After a few moments, he heard a splash, waited a few more seconds till she had a chance to cover herself with the water, then turned to find Inanna, three feet away, almost eye to eye. The water rippled around him again, but this time, he didn't break eye contact to look at it.

"I haven't learned that trick yet. You must teach me," he said of the effect on the water, his own tone of defiance evident. The way she was looking at him was thrilling but at the same time, frightening. *I don't think I want to turn my back on this one again. At least not while she's this close. What a beauty!* He pulled back from that thought, rising above the situation, trying to focus on her as a person, instead of a sea nymph. This is certainly a compromising situation, *but innocent enough, so far,* he thought, pulling himself together.

"There is much I can teach you," she paused, the tone of defiance still present which Johnny took as a bluff. Then she completed her sentence, "Profligate."

He smiled at her innuendo that he was a fallen man, a sinner, a backslider and the insinuation that he was about to become her lover. "And there is much I could teach you," he answered softly, allowing her to believe what she wanted, but realizing that even with the close proximity, he was still in command of his faculties.

His smile broadened as he remembered his younger sister's warning syllogism, "When the little head gets hard, the big head gets soft. Men don't have enough blood to operate both at the same time." *Not this time, little sister.* He thought to himself. *I'm here to do a job, not to play.* Then the Marine Corp paradigm flashed past his consciousness, "This is my rifle. This is my gun. This one's for killing. This one's for fun." All the while he kept his eyes on Inanna, puzzled at the range of emotions and the speed of the thoughts flashing through his mind.

"Who are you?" she asked softly. "Are you a god?"

His smile returned, as he saw for the first time, signs of vulnerability in her eyes, of hope, longing. His caution levels came down a notch without fully relaxing. *She's a person after all,* he thought to himself.

She contains good as well as the mixture that leads us all astray from time to time. Oh, how I would like to reassure her. But instead of revealing these feelings of compassion or tenderness, he felt it important to keep up the façade of bravado and machismo. "You know," he said lowering his eyes for a second, then smiling and looking back at her, "you are not the first woman to make such a mistake."

She looked at him for a moment in shock, watching his widening grin, then for the first time, smiled. Then she threw her head back and laughed, relaxing for the first time since he had seen her. "Such arrogance is so refreshing. People are usually so frightened of me. Who are you, - Profligate?"

"I think you called me ... what was it? A cloistered sleeper? They call me DeMuzzi." *Such a strange name,* he thought to himself again. *I wonder what its significance is. I wish they had given me some more interesting name like Caleb or Lucias. I wonder how she'll react to this: DeMuzzi, the Cloistered Sleeper.*

She lowered her eyes, a deep disappointment for Johnny. He was close to becoming addicted to looking at them, but then, praise the Lord. She raised them again to meet his, but with furrowed brow. "Would you mind repeating that again. The name, that is?"

He repeated it, "DeMuzzi." He watched as her eyes grew hard and cold again. Then she gazed off toward the horizon for a moment revealing the vulnerability he had seen earlier.

"You even look like him," she muttered so softly he barely heard it.

"Who do I look like," Johnny asked her, softly. *Why is it when I find a rare beauty like this she always has some miserable baggage? She's got to be longing for some mystical lost love of the past, some fool who failed to see what he had and dumped her for some stupid reason. If my wife had been a woman like this I would never gone back to the seminary, never have joined Ha Agudoss, and certainly never have chosen a life of celibacy. Why can't I find the rare beauty first, for a change? Why am I always last in line? Shit.*

She met his eye again. *She looks troubled,* he thought, *but with some hidden agenda. Those opaque eyes simply can't be read very well, and certainly not by me.*

"Where did you get this name, DeMuzzi?" she asked, one eyebrow lifted. "Do you know who I am?" The questions were innocent enough, but there seemed to be a barb at the edge of it.

She's trying to take control of the interview, he thought to himself, *the old control dance again. What a powerful personality she has. Shall I let her? I don't think so.*

"I don't know where the name DeMuzzi came from, but I suspect you gave it to me. And do I know who you are? Yes. You are a magic sea nymph who has come to look at her own reflection in my eyes. *Talk about tossing it in her face,* He chuckled inwardly. *Never let the prospect take control of the interview, Al Vogel used to say. Either they get sold or you get sold. It's all in who controls the interview. Is this a sales interview?* He asked himself. Then he answered himself, *I'm afraid so. This may even be a contest about whether I make it back to the monastery or not. Was that rippling of the water some sort of attack? Maybe I will be the first one who is able to return from here. Now, will I sell or get sold. Let's do the dance, Babe.*

He was surprised by her reaction, again. She grinned broadly. "You're closer to the truth than you suspect." Then her eyes grew soft, almost sad and she said, "I know what I'm about to ask you may be an imposition but..." she paused, glanced off toward the horizon again, then back to him. "Would you hold me? Just for a moment. Nothing else, just please hold me, in your arms?"

Johnny's thoughts became erratic, a confusion of electrical impulses which normally could have resulted in unconsciousness. His heart was pounding so hard that his chest was causing ripples on the water. *Good Lord! Talk about taking over control of the interview. I may be lost. She's giving me an aqua-cardiogram!!* Before he could answer, she slid in closer through the crystal clear water, turned sideways and was seated on his lap, arms around his neck, her head on his shoulder. He put his arms round her, and held her, as she asked, nothing more. He was close to being overcome with the sensations when he realized she was sobbing. Her back heaved with the tears. The harder she cried, the tighter she clung to him.

He waited and after a few minutes. She stopped crying, but still held him, gazing out to sea. Then she broke off, pushing him away and said, "You must leave now, Profligate. The sun nears the horizon."

Johnny was a bit stunned. He didn't know where this sales interview, as he thought of it, was going, but this was not the direction he expected it to take. He was slightly off balance. "I... I.... Uh, don't even know your name?"

"And you may never," she snapped. "You may never. But, you may call me Anna. Now go."

"How will we do this, Anna? Will you turn your back while I leave, or should I turn away again."

"This is how we will do it, Profligate. You will leave and I will watch."

Johnny kept his back to her as he dressed. He turned for one last look in the failing light. Her hair was spread out over the water. Her long straight nose and strong chin cast a profile that would stay with him for a long time. Without another word, he turned to the lava flow and began to climb. At the top, he turned again. She was directly behind him. She had not yet dressed. She said simply, "Muzzi. Thank you for the hug."

಄   ಎ

A large owl, perched in the highest palm tree, not far from the beach, watched quietly while Johnny made his way back to the path and Inanna walked naked back toward her own quarters, carrying the sarong. When they were both out of sight, the owl closed its eyes, seeking the peace of sleep.

Two more beings, the ones who watched Johnny with Belili at the airport, waited at the edge of the forest, observing in silence from the ether. When Inanna had finally gone, the one called Chaim said to the other, "Matziel, my friend. I was fearful for him. He had no idea the danger he was in. That seemed like a close call to me."

"And to me. He has no idea, the dangers awaiting him," came the reply. "But he does have certain protections."

"What about the hag, Belili? She is no friend. I think she has her own cause to battle."

"She gave him the amulet, did she not, the stone of Lapis Lazuli?"

"'Who fights my enemy is my friend,' is not always true," said Chaim.

"Until she proves otherwise, we will not interfere with her."

಄   ಎ

When Johnny arrived at the top terrace, he was surprised to find torches and a large group of men preparing to go in search for him. Lucias was among them, and Cardac.

Cardac was the first to speak, his eyes bulging more than ever in his excitement, "Where have you been? Someone said you were seen climbing over the lava flow. Don't you know that usually marks the border between our side and the western side? Do you have any idea the danger you were in? How did you even make it back? Why did you go over there?"

Lucias, strain showing in his face, edged Cardac aside saying, "Let him answer for heaven's sake. Tell us what happened, DeMuzzi? Tell us what happened? What did you see? What's over there? Do you know that while you were there, the shimmering wall fell? There was a pause in the resistance. Now it is back, of course."

Everyone fell silent, waiting for Johnny to say something. He looked out over the night-covered sea and at low breath he said only, "She needed catharsis, love. I gave it to her."

Chapter 8: The Hymn of Enheduanna

Chip and Joyce were seated with the fishing party for dinner as before, but no longer on the dais. They were among the Polynesians seated on the main floor. The Smithsons and the Johns were quiet this evening, still chilled by the day's events. Jorge, seated at the end of the table was sullen. The room was decorated with fresh flowers and potted orchids.

The glowing blue 'throne' of Lapis Lazuli was placed facing the lower floor with a table beside it laden with several types of fruits and what Chip took to be a slab of pork, complete with pineapple slices and cloves sticking out of it. All seemed to be waiting. Finally, a young woman rose from one of the tables, clothed in a white sarong and sandals. Her hair was done in a large wave with a blue orchid completing the effect of soft beauty. Slowly she made her way toward the dais, stopping at the bottom of the three-step stairway to the higher level.

Ever so softly, the girl began to sing in the lilting tones of the Polynesian tongue. After each line, she paused. Another girl in the back of the room, echoed the melody but in Spanish, also pausing at the end of the first line. A third girl at the other side of the room, echoed the melody a third time, but in English so that each line of the poem was repeated three times. A young man seated near the center of the room accompanied them on a stringed instrument, which Chip did not recognize. The tones of the instrument seemed Oriental. One note was struck and one line sung. Then two notes were played on the stringed instrument, and the second girl repeated the line in Spanish, and so following. The English words to the song were:

A Flame burns for Inanna.
May she bless those who love her with fertility.
With Fertility may she bless those who love her.
Oh Queen of all power.
Oh Queen of the bright burning light,
Triumphant woman clothed in brilliance,
Beloved in heaven and earth.
Chosen to wear the grand adornments
Crowned with goodness, rightfully.
In your hands are the seven fixed powers.
The Fundamental Forces are in your grasp.
Guardian of the cosmos, the universe.
You bind the elements with your hands.
Press the powers to your breast.
You kill the evil poisoning the land,
The Storm god you subdue.
You cause bread to spring from the earth.
You are Inanna, supreme over heaven and earth.

As the song was presented, Inanna entered the room from behind the dais. She seemed much larger, to Chip, taller, somehow, changed. *This has got to be my imagination,* he mused to himself. *Is she glowing? Walking a foot above the floor? There must be something in the water they gave us today.*

"My gawd, jist look at that woman," muttered Teri. "She muss be twelve feet tall!"

Jorge's demeanor changed from sullen anger to shocked disbelief. *"Por Diós,"* he exclaimed. *¿Y este mujer, de donde viene?"*

"This isn't possible," said Joyce very softly.

"She's obviously an illusionist," said Al John. "No one can really do that."

Rosemary Smithson, Jimmy's wife muttered, "She's done enough other things no one can do that I'm not taking any chances challenging her on it."

Inanna's glare silenced them. She seemed to grow even larger and as she did so, the congregation of islanders among whom the Americans were seated began to chant the same song that had just been presented by the three young women, each in their own tongue. Inanna closed her eyes and lifted her face slightly. She extended her palms, as would a person standing before a fire, absorbing the warmth.

When the song was finished, Inanna appeared to resume her normal size and sat down on the blue throne of Lapis Lazuli. She began picking at the food on the table beside her. She seemed moody. The three singers returned to their seats and everyone began eating. Chip noticed that Leelee was seated in a rear alcove of the room, not quite out of Inanna's sight.

"Talk about self love!" muttered Jimmy to his wife.

Rosemary Smithson was of a generous figure, a strawberry blond. When whispering she tended to speak out of one side of her wide mouth as she then did. "It almost seemed like she was recharging or something; as though she could feel power or electricity or something coming from these people."

"They were actually worshiping her," Jimmy replied. "Feeding her?"

"Well, now we know why she said she thought them islanders was food," whispered Teri. "I wonder what's got under her skin tonight, anyway. Last night she wanted to be a reg'lar Chatty Kathy. Tonight she's jist moody lookin.'"

CR   SO

Later that night, Chip was unable to sleep and found himself strolling toward the pier. The stars were very bright, the view undisturbed by streetlights, neighbor's porch lights or city lights that so clutter up the air on the mainland. He was enjoying a direct view of the Southern Cross high over head when he noticed someone else standing on the pier. It was Jimmy Smithson. "Hello James," he greeted him when he got close enough. "Couldn't sleep. Joyce is doing all right though. She's out like a light."

"So is Rosemary. I don't know how she does it. I'm just about frantic to get out of here. The folks back at the office are going to think we're dead, lost at sea in that Rapanui Storm."

"How did you guys get stuck in it? Weren't you chartering off of Easter Island? Jorge seems to know better than to run under those bronze clouds. It was him I heard talking with his cousin about the Rapanui Storm. He seemed afraid of it."

"They were afraid alright," said Smithson. "It was Al. That's why he's so quiet now. We had planned to run a hundred miles south of Easter Island. There had been reports of good fishing down there. When we got out about fifty miles, we spotted the phenomenon. Jorge and Alphonso didn't say a word. They just changed course and headed back for the main island. Big Al demanded to know why we weren't still headed south. When they told him, he ordered them to turn back. 'Plan your work and work your plan,' he kept saying. They refused until he offered to not pay them. His last words before the engine failed were, 'it's my gawd damned charter and it's going to go where ever I gawd damned want it to.' He more or less bullied them out of the wheelhouse. He actually, physically threatened them, then turned the boat himself. Half an hour later, poof, the engine quit and here we are."

"Has she been like this the whole time you've been here?" asked Chip.

"Worse," Smithson responded. "She's been on good behavior since you and Joyce got here. It's like she's embarrassed or something, to spring herself on a person all at once. I think she really wants to be loved, but hasn't a clue how to go about it. Or else, she's so frustrated and angry about something that she forgets and lashes out, like she did at Alphonso this morning. Did you see him when Jorge brought him in?"

"Yeah. He looked like he was about a hundred and fifty years old all of a sudden and died of old age." Chip continued, "Have you seen her do this before?"

"Yup. Several times. Once she did it right in front of us. It was like she was draining the man's life and all the life he would ever have in the future, right out of him. She can be a real monster."

"How can something that beautiful be so..."

Smithson interrupted Chip with, "Shhh. Look."

The door was opening in the main ballroom. Light from the glowing throne could be seen coming from inside and by that light, they saw the figure of Inanna exiting the building, walking slowly in their general direction.

"What ever you do," said Smithson, "be polite. Don't ask her anything especially about leaving the island. I've seen her really get upset when people ask about that. Trust me. You don't want her to get upset with you."

"Thanks for the advice," answered Chip. "I was planning to ask her about that."

Inanna had changed her color from the blue sarong to one of magenta, the love color. Her walk was moody, head down, not paying close attention to her surroundings. As she passed, they could hear her humming to herself, a tune neither of them recognized. To Chip's amazement, the path seemed to brighten slightly a few feet ahead of her as she walked, then fade again after she passed. Before actually reaching the pier, where the men were standing, she turned toward the path in the forest, the one where Leelee had appeared that morning.

After she disappeared into the forest, Chip said to Smithson, "Let's follow her and see if we can learn anything."

"Following her could be a fatal experience," Smithson said.

"If we're going to spend the rest of our lives on the island," Chip retorted grimly, "it's okay with me if my life is going to be short. My programming design doesn't include a slavery subroutine, if you get my drift. I also don't make a very good prisoner."

"I'm going to go back to bed," said Smithson. "I've seen her when she's angry and following her could make her angry. Don't do it."

"I just got out of the service a few years ago," said Chip. "Rain forests and jungles are a specialty of mine. I'll make sure she doesn't catch me."

"Live long and prosper," said Smithson sarcastically. "Hope to see you at breakfast. So does Joyce." He walked away, as Chip moved silently toward the opening in the forest.

This may be the stupidest thing I ever did, thought Chip. *But it has to be done. The more I can learn about her, the better I'll know how to fight her, and escape her. It's a nice island. I could live here if it was by my own free will, but I owe it to Joyce to get home safely. I owe it to our families to make it back in one piece.*

Further, ahead on the path he could see a dim light. *That has to be her.* He moved rapidly down the path, not making a sound, trying to get a little closer. The night sounds in the forest are different than in the day. There are different birds, whole species and families of insects prefer the night. Predators choose darkness for finding their sleeping prey. He paused, closing his eyes, allowing his consciousness to fill the forest, feeling it, making himself one with it, himself, becoming the forest. Open your senses, he heard the voice of his Kung Fu Master back in Jacksonville echoing in the recesses of his memory. No one needs eyes to see. We are spirits. Let your spirit walk beside you and be your eyes. No one needs ears. Let your spirit walk beside you listening. Nothing can strike from behind while your inner senses guard you...

Chip straightened his back in a gentle stretch. He opened his eyes and felt the forest stretching in the distance. Inanna was still far ahead. He closed the distance as silently as the unseen owl above him. Inanna took a branching path to the right heading toward the south side of the island. The path began descending sharply. Chip was hard put to not slip on the path, creating sounds alerting Inanna to his presence. Finally it leveled off and Chip realized that Inanna had stopped. She was on the beach.

The owl, silently shadowing Chip, now passed and alighted on the sand beside Inanna, transforming into Belili. Chip saw nothing of this, but was now surprised to hear voices, conversation. Chip moved silently off the path, disappearing into the foliage in case Inanna decided to return too suddenly for him to react. Slowly and methodically, he worked his way closer so he could see as well as hear the voices.

Inanna was seated on the ground, while Belili stood watching out to sea. "You were watching this afternoon," Inanna said. "I could feel your eyes."

"I am always near you, Inanna," answered Belili.

"I no longer need a nurse," snapped Inanna. "Why do you watch me so closely?"

"We have had this conversation many times," Belili answered. "I will tell you again. When the others left this primitive place, you chose to stay. You were angry and broken hearted. Then, when Anu, Ea, Enlil and the others imprisoned you on this island to protect humanity from your rages, Anu personally ordered me to stay with you to help you work through your pain. This has become a litany. Have you not memorized it yet? You know you can rejoin them any time you want. Why do you stay and tease these poor LULUs?"

"Because they don't love me as they should. I have to force them," muttered Inanna, almost too low for Chip to hear her. "They are ungracious. We created them. They owe us. They owe me." The anger in her voice was so intense that Chip actually felt pain from its proximity.

Created us? Ha, thought Chip. *She really does have a god complex. So, this is an elaborate nursing home for the daughter of some fabulously rich, middle eastern tycoon, probably from oil. It's a wonder they don't make her wear a berka and stay indoors all the time. God knows everyone would be safer if she were confined.*

"And what do you think they owe you, oh great goddess of love," asked Belili in sarcastic tones. "That time was so long ago barely anyone remembers your name. In fact, no one does unless they study ancient manuscripts in such a little known tongue that few have ever bothered to learn it. They owe you nothing. You aren't a creator. You're a criminal. Look what you did on Easter Island! You were so vain you even planned it so Roggeveen would land there, discover the place for Europe on your old feast day that no one remembers. The feast day of Ishtar now belongs to a new religion and they don't even know where the name came from. They call it "Easter." Even then, people had forgotten Inanna. They called you Ishtar, Istarte and a number of other names. The gods alone know where these names come from," shaking her head. "Even then you were here, a prisoner on the top of what's left of your sunken lands of Arrata."

Ishtar? Easter?! They're both nuts, thought Chip. *Yes, Leelee looks old but no one lives that long and Inanna couldn't be over thirty-five if she's even that old. She's just a spoiled, headstrong nut case. However she does her tricks, there has to be a rational explanation. These other names, they mentioned are new to me. Never heard of 'em - probably her family or something. And what unusual names they are too. Probably middle eastern.*

Inanna was silently staring at the reflection of the moon and stars off the surf. "I miss my husband," she said simply. "Leave off with the litany, old bird. I want to talk about DeMuzzi." She raised her eyes to look into the old woman's face.

"If you had managed to stay out of Tessub's bed, he wouldn't have left you. You know this. Why do you bring it up?"

How does this old crone get away with being so rough on her, Chip wondered? *If any of us talked to her like that, she'd fry us in our own fat.*

"You saw him today," said Inanna. "Was this DeMuzzi, my Du-Muzzi?"

"You know that it couldn't be," said Belili.

"But he looked so much like my DuMuzzi. He even smelled like him. His body... Oh how I wanted him. But I could tell that he would have refused me. At first, I was angry at his arrogance. Can you imagine a mere human propositioning me? Even when he did it, I knew he was calling my bluff, challenging me, taunting me. I tried to kill him, take his body's life into my own but he managed to resist me. He resisted me!" she repeated angrily.

Inanna was on her feet gesticulating in emphasis. "How could he resist me? How could he?"

Belili started laughing. Then she said, "It would appear you have found a man you cannot control and you are drawn to him like a moth to a flame." She started laughing again.

"I'm not drawn to him at all. He's a stinking Monk from that monastery on the eastern end of the island. Why did they come here? It seems their sole purpose is to fight, to resist me. And they keep invading my domain. Their very presence is an invasion of my privacy but as they work together, I can't get at them. I've tried and tried. Only a few times have I managed to get into their lands, but they drove me off."

Belili answered with, "I don't know why they're here. I suspect they came to find out why such devastation was taking place among the peoples of Te Pito Te Henua. You caused that devastation. You even drew Hotu Matua and his people to that island in the first place just so you could drain their energy for your own power. 'A farm' you called it."

"Worship isn't draining," stated Inanna. "It's uplifting."

"Not the way you get them to do it," said Belili. "Look at that poor man this morning, Alphonso. Was he uplifted? I don't think so."

"I was angry," said Inanna. "He was going to call for help, and try to motor away. I couldn't handle the invasion that would come here if he went for help. That's why I retired to Arrata in the first place. Too many people in concert against me would overwhelm my power."

"You didn't retire here," said Belili. "You were imprisoned here, on the most remote island in the world. Remember when that old king, I forgot his name, adopted a different god? You became the goddess of war for a while and never got over it."

"Do you think DeMuzzi will come back to me? The Monk, I mean."

Chip had been lying in the same position for almost half an hour. Underneath him was a dried tree branch he had chosen to lie on so he wouldn't get his clothing as damp as he would if he were lying directly on the ground. That branch chose this moment to crack under Chip's weight, drawing Inanna's attention to the fact of his presence.

⋄ ⋄

Joyce woke up at the sound of a night bird, rolled over and Chip was not there. She climbed out of bed and went to the window calling out softly, "Chip. Are you out there?" There was no answer. She checked the anteroom. "Chip. Are you in there?" There was no answer.

A few minutes later, Joyce was fully clothed and headed across the grounds in the direction of the pier. No lights were showing in any of the windows of the compound. The moon had set so the light was much lower than when Chip and Smithson were talking earlier. Joyce walked all the way to the pier, watching the shadows and the complex for signs of life or light.

Finding nothing, she turned back in the direction of the palace complex, walking slowly, still watching and listening. When she made it all the way back to the door of their private quarters, she turned to the left and walked the length of the building. She passed the entrance to the ballroom, and the sleeping quarters of the Smithsons, the Johns, Jorge and *probably all those Polynesians live in these rooms too. Where could he be? Is he all right? What would I ever do without him? Could that crazy woman have hurt him, taken him?*

She reached the end of the building at the edge of the forest, hearing and seeing no sign of her husband. She was on her way back toward their sleeping quarters, when she saw Inanna's light emerge from the forest. The path miraculously illuminated itself a few feet in front of her, at the far end of the grounds. Joyce turned in that direction, determining to ask her for help or confront her if necessary. Before she had taken ten steps, she saw second and third figures appear from the forest behind Inanna. Joyce began to hurry toward them.

As she got closer, she began to recognize that the second figure was Chip and the third figure was helping him to walk. She rushed toward them to find that the third figure was the old woman called Leelee. She must have been incredibly strong for her age, since she was almost carrying Chip.

Joyce rushed right past Inanna, straight to Belili and Chip. "Is he alright? What happened?" she demanded of Belili. "What happened?"

Chip raised his head slightly and recognizing his wife, said, "Joyce. Oh Joyce. Take me home."

"He angered the goddess," said Belili. "I managed to be his intercessor, so he is not dead. She drained him of most of his life's force. This calmed her. We must get him back to his bed so he can rest. He will recover in a few days."

Back in their sleeping quarters, Belili helped Joyce get Chip onto the sleeping mat and cover him. "He seems out of his mind," said Joyce worriedly. "Why did she do this to him?" Joyce was furious but trying to conceal the full force of her rage from Belili. *How can I trust this old woman,* she thought. *She's some kind of a friend to that monster. I don't know anything about any of them. The old woman could well be a spy, soothing me with nice tones and complimentary remarks. Does she really think I can't see right through this kind of nonsense?*

Belili answered, "She did this to him because she was angry. He followed her and was eavesdropping on a private conversation between us. His crime was curiosity. Inanna was not patient with him nor was she forgiving until after she punished him. He's lucky to be alive. Keep him away from her until he recovers, if you value his life."

Chip was mumbling and nearly incoherent. After Belili left, Joyce stretched out beside him, on her side, facing Chip. She watched him intently as he mouthed words she couldn't understand. She put her arms around him in what seemed an impotent attempt to protect him as well as provide comfort. As she got closer, some of the words began to grow clear enough for her to understand them. They were the words to the song they had heard earlier at dinner. Inanna this and Inanna that. She heard the words 'Lapis Lazuli,' several times, but couldn't make out the context.

"Chip," she whispered to him. "Can you hear me?"

He opened his eyes and tried to look at her, but she could see that he was unable to focus. His eyes were glazed red and functioned like those of a blind man, looking into the distance while addressing someone close up. He seemed to be trying to catch his breath enough to form words, then managed to get out, "Yeah."

"Are you in any pain?" she asked.

"He furrowed his brow with the effort, and managed to say, "No. Tired." He closed his eyes. Joyce decided to let him sleep, but after a few moments, he opened them again. With what was apparently great effort, Chip managed to get one of his arms around her, and pulled her closer. Speaking very slowly, he began talking. "Monastery at other end of island. We gotta' get there. Safe."

"I thought I'd lost you, " she sobbed. "I was afraid, well, she's so beautiful."

"Bad temper," he muttered. His words were coming a little stronger than before. "Gotta save you. I love you Joyce. I always will."

Chapter 9: Dramatic Meditation

The let down was as sharp as it was a surprise. *It's the morning after. Does she still respect me?* Johnny chuckled to himself. *I didn't do anything wrong. After the intensity of Inanna and the questioning of the brotherhood the night before, the morning's solitude and silence was hard to take.*

He had been taken to the refectory and although the Essene community did not cook anything, he felt he had been grilled alive with questions, more slowly this time than how Cardac and Lucias had begun. Each brother who had questions was given a turn with Johnny.

"Who is Anna?" they discussed endlessly. "Is she a perverted Angel? Is she a demon of some sort? Is she Shatán in disguise? Who is she? What is she?"

"She's a woman," Johnny insisted, visualizing those haughty eyes, her sarcasm echoing in his ears as she called him again in his thoughts, 'Profligate.' He smiled at the thought. "I met a beautiful woman," he told them. "I felt tempted by her. It was a temptation I would have fallen to had it been available. I may even be a little bit in love."

"Or maybe in heat," someone who Johnny did not see, interjected near the rear of the room.

"I need to sort out my feelings a little more," Johnny finished the thought, straining around to see who had made the other remark.

"Those of our fraternity have given up such pleasures," Lucias reminded him. "We are a celibate society. How could you make such a choice? You know the damage it would do to your years of building your strength in meditation."

"Perhaps it was a mistake," Johnny said. *Maybe joining the fraternity was a knee jerk reaction, a rebellion to the pain I was feeling over my divorce. The thought washed over him like a betrayal. I wasn't brain washed, exactly, just overwhelmed with the experiences. Maybe joining this group was a major screw up. What am I doing on this remote island and what kind of sense does it make to be practicing celibacy when such a woman is naked in my arms?* "I guess I shouldn't have wandered over there," Johnny said. *And how long has it been since I've had a woman?* His thoughts continued against his will. *Since long before my divorce, actually. I decided to become celibate, but my body made no such promises. It proved that today. And I recognize the incredible power of Nefesh, the animal soul animating my flesh, when it raises its voice in passion.*

Lee Moy, who had been lurking in the background, his eyes closed, hands folded in his lap, cleared his throat to gain the attention of the group around them. He raised his eyes, glancing at each of them, saying, "We have been in a repeating loop for a long time playing with this problem, afraid to touch it, afraid to retreat from it. We have lost seven brothers who were brave enough to cross to the other side, in the years we have been in this loop. In our meetings, we castigated their memory for the foolishness of the risks they took and pitied their fates, while in our hearts, we admired their courage and envied the secret knowledge they had gained. In the face of our desire for that knowledge, we have made, not crossing the line, an unspoken tenet of a spontaneous religion which has arisen here among us and regarded those who violated that taboo as profligates."

Did she know this? thought Johnny in alarm. *How could she know they used this word here to describe people who visit the western side of the island?*

"Now," Lee Moy continued, "we have a so called profligate who managed to return."

Or does Lee Moy somehow know that she called me that and he's taunting me even as he addresses the brotherhood? Johnny was becoming concerned over whom he could really trust. *Is it Anna, who is being open and honest with me, or is she the betrayer, while Lee Moy is the faithful brother? Which? Which!*

"On the other hand," said Lee Moy, "our brother DeMuzzi, as he is called, may have been turned by the evil of the western side of the island. He may have perceived this evil to be a beautiful, innocent young woman, but we have known this evil to take many forms, to have many faces. He could now very well be a spy representing the best interests of our enemy, here in our very midst, himself completely unaware of his situation. She could have somehow used the close proximity DeMuzzi describes to gain a psychic contact with him so that it, or she, can watch us through his eyes."

"I think that's the epitome of paranoia," Caleb blurted out with disgust.

An undercurrent of conversation erupted in the background that Lucias quickly called to order. "It's necessary that we consider every possibility," he said. "It's true that none who have gone there before DeMuzzi ever returned. We believed them to have been murdered. It is true that we have regarded crossing that threshold of evil as profligacy for many years. It truly is a violation of what Lee Moy has called an unspoken tenet of the unwritten conventions we practice here. We have made exploration and courage a taboo of the micro-culture we have constructed between us on this island. Perhaps this type of profligacy should not be so discouraged?"

"What about the spy angle?" Cardac inserted.

Johnny winced at the thought that she might be using him in this way. *On the other hand,* he thought, *If I'm a spy, maybe Caleb is too. He is the one who called Lee Moy's suspicion, paranoia. Or maybe Lee Moy is the spy, because I represent the first successful attempt to communicate with that side of the island, ever, since the fraternity has been here. Was Lee Moy speaking for or against me? Maybe they're both completely loyal and I really have been turned. My head has certainly been turned. What a woman! Do I feel loyalty to her? Yes. Do I feel loyalty to my brothers? Yes. I see no conflict, yet. It seems we're all fighting the same battle. Anna and the fraternity, looking for ultimate love, acceptance, trust, peace, trying to overcome the angst of the past in favor of a more joyous future.*

"I don't think he's become a spy," said Lucias. "I can sense no duplicity in him."

"Neither do I," said several others. While some, remaining silent were wearing doubtful expressions, none objected. Some, satisfied with the outcome so far, rose and exited the room. The remainder had more questions to discuss. "Lucias. Do you feel that we should send him back to see if he can find out more?" asked one.

"I think we should order him to never go there again. I don't think he's been turned yet, but who knows what could happen to him if he returns," said another, a portly, bearded man, dressed in a brown wool jerkin.

What a weird looking shirt he's wearing, thought Johnny.

Lucias stood and raised his hands for silence. Having received it, he fixed his gaze on Johnny and after exhaling sharply as if with exasperation, he said, "I think we have a consensus that he's not a spy, not been somehow turned." He returned his gaze to those in the room who had posed the above questions, saying, "As we all know, Ha Agudoss rarely issues orders to any of the brothers. We are a voluntary organization. Our membership is composed of like-minded men, mostly; who have chosen a life of meditation and prayer. So, we won't order him to come here or go hither. He is not subject to our orders, but to those laws and rules written on his heart, by the Supreme Architect of the Universe, God Almighty. If he returns into the valley of the shadow of death or remains here as we always have done, it will be with a mightier hand than ours leading him, and more courage than any of us have shown, protecting him."

Lucias turned to face Johnny again, saying, "It is my recommendation that he not go back, that he join into the regular routines of the community, working and meditating. But I speak through my own cowardice. I fear for him as much as I admire his courage, pity the weakness leading him there and dread his possible loss to us. I'm as confused on the subject as he appears to be. What say you, DeMuzzi? Will your desire for this woman lead you to return to the west, again, or will you conform to our sedate cowardice, or conservative defenses, however you wish to regard it?"

He wants me to make a decision? Thought Johnny. *I have so much to think about. There are too many options and possibilities to consider.* "This is all happening a little too fast for me," he said. "I don't know what to do or what to say to you. At the time, I was unaware, I had crossed the line. It was only after I got there that I realized it. At no time while I was there did I feel threatened in any way and it was a nice beach."

Some background snickering made itself heard, but Lucias again called for order and said, "Let's hear him out, brothers."

"I think for the moment," Johnny continued, "I would like to spend some time reflecting on the experience and considering the best course of action or inaction. When I make a decision about what to do, I'll discuss it with Lucias first, before acting." Johnny turned to face the Head of the Monastery. "Will that work for you Lucias?" He turned to look at the gathering again and said, "And you, my brothers?"

C3   80

His dreams, that night, were filled with horrific action. He found himself fleeing from a fire-breathing dragon, then riding on a chariot through the clouds, Anna at his side. When the chariot rose too close to the sun, he woke up in a heavy sweat, greatly alarmed. Finding himself in his meditation cell calmed him and he was able to return to a troubled sleep. New dreams had him thrashing through the rest of the night, wrestling with his demons, not the least of which was a beautiful black haired woman with wide intense eyes who kept sardonically calling him 'Profligate.'

Johnny was the first to arrive on the main terrace to 'open the day.' He had given up on trying to sleep and decided to wait out the rest of the night, however much of it was left, watching the stars and listening to the night sounds from the patio. There was dew on his chair, that soaked through his pants when he sat down. He immediately jumped up again, startled by the sensation of cold and wet. When he jumped up, it seemed that he disturbed a large bird perched nearby, which swooped past him in its flight. It was an owl. It screeched once and was gone.

He was unwilling to sit down on the damp chair again. He was a little spooked by the owl and too wary to walk down through the terraces in the dark. He went inside and sought out the chapel where the sixty brothers were nearing the end of this night's meditation. His turn to join them would come up in twelve hours. On this day he would work with the Brother, Caleb had called Agricola. *Cute name for the head gardener,* he had thought. *It's Latin for 'Farmer,' and the chef calls himself Cook.* He had chuckled inwardly. *It's nice that they can keep their sense of humor. I hope I can keep mine.*

Finding solace in routine and ritual was not something Johnny could readily do since all of the routines and rituals of the monastery were new to him. But the mindless work of weeding a garden quickly became a ritual freeing his mind to wander. The jarring experiences of the day before finally began to heal with the repeated review and so, begin fading into the past. Review them he did. From the exertion of climbing over the lava flow to the questioning of his brothers in the Refectory, it all replayed itself in minute detail. By mid morning he was into the game humans so often waste time with, "What if."

What if she had... thought Johnny. What if I had... What if Lee Moy really is the spy? He is quite secretive and disappears into the forest all the time - TOWARD the west. Lucias thinks he has an herb garden back there and maybe he does, but that could be just a cover for some other activity.

His mind wandered back to reality, called there by the sting of a broken blister on his right hand. *Okay, so I'm not used to this, yet. Weed this. Trim that. Water here, it seems a bit dry. More sheep manure is needed on the next level. Will I please fetch some from the meadow above? I could get used to this,* he ordered himself. *I need to stop focusing on yesterday and start doing this in meditation, as Agricola suggested.*

"Listen to the spirit of the plant and it will tell you what it needs," Agricola, a tall thin man wearing coveralls and a wide brimmed hat constructed from palm tree leaves, had told him. "Sometimes what it will tell you is simply, 'You're blocking my sunlight. Please leave.'" Agricola had given him a cloth to protect the back of his neck from the burning light of the rising sun before leaving him to his labor.

Johnny was glad when the noon meal was announced. It marked the end of the day's period of work and the beginning of his free time. *Today,* he determined wryly, *I don't need a swim in the ocean. Maybe I'll just go and watch them make sandals.* He was aware that many were watching to see what he would do after the noon meal. Lee Moy was one of them and when he saw Johnny was headed for the cobbler's shop he signaled him to come and talk for a minute.

He followed Lee Moy through the winding corridors of the complex and out through the upper entrance past the sheep. He was about to object to the hike, when Lee Moy gestured for silence with his finger to his lips. In a moment, Johnny saw why. They had started down the path through the forest where he had seen Lee Moy emerge two days before. Just around the first bend, there was a small clearing filled with many colorful birds. Since it was the beginning of summer, many of them were engaged in nest building while others were tending to their young in already constructed nests.

"I try to not disturb them when I pass through here," Lee Moy whispered to him. "We will walk slowly and maybe they will accept you as well."

As they passed through the clearing Johnny was surprised to see one small bird leave her nest building, flutter once around Lee Moy's head then land on his shoulder. Lee Moy carefully ignored it while it chirped loudly at him and pecked at his hair. When they reached the other side of the clearing, Lee Moy turned slightly as they walked and remarked with a smile, "I call this one Jezebel because sometimes she prefers me to her husband."

Soon they entered Lee Moy's garden. It was just as Lucias had described it, herbs of all sorts, carefully labeled, weeded and tended. There were two short benches beside the tilled earth where Lee Moy indicated Johnny should take a seat. When the Anasazi sat down, Jezebell fluttered to his knee then into the herb garden. "Those are not for you. Go back to your husband," Lee Moy addressed it sharply. The bird lifted off and disappeared around the bend in the path.

"This place gives me peace," he said to Johnny. "It's like my own private den. I come here to be alone. The others seem to respect that." Lee Moy appeared to be much older than Johnny had at first realized.

His eyes were small, sunk into a wrinkled and lined face. That Lee Moy avoided direct eye contact led Johnny to believe that he was shy rather than hiding something, a very inward sort of person.

"It is a very peaceful place," Johnny said carefully, waiting for Lee Moy's real agenda to be revealed. It came more quickly than he expected. Lee Moy was apparently not one for wasting time.

"You know, DeMuzzi, You have caused quite a stir; over there," he said nodding his head toward the west, "as well as here. Those meditating last night reported that the energies in the west became very agitated yesterday and last night as well, that was after the wall returned, that is. You know it fell briefly, don't you?"

Johnny nodded in acknowledgement.

"They described a sort of pulsing anger rotating to pain and passion. It didn't return to its normal levels until nearly midnight."

"What do they think caused that?" asked Johnny.

Lee Moy kicked a small pebble across the path toward the garden. "They think you caused it. Did anything else happen while you were there that you did not share in the group last night? I understand that it was a highly personal experience, but was there anything else that you may think could shed light on what I just told you?"

"I didn't make love to her, if that's what you're asking." Johnny's answer came with more energy than he intended, something more like a defensive retort than an answer. "But I think I might have, had there been more time," Johnny continued, still defensive.

"Lee Moy looked directly at him with a warm smile and said, "From the way you described it, DeMuzzi, I think I might have done so myself. How could you be blamed had you succumbed?" His face turned more serious, "Still, it would have been a shame to break your stride." He made eye contact again, "spiritually, that is."

"Tell me what is known about the other side. Who lives there? Does anyone know?" asked Johnny.

"I was hoping you could tell me," Lee Moy smiled again. "Here's a suggestion. You are the only one of us who has a visual link and a personal contact. In your meditation tonight and in the following nights, perhaps you can use that visualization to visit the other side spiritually. If you can do this, you will be able to answer that question yourself and for us."

ෆ ෨

The evening meditation shift was beginning to take place. Johnny had not considered how it might be done, and was surprised to see that those meditating were replaced one at a time, so as not to break the intensity of the defense they maintained. The process took over an hour. A person entering on the new shift would go the person he was to replace, tap him gently on the shoulder, and then take a seat where that person had been. Then the next would enter the room. It was an orderly procedure, but slow.

When his turn came, he was relieved to find himself in a comfortable chair with a high back, high enough that he could rest his head on it. As he began to sink into the meditative state, he became more aware of the amazing energy in the room, and gradually allowed his own energy to merge with it. In an attempt to comply with Lee Moy's suggestion, he called to his mind's eye the face of Inanna. He consciously practiced the procedure of looking at each tiny detail in his mind's image, knowing that this helps deepen the meditative state. When he had Inanna's image perfectly in his mind's eye, he released to that image, the intense emotions he had been repressing.

Then the visions began. In his mind's eye, the image of Inanna suddenly stood bolt upright. She gasped. A look of uncertainty, or searching passed though her eyes, and suddenly it was as though Johnny stood before her. She had taken a seat in her 'blue chair.' It seemed to him that he was seated very close to and directly in front of her, their knees touching. The sound of her voice almost shocked him out of his meditation.

"What are you doing, Profligate," she demanded. "You invaded my realm yesterday and today you invade it again."

In the vision, Johnny said nothing. He merely continued to release the emotions he felt toward her. He could feel them growing much stronger as the image of her face clarified in his mind's eye, as she called him by this new pet name, 'Profligate,' that he enjoyed hearing her enunciate. He could feel himself smiling in his meditation.

She stood, suddenly. "You smile at my rebuke? How dare you!?"

Johnny continued emoting as she stomped her foot. Blue light flew from her hands. It buffeted around him as though he was being charged with static electricity. Your rebuke, Johnny thought, is as full of longing as my gaze, Anna.

"The passion you are directing at me is rising in my gorge like indigestion," she muttered. Then in his vision, Johnny saw her sit back down on the blue chair. He looked at it more carefully now and saw that it was carved from the same type of stone as the amulet given him by the old woman at the airport. It was Lapis Lazuli.

In his vision, Inanna closed her eyes, elevated her face and suddenly Johnny began to lose the clarity he had earlier achieved. It seemed to him that the image he was watching began to shimmer, like the wall he had seen beyond the first mountain peek, the divider of the east and west sides of the island. Then he heard her voice again saying, but with tenderness, "I'll show you passion, Profligate."

The vision now brought him back to the chapel, to his very chair where in his mind's eye, he saw Inanna standing before him. She took him by the hand and suddenly they were whirling through the clouds and above the clouds. The sky flashed from night to day to night to day.

The sun became like a strobe light, hot then cold then hot, spinning as fast as a shooting star from east to west repeatedly; each trip interspersed with star-studded darkness. The stars became lines of light across the sky, each revolution drawing their fiber-optic appearance to the north, then back to the south as the seasons changed. But Johnny was barely aware of the heavenly bodies racing over his head. Inanna had captured his full awareness. He could see only her.

Every fiber of his being was filled with her. The emotional intensity was beyond anything he could have conceived. His head was spinning with her breath on his cheek. Her hair was wild in the wind, wrapping around his head and neck, then flaying back behind her. Her eyes held his with an intensity beyond any ability he had for dreaming. His own emotions returned the intensity with equal force, and between them they became a stationary light in the spinning sky, a fixed satellite reflecting the flashing sun and racing stars, Arrata lying still in the undulating sea below. Then she was gone. Johnny's last impression was that he had heard the words in her voice saying, "These others are most annoying. Come to me."

Johnny came out of his meditation lying on the floor of the chamber, thrashing back and forth. Those meditating had continued without interruption, but some fifteen others were standing around Johnny, staring at him in amazement. Tarek, seated on the floor beside him was the first to speak. "Are you okay?"

"I think so," said Johnny. "Don't get too close to me for a while. Don't touch me."

He stood, noticing that someone had already replaced him for the meditation shift. Glad to be relieved of that responsibility for the time being, he headed for the door to the chamber and reaching it, continued to the patio at the top terrace where he remained standing, looking out over the night enshrouded ocean. Those who had been watching him continued to do so in amazement, while the occasional magenta spark leaped from his fingers, one from an ear, and the path ahead of him appeared to illuminate itself as though concerned that he might stumble.

He remained quietly looking into the night sky for a time, then extended his arms, palms out and released the remainder of the energy with which she had filled him. His entire form glowed with the magenta light, beams of light, colored with a little more red than the pure magenta, extended straight up into the sky, broadening with altitude and distance until the grounds were almost as bright as day, for a few seconds. Then Johnny sat down, not minding the dew already appearing on the chairs.

Lucias sat down next to him with many brothers standing around close enough to hear. Lucias asked, "What was that all about?"

Johnny seemed to be in some sort of shock, but he turned his head to Lucias and said, "I haven't a clue, but it was wonderful. What did you see?"

"What we saw, DeMuzzi, was this. The wall fell again shortly after you began meditating then reformed within the very meditation chamber, in a dense whirling column completely consuming any view of you. We heard voices inside the column, yours and another's, a woman's voice. It lasted more than an hour. It awakened the whole community. I'm afraid you've become somewhat of a celebrity, in that short time. There is no longer anyone among us who does not know your name."

"Lee Moy. Is he near?" asked Johnny.

"I am here," he heard Lee Moy's voice among those standing nearby. Lee Moy stepped forward.

"You said to use the visual link for a meditation focus to see what I could learn."

"Yes," said Lee Moy. "Is that what you did?"

"I used her face as a meditation focus," Johnny began explaining. "When I had her face in my mind's eye, she began speaking to me as though I were really seeing her. Then she took over my meditation."

"It would appear," said Lucias, "that she also used your face as a meditation focus. The sounds which came from the shimmering column... Well, let me tell you this. I once stayed in a cheap motel in Amarillo Texas. The beds were a bit shaky with a large headboard against thin walls. The sounds I heard from the couple in the next room were timed with the sound of their headboard hitting the common wall. If those two had been Anthony and Cleopatra, the sounds I heard from you inside that column, would have turned them to dust."

"I must go back there," said Johnny.

"I agree," said Lucias. "I have never heard of love making on a spiritual plane before, but now I think I have witnessed it and each time you are near her, it seems, the wall either recedes or disappears completely. Even when you think of her intensely the wall disappears. Go back to the western side of the island, DeMuzzi, and consume her attention. We could use the rest. Maybe in so doing you can learn enough that we can finally prevail."

Chapter 10: Water Games

Chip felt weak, but with the help of Jimmy Smithson and Al Johns, he managed to come outside to sit in the morning sun to eat some fruit when he woke, late in the morning. Joyce looked as though she hadn't slept at all. As soon as he woke she splashed some water in her face to try to freshen up, but the rings under her eyes from not sleeping didn't go away. "What happened to you last night?" he asked through a mouthful of pineapple. "I thought it was me that got slammed."

"I was so worried about you," she responded. "I woke up and you weren't there. I looked around for you, went outside and wandered all over. Then Anna showed up from the forest. She was glowing in the dark with you and Leelee not far behind. What happened?"

"I told him not to do it," Smithson volunteered.

"Told him not to do what?" asked Al Johns, his face still red from the exertion of helping Chip to his chair outdoors.

At that moment Inanna made her appearance from the ballroom doors. Chip remained silent, indicating to Joyce and the others that they too should keep quiet until Inanna was gone again. Inanna seemed to glide down the steps and across the grounds, ignoring them. The Polynesians working in the gardens stopped work, kneeled toward her as before but kept quiet this time. Inanna made no sign indicating she saw anyone. She continued across the cultivated area and again disappeared down the path through the forest. She seemed somehow distracted, head down, and sullen.

When she was out of sight, Chip, still keeping his voice very low said to Joyce and the others, "Be wary of her. I don't know what she is but I don't think she's human. She isn't ruled by any of the social or cultural conventions that we follow. I think she's very dangerous. We would have been safer when the boat went down if we had tried to swim to Easter Island."

"You still haven't told me what happened," said Joyce. "I saw her kill Alphonso yesterday. I think I already know she's dangerous. What did she do to you and why?"

Chip described his following Inanna and Belili, his eavesdropping on the conversation and the snapping branch betraying his presence. "It was as though she had been turned to stone. She froze, listening. Then it was as though she could feel exactly where I was. The underbrush between us separated like the Red Sea must have parted for Moses. She walked directly to me. The strangest thing was that I was frozen like a rabbit under the fangs of a lion. I couldn't move."

"Are you crazy?" demanded Joyce. "You know what Leelee told us. You saw what she did to Alphonso. The others told us she's done this before, too. She could have killed you."

"You're right. I know, but I don't want to spend the rest of my life here. I don't want you to have to do that either. I have to find out who and what she is," said Chip. "I did manage to find out about the monastery at the other end of the island."

"You mentioned that last night," said Joyce.

"What monastery?" Jimmy and Al said at almost the same time, but Smithson stopped in deference to Al, who completed the question. "What do y'all know about the monastery, anything?"

"Just that she thinks of them as an enemy," answered Chip. "If we could make it there, I think we'd be safe from her."

"I think that's crazy as hell," remarked Teri Johns who had arrived on the scene in time to hear the last exchange. "You know what she'd do ta' us if she caught us tryin' ta' git away. You seen that poor boy, Alphonso. He was shriveled up like he'd been dayed a hunderd years. I'm stayin' right chere till somethin' better suggests itself."

Big Al put his arm around his tiny wife making her look even tinier by comparison. "Now Honey," he said. "We'll jist have ta' talk about this a little bit."

"Teri may be right," said Smithson. "The risks are horrendous."

"Whatever we decide," said Joyce, "we better decide it soon. Anna is just too explosive to be around her too much, especially if she hurts people like she does when she gets angry."

"I'll go," said Chip.

"Like hell you will, buster," said Joyce. "You just stay right here and heal and we'll talk about it later. Now. What did she do to you?"

"She made me sing to her," said Chip. "It was as though she took control of my voice and throat and suddenly I was singing…"

"Singin'," Teri cut him off disgustedly. "Fer Gawd's sake. How did she do that? What did y'all have ta' sing, anyway? Does she like Elvis 'er what?"

"Remember the song the girls sang while she made her grand entrance the other night?" asked Chip. "That was what she had me singing and in some strange language I never heard before. At least it was the same tune."

"Quite an ego on that' n," smirked Teri.

"A hymn of worship," remarked Smithson. "What the hell does she think she is; some kind of god?"

"Exactly," said Chip. "She thinks she's a god. Her husband left her a long time ago and she's been raging about it ever since. It seems he caught her in bed with another guy and that was it. He was gone."

"Well, wouldn't cha' jist know it," said Teri. "She couldn't keep her panties on, 'er that sarong thingy she wears and now she's payin' the price and makin' everyone around her pay it with her."

"We need a volunteer," said Big Al. "We need ta' find out what's on the eastern end of this bubble a' dirt. If Chip's right, we might jist be able ta' git away from this wild woman."

"Let's talk about trying to do this with the least amount of risk," said Chip. "We need to out smart her, if that's possible."

"Well how can that be done," asked Smithson. "She seems to know about almost everything we do. I'm surprised she didn't catch Chip sooner."

"She was upset about something," said Chip. "She was distracted about something. She was talking about her husband and being stranded on this island. She wasn't paying attention. Leelee was there, thank God. Leelee saved my life, but you should have heard how rough Leelee talks to her, almost like a mean schoolteacher to a third grader. The only thing missing was the foot long ruler."

"Leelee?" echoed Joyce. "That old woman stood up to her and saved your life? How?"

"It felt like while I was doing this singing," said Chip, "that she was somehow draining my energy, my life force, if you will. I think she was well on her way to taking all of it when Leelee stepped in and talked her out of it. She said, 'Don't kill the goose that lays the golden egg.' She said, 'if you take all of it, there will be no more tomorrow and you know how hard they are to come by.'"

"Good Gawd," said Teri. "What did she mean by that?"

"I think she was talking about whatever energy she was taking from me," said Chip. "Anna apparently has some need for being worshiped. Didn't you see how she soaks it up when the islanders sing to her, when they kneel and start this 'heena heena' thing that they do?"

"I think," said Al, "if we're gonna' escape from here, before we go we need ta' fix her little red wagon. We at least need ta' take all these people with us so she can't do whatever it is she does no more."

"How do we do that," said Smithson. "None of us know any Polynesian languages."

Big Al continued, "There's a difference 'tween a man an' a animal. When a raccoon, 'er some other critter gits in a jaw trap, it'll chew its own leg off ta' git away, if it has time. A man 'll stay there and wait so he can kill the son of a bitch that trapped him and protect others of his own kind. I ain't no damned critter. I aim ta' put a stop ta' this if I can. She ain't no god. I don't know what she is but she ain't no god. She's got a weakness somewhere. We have to find it."

Belili emerged from the forest at the far end of the building complex and the conversation ended, for the time being. A moment later, Inanna appeared at the top of the path across the grounds. Belili came walking toward them. Inanna paused at the pier and stood looking out to sea. She still seemed to be distracted and sullen.

Belili disappeared into one of the many doorways lining the walk and re-emerged a moment later with a tray loaded with a pitcher of tea and glasses. She continued toward them. When she reached the group, she placed the tray on the lawn table and drew up a seat to join them.

"We don't know whose side your on, old woman," said Al. "We don't even know who you are, but thanks for the tea." He poured himself a cup then offered to pour for the others.

Belili smiled, her eyes sparkling with good humor. She answered with a question, "Tell me, Mr. Johns. When the human is captured in the trap, does he really stay to kill his captor to protect others of his kind? Or does he kill his captor out of revenge? Perhaps a more enlightened human would consider it better, or safer if he left without harming his captor and simply warned others of his kind about the danger. Perhaps the captor is only doing what comes naturally to him, or her and is only trying to survive in the only way he or she knows how, in which case, the captor means no personal harm to the captive. When you trap a raccoon is it because you hate raccoons or because you want the pelt and the meat? What do you say about that? Should the captor then be hated and executed or pitied and avoided?"

Chip enjoyed Big Al's discomfiture. Not only had Belili informed him that the tones of their conversation carried farther than they had thought, but she trumped him on being human, as well. Smithson was smiling too, Chip noticed, and trying to conceal it from Big Al, who sort of blustered for a moment. Then recovering he stated with indignation, "You been listnin' in."

"Hardly a sin in this company." Belili laughed at him and sobering looked at Chip. "Feeling better?"

"Yes, thanks to you," Chip answered.

"And to this fine lady," Belili added, patting Joyce on the knee. "You should take my advice. Has your stay here not been pleasant? Except for last night of course. Have you plenty to eat, a comfortable place to sleep. No work has been required of you. Why not enjoy it. She asks so little. Why not stop fighting her? All she wants from you is your love."

"But love isn't something which can be taken like a ransom," offered Joyce. "It has to be freely given and freely received, otherwise it has no real value. God doesn't appear to us like some sea monster and demand our love or He'll kill us. He gives us the message, leads us in His way, loves us unreservedly and asks that we love Him back."

"That is a lesson Inanna has not yet learned," replied Belili. "Intimidating humans has been too easy for her, but in the world today there is a new kind of human. This new kind of human does not worship gods of the moon and gods of the sea. They are not frightened so easily by the old ways, just angered. The Pantheon of old is forgotten and gone, except for Inanna and a few others. Some day they all will follow their families and Arrata and the Earth will be at peace."

"That answers my question," said Big Al. "You're on her side."

Belili looked discouraged and thoughtful. "Perhaps," she said slowly, "but not in the way Inanna would have me be on her side. I am here to force her to grow up. Have you ever taught children?"

"She ain't no child," interjected Teri with an angry look on her face. "I don't know what she is but she ain't no child."

"Looks pretty grown up to me," cracked Smithson.

"And to me," said Joyce. "What's your point?"

"I've taught many," reflected Belili. "Most children can be guided along a course of study, systematically building one block of learning upon the next. Then sometimes you get a child who can't think in this same way. They think outside of the box, as Mr. Johns might put it. Their questions are challenging and creative. Those children need a special kind of prodding, or herding. That kind of child needs a very special kind of shepherd. I am Inanna's shepherd. I challenge her. I make her think."

"She said last night that she was trapped here, like us, imprisoned," said Chip.

"Anyone can make his or her own life a prison," answered Belili.

"Tell me you don't know that this is true."

"Anna also mentioned a monastery on the other end of the island. Is there a monastery there?" Chip continued.

"If you try to go there, you will share Alphonso's fate," Belili said grimly. "You are Inanna's play things, like it or not. If you are human, as Mr. Johns defines it, you will try to kill your captor and die in the process. If you are enlightened humans, you will stay and pacify her so she lures no other humans to this place. I would prefer to see no one else of your kind injured."

"'Of your kind,' you said," Joyce picked up on the phrase. "'Of your kind.' What kind are you, Leelee? Are you not human?"

Belili began laughing and as she did she stood up, morphed into the owl figure and flew back toward the forest, screeching.

"Well I'll be damned," stated Teri emphatically.

"What was that?" Asked Rosemary rubbing her eyes as she stepped out of the Johns' sleeping quarters. "What did I miss?"

"Not a thing, dear," said Joyce. "Have a cup of tea."

"I feel like a swim in the ocean," said Smithson. "How about you, Chip? Do you feel good enough to see how far the envelope reaches?"

Inanna was still standing on the pier, but she had turned to face in their direction. It seemed to Chip that she was looking at the mountain, rising behind the building complex. Chip turned so his eyes could follow her gaze and was surprised to see a sort of shimmering haze in the distance, like a heat wave rising off of pavement, but far too big, and high.

"You stay here and rest," Joyce said to him protectively. "I don't want you getting hurt."

"How about it Rosey," Smithson said to his wife. "Feel like a dip in the surf?"

"Sounds good to me," she said smiling. "It'll have to be just the two of us. I don't have my swimsuit. It's on the boat."

"I'll join you," said Big Al, absentmindedly.

"Oh no you won't," said Teri, taking him by the arm and dragging him toward their quarters. "They're goin' skinny dippin.'"

"Maybe I can get Jorge to take me out to the boat. Then we can get our swimming gear?" said Smithson. "And we can all go."

"What about Inanna," said Big Al.

"Hell," said Teri. "You jist let me handle that. Nobody never got offended by a little Texas hospitality. I'll invite her to join us. Maybe we can even set up a little barbecue down there in the sand."

Chip and Joyce grinned at each other briefly as the others walked away. "I wonder if they got any jalepinos 'er chile peppers 'er datils 'er something we can liven up the food with," they could hear Teri talking as they vanished into their quarters.

In a few moments, the Smithsons reappeared with Jorge in tow. The Johns were close behind. Chip sipped some more tea while he watched them approach the pier and Inanna. She was wearing a pink sarong today and had an orchid in her hair. They spoke briefly and to Chip's surprise, Big Al and Jorge climbed into the boat and they began rowing out to the yacht.

"Do you think she went for it?" asked Joyce with concern.

"Yeah. I do," said Chip. "Leelee told us how to treat her and it seems to be working."

"How's that?" asked Joyce. "How do we treat her?"

"Like she's a very head strong five year old with a loaded shot gun," he answered grimly.

"Oh God," she answered. "What an analogy. But I think you may be right."

They sat in silence while Jorge and Al rowed out to the Yacht. They climbed aboard, with Inanna standing on the pier watching suspiciously. In a few minutes, the two reappeared on the deck of the yacht and climbed back into the skiff. "Oh look," said Joyce. "They have a beach ball and an inflatable mattress. Is that thing Al has one of those floating nets for water volleyball?"

"I think it is," said Chip with a smile.

"If they're going to try to get her to play volleyball... I've got to see this," muttered Joyce.

"They may be making a really big mistake," said Chip softly. "They're going to try to win her as a friend then betray her by trying to escape. It's a dangerous volleyball game if you ask me. Not only will she be angry about our trying to leave, she'll be hurt by the betrayal of friends."

"If we succeed in making her a friend, maybe she'll allow us to leave," answered Joyce.

"Don't count on it."

"Try looking on the positive side," she continued. "If the lesson she has to learn is that love must be freely given and received to have any value, then what we have to do is to make her love us. If we can do that, then she'll realize that we have lives back home that we want to get back to and that no matter how easy she makes life for us here, we are never going to be happy unless we can go home. If she loves her friends, she'll want us to be happy. She'll not only let us go, she may even help us get there."

"Twisted logic if you ask me," said Chip. "But it's certainly worth a try. Let's see if we can join them. I think I can walk that far. I think you need to tell this to the others, too; before they screw things up and make her distrust us by trying to escape."

Inanna and the others had long disappeared down the path by the time Joyce and Chip got to it. Chip's progress was slow, but he made steady headway and finally they arrived on the scene at the beach.

The water volleyball net was set up and securely anchored at each end. The gentle surf caused the net to dance erratically, but it was steady enough for the game. Inanna was seated in the sand watching, trying to keep her haughty look, but obviously interested. The Johns were on one side of the net and the Smithsons on the other. The first set was under way. Big Al was serving.

"Now don't y'all make this too hard lookin,'" Teri admonished her husband. "No spikin' an' none a your tricks Mr. Al." Al hit the ball. It flew over the net directly to Smithson. Smithson hit it back but the breeze carried it a bit to Teri's right and she had to dive for it. She got it just in time and drove the ball back toward Rosemary who missed it entirely, lost her footing, submerging herself in the water. Rosemary came up laughing.

Big Al called out, "Point. One ta' nothin.'" Then he served again, this time to Rosemary who missed the ball again, swore, giggled and threw it back toward Al.

"Y'all come on in an' join us any time y'all feel ready, Darlin,'" Teri called out to Inanna, then ducked as Smithson returned Al's serve.

"One up," Smithson called out. "Our serve." Teri retrieved the ball and threw it back to Smithson who tossed it to his wife. Rosemary stepped back through the water, over the imaginary boundary line. She set the ball on her fist, cocked her arm and sent it skimming the net directly to Teri.

Inanna's defensive expression had faded to one of interest. She even giggled with Rosemary when Rosemary fell again. Chip and Joyce exchanged "see I told ya' so" glances and sat down next to Inanna in the sand. They watched Inanna as much as they watched the game. After a few minutes, Inanna leaned over to Joyce and asked, "What do they mean by 'up?' Sometimes they say 'one up,' or two up. What does this mean?"

Joyce smiled before she answered. Inanna seemed satisfied and watched for a few more minutes. Then she said, "I think I would like to play too, but if I join the game, one side will be off balance."

Joyce said, "I'll take the other side and keep it balanced. How's that?"

Inanna nodded acceptance and Joyce entered the water in her clothes, joining Teri and Al Johns. Teri jumped right on that with "didn't y'all bring no swim suit Honey. I think I got a extra one on the yacht but I don't think it'd fit..." Teri was totally silenced by the fact that before entering the water, Inanna dropped her sarong to the sand, and began walking into the water on the Smithson's side, in the nude.

"Don't you say one word," Joyce cautioned her.

"But she's buck nekked," Teri whispered, still in shock.

"My mother always told me," Joyce said to her, loud enough for all to hear. "If you want to make a friend, you have to be a friend. I think we need to make a friend. What do you say Big Al?"

"Looks mighty friendly ta' me," he replied and served the ball very gently toward Inanna.

Chip watched their discomfiture with amusement, catching Joyce's warning glances. Teri was flushed with embarrassment. Big Al was as pleased "As a man my age can be," he said later.

Smithson was studiously not looking at her. Rosemary was successfully pretending that nothing unusual was happening. Inanna missed Al's serve. Chip could see her hair trigger anger about to burst. So could Al Johns, evidently. She was about to blast the ball when Al called out to her, "It's the only one we got Darlin.' We all miss now an' then. It's part of the game. No one laughed.

After only a few minutes, everyone appeared to have forgotten that Inanna had no swimsuit. The volleyball game went on with splashing, laughing and point calling, just as though it was a school picnic in Idaho. At one frightful point, Teri served the ball to Inanna, gently, but Inanna missed it and it hit her on the head. Everyone gasped in unison. Inanna looked about uncertainly for a moment then dived under the water to straighten her hair and came up laughing. The momentary tension was broken.

After the game, they changed sides and played another one. With the sun nearing the horizon, everyone picked up their clothing and headed up the path toward dinner, laughing and talking animatedly about the game. Inanna was strangely silent even when Al and Teri tried to include her in the joking and general camaraderie. When they reached the top of the path she separated herself from the group and went straight to her quarters, through the ballroom.

When she was out of sight, Teri broke the silence. "I sure hope she ain't upset about somethin.'"

Later the group gathered in the ballroom for dinner. The same three girls presented the usual song, this time with a different accompanying instrument, also stringed. The dais was set up differently. "I wonder who she's havin' for dinner," Big Al ventured when they saw the extra seven places at Inanna's table.

Inanna then rose from her throne of Lapis Lazuli and announced. "I wonder if my volleyball friends will join me?" Then she took a seat at the table set for seven, in a hand made wicker chair like the others, leaving her throne unoccupied. She indicated that Al should sit at the head of the table at one end and Joyce at the other. As they joined her, she said, "I decided to set the throne aside for special occasions and sit with my friends in the same kind of chair you are using."

Jorge, who had not joined the game in the surf, was left sitting with the rest of the islanders. The look on his face did not indicate pleasure with the arrangement. He sat restlessly watching the conversation at the head table, fidgeting and frowning. He was the first to leave the room after finishing his food. Chip kept a watch on him, glancing in Jorge's direction from time to time. When he left, Chip thought to himself, "I hope he's not going to cause trouble. This is going so well, now."

Chapter 11: Duplicity?

The Fraternity's council chamber was located on the second floor of the main building. Its arched windows overlooked the cultivated terraces below and the sea beyond. A fireplace at the north end of the room had charred walls and an empty grate, since the late spring weather didn't require artificial warmth, but Johnny was shivering, nevertheless. He was seated on a cut off palm stump which had been carved to the shape of a low backed chair, like all the other chairs in the room, only his was beside the fireplace, next to Lucias' at the highly polished conference table. Some enterprising group of brothers had cut and polished it from one of the native hardwoods. It was an eight-foot long, vertical slice of a four-foot thick tree. The edges of the table were irregular as though the artist had deliberately allowed nature's superior beauty to remain in the form of the tree's original contours.

There was a pitcher of tea on the table with numerous cups. The brothers helped themselves as they filed into the room. Lee Moy was seated beyond Lucias with Cardac next to him and Caleb at the far end of the table, all facing the growing congregation on the other side of the table. Johnny tried to ignore the dozens of private conversations going on between individual brothers as the crowd gathered. Tarek was seated on Johnny's right at the far end of the table from Caleb. Tarek leaned over to Johnny and whispered, "How does it feel to be the center of attention at our first town meeting?"

"It feels more like a hot seat than a center of attention," Johnny whispered back. "I guess I've stirred up a lot of attention from the community and they want answers. I really don't have any. I don't know anymore about what happened than those watching."

Lucias stood up. He rapped his gavel on the table three times. The whole company stood. The talking stopped and all waited to hear what Lucias had to say. He opened with a prayer. When he had finished he rapped the table one more time and everyone sat down.

"I think everyone is here," Lucias began, "except for those in the morning meditation shift. We have been on this island for a long time and before us, our people have been serving here for much longer. During those many years, we have made little progress that we know of for sure. We have managed to stabilize a sort of polarity between us and what we perceive as a threat from the west side of the island."

There was a hue and cry about Lucias' use of the word 'perceive.' Lucias rapped the gavel once more for silence and got it. Then he continued with a determined look on his face. "I'm trying to not make any absolute statements about it, based on fear or the subjective conclusions drawn by third party observers. I think we all agree that we perceive a threat from the west. Do we not?"

There was a resounding "yes."

Lucias continued. "During our years of occupying this end of this island, we have managed to erect and maintain a barrier which protects us from the influence of what ever is over there. As our energy varies in its strength and the energy of the opposition, what ever it is, varies in strength, the barrier vacillates back and forth, like a continuous tug of war. Recently it fell completely, twice. We have seen it fall before. We have also seen it completely overwhelm us temporarily.

"It is my opinion that the reason it withdrew after overwhelming us was that it was unprepared for victory and having achieved it unexpectedly was uncertain as to how to proceed, to complete our undoing. On the same token, when the barrier fell, recently, we also were unprepared for victory and subsequently, let down our guard when perhaps we should have charged forward to complete the rout and finally conclude our business on Arrata. Why not discuss this among yourselves for a few moments? Then we will discuss it together."

Johnny was a miasma of confusion. *Is Anna the source of the evil we fight, as they seem to think, or is she a victim of it?* The confusion of conversation in the room was difficult to follow so he didn't try. He wrung his hands, stretched, squirmed in his seat, and waited for Lucias to call the meeting to order again, which he soon did.

The first person whom Lucias chose to speak was Broesseus, a middle aged man of average height and extraordinary girth wearing a sleeveless, wool, knee length shirt exposing thick muscular arms and shoulders. He shook his long dark hair out of his eyes as he spoke.

Beards seemed to be the general preference but Broesseus' reddish beard was apparently itchy, the skin around its edges scarlet from his scratching it. "We think there's a new and unknown factor in the equation," he said. "Things began changing quickly after DeMuzzi arrived. In the last few days alone, the barrier fell twice, and then there was that little distraction in the meditation room. It was as though the barrier had formed a column and moved right in among us - and settled on top of him. We think we should look into this more before we start planning a direct assault or something along those lines."

Lucias next recognized a thin elderly gentleman called Damian who rose as though his joints were stiff. Damian wore a white cotton shirt and shorts with a wool lap blanket bunched up and thrown over his shoulders like a scarf. His hair and beard were short as though trimmed frequently. He began by clearing his throat and removing the lap blanket from his neck. "Brothers," he began. "Here's a thought we may want to consider. In the past, our ancient brothers placed much greater emphasis on the meaning of the letters we represent in our Aleph-Bayts and their corresponding numbers. Today we tend to work more as a team than as individuals with personal crusades, but in the past, we worked more or less separately, gaining help from the rest of the team as needed. Is this not true?"

"It is said to be true," replied Lucias and several others.

"Then consider," continued Damian. "In the past we have lost seven brothers to the evil of the island's western side. Brother DeMuzzi is the eighth of us to venture in that direction and only he has returned to us. Brother DeMuzzi tells us that his Aleph-Bayt designation is Hjet, the number Eight. Hjet, as we all know, means 'a fence.' Furthermore, this designation of his was not given to him by the Aleph-Bayt of his initiation, but by a much more ancient Aleph-Bayt. DeMuzzi still bears upon his body, the baton passed to him by our brother Prill and he has yet to execute his chosen task. Further, consider that our main task on this island for so many years has been to maintain a FENCE. Now, after all this time, has the Ascended Brotherhood finally sent us a HJET and suddenly everything changes? Is this really such a surprise?"

"He's too young," objected one.

"He lacks the maturity of spiritual strength. Did you see how flushed he was when the column receded?" said another.

"He has no discipline," interjected yet another. "We told him not to go to the western side and did he follow our advice? No! He immediately on his first day, even, headed directly to the west."

The meeting descended into dozens of vehement, simultaneous conversations until Lucias again rapped the gavel to regain their attention. Gradually the volume decreased and the group waited for Lucias to speak. "Caleb," Lucias said, beginning to poll the head table. "Do you have anything to add?"

"No," responded Caleb.

"And you, Cardac?"

"Like the rest of us, I'm afraid of this unknown on the western side of the island. And now, I am also afraid of the unknown on this side of the island. I don't know whether to be awed or scared. We know the evil of the west can spy on us somehow, or at least it has seemed that way in the past. For all we know, what was said the other night might be true. DeMuzzi could have been converted or turned somehow to work against us. That could be the only reason he was permitted to return to us alive. On the other hand, he may be under the protection of the Ascended Brotherhood or some other power unknown to us. Sometimes the best decision is no decision and that is my feeling about what we should do right now. We should wait and watch. That's my opinion."

"Well said," replied Lucias as Cardac took his seat. "What say you Lee Moy?"

Lee Moy rose from his seat. *He seems like an old Indian Shaman,* thought Johnny, *infinitely wise. I'm glad I got to see the lighter side of him. I'll never forget the image of that bird on his shoulder and him calling it Jezebell, or the herb garden and how the bird obeyed him when he told it not to eat his seeds.*

Lee Moy cleared his throat. "Our brother Damian spoke of our modern time and how our priorities and focuses have changed over the millennia. Those changes he spoke of are true, but many other changes have taken place. Our ancient brothers recognized more fully than we do that a human is more than a mind and a spirit and a body. We also contain emotion and passion, each quality more complex and more intricately designed than any of us has ever been able to fathom. Our ancient brothers recognized this and utilized these parts of us in ways our modern culture no longer believes is valid or valuable.

"Those of our fraternity, however, are still taught to focus passion and to spiritually rise above its urgency so that we can use it constructively. That our brother DeMuzzi is young does not communicate to us that he is unable to do this, only that the power of his passion is nearer its peak. That he was led to the west side of the island on his first full day among us does not necessarily communicate to us that he is undisciplined, but perhaps it communicates to us and perhaps should communicate to him, that his higher purpose lies in that place.

"It is my belief," continued Lee Moy, "that we should be reminded that none of us is here by chance. All of us have been selected especially for this service because of some special skill that we individually possess. That DeMuzzi is among us is not an accident. It is my opinion that we should encourage DeMuzzi to go where his spirit leads him to go and that we should maintain our faith in his purpose and in those who selected him."

"I think we should lock him up," said a voice from the rear. "We need to stop what ever that was from coming back."

"Yeah, right, I agree," several answered.

"No leave him alone," responded a few more.

Lucias arose and rapped his gavel again. Johnny semi-consciously looked to see if a dent was appearing where Lucias was rapping. "There is quite a diversity of opinion among us," Lucias commented. "It's so much nicer when we're all in agreement. I myself prefer a sort of laissez faire approach to life and to my fellow beings. Like Lee Moy, I believe we should have more faith in those who selected and watch over us, that we should allow DeMuzzi to continue to explore, as he believes is good. That changes are taking place in the status quo of our ongoing struggle may well be a good sign, rather than a harbinger of worse evils to come.

"DeMuzzi has already told us all he knows of the other side of the island, which is not much. He told us about meeting a woman who treated him as a man. He told us of the meditation in which he used her face as a focal point hoping to see more of that area. We know the results of that so we must assume that this woman is more than she appears to be.

"DeMuzzi has returned to us. So, we have every reason to believe in his integrity and his good intentions toward our purposes and us. We have no reason to suspect otherwise except through our own fears and superstitions. Fear and superstition are two things we hope to rise above as brothers of this order. It is my recommendation that we make no decision at this time, but that we wait for a few weeks and if conditions change more radically, discuss it again."

Lucias called for a vote which when counted, supported his recommendation.

"It is my further recommendation that we try to find a correlation between DeMuzzi's activities and when the barrier disappears and once we find that connection, that we plan a direct assault to be timed with those disappearances." He called for another vote, which was unanimously in favor.

CB   BD

That was a lot of talk for nothing, Johnny muttered to himself as he left the chamber. After the noon meal, he headed for the beach. On the way down the path, he argued with himself, introspecting and worrying about his mixed agenda.

I can't get her out of my mind, was his most repeated thought. *But it's not the life I've chosen. It's not where I want to be going. It's not what I want to do. But is it? I want her more than any woman I ever wanted. My heart pounds at the very thought of seeing her again. I will my feet to take me to my cell and look where I'm going. Right back into harm's way, if I'm to believe what I've been told.*

The surf looked more inviting than ever, clear blue water, gently lapping against the shore on the lee side of the island. He could see a crab making its way across the bottom and idly wondered if it was the same one he saw the first time he came this way. This time there were more tracks on the beach, of birds and other small animals. The tide must be rising, he thought. The beach hasn't been swept clean of tracks yet.

The lava flow looked the same as before but this time there was a large owl sitting on top of it which took to flight as he approached. Before climbing the flow and crossing into the western side of the island, he decided to try to center himself and proceed in a meditative state with the intention of sensing any change in the spiritual ambience of his surroundings. When he was ready, he began to climb the flow. When he got to the top, he was pleased to see Anna seated in the sand, wearing a magenta sarong. Her hair was tied back and hanging over her shoulder with an orchid in it, matching the color of her clothing.

"I am glad you have come to me, DeMuzzi. Still a Profligate, I see."

Her demeanor is different, he observed. *No longer so challenging as though I'm a trespasser. She seems, somehow more subdued, friendlier.*

"I'm just a devoted swimmer," he replied with a smile. "I'm glad to see you too, Anna." He jumped down from the lava flow, fell in the sand. After standing to brush himself off he took a seat in the sand beside her.

"A somewhat clumsy Profligate too, if you ask me," she said with a chuckle. "Why don't you just fly down? Why jump?"

"Flying takes longer," he said with a smile. "That was nice last night."

Her eyes flashed suddenly with what Johnny took to be anger, then quieted again as quickly. "How did you do that?" she demanded. "I think that you must be a god, who has come to rescue me."

"I'd ask how you did what you did, too, but I think I know," he replied.

"First," she said. "I want to share a unique experience I had yesterday. It was something I never did before." She leaned toward him playfully. "I played water volleyball," she paused again for effect, grinning, then added, "with some friends."

"What was it you enjoyed most about the experience?" he asked, being careful.

Her eyes changed again to uncertainty, then to discovery. "I guess I shouldn't be surprised because I felt this last night. You love me. Don't you? And I didn't force you to. This is so amazing. Have you ever played water volleyball?"

Johnny was beginning to feel off balance, again. "Yes," he answered remembering the pool in his parent's yard and the wobbly net crossing its center.

"I have six friends, well seven counting you. Are you my friend?"

"Yes," answered Johnny.

"Maybe you will play water volleyball with us sometime."

"Why are you so excited about having played water volleyball with six friends?" Johnny risked asking.

"Well, there were only five," Anna responded. "Chip watched from the beach."

"Chip?" asked Johnny.

"Oh," she said comforting him. "He doesn't love me like you do. Chip has a wife, Joyce. There were Joyce, Al, Jimmy, Rosemary and Teri. Al and Teri talk funny. They're from Texas."

"Texas?" Johnny was growing increasingly surprised and alarmed. "How many people live over here with you?"

"The nicest thing?" she turned serious. "They accepted me. It was as though nothing bad had happened between us. They forgave me and included me in their friendship."

"Are these your first friends?" asked Johnny, trying not to be too intrusive.

"Yes," she said. "I received their love and gave it back and we were all uplifted. That's how it's supposed to be, but I've never managed it before. Well Belili is a friend, I suppose, a very old friend, but Belili scolds me more than she shares with me."

Belili? Thought Johnny. *Where have I heard that name before, and recently, I think.* "How is my love different?" Johnny asked.

Inanna stopped talking, looking directly into his eyes. Her expression was almost fierce, but softened. He could feel her intensity and gradually allowed his heart to sink into those eyes. As he did so, she took his hand, saying, "Let me feel your energy again. Like last night."

His hand felt a tingling sensation. When he glanced at it, he was shocked to see magenta sparks coming from his fingers, again. He held up his other hand, palm up, focusing the energy in that hand. When it began glowing, he put his arms around Inanna, encircling her in the magenta light. She did the same, then suddenly pulled back. "I know you are going to refuse me," she said simply. "Why? Who are you? Why are your people here on my island? What do you want from me?"

"Well," Johnny began to answer.

"I know why you're here," She announced. "You're here to fight me. That's all they've done since they arrived, is fight me.

Good heavens thought Johnny. *She just told me that she has been here as long as the brotherhood and that she is the one we have been fighting.* "You couldn't have been here when they arrived. That was hundreds of years ago," he muttered, then added, "I'm not here to fight you, Anna. I'm here because I'm in love with you. I couldn't stay away."

She leaped to her feet and before Johnny knew what hit him, he was surrounded with a bright blue light emanating from her hands. It struck him like the hot air of an opened oven door, blew through his hair, and singed his clothing. "Wow," he said with a surprised laugh. "You have got to teach me how to do that. That is so cool."

Then, slightly understanding that she just tried to take his life again, he responded. He elevated his hands just above his waist, palms facing her and released his own energy which he had just had augmented from her only moments before. Inanna found herself surrounded with magenta light, the light of love.

She stood quietly for a moment, digesting the experience. Then she said in low tones, "I don't know whether to be infuriated or flattered. No one has ever survived my fury, but you laugh at me and return love in exchange. You are a most peculiar Profligate, DeMuzzi." She plopped back down in the sand, dejectedly. "What do your people want from me, DeMuzzi?"

"They want to spread peace and love over the rest of the island. They want to find out why such terrible things happened to the Easter Islanders and what causes the Rapanui storms that bring shipwrecks here. They want the threat these things represent to our kind, to go away."

"So. They think I am a threat to your kind," she said angrily. "They have no idea what kind of threat I can be."

"Why does this anger you, Anna? It's not a big thing that they want."

"They want to take away my power, my control," she snarled. "They want to take away my people and for me to be like them."

"Anna. Why must you be in control when sharing is so much more fulfilling? Did you control the water volleyball game? Did you control my gift of love? Which is more rewarding; to give and receive freely or to take and demand?" Johnny sat down beside her again. "Give me your hand," he said to her.

"Is that a command?" she asked sullenly.

"Of course not," Johnny answered. "Friends don't command friends. It's a request. Give me your hand and you may trust that I will put something good into it."

She extended her hand, one eyebrow lifted in defiance. Johnny took her hand, turned it over and kissed her palm. Then he turned it over and kissed the back of her hand, allowing her to receive his tenderness.

"I want you to come back to my palace and stay with me, DeMuzzi. Come with me. I will be yours and you will be mine."

"Is that a command?" he asked mischievously.

"No," she stretched the word over three octaves. "It's a request, as between friends."

"I want to," he said simply. "But I have to give it some thought. I'll let you know. Maybe I'll see you tomorrow."

They were still seated in the sand with the blue surf, rolling gently toward them, lapping the shore. Johnny could hear some birds twittering in the background. He did not see the large owl perched in the palm tree overhead. Inanna rolled out of her sitting position on top of him. He allowed her to pin him in the sand, and with a wide smile, said, "Kiss me you fool."

"How dare you call me a fool," she said, her eyes wide with anger. She kissed him. Then she hopped off of him sputtering. "Want to think about it. I've never made such an offer to a mortal man and he wants to think about it. He expects me to wait while he thinks."

"Mortal?" smirked Johnny. "I thought you knew that I was a god."

"See?" she demanded. "I knew it. You are a god."

"Only in my mind. Only in my mind," he smiled over his shoulder as he headed for the lava flow.

"Before you go, DeMuzzi," she started. "Let me ask you a question."

He paused and turned to her. "What is that lump I felt between us when we embraced? Are you wearing some jewel?"

"Yes," he said before he caught himself. *Now I remember. Belili was the name of that old woman in the airport that gave me the blue obelisk. What did she call it? Yes!, Lapis Lazuli! Anna said Belili is a friend of hers. What's the connection? She said someone gave it to her to give to me. It wasn't Anna. Who was it?* "I have an amulet given to me by a friend," he said evasively. He pulled the chain around his neck to bring the stone above his shirt so Anna could see it. To his amazement, the stone was glowing and the glow was bright enough that he could notice it in the direct afternoon sunlight.

"That must have been a very good friend," said Anna secretively.

"It would seem so," said Johnny.

Back at the monastery he sought out Lucias and told him of the day's events. "It is the woman I've been meeting who is the source of the energy we've been fighting. She talks of having been here when the brotherhood first arrived. When was that?"

"Eighteenth Century," Lucias replied. "It's impossible. You say she appears to be about your age, 35 more or less?"

"About that," replied Johnny.

"Well she's crackers," said Lucias. "But then there's the business of the blue light she keeps flashing at you. Do you think it's dangerous?"

"I'm beginning to think so," said Johnny. Then he told Lucias of meeting the old woman who called herself Belili at the airport in Santiago and showed him the amulet of Lapis Lazuli.

"It's a pretty thing, isn't it," Lucias remarked. "You say it was glowing? If that's what has been protecting you, I'd suggest that you never take it off, but I don't see how a semi-precious gemstone would have any effect against what we've been fighting. Maybe we should send for some and try it out?"

"I wouldn't know where to send," Johnny said.

"I'll ask Agricola what he knows about it. It's my understanding that he used to collect rocks. He might be able to tell us something about it."

Chapter 12: DeMuzzi Meets the Castaways

Johnny found this evening, that he was not welcome in the meditation group. The experience of the previous evening had adequately frightened some of the brothers that they thought his presence to be too disruptive. So, he was excluded. *That's okay with me*, thought Johnny. *I'll sit outside and enjoy the evening.*

The setting sun was not visible from the main terrace. It was lying in the shadow of the twin peaks. Johnny amused himself by watching the birds circling in search of the most favorable roost for the night and the tiny bug eating lizards of the island trying to make themselves invisible by snuggling against thin twigs and branches of the foliage while their body temperatures dropped. That they could change their skin color to match their immediate surroundings continued to amaze Johnny and excite a little bit of envy. Sometimes I wish I could just disappear like that, he moaned to himself.

As the last light of the day began fading, he picked up his chair and moved it away from the overhanging roof of the top terrace. He carried it to one side to where he could see the eastern volcano and the shimmering barrier beyond. He placed his chair on the ground facing west and slouched in it, arms folded defensively. *I wonder if the barrier can be seen in the dark,* he mused. *If Anna is causing it, it should be relatively calm tonight. She seemed relaxed when I left her, but I did reject her and after reflecting, she may have reacted differently.*

On previous evenings, he had not noticed the shimmering barrier in the darkness, but tonight, there was a faint color emanating from where the barrier should be. *Like a stationary aurora borealis*, his mind wandered. The colors gradually fluctuated from magenta to blue then back through magenta to red. As the hue reached the red end of the spectrum, it seemed to him to become more turbulent, like the chop on an enclosed bay in a high wind. As it fluctuated back through magenta it seemed to recede slightly and grow calmer, then as it reached the other end of the visible spectrum, blue, it began charging closer again. Bolts of blue, like that from Anna's hands, shot from the aurora like rams trying to punch through a rubber sheet. The passions displayed in this color range frightened Johnny because they came so close to the compound. *What is she doing?* He mused; unaware that he had finally accepted that it was indeed Anna who was causing the display. Anna was the source of the energy that the fraternity had been struggling against for so long.

Gradually the realization of this acceptance sunk into his consciousness and as it did, his face turned very grave. *I survived that? Why did she let me live? Why did she let me leave when she wanted me to stay?* He turned reflective, submerging his new fear into the safety of disbelief. *She couldn't be doing that. She's just a young woman ... but she does have some unusual abilities,* he admitted to himself with a puzzled frown.

The aurora had faded beyond the visible violet end of the spectrum. When it had completely vanished, the ground suddenly exploded with a gust or whirlwind of violent air movement. He was covered with dust and bits of vegetation from nearby plants, torn from the ground. He leaped to his feet, startled. As the wind stopped, he began brushing the dirt off of himself. When he finished he sat down again and looked toward the barrier. It had returned through the ultra-violet into the visible spectrum and was now blue. The invisible ram was again plunging into the elastic barrier, plunging almost near him only to be pushed back.

Lee Moy stepped out of the shadows of the terrace. Johnny could see him approaching in the moonlight. "For the time being," Johnny said to him, "It may be unadvisable to get too close to me. Did you see what just happened?"

Lee Moy stopped about ten yards away and said, "Indeed I did. Are you alright?"

"Yes," said Johnny pointing at the aurora. "I'm just a little dusty. Have you seen the light show that's going on tonight?"

Lee Moy stepped farther from the overhead cover provided by the top terrace, carefully maintaining his distance from Johnny. The barrier had receded slightly and was fading into the Magenta phase of its cycle. "Very pretty," said Lee Moy. "How long has this been going on?"

"I just noticed it after the sun went down," said Johnny. "Now watch this. It's heading into its red phase."

The light continued to fade toward red and as it did it became choppy as before, but this time, the barrier approached much more closely, even passing east of the eastern most peak before it faded into the invisible infrared range. "Best to get back under the canopy," Johnny called to Lee Moy. Just as Lee Moy followed Johnny's suggestion, Johnny felt a rush of heat wash over his body. Plants on the ground near him appeared to have been wilted by its intensity and Johnny's clothing was slightly smoking. "She seems to be working herself up," Johnny called to Lee Moy who stepped back out under the sky so he could continue to watch.

The barrier had returned through the spectrum into the visible red range and was going back to magenta. "Vacillating. I'd say," said Lee Moy. "What do you suppose we're looking at? Her aura?"

"Now there's a thought," said Johnny. "Wouldn't it be interesting if that's what the brotherhood has been holding off, all this time, being enclosed in her aura."

"If that's what it is," offered Lee Moy, "it's a very powerful aura."

The color of the barrier was now fading toward the blue range. "Still," said Johnny. "If it's aural energy, after all, we do know how to manipulate and change the energy in a person's aura, do we not? You'd better step back a little farther. The light is reaching toward the ultra-violet again. Last time it did that you saw what happened."

Lee Moy kept his distance. A moment after the blue faded to violet and disappeared, the whirlwind hit Johnny again. Light danced around him and lifted him slightly off his feet before dropping him. "Wow!" Johnny exclaimed. "That was a good one." He started laughing.

"It's nice that you're enjoying the ride," remarked Lee Moy, sarcastically. "Why are you laughing?" He stepped out of the shadows again to watch the changing light.

"Blue is her angry color," said Johnny. "It annoys her when I laugh at her anger because she can't hurt me." He continued chuckling. "Watch. I bet the light won't make it back to red. It will stop in the blue range and return to violet. Then she'll relent and it'll settle in the magenta range, her love color. She can't make up her mind whether she hates me or loves me." Johnny and Lee Moy waited to see if Johnny's prediction would come true.

Johnny was right. The color of the barrier stopped changing momentarily in the blue portion of the spectrum then began fading back to the invisible ultra-violet range. "If the last time was any kind of guide, I better hang on to something," laughed Johnny as he wrapped his arms around a nearby stump. Lee Moy ducked for cover as the next strike hit Johnny, tearing up vegetation in a radius of nearly 12 feet. The stump held, and Johnny remained, waiting with anticipation to see what would happen next.

The barrier did not reappear into the visible spectrum. Instead, a bolt of visible blue lightning flashed out of the clear night sky from the direction of the barrier and sparkled around Johnny, making his hair stand straight up. When the bolt had unloaded its power, Johnny stood up laughing again and said, "That was a good one. Watch this, Lee Moy."

Johnny stood straight up, raised his face toward the barrier, closing his eyes and released the energy he had accumulated from the lightning bolt, only the light he released was magenta, the love color. To Lee Moy's amazement, the barrier reappeared but in a color matching Johnny's aural energy. Not only did the shimmering wall begin emitting the magenta light; it was bright enough to illuminate the entire western end of the island.

"I think it really is her aura," Lee Moy said. "And you have changed its energy. Fascinating. Is she really that predictable? I wonder why we never noticed this before?"

"I don't know for sure," said Johnny, "But I think I'm getting to know her a little bit. She seems to like a man who will stand up to her rages. I don't think anyone else ever has, or maybe, been able to. She'll hit me with this lightning and all it does is charge me up. Remember after the session in the meditation room? I had sparks jumping off my fingers. It happened again this afternoon on the beach. It's like she tests me and when I pass the test, she gets all loving."

"Maybe you should marry her and settle her hash once and for all," said Cardac appearing out of the shadows followed by several others. "If all she needs is a little loving and she wants you, go for it, I say."

Johnny was a bit startled to see how many of the brothers had been watching his light show and listening to the conversation. *Why not,* he thought. *This is their battle too,* but he only said, "I've been married. Now I'm a real Monk."

Lucias was the next to emerge from the shadows. "Sometimes a man's highest calling is in union with his mate. Do you think she's watching you - can actually see you and is directing these attacks deliberately?"

"No," said Johnny thoughtfully. "I think she's in turmoil and that this is her aura we've been watching. It reaches out, just as does mine or yours when we're thinking about someone."

"Those meditating are reporting unusual turmoil," said Lucias.

"You may be right. This turmoil they're reporting, they say, seems unfocused."

"I'll go back tomorrow," said Johnny and see if I can defuse her."

⁂

The air was cooler the next morning, like a last moan of the winter's passage, but the sun was shining in promise. Johnny waited till after the noon meal before heading for Inanna's beach. The energy contained in the barrier the previous evening had seemed to calm down considerably. *Maybe she finally wore herself out and went to sleep,* he thought.

He glanced toward the barrier. It was still shimmering but the color had faded with the sun's light. It seemed to be steadier, now. The intermittent throbbing, he and the others watched the night before had settled. *If that energy we've been battling really is simply her aura trying to extend itself over the rest of the island, it answers some long-standing questions. Manipulating the energy of an aura isn't that hard, but then, Anna's is not the usual kind of aura. I changed the energy easily because she had just charged me up with her own energy, plus, she was tuned into me. I think others would have a harder time with it.*

Caleb confirmed this a few minutes later. He joined Johnny on the fourth terrace where he was staking up some cucumber vines as part of his morning contribution. "I just came off the meditation shift," he said, his long face seeming a little longer than usual. "The energy from the west stayed as you said it would, then faded toward morning. Just in the last hour or so, it has begun strengthening again. As usual, it receded while it calmed and now it's pushing at us. See?" he pointed. "It's nearing the eastern peak again. I thought you were going to go back there today."

Johnny glanced up again at the shimmering barrier he had watched the night before, now colorless in the morning sun. "I thought I'd go after the noon meal," he said. "When one only eats once per day, one doesn't want to miss meals, eh?"

"Well, you've got a point there," Caleb chuckled.

"Also, waiting stirs the heart. I'm getting quite a crush on Anna and I think she feels something for me, too. If that's so and if she's the evil of the western side of the island, stirring her passions by making her wait a bit, can't hurt. I hope I'm right in that."

"I think you may not want to make her too angry with you. It could be dangerous for you."

"True, it could be dangerous, but I think probably the only thing I have going for me is that I laugh at her anger, unless it's justified of course, then I apologize. It could be that she's just curious about me since it seems she keeps trying to hurt me when she gets angry and can't. She's sort of like a child who lashes out, not really wanting to injure, but hoping for better quality attention. I'm hoping to explore some of those ideas today."

CȜ ȣ

As Johnny approached the lava flow marking the beginning of Inanna's territory, he could feel his pulse picking up. This time it was not only in anticipation of seeing her again, but out of a certain sense of danger, he had not felt before. He noticed there were no tracks on the beach signaling the presence of birds and fiddler crabs. *Maybe it's because it's cooler today,* he thought to himself. *At least I hope that's why the wildlife is in hiding.* As this thought presented itself to him, he noticed with a shudder that no birds were singing. *This reminds me of the doves and squirrels back home, how they go into hiding when Ole Armageddon, the broad tailed hawk is nearby. Even the mourning doves take a dive when the hawk is hunting. Who's the hawk this time? Who is the squirrel?*

As Johnny walked toward the barrier, he remembered the first time he saw Ole Armageddon. The large hawk was standing along the side of the road as Johnny drove toward it. One wing was hanging down as though injured. Johnny stopped the car with the intention of seeing if he could assist the hawk, take it to a wildlife center where it could receive medical treatment. But as he stopped, the hawk lifted off, climbing heavily into the sky, apparently close to its maximum weight limit, with a full grown and frantically struggling gray squirrel in its talons. He gave a shiver at the thought, then climbed the lava flow. *Where is my lovely hawk today?* He thought.

His pulse peaked as his head popped above the rock obstruction. Then he sighed deeply with disappointment. *Tit for tat,* he chided himself sarcastically. *She's going to make me wait instead. I haven't played this game for a long time. I must be getting rusty.*

He jumped down from the lava flow and waded into the water up to his ankles, sandals in his hand. Tiny fish darted away from the shadow of the unknown he created in their habitat. He smiled, glad to see so many of them, then smiled again as a large school of finger length fish leaped from the water avoiding a predator. *I'm glad to see it's really fish jumping this time and not some pulse of energy from an angry, whatever she is.*

He continued wading slowly in a westerly direction, working his way farther into the area of danger than he had so far gone. His senses were tuned carefully to the surroundings, not knowing what to expect or when to expect it. *I still don't altogether believe the problem is Anna, he thought. The idea is too unlikely. She's a spectacular woman, but still, she's just a woman. Maybe there's some evil jinni or demon, controlling her and using her. That's more believable than thinking Anna herself is the cause of this disturbance. Maybe she's the slave of this jinni. Maybe that's why she was crying in my arms, the first time I met her. Don't want to think about that too much,* he cautioned himself, feeling his pulse suddenly quicken at the thought of her nakedness.

In the distance, he could see another obstruction of some sort on the beach. As he neared it he could see that it was the wreck of a large fishing boat, double booms lowered and rusting in the water, remains of the ragged net strung out behind. The hull had a large gaping hole across the length of the starboard side. The sea was gradually consuming it, piece by piece. *The process could take several years, unless there's a storm,* He thought. Across the stern of the boat, he could just see the words, "ERIKI." *I guess that's the boat's name,* thought Johnny, looking more closely to see if he could discover the boat's origin. Under "ERIKI," were the words, half buried in the sand, "Hanga Roa," and under that Isla De Pascua, Chile.

He approached the boat cautiously, concerned about its stability on the beach sand, that it not roll over on him if he got too close. He could see through the hole in the side, that the boat was nearly half filled with beach sand. It had been there long enough that there were actually barnacles on the inside of the hull. When he peeped through the opening, small fiddler crabs darted away to hide in shadows and in small holes in the sand. He could now see that part of the boat's stern had been crushed. As the gentle seas rolled in over the reef, the water rose and fell inside the boat's hull.

A narrow circular stairway rose from the sand filled hull to the deck level. Johnny approached it wondering just how adventuresome he wanted to be. He felt the stairway and shook it with his hand. It was steel and remained strong enough, in his opinion, to support his weight. The remaining question to be answered was if the deck supporting the stairway was equally strong. He cautiously placed his weight on the first step. The deck overhead creaked, startling him, but before he could step back onto the sand, something else startled him even more. It was a voice.

"Thinking of entering the salvage business, Profligate?" The tone was more playful now than threatening, as it was the first time she had called him that.

Johnny turned in surprise, saw her and smiled, "Anna. I was looking for you."

"Did you think you would find me in a shipwreck?"

"Not on a shipwreck, but on a beautiful island in the South Pacific, on a pristine beach with crystal blue water, on a cloudless day at the beginning of summer."

"I think I like your praises better than those of Enheduanna, though she probably sings better than you do," Inanna replied. She was standing on the beach outside the hull of the boat talking to him through the gash in the side. Johnny sloshed through the soggy sand in the boat's hull toward her. She stepped back as he crawled out through the boat's fatal wound.

Without another word, he took her hand and drew her to him in an embrace ending in a light kiss on the lips. The surprised look in her eyes quickly changed to one of enjoyment. She closed her eyes and said, "That was nice. Do it again."

He kissed her again, but she broke out of his embrace and ran down the beach, toward the west. Over her shoulder she called out "Come." In a few minutes he caught up to her and found they were at the foot of a path leading off into the forest, and up the side of the western slope. Absently he glanced toward the east, to see if the barrier was visible. It was not. He continued to follow her up the path. As they walked, he tried to still his mind to watch her aura. To his amazement, he could see no end to it. It extended beyond his vision, in magenta, vacillating toward the red end of the spectrum and back into magenta. He looked inwardly to see if he had acquired any of her energy in the embrace and was pleased to see that he had, somewhat.

At the top of the path, he stopped in awe to admire the sights around what she called her palace grounds. There was a sullen looking, whiskered man fishing off the end of a short pier with a large yacht anchored beyond. Several people were lounging in front of one section of the building complex to the right of what appeared to be a main section of the building. There was a large number of islanders, Polynesian by appearance, working in a wide cultivated area, a garden of sorts between the building complex and the water. What stunned him most was that upon their appearance the islanders kneeled in their direction and began chanting "Heena. Heena."

Anna ignored them, leading him hand in hand long the path through the gardens toward the main building. As they passed among the islanders, Johnny could hear an undertone of conversation among them, apparently in some language of the islands. One word he heard repeated more than any other sounded like "Mawkee," and it was always repeated in doubles as though they were talking of someone named "Mawkee-mawkee."

"What is this mawkee-mawkee I keep hearing?" he asked Inanna.

In response, she waved her hand at them and the chanting stopped. "They are very superstitious," she said. "They think I am Hina, their moon goddess. But I'm really the goddess of love," she smiled at him with mischief in her eyes. "And they think because they have not seen you before and because you are holding my hand that you are Make-make the chief of the island gods. They are hoping I have found a mate because they think this will make me happy."

"Would it make you happy, oh goddess of love?" he asked returning her look of playful mischief.

Anna lowered her eyes. Then she looked around the grounds, at the Polynesian workers and the people lounging in front of the building complex. Then her eyes searched the treetops, then the front of the building complex again before looking directly at him. "Yes," she said thoughtfully. "Maybe you are Makemake. Maybe it will even be you," she added, but Johnny could see in her eyes that something was troubling her. Her smile brightened, suddenly as with a new idea. "Let me introduce you to my friends."

As they approached the people who had been lounging in front of the building, they stood to greet Anna and her new friend. Johnny counted three couples who Anna introduced as Chip and Joyce, Jimmy and Rosemary, Big Al and Teri. Then she said, "I'm going to go and change for dinner. We can eat early this evening. DeMuzzi and I have plans for after dinner." Leaving Johnny with the group, she disappeared inside the main building through the ballroom.

Johnny tried to make small talk, but the group seemed very guarded in their responses to him. "Where are you folks all from?" Johnny began. "It seems strange to bump into six Americans, in a remote spot like this. I guess you're Americans, from your speech at least."

"We're all Americans," said Joyce, except for Al and Teri. They're from Texas."

"Well, America's part a Texas. Ain't it?" said Teri with a smile. That seemed to break the ice, in part. Everyone smiled at the joke. Rosemary went inside and brought a chair for Johnny.

"Have you folks noticed anything unusual over here?" he asked. They began exchanging looks fearfully, again beginning to distrust him. "I'm from the monastery at the other end of the island. You did know there is a monastery at the eastern end of the island, didn't you?"

"We have heard of it," ventured Chip, cautiously.

"We'd love to visit it, but we really can't leave here," added Joyce, the buried anger over Chip's injuries beginning to show itself in her eyes. Chip patted her back affectionately cautioning her.

"We don't know who or what he is," he said softly, concern evident on his face, but Johnny overheard.

"Have some tea," said Teri, trying to cover for Chip and salvage what might be a declining safety level.

"Jist who are you?" Big Al angrily directed the question at Johnny. "Y'all come up here hand in hand with that woman like boy fren' girl fren.' Are you another victim she somehow sucked in, or are you in with her, somehow? I'd like ta' know right now."

Johnny wasn't expecting a confrontation. His answer sounded defensive. "I'm a friend of Anna, like she says you are. She thinks of you as her friends. You should have heard how touched she was by your including her in the volleyball game the other day. I'm assuming, it was you she was playing volley ball with. Was it?"

"Yes," Smithson began. "Including her was like a survival skill."

"You can say that again," muttered Chip.

"Remember," Joyce addressed the group. "If you want a friend, you have to be a friend. And friends talk nicely about their friends, so just let's back off a little bit. I know we've all been through a lot here but if we want things to get better, it's up to us to make them better. Bad talking her isn't going to contribute to the goal."

"Joyce is right as rain," Teri interjected.

"But she can be very dangerous when angered," said Smithson.

"That's fer damn sure," stated Big Al. "We seen her kill a man a few days ago and she damned near killed ole Chip here, a couple of nights ago."

Kill? Thought Johnny incredulously. *Kill? Could Anna have done that?? Did she really try to kill me with that bolt of blue that she sets off? But when she does, she warms up to me again right away. There's something off kilter here.*

"All she had to say for herself was, 'he shouldn't have made me angry.'" Said Smithson.

"You know, doncha'" Teri said to Johnny. "She ain't gonna' let y'all go home. None a' us can leave here."

"I can leave," said Johnny, shaken by the message of these mariners, guests of Inanna. "Why do you think I can't?"

They all drew back in their chairs with looks of fear on their faces. "That's how Chip got hurt," Joyce offered.

"The monastery has been at the east end of the island for a long time. It's there because we've discovered, uh, problems in the area. We've been trying to discover what the problem comes from. Over the years, seven of our brothers have come here, to the west end of the island to find out. None of them ever returned."

"They're probly all dayed," said Teri, "like y'all will be if you try to go back."

"I can go any time I want," said Johnny. "When I do, I need to go back with information. First; is there anything else over here that might be causing the troubles? Do you really think it's Anna."

"We may as well tell him," said Chip. "He's going to find out sooner or later."

"I'm for it," said Big Al.

"Me too," Added Smithson with Rosemary affirming his statement.

"First of all," Teri began. "Her name ain't Anna. It's Inanna. That's where them islanders git the name Hina; sounds like the first part of her name."

Inanna, thought Johnny. *So that's what her real name is. I wonder why she wanted to conceal it from me. Maybe she's afraid it would reveal something to me about her. Inanna. I don't think I've ever heard that name before.*

"She's very powerful," said Chip. "She can suck the life right out of you from a hundred yards away."

"Farther than that, I believe," interjected Johnny, thinking of the pulsing light from the night before, the shimmering light striking out at him like bolts of blue lightning, the whirlwinds that threatened to lift him off his feet and dash him on the ground far below.

"An' she's stone crazy," added Big Al. "She thinks she's some kind of a god, but not any kind a Polynesian god."

"Is she an alien?" asked Joyce of the group. Then to Johnny she said, "We don't know what she is, but we don't think she's human."

"She ain't no alien," said Teri. I ain't seen no flyin' saucer around here no where."

"I don't think she's an alien," said Chip, "but anything could be possible. She says she's stuck here on the island like the rest of us, but I suspect she can leave if she really wants to."

The conversation was interrupted by some of the Polynesians waving to them to come to dinner. Johnny noticed the sun was nearing the horizon and considered declining dinner because of his regular routine of one meal per day. Then he decided to go with the flow and see what else he could learn.

Johnny was not expecting what he found in the ballroom. The raised dais was a surprise to him with the throne of Lapis Lazuli and the dining area below with the many tables where the islanders who worked in the gardens seated themselves for dinner. Chip and Joyce took him in tow and seated him with their group on the dais. Inanna made her usual grand entrance accompanied by the three singers and the young man with the stringed instrument.

The islanders sing to her as though they think she really is a god, thought Johnny trying to conceal his surprise. He turned his attention from the singers to look at Inanna who had seated herself on her blue throne. She was wearing a cotton sarong as usual, but this one was a print design with shades of blue flowers on a white background. In her hair was a blue orchid, matching the flowers in her clothing design. The Lapis Lazuli he recognized as being of the same stone as the obelisk given him by Belili. Then he saw Belili seated at the front of the ballroom in her alcove, looking at him with a smile. When he made eye contact, she raised her finger to her lips indicating to him to not mention their earlier meeting or that they were acquainted.

What is she doing here? He thought to himself. *How did she get here? If she's here, how did she get to the mainland to meet me at the airport?*

As the song ended, Johnny noticed a flaw in Inanna's blue throne. There was a deep nick from its thickness near the floor. The rest of the stone was polished to a high sheen. It literally gleamed in the low light of the large room, except for that flaw near the floor. Then it occurred to him that this nick in the perfectly smooth surface of the throne was about the same size as the amulet of Lapis Lazuli given to him by Belili. Before he could give this much consideration, Inanna joined them at the table set for eight.

How appropriate, he mused. *I am the number Eight, Hjet, the fence, come here to stand between the good and the evil. Now, all I have to do is find the good and the evil and figure out how to separate them one from the other, or better yet, how to stand between them. Anna isn't evil, but she apparently does evil things. None of the people here are either good or evil but they contain both, just as I do. To begin, I am told, I must first polarize the good and evil within myself. How do I do that? Where do I start?*

Chapter 13: Inanna's Rage

They'll be worried about me, thought Johnny. *It's past sunset and I haven't returned to the east.* Ignoring whatever dangers awaited him, he allowed Inanna to lead him from the ballroom toward her private quarters. The winding, torch lit corridors leading east toward the mountain were elaborately decorated, unlike those of the monastery which were mostly rough stone. Murals of all sorts adorned the plaster-covered walls. Some depicted pastoral love scenes. Others illustrated ancient battles with warriors clothed in body armor bearing primitive weapons; spears, pikes, halberds, axes, war hammers and swords. A reappearing female figure seemed to have a sort of secondary prominence in most of them. Johnny was trying to digest the images in his mind when Inanna turned into a large chamber overlooking the south side of the island through two large, arched windows.

I don't know whether to be fantastically aroused or fearful for my life, he mused. The décor of the room was sparse compared with the corridors where he had just passed. The walls were unadorned with one other entrance through a closed door to the left, with a large carving on it of a native scene involving parrots and date palms. Columns on both sides framed the door. The columns bore the images of large serpents coiled around them at the bottom. The room seemed to have a natural lighting whose source Johnny couldn't see. The room was furnished like a den or family room with several comfortable looking chairs a fireplace opposite the carved door and a love seat with stuffed cushions.

Inanna had stopped in front of one of the two windows with her back to him. *Now what?* The thought emerged uninvited. *Will I break my fast of many years? Am I going to make my rusty sex odometer turn one more notch? Or will there be some other way to subdue this wild tiger? Oh God! How I want her!* He mentally began standing beside himself, watching curiously. *Can I rise above this passion or can I subdue my passions and improve myself in this fire of temptation? If I refuse her, what will she do this close to the fact? If I take her what will it do to me? Physical love isn't wrong unless it's fraudulent or controlling or... Or what!? Do I love her? Yes. Is physical love wrong when it's a manifestation of a spiritual truth? No. Then why does the fraternity insist on celibacy?* "To learn to divorce the spirit from matter so that the ultimate ascension can take place." *What dribble that sounds like with such a beautiful woman who wants me, so close.*

He was beside her at the window, watching the stars. "Stop intellectualizing and kiss me," she said. "I can feel the turbulence of your thoughts. You want me as you have wanted no other. I can feel the power of your passion. It fills the whole palace."

Her eyes are so intense, Johnny continued trying to divert himself. *This is like a dream.* "As your passion reached to me even beyond the barrier, last night, Inanna."

She pushed him away and stepped back into the room. "They told you my name," she said with annoyance.

"Yes," said Johnny. "It's a beautiful name. Why didn't you tell me yourself?"

"Does it mean anything to you?" she answered. "Have you never heard the name before?" Her demeanor was gathering a touch of hostility. "They shouldn't have told you."

"I... I don't think so," said Johnny. "Should I have heard the name somewhere?"

"If you are DeMuzzi, come to rescue me..." She didn't finish, but instead stepped into his arms and kissed him with gathering passion, then tightened the embrace. Johnny's senses were again reeling. The feel of her warmth through the light, cotton wrap of her sarong and the pervading flower scent of her hair, filled his awareness, driving away his thoughts of polarizing intrinsic qualities, rising above his passions and any other spiritual teachings of his Order, leaving only one thought.

She pulled back and taking his hand said, "Come."

He followed dumbly, like a sheep on a tether as they approached the carved door and passed between the serpents. Beyond the door was a large bedchamber with a four poster bed in the center, like the stage in theater-in-the-round. Two more windows overlooked the sea, starlight illuminating the room. She led him toward the bed, then stopped just before reaching it and turned to him. "Please remove the stone that hangs around your neck, my love. It's such a hard lump between us. I want to feel only you when we embrace." She kissed him again, snuggling up tight, then pulled back again. "Can't you feel it? It's like a barrier between us."

Johnny reached up to his neck taking hold of the chain and pulled it up over his head. He tossed the stone of Lapis Lazuli and its chain on the bed and turned back for another embrace. To his astonishment, as soon has the amulet hit the bed, she leaped back and blasted him again with the bolt of blue lightning he had seen so many times before. He just had time for the shocked impression; *She's been faking! Damn!* when the bolt struck him.

It was different this time. It didn't deflect all around him as before. This time, to his utter amazement, it reflected directly back and hit her, as though he had been holding a mirror. She stepped back in stunned disbelief, herself, glowing blue from the effect of her own attack. Then she plopped into a chair beside the still open door. "Well," she said thoughtfully. "I don't think I'll do that again. That was very unpleasant."

Johnny sat down on the bed, picked up his amulet and put it back on. "So," he said to her in anger. "Tell me something, Inanna. Is anything about you true or are you always just a fraud - a cheap, phony imitation of a real person, a real woman - luring people to your prison with empty promises, blowing smoke in their eyes so they can't see the lie that you really are? Do you betray every friend? Are you nothing but some demonic imitation of joy. You think I'm protected by this piece of stone and the minute I take it off you try to kill me again. How can you ever expect to have any friends if you can't be trusted? You can rot. I'm leaving."

CB   EO

Two spectators existing on a spiritual plane just beyond Johnny's ability to sense them stood by the window of Inanna's bedchamber. They were both one step beyond speechless for a moment, breathless, if that could be said of incorporeal beings. Then Chaim said to Matziel, "I hope he doesn't take it off again. I don't think we could protect him a second time."

"We would need some help, I think," said Matziel, obviously depleted from the effort.

"Maybe we should have reflected it out through the window," said Chaim. "We could have hurt her."

"'Is that a bad thing?' is my first reaction to your statement," said

Matziel. "In all things we must remember that we are bound to cause no harm to anyone. So, you are correct. If it happens again, we will try to deflect her bolts elsewhere. Though, she does seem to have taken it well enough. Maybe the result will be her reluctance to try harming him again."

"I don't think her desire was to harm him, exactly," said Chaim. "I can feel her passion for him. I think, rather, she was testing him, wanting him to be the real DeMuzzi but knowing that he is not."

Let's bide our time as this scene unfolds," said Matziel. "He may need our help again."

"I wish he had been more gentle with his anger. It was better when he laughed and returned love for her rage. Now, I'm afraid, there may be a rift."

ଔ ଓ

Inanna was on her feet, fury leaping from her eyes, sputtering in her heated attempts to speak, but so filled with rage that she could only gasp. To Johnny's dismay she seemed to explode into a twelve-foot tall image of herself, bursting with blue light fading at the edges to the ul-tra-violet he couldn't see. But he could see the results of the violet fire singeing the ceiling and walls where it touched.

"Don't think you can intimidate me with your pitiful light shows," Johnny muttered loud enough for her to hear. "Go frighten your Poly-nesians." He rose and headed for the door. As he did so, a bolt of blue lightning leapt from Inanna's hands, large enough in circumference to completely engulf him. He could feel his hair standing on end with the electricity in the charge. His skin tingled and his feet slightly left the floor. Then the bolt ended.

"You'll stop feeling like a fool, " he said viciously, "when you quit act-ing like one." He walked out the door, pulling it shut with a resounding slam and headed quickly for the exit to the antechamber. The sounds of rage were clearly audible from the corridor. Johnny turned to the left and nearly bumped into Belili who was hurrying toward him.

"Come with me," she told him. "The other way. She's angry enough that you may not be able to hold her off." The sound of the heavy wood-en door shattering drowned out what Belili was saying. She grabbed his arm and with strength unexpected in a woman of such apparent age dragged him along the corridor. As they hurried through the pas-sageways, she said to him, "It is well that you did not tell her it was I, who gave you the amulet. It would have been dangerous for both of us."

"Is it really the amulet that protects me from her?" Johnny asked.

"Yes," she said, "But even this magic has limitations. As angry as she is I am surprised that it was enough."

"Did you see that last bolt she hit me with? She became twelve feet tall and blasted me with a bolt big enough to swallow a full grown cow."

Belili looked at him in surprise and responded, "Maybe you really are descended from DeMuzzi. Only a real god, one of us, could have withstood such an attack."

"I'm not a god," said Johnny sarcastically.

"Then the Great God must be your protector. None other has such power."

Belili led him uphill instead of down, through another series of corridors and finally through an exit to the building. "That path will lead you to the beach. I think you can find your way back from there. You had better hurry," she added with a frightening, hushed urgency. Then she vanished back into the building.

Johnny was left standing in the darkness, but to his surprise, he was glowing as in his previous experiences with Inanna's passion. His hair still contained some of the charge from the blue lightning. His fingertips were sparking. The path in every direction he looked glowed enough that he could see his way as well as if he had a lantern with him. His adrenaline was dropping enough now that he began at last to be frightened. *Gees. What was that? I know I've got a wicked tongue in my head, but I never made a woman that mad before. I thought for a minute that she actually exploded. Well, I guess she did but she stopped exploding when she got to twelve feet tall. I wondered why the ceilings were so high in those rooms. Now I know.* His feet were carrying him quickly along the path toward the sea, as he reviewed the experience.

Glancing over his shoulder toward the palace, he could see flashes of blue light washing down over the landscape, from the windows. He did not pause to watch, but continued down the path as quickly as he could.

When he reached the beach, he nearly collided with Jorge, the man who he had seen on the pier fishing that afternoon. Jorge leaped back in terror then made as if to attack him. Johnny jumped aside as Jorge dived for him, landing in the sand on his stomach. He again leaped to his feet to renew his attack when Johnny managed to say, "Hold on, man. I'm not your enemy. I'm not your enemy." Then as understanding took hold he said, "Are you trying to escape her?"

"Si, si," Jorge grunted. "They say there's a monasterio in the east. I must get there."

"That's where I'm going," said Johnny. "Come on. I'll show you the way." The two hurried off into the night, east bound across the sand. Johnny could still see flashes of blue light behind him. That they seemed to be drawing closer added a chill to his skin and urgency to his footsteps.

"She keel my cousin, the son of my father's brother," said Jorge. "Alphonso. She blast heem with el relampago azul [blue lightning]. I saw thees. She was far away from heem. We must hurry. She will keel us too."

The moon had not yet risen but the starlight was enough combined with Johnny's mysterious glowing for them to see their way. The blue flashes from behind had seemed to stop overtaking them, remaining in one location, but close enough, on the beach to be cause for serious concern. Johnny didn't pause to try to figure out where she was. He and Jorge kept up a rapid jogging eastward. When the hulking image of the shipwreck appeared, Jorge stopped in his tracks muttering in fear.

"That's ERIKI," said Johnny. It's a fishing boat out of Easter Island."

"It is the boat of el abuelo mio, my grandfather," said Jorge. "He go to feesh more than a year ago. He not come back. Now I know how he die." This realization seemed to anger Jorge rather than discourage him. He quickened his pace so much that Johnny began having a hard time keeping up.

CB   BD

After dinner, Chip, Joyce and the gang retired to the patio where they had been seated earlier. They wanted to discuss Inanna's unusual behavior. "What do y'all think she meant by 'plans fer later," Teri asked the group in general with a sly smile.

"I think we all know exactly what she meant," responded Rosemary with an equally knowing smile. "She had that glint of lust in her eyes. I wonder if DeMuzzi, who ever he is, will survive the experience."

"Ah donno," said Big Al with a chuckle. "That fella' bein' a monk an' all. She might be in fer a big disappointment."

"He looked pretty intent on the object of the chase," said Chip. "I don't think she's going to be disappointed."

"Well, what ever happens," said Big Al. "I think that fella' might jist cool her jets for a little bit. If he can make 'er happy, maybe we won't have ta' play no more water volleyball fer a while."

"That'd be fine with me," sighed Teri with one eyebrow raised.

"Me too," said Smithson. "I never was much into sports. Too strenuous."

"A bit of a strained gathering it was, too," added Joyce, "With death staring us in the face if we make one wrong move."

As they talked, the light show began in Inanna's quarters. They could see the flashes of blue light playing out over the landscape. The conversation paused. Then Chip ventured, "It looks like the sparks are getting bigger than any of us hoped for."

"Boy, you can say that agin,'" from Big Al. "Looks like things 'er gittin' outa' hand. Maybe it's time fer' us ta' make ourselves scarce."

"Do you mean hide in bed, or flee?" asked Joyce with a wry smile.

"I think this may be a good time to head for the hills," said Teri.

"Or maybe the beach," said Chip. "Let's go." Chip took the lead because he knew the way to the beach on the south side of the island. "The north side has those cliffs blocking the way. We can't walk the beach all the way to the other end of the island that way."

"How do you know we can walk the beach all the way on the south side of the island?" asked Smithson.

"I don't," said Chip, "but I do know we can't do it on the north side."

"What if she catches us?" asked Teri. "She'll fry our butts."

"If we're near the water we can dive in and say we wanted to go for a night swim and ask her to join us," offered Joyce. "She seems to be a real sucker for being included in the party."

"Ah donno," said Big Al. "Them flashes is gittin' bigger all the time. Looks like she's havin' herself a real tantrum. I feel sorry fer' that De-Muzzi fella.' He musta' said 'no,' after all."

"Or he was a quick draw McGraw," quipped Teri with a snort. "That always makes me mad too." She slapped Big Al on the arm as she guffawed at her own joke

As they hurried down the path toward the southern beach, the flashing lights seemed to be coming closer. They had barely made it to the sandy beach when Inanna's huge image could be seen storming down the path behind them. "We best dive in right now," whispered Teri to the rest. Six splashes followed just before Inanna arrived on the scene.

"Why hello honey," gushed Teri. "Are we ever glad ta' see y'all. Joyce here was jist sayin' 'too bad Anna ain't with us fer' a nice nighttime skinny dip. She had sa' much fun with us last time, it jist don't seem right goin' swimmin' without 'er."

Inanna stopped in her tracks, still seething with rage. This pause gave Teri the opening she needed. "Oh Darlin.' You look upset. Come on in. The water feels real good. It'll help y'all calm down a little bit. Gittin' upset over a man like that ain't no good fer' nobody."

"Hey Anna," called Smithson. "Come on in the water's great. Look at how it's reflecting the light of the stars. There never was a better night for it."

"Look," called Joyce. "We were all here hoping you'd come along. Maybe we could even get up a game of night water tag."

Inanna gazed down the beach after Johnny, the distraction working its own kind of magic. Her size began to shrink back to normal and her towering rage to dissipate. In one last fit of anger, she cast a single bolt down the beach toward the lava flow. It missed Jorge by a yard and Johnny by inches. It struck the lava flow, now in front of the fleeing twosome and blasted a whole right through it, but not big enough a hole for the two to walk through. They still had to climb over the rock.

Inanna dropped her sarong as before and walked into the water, which sizzled around her at first, slowly cooling her flaming rage. The others stepped aside to give her plenty of room. She walked until she was up to her waist then dropped to her neck and swam toward the deeper water without saying a word. They watched as she continued swimming until she reached the reef, then turned and swam back. When she reached them, she was crying. She allowed them to gather around her as she tried to rinse the tears from her eyes with the salt water.

"Ah honey," said Teri. "It'll be all right. There ain't no point in gittin' all worked up over him. He's jist a man. Where there's one that hurts ya' there's twenty more that won't."

"He said awful things to me," said Inanna, beginning to glow again, visibly clinging to her anger, reliving the insults in her mind. "I hate him," she said casting a longing glance toward the east.

"Ah you don't mean that," drawled Teri. "That boy's flat in love with you. We could see it in his eyes. When he looked at you he almost glowed as much as you did when you looked at him. This is jist an ole lovers' spat. He'll be back."

"Lovers' spat?" Inanna looked quizzically at Teri.

"Why you know," said Teri. "People that's in love sometimes fight a little bit, while they're tryin' ta' make up. It all blows over in a day 'er two. You'll see."

The rest of the group stood back watching in awe as Teri skillfully worked her way into playing the doting duenna for the angry woman. Chip was relieved to see her furiously glowing blue, fade as she cried her angry tears into the sea. "He said I was a phony and a liar," said Inanna. "He accused me of being a false friend, to him and to you."

"You ain't no false friend," cooed Teri. "Yer' as good a buddy ta' us as we ever had. Ain't that so, Al?"

Al, taken a back that he was being called upon to participate in this charade took a second to pull himself together enough to say, "Uh, yeah. That's right." He sounded sincere, even to Chip who knew they had been trying to escape while Inanna was distracted with her lovers' quarrel.

"I bet you got some good licks in too didn't cha' honey? What did you do that made him sa' damned mad as ta' say things he didn't mean, like that?" from Teri.

"I believed he had a shield that protected him from my power," said Inanna. "I fooled him into lowering his shield then I tried to take him, again. It never made him angry in the past. He always laughed at me and returned it with love energy. This time it made him angry. Then I became angry and he left me." She began crying again. "He said I was a fool."

She got him to drop his protections and when he did, she tried to take his life, thought Chip. *That'd be enough to make the best of us angry. Looks like DeMuzzi is finally realizing that what we told him is true. How did he survive it? Some kind of shield, she said. What shield could we use against her?*

"Don't y'all fret none, now," said Teri. "He'll be back when he figures y'all might have calmed down a little bit. You'll see. Don't y'all think so Joyce? How 'bout y'all Rosemary."

Chapter 14: The Goddess of Love and WAR

Although it was dark when they arrived back at the monastery, the moon was rising, casting more light over the setting. Johnny was gratified by the surprise of Jorge when he first set eyes on the complexity and size of the antique project. The sight of the buildings' silhouette against the blue shimmering barrier stopped him in his tracks.

"¡Por Diós!"[For God's sake!] he muttered. "¿Que esta, el monasterio?" [What is that, the monastery?] He looked at Johnny for an answer.

"Yes. With Inanna beyond," answered Johnny simply, correctly assuming the translation. "Come on. Let's hope someone of the brothers knows enough Spanish that you don't have to struggle to answer all the questions I know they're going to be asking."

They continued up the path beside the cultivated terraces, Jorge observing each level carefully, apparently looking for any sign of danger. "Mis Englesa is okay," he responded. "I can answer in la Englesa if it can help."

Johnny watched the barrier with an undercurrent of fear as they climbed the path. *Why was I so mean to her?* He asked himself. *Well, I guess when I was looking for a kiss and got a slap instead, it sort of set me off. Still, when she did that in the past, I laughed at her and was kind. This time I went off like a terrorist's bomb, unexpected and murderous. I think I need to go and apologize. I hope she'll forgive me. If this means the end of our relationship, I'll never forgive myself. Then there's this fence business. If my task is to somehow polarize the situation here, I've really blown it if I screwed up the lines of communication. But it looks like the situation is already polarized. She's over there and we're over here. Okay that's a rationalization. I know it, but....*

Jorge interrupted his thoughts with, "People are there in the shadows."

"Don't worry," said Johnny. "You're in no danger here."

"When she finds out I'm gone," Jorge said, "Will she come here to get me? I put everyone in danger; in this whole place."

"This place has always been in danger from her," Johnny answered. "No where on this island is really safe, but over here we're pretty much out of her reach."

As if to put the lie to Johnny's statement, the barrier faded to the ultra-violet, beyond the visible range and a whirlwind just about knocked him off his feet. Jorge was close enough that the blast left him seated on the ground in shocked terror. "Don't worry, Jorge. That was meant for me. While she's at it, though it'd be best if you keep at least ten feet away from me or you might get hurt."

The two hurried to the top of the terrace and into the shadows under the patio cover, with Jorge carefully keeping his distance. Half a dozen of the brothers were sitting there talking of the day's events. When they saw Johnny and Jorge approaching, someone was sent to fetch Lucias, Lee Moy and Cardac. When Johnny and Jorge arrived in the shelter of the patio, the three had joined the group.

"We thought you were dead," said Lucias, a worried look on his face, "or trapped over there. "And who is this?" he added, welcoming Jorge with a smile and an offered handshake.

After the introductions, Lucias volunteered, "Her energy has been chaotic today, especially this evening. We thought for a while we had a full fledged battle on our hands."

"Her name is Inanna," said Johnny. "Does that mean anything to anybody?"

There was some mumbling conversation among the brothers, but the consensus was that no one had heard the name before, except for Lee Moy who rose from the rear of the group and said, "Heena-nna is another way to say it. The daughter of Nanna and Ningal, the moon gods of Sumer, Shin'ar in the Bible. Ancient religions used to be a hobby of mine. She was the goddess of love and war, in that tradition. Quite a confusion of issues, in my opinion." He sat down again with a smile. "This belief, I might add, existed roughly six thousand years ago, hardly an application to our situation."

"Heena," muttered Jorge, his eyes wide in terror. "She is el demonio [a demon]."

"She's no demon," answered Johnny. "She's a confused female and I still think she's human, in spite of what they say."

"They?" Lucias picked up on the word. "How many people did you see over there?"

"How many would you say, Jorge? Maybe a hundred or more? I met six Americans who told me the Rapanui Storm captured them in two separate boats. The rest appear to be native peoples, and by the way, they do call her Heena. I'm told the name belongs to the Polynesian moon goddess."

"Excuse me one more time," said Lee Moy. "It has been a long time since I studied these matters and it comes back to me slowly, but here is another interesting coincidence. The name of Inanna's husband's was DuMuzzi. Isn't that interesting? He was also known as Tammuz, a sort of pet name between lovers. He's even mentioned in the scripture in Ezekiel, as I recall."

(Then he brought me to the north entrance to the House of the Lord; and behold there sat women weeping for Tammuz.)

"In the old religion of Sumer, he died every year and was resurrected for six months for the growing season then he had to return to the underworld. He annually gave his life so that Inanna could live. They referred to him as the sacrificial lamb - and as the "lamb of god" in the traditions of that predecessor religion that came long before Judaism or Christianity. The Christian and Jewish traditions have numerous parallel stories in those ancient times. Presumably, the women weeping in the Ezekiel verses were adherents to this older religion and the time indicated was fall, when Tammuz had to return to the underworld. And now, on the Island of Arrata, coincidentally, it is spring, when Tammuz or DuMuzzi traditionally returns from the dead.

"If this entity we fight is indeed the real Inanna, it makes me wonder if the real DuMuzzi is going to make an appearance, this spring. It also explains to me why she so readily welcomes our DeMuzzi. He may be in even greater danger than we suspected."

"That's ancient mythology, isn't it?" said Cardac. "It certainly has nothing to do with us."

"Heena," Jorge continued to mutter, anger edging out the fear in his eyes.

"It's fun to speculate about it," said Lucias, "but mythologies that old are probably as pertinent to our situation as the Polynesian belief that the world rides on the back of a turtle."

"Next we'll be looking for the god Hermes to appear with a message from Zeus," chuckled one of the brothers, "and Hercules to arrive to save the day."

More chuckling arose in the background. *She couldn't be that old,*

Johnny half mumbled to himself, considering the possibilities introduced by Lee Moy. Then he dismissed the thought.

Tarek who had been silent, listening to the conversation now said,
"In Israel today, there are still vestiges of the worship of some of the
ancient gods. It's believed that these ancient mythologies had some
grounding, some beginning in truth. Maybe at one time, there really
were some powerful leaders by these names. Maybe DuMuzzi had a
summer home down south, somewhere he went every winter and his
wife objected to going which resulted in an annual argument. Many
of the ancient monarchs forced their subjects to worship them as gods.
These things come down to us today as mythology in which these ancient monarchs really were thought to be gods. But I can't believe that
Inanna of our island is the Inanna of the myths. Can anybody?"

"Well, it makes no sense at all to believe that she is," said Lucias, so
let's move on, shall we?"

"What are the alternatives?" asked Lee Moy. "I don't think it's reasonable to believe she's the original Inanna either, but what do we know
about her? She's very adept with the use of her aura. She apparently
uses it as a weapon. She has a large group of followers whether they're
willing followers or unwilling seems to vary. Are they willing?" he
asked Jorge and DeMuzzi.

"The Polynesians who call her Heena seem to worship her willingly
enough," said Johnny. "And before dinner was that song of praise that
she seemed to drink in almost as though it was nourishment."

"She can drink life," said Jorge. "When Chip followed her she almost drink him completely but Leelee stop her."

Lucias asked, "It sounds like you seem to think that she draws some
kind of nourishment or energy from the worship and when the worship
isn't offered freely, as with the Polynesians, she has the ability to take it
by force. Is that your understanding of the matter, DeMuzzi?"

"I haven't seen her do this," said Johnny. "Maybe that's what she's
trying to do when she hits me with that blue lightning bolt of hers. But
when she hits me with it I just sort of soak it up like now." He raised
his index finger and emitted one blue spark. "I'm still all charged up,
as you can see."

Jorge jumped back from Johnny when he saw the spark, the fear
back in his eyes. "You are like her," he said angrily. "What are you?"

The others drew back as well, but more out of awe than fear. "She
told me the other day, " began Johnny, "that she had some new friends,
that they played water volleyball together and that when they accepted
her as a friend there was an equal give and take of energy. She was
happy about that and she said that's how it was supposed to be but she

had never before been able to manage it."

"Well she's not a god," said Lucias. "The alternative is that she's a mutation of some kind or a person who has somehow evolved slightly beyond where we are. We use the energy of the aura in much the same ways in healing, helping the plants to grow, even to communicate sometimes. But our aural energy doesn't have the power hers has. Even if we work together in teams we can't approach her strength."

"If she's so powerful," said Cardac, "Why doesn't she just come over here and take control? Is it just too much bother for her or too much of a strain on her energy? Why do you think, DeMuzzi?"

"We know she's powerful," said Johnny. "We know her power fluctuates. It appears to be weakest in the morning before dawn, but then it seems to pick up strength again, as though she's just getting awake."

"It's when the native islanders begin to chant," interjected Jorge. "At dawn, she comes out and stands in front of the building while those people who work in the gardens sing to her and chant Heena Heena."

"So," said Lucias. "She soaks up her energy from them, like having breakfast?"

"Si," said Jorge. "That is how it is."

"There," said Lee Moy. "There's proof that she uses the energy she receives from her worshipers. Maybe when she deliberately drains someone, she gets a rush of euphoria or something like that."

"It still doesn't prove that she's one of those creatures they used to call gods," said Lucias. "What does the Torah call them? Oh yes, 'Nefilim,' giants. Literally 'those from above.'"

"The practice of using the aural energy of others is not new to us," said Tarek. "This is how healing is done with the laying on of hands in certain ways. That she soaks up the energy of others doesn't make her any different than us."

"I have to admit she's different, though," said Johnny. "We can't do it to the extent she does it and we can't take the energy of another's aura without their participation and willingness."

"Well it looks like we're back where we started," said Lucias. "She's not a god and she's somehow more than a human. What is she?"

She's a woman, thought Johnny. *She's a woman who I have made terribly angry with me.* "Let's assume that she's a woman with extraordinary capabilities, for the sake of argument and start trying to understand her. It's clear that we can't overpower her, but with understanding we might be able to accomplish our goal here, which is what? As I understand it, the goal is to try to get her to stop hurting people, not just here but on neighboring islands, assuming she's the cause of the troubles on Easter Island as I've been told about it. Am I right?"

There was a murmuring of assent. "I don't see how that's going to help at all," said Cardac "I've never been able to understand women."

"A complication with the idea that she's only a woman is that she thinks she's a god and that no matter what she does, the fact that she does a thing makes it right because she's a god. She seems to have no sense of accountability," said Johnny.

"What leads you to think that?" asked Lee Moy.

"Well, every time we've been together, she snuggles up to me then steps back and hits me with this blue lightning bolt. That's what happened last night. She's never managed to hurt me with it but the others say that's how she kills, so I have to assume that she has tried to kill me every time I've gone to see her. I don't think she knows herself whether she wants me for a friend or for lunch."

"Sounds like a typical woman to me," chuckled Cardac.

ಐ   ಐ

Although Lucias and some of the others thought it unwise, Johnny resumed his duties that evening among those meditating against the pressures from Inanna. Concerned about not making direct contact with her again in meditation as he did the last time, he focused primarily in the same manner as the others, simply spreading peace around himself and the others. In his meditative state, he could feel the aura pressing on them from the west. He could sense its changing moods almost as well as he could see them reflected in the changing colors of the shimmering barriers. More than two hours had passed since he started when he began to feel a change in the energy. It was subtle at first but it began building. It felt to him almost as though it were trying to seek him out, trying to find him among those meditating. Then it succeeded!

For a moment, only, he could see Inanna's face looking at him mentally, seeking contact. He avoided it, focusing away from her, but then she had him. He could feel her touching him, his face, his hands. He could feel her trying to reassure him somehow. It felt to him then as though she was taking him by the hand and was leading him somewhere. Then the visions began.

They were flying at high altitude over a cultivated plain. Some areas were laid out in groves while others had fields of green crops in arrow straight rows for what seemed like miles. There were two large rivers on either side of the area, many miles apart, emptying into the same sea. Descending, he could see dark headed people working in the gardens, much like Inanna's Polynesian gardeners did in her grounds, but there were many more in a much larger area.

Ascending again, he could see cities and villages all surrounded by farmland. People were moving from these cities as their numbers increased. They spread in all directions from the original plain. *What am I seeing?* He allowed the thought to surface. *It seems that I'm watching entire populations rising, falling off, rising again, moving to new lands. A large temple appears here and then vanishes, while another even larger one appears nearby or in the same place. I see large sailing ships arriving and leaving, up and down the rivers, across the seas. There is mining farming, technology, space travel, and disease.* Then the vision suddenly changed.

Now there is only one large river, different than the other two. It runs from mountains in the south into a sea in the north. Oh yes, there are the first two rivers over here on the right and that other sea. Then this one must be the Nile and the sea the Mediterranean? Wait! Those buildings are bigger than any others that I've seen so far. Then he allowed his thoughts to quiet while he watched in awed reverence, pyramids rising out of the north African deserts, pyramids which are now unknown, their foundations yet to be discovered. He watched the construction of the sphinx, its body carved from native rock, then re-carved, then carved over, yet again. He watched as the climates changed, the rains washing erosion lines in the rock, then the return of the desert in the never ending cycle of the Earth's changes. He watched the ice slip from the poles causing horrendous flooding of the sea, the collapse of the land bridge creating the Black Sea, the slip of continents, the births of volcanoes, the uplifting of mountains and the sinking of others. The Earth became an undulating living entity gathering life and then killing it off with new cataclysms, spawning a species of animal then feeding that species to another in a never ending, shifting cycle of life and death. Then the vision changed again.

Johnny found himself on a large plain with thousands of others, trampling crops, slipping on furrows. They were mostly men clothed in widely varying ways with primitive garments of cotton, wool or leather. Many were brandishing bronze colored swords, spears or other implements he didn't recognize. Not far away he could see another large group of men similarly armed charging toward them. There was shouting, cursing. The smell of unwashed bodies nearly overwhelmed him. Then the groups clashed and the smell of blood added to the medley of insults to his senses. He could hear shrieks of pain above the sound of the clashing instruments of death. The group he was part of charged on, gaining ground. The sight of someone's arm lying at his feet, sickened him. He had nearly overcome the nausea when the body it belonged to appeared next. Then he saw a disembodied head on the ground to his left. It was missing one ear. A large gash separated the flesh of one cheek and the gaping sightless eyes were sunk into its gray, dead flesh.

Johnny tried to rise out of the nightmarish meditation but was held there, by what he didn't know. The melee continued growing in sound and momentum. Suddenly he heard someone shout in an unknown tongue but somehow, he knew the meaning. "Look out! Here she comes!"

Men began turning to flee as a slow moving aircraft approached, guns blazing, bombs falling out of its belly. Then as fast as he saw it he realized that this was unlike any other aircraft he had ever seen and they weren't guns that were blazing, but bolts of blue light, lightning, like Inanna's bolts of blue. He stopped fleeing with the others so he could see better what this strange craft was and who was at the helm. He could barely see through the protective shielding. Glass? Plastic? It was the face of a woman. She was wearing a helmet, like those he had seen of the forces attacking his forces. The craft descended and landed. The main hatch opened and the woman stood inside it. She was wearing bronze armor bearing strange markings he did not recognize. Just as he realized that the woman was Inanna, she fired one of her lightning bolts at him. It was large and intense in color, blue, striking him with such force that it knocked him off of his feet. To his surprise, he got back onto his feet and sent another bolt of his own, back at her, one just like she had used to strike at him. And the vision changed again.

He was on his back on a cold stone floor, torch lit walls rising all around him with men standing around looking at him in concern and wonder, while others were seated nearby seemingly asleep. Then he realized he was in the meditation chamber with his brothers on the Island of Arrata. "It happened again. Didn't it?" His question sounded more like a statement. "How long this time?"

Chapter 15: Another Rapanui Storm

"Inanna's demeanor seems different today, somehow," said Joyce, "More sullen. More withdrawn. More dangerous. And what's she doing with the islanders?"

The coming of summer was more apparent this morning. The air was much warmer and there was no dew on the shrubs and plants. Joyce and Chip had walked to the pier to watch the fish jumping in the small bay. The sun had just crested the horizon. They watched as the shadow of the two peaks gradually diminished over the water.

Inanna had emerged from the ballroom doors just after they reached the pier and began gathering the people she used in her gardens. Some had gone into the forest and were now returning carrying poles and vines they distributed among their number.

"What are they making, Anyway?" said Joyce softly to Chip.

Inanna moved among them speaking to one here and one there, then to the group as a whole in a language neither Joyce nor Chip understood. As she did this, they would chant among themselves with the one word Chip and Joyce had come to recognize being prominent. It was "Heena. Heena."

"Are they making what I think they're making?" Chip asked as the first man to finish is project raised a spear on a long pole. The head was a piece of steel that looked like the remains of a whaler's harpoon. Then another finished and raised his so others could see it. This one had a heavier pole with a smaller head carved from a large mollusk's shell.

"It looks like she's beating her plow shares into swords," said Joyce.

"And spears," added Chip.

The first man to wave his handiwork in the air for the others to see was now busy again, seated on the ground, chipping away at another sea shell, while still others were finishing spears and other weapons. Apparently satisfied that all was going as she wanted, Inanna began encouraging the large gathering to carry on with the chanting adding some ritual songs to their work. The sound of many voices crying "Heena Heena," brought Al and Teri out of their cottage, followed closely by James Smithson and his wife.

"What's that new sound I hear?" asked Joyce. "It sounds like a flute. Do you hear a flute?"

The sound grew louder. Soon they saw a young man emerge from the forest playing a flute carved from one piece of Lapis Lazuli. He wore a cloth around his waist and his feet were bare. One piece of cloth was slung over his shoulder, like a cotton suspender holding up his lower garment. His bronze skin glistened in the early morning light. His jet-black hair hung straight to his shoulders and his well-muscled torso seemed focused completely on playing the hymn of adoration to the goddess.

Ceremoniously he began walking among Inanna's army of gardeners devotedly playing the ritual tune that was usually sung to Inanna at dinner. The voices were raised in her praise and she stood on the porch in front of the ballroom, soaking it up like a serpent basking in the sun.

Al, Teri and the Smithsons began to walk toward the pier to join Joyce and Chip, but suddenly they stopped, turned toward Inanna and kneeled, joining in the chanting and singing. The young man circled them three times with his blue flute. Inanna watched in stony silence. Then she turned to face Chip and Joyce, still watching from the pier. They could hear her voice ringing inside their heads, like the echo of some old memory growing more and more demanding.

"I am Inanna," it said. "I am the goddess of the Earth and the Sky, of love and of war. It is I, who causes the sun to retreat into the darkness of the night and the moon, my father and mother, to arise in its stead. It is I, who brings fruit to the trees and the lush vegetables to sprout from the ground. It is I, who calls the fish into the fisherman's net and I who allows the sweet sound of music to reach your ears. I am Inanna. You will fall down and worship me."

Chip rebelled and he could see that Joyce also heard Inanna speaking to them and that she too was rebelling. "There's only one God, Inanna, and it's not you," Chip stated simply. Then he felt his knees buckle and hit the boards on the pier. Joyce lasted a moment longer, but shortly she too was on her knees beside him.

"Do you think God will get mad at us for this?" Joyce whispered to him.

Inanna's fury seemed to be aimed at them now. Although she was still standing on the porch to the ballroom, Chip could feel her breath on his face and hear her commanding voice in his ears. Still in defiance, he replied, "God must already be mad at us or we wouldn't be here. Besides, I have no more control over my knees right now. She's made me do this against my will. If someone steals your knees and misuses them, how can you be blamed?" Still struggling with all he had against Inanna's control, Chip began to recite, "Our Father who art in Heaven, hallowed be thy name..." tears streaming down his cheeks.

Chip heard Joyce joining him in the prayer then found himself suddenly silenced. Joyce's voice came first singing the hymn of praise to Inanna, then very much against his will, his lips began to move. His throat restricted causing his voice to sound, pushing the unwelcome words of praise through his mouth. "Queen of all powers, revealed light..."

Through his forced singing, Chip could hear Inanna speaking to him. "I have tired of the enemy on my eastern shore. I have tired of his presence. I have tired of the battle he wages against my will. I have tired of his disturbance of my sleep and my peace. I first hated him. Then I loved him. He is a mortal man among mortal men. All of them are my enemy. He has rejected my love. He has refused to worship me. This is not acceptable. I am the goddess of war. I shall now wage war."

"We have to warn them," Chip managed to squeeze out the words between lines of the song."

"You will warn no one," Inanna's voice rang loudly in his ears. "Instead you will join my people. You will make weapons. With me and the others, you will come to the eastern side of the island and with me you will kill my enemies."

Chip suddenly found himself on his feet again, walking toward the group making spears and knives out of seashells. Joyce followed woodenly behind him. And so went the day. Chip and Joyce by sunset had made several spears and knives each constantly interrupted by new demands for singing and praise. The Smithsons and the Johns had also been recruited to the garden area and had done the same. Between working in the hot sun all day and Inanna's constantly feeding on their emotional and mental energy, by the end of the day Chip felt drained, weak and exhausted.

The group found that they no longer shared Inanna's favored spot on the dais but were seated among the islanders with whom they had spent the day at labor and in praise of Inanna. Inanna made her usual grand entrance accompanied tonight by the young man with the flute of Lapis Lazuli. She was at full stature, nearly twelve feet in height and glowing with the light they had seen around her before, brilliant blue, like that of the stone chair of Lapis Lazuli which she liked to call her 'throne.'

"I feel like I could sleep fer' a week," drawled Big Al in hushed tones. All of them felt cautioned by the change in Inanna's demeanor and appearance. The conversation took the form of whispers and asides. "It looks like all that singin' an' stuff we did today made her swell all up - not jist her head," Al added.

"I think we're all tired," answered Rosemary. "Best not to notice."

"I wonder how long her war will last," said Smithson.

"Depends on how well armed they are at this here monastery," answered Chip. "We don't know what they have over there. It could be a military installation for all we know and if that's true, Inanna doesn't stand a chance with her gardeners and their spears. One good man with an automatic weapon could hold off the lot of us indefinitely."

"That fella' that was over here the other day didn't look like no warrior," said Teri. "He was too skinny. But he coulda' been one a' them there Kung Fu Ninjas 'er somethin' like that. What do y'all think, Big Al?"

"I thought he looked like a wide eyed divorcee in the throws of mid life crises," said Joyce. "If I ever saw a man who's fallen in lust, it was definitely him. I'm surprised he even survived the experience, if he even did. We haven't seen him today. Have we?"

"Well I guess you have a point there," said Smithson. "He was almost worshipful in how he looked at her, and I don't think it was the kind of worshipful that Inanna likes."

"For all we know he didn't survive the encounter," said Chip. "I haven't seen Inanna that angry before and she doesn't have to get as mad as that to start killing people. Remember Alphonso? And what happened to Jorge? I haven't seen him today, either."

"Ya' know," said Al. "Y'all got a point there. I ain't seen Jorge today neither, or 'is dried burned body. Maybe that ole boy up and got clean away? Maybe that's why she's sa' damned mad today? Raisin' a army an' all."

Without warning, the singing and even the flute became silent. Inanna rose from her throne of Lapis Lazuli, glowing a little brighter than before. "Hell," said Teri. "She didn't even eat nothin.'"

"Neither did we," answered Joyce.

The room suddenly reverberated with the voice of Inanna at a near deafening pitch. "Silence," she commanded them. Dishes rattled with the volume. A gust of wind accompanied the command, blowing napkins and some of the food off tables. "Your worship has made me strong," she continued, "but not strong enough. I have found others to join you. They are many. You will come with me, while I summon them."

☙ ❧

Six hundred miles northwest, more or less:

Captain Francis Xaviar Dudely paced the bridge of the ADRIANNA as he had been doing all evening. Southeast bound from Fiji toward the last foreign stop on the cruise, Easter Island, Captain Dudely had not been expecting rough weather. He was a spare man, short, thin with weathered skin, worried, gray eyes, a Camel cigarette and a pin on his shirt pocket bearing his name and the slogan, "ADRIANNA," and "Pacific Vacation Cruise Ships." He stopped in front of the main control board, looking over the shoulder of Seaman First Class Kenneth Fleeson who was studying the weather radar.

"Exactly where the hell did this damned weather come from?" demanded Captain Dudely for the fourth time in the last half-hour.

Fleeson was slightly overweight exceeding the maximum limits of the Company for a man of fifty years and six feet of height. If he had any other black marks on his record it could cost him his job and it was up to the Captain to make that decision. Company requirements were very specific about the good physical condition of its seamen. Fleeson had been forced to abandon his exercise program months before because of injuries from an auto accident in New Zealand. The weight gain had been minor, he thought, but not minor enough for the Company. "Appearance is everything," his examiner had quoted the Company Manual. "Eat less."

"I don't know sir," Fleeson replied to Captain Dudely. He took off his glasses, wiped his face with his handkerchief and looked up at the Captain. His tan uniform shirt was pulling at its buttons from his weight increase and it was ringed with perspiration at the armpits and collar. "The barometer was steady with no sign of the storm anywhere, an hour ago. It seems like it just popped up out of the ocean. It looks like a real honey too, sir. Look at that lightning on the weather scope."

"See that we steer clear of it, seaman," said Captain Dudely, exhaling a cloud of Camel smoke. "The last thing I need on my hands is thirteen hundred seasick passengers. If that storm actually hits us, I'm going to put you in charge of the goddamned mop and bucket brigade. I was on the MY SWEET LADY a few years ago when they hit a small hurricane. The whole ship smelled like the toilet in a cheap bar. It took weeks to get her hosed down enough to get rid of that smell."

"It's coming at us too fast, sir. I don't think we can avoid it."

"Let's try. Change your course heading. Turn port to seventy-five degrees. We'll run a little north and maybe it'll pass us by. Make that a very slow turn. Don't want to spill Darlene Hodge's martini down below. It embarrasses the Senator when his wife spills her drinks. He's afraid people will realize he's married to a lush. I wish these damned politicians 'd worry about running the country instead of how the media sees 'em."

"Turn port to seventy five degrees. Aye, aye, sir," replied Fleeson.

At that moment, Raymond Blunt came through the door. Blunt was graying, husky and very pale. His tan, uniform shirt showed a few drops of rain. His short cut, salt and pepper beard had a few visible drops in it. Fleeson noticed that First Officer Blunt was out of breath and that he had a gravy stain on his right trouser leg. When are they gonna' make this guy clean up his act, thought Fleeson. I may be a tad overweight, but at least my clothes are clean.

"First Officer Blunt reporting for duty sir," Blunt said to the Captain.

"Right," replied Dudely. "We have some weather coming at us from the southeast, Blunt. I ordered a course change to try to avoid it. Keep an eye on it. It looks like a small hurricane."

"It's already clouding over, sir," replied Blunt. "The wind is freshening and we have rather large following seas, in the neighborhood of about thirty feet. It's nothing the stabilizers can't handle, yet, but if it picks up much more, even four hundred sixteen feet of the ole ADRIANNA is going to start surfing a little bit."

"As long as we're running faster than the seas, this boat doesn't surf," replied Dudely. "She just plows on through. She may pound a bit, but she won't surf. I'll see you in four hours, Blunt. If you need me I'll be in my sea cabin." Dudely had two cabins, one provisioned for entertaining and gracious living while in port and one, the sea cabin, rigged for efficiency with a cot, a change of clothes and a small head.

"Yes sir, Captain," Blunt said with aplomb.

Gees, thought Fleeson. *Another four hours with this dickhead. He's a classic example of the Peter Principle, risen to his level of incompetence and will go no farther. If any decisions have to be made tonight, rest assured, he'll call the captain or even ask me to make them.* "Good evening Mister Blunt," he said with a smile reserved for superior officers. "Looks like a nice night for an off season storm, aye?"

"It looks promising," Blunt answered, glancing at the weather radar. "But I think we'll keep our feet dry, maybe even do a little fishing," he added with a patronizing smile.

One thing I really wish he would quit doing, thought Fleeson, *is this constant good-ole-boy crap.* "The storm appears to have changed course again, sir," said Fleeson. "It's on a collision course for us at about three hundred forty degrees. We changed our course heading and so did it, almost like it could see us coming and can't pass up the chance to bounce us around a little bit."

"If it's going to run north and intercept us," said Blunt, "maybe it would be better if we head south and let it pass us to port. Change the course heading again. Turn starboard to one hundred eighty degrees. Let's see if it follows us again."

Oh my God, thought Fleeson. *This good ole boy actually made a decision on his own. He didn't even ask my opinion. That's rare.* "Turn starboard to one hundred eighty degrees. Aye aye, sir."

"Sure is smoky in here," remarked Blunt, propping open the starboard hatch. "I guess it's too late for ole Doodily to stunt his growth. I wish he'd worry about mine and yours and do his smoking outside." He walked to the port side and opened the outside entry there too, providing a cross breeze.

I wish the old man would hear him call him that just once, thought Fleeson. *He'd bust ole Blunt brain down to steward. Then we'd see who was slopping vomit in storms.* "The weather station aloft is reporting winds to sixty knots, sir," said Fleeson to Blunt. "The barometer is down to twenty eight and a half inches. And sir?"

"Yes?" said Blunt, sounding distracted.

"Take a look at the weather radar, sir. The storm has changed course again and it's back on an intercepting vector."

"Well I'll be damned," said Blunt. "Well, if you can't beat 'em join 'em. That's what I always say. Change the course heading again, seaman. Turn port to our original heading of one hundred five degrees. We'll push old ADRIANNA right down its throat. If it holds its present heading, it will still pass us to the south. If it has some weird kind of internal guidance system, we won't be able to escape it anyway. On second thought belay that order, seaman. I think I'll check with the captain before we ram the storm."

"He could be asleep by now, sir," said Fleeson. *Watch his silly ass squirm now. He can't decide whether to risk the captain's wrath for waking him or risk his wrath for making the wrong decision. I love pushing this jackass's buttons. And old Doodily makes it easy because he doesn't support his officer's decisions and gives them hell in front of the crew. No wonder he's just a cruise ship captain. No wonder he washed out of the Navy.*

Blunt was pacing just as Dudely had before him, less the Camel. Fleeson could see that the raindrops had dried from Blunt's shirt and beard, but drops were now appearing on his forehead. "Execute the order, seaman," said Blunt. One thing we can be sure of is that the old man is going to raise hell whether we miss the storm or not."

"Turn port to one hundred five degrees. Aye, aye, sir," replied Fleeson trying to hide his smile.

Blunt paced between the weather radar and forward portholes, alternating every third or fourth pass to the starboard hatch where he stepped outside to the deck to eyeball the sky first hand. He was visibly frightened and trying to conceal it from Fleeson. *It doesn't look good for the officers to be scared,* thought Fleeson. *How did he get this job anyway? Does his daddy own major shares in the cruise line? I bet I have twice the experience at sea that this guy has. It's silly to be scared of a little storm in of boat this size. 'Course, he's worried about getting his butt reamed out by the old man more than he's probably scared of the storm.*

"How stands the weather?" Blunt asked the ritual question.
"Twenty eight point three five inches, seventeen degrees at seven zero [knots], dew point is at six two degrees Fahrenheit, ambient temperature at six zero degrees Fahrenheit. The weather station aft indicates that we still have following seas standing at about forty five feet, sir," Fleeson said.

"With the dew point at sixty two degrees and the outside temperature at sixty, it would be raining," mumbled Blunt.

"That is correct sir," said Fleeson. "It is raining. I expect the temperature to drop another twenty degrees in the next half-hour, sir. It will soon be raining very hard, sir, sideways." Fleeson switched on the automatic wipers to clear the windshield for better visibility. The ship had begun pitching slightly and pounding into the backs of the seas it overtook.

"What is our speed, seaman?" asked Blunt.

"Twenty two knots sir," answered Fleeson.

"Reduce our speed to fifteen knots, seaman."

"Reduce speed to fifteen knots, aye, aye sir," responded Fleeson. *Well he did that right. If we keep pounding like this, it could damage something.*

Blunt had stopped exiting to the deck for his first hand looks at the clouds. Now he hung out at the front windshield, watching the sky, stepping back startled from time to time when particularly heavy sheets of rain struck the glass. Suddenly there was so much light from the windows that both men were temporarily blinded.

"What the hell was that?" said Blunt.

"I think it was lightning sir," said Fleeson. "The system's going wild sir. The lightning knocked out our main power. The secondary system kicked on right a way, but then we got a second flash. Lucky we have triple redundancy, sir. We still have power."

"State of the art," grinned Blunt. "Nothing the old man of the sea can throw at us could take out modern vessels. We're all electronics. Even those big Diesels down below have little computer brains that keep the fuel flow just right for the temperature and the demand on them."

Nothing like a little bravado to calm down the help, thought Fleeson. *Another strike like that and those little computer brains in the hold will all be fried like overcooked eggs, crisp on one side and this big tub will lay in the water like a bloated whale. In fact, two of the three are probably already fried. That's why the lights went out, twice!* Fleeson was getting nervous. *These big boats don't row very well. I wish he'd cut power and disconnect that last computer till the storm passes so we don't have to float around waiting for help.*

"Oh my God," said Blunt in a hushed voice.

"What is it sir?" asked Fleeson.

"I'll stand the helm, Fleeson. Go get the Captain."

"Me, sir?" pleaded Fleeson. "He'll bite my head off if I wake him."

"Better yours than mine. Get him," Blunt commanded with more authority than Fleeson had ever before heard in his voice.

Dudely had been sound asleep, but before raising hell with the crewman for waking him, he first came forward to the main bridge to see what the problem was. He had been roused nearly every time Blunt was in command but Fleeson didn't know what to expect this time. Blunt had not told him the problem.

"What is it?" Dudely demanded.

"The storm's not that bad sir, but you had ordered me to wake you even if you were dead, if I ever saw what I can see ahead now. Take a look for yourself, sir." Blunt was paler than usual, and sweating.

Captain Dudely walked to the forward most portholes and peered out through the sheets of rain. "It looks like it's clearing up a bit in the distance. We've about come through it." He was about to turn back toward Blunt when he stopped and said in fearful amazement, "Oh my God." Then to Fleeson, "Reduce speed to ten knots Seaman and once you've done that come about. Turn left to a heading of two hundred eighty five degrees, and once you've done that, Seaman, increase our speed to the maximum this tub can do, twenty five knots."

Fleeson glanced out the window as the ship was slowing to ten knots. In the sky in the distance he could see a swirling cloud formation glowing in an eerie, blue light, almost as though a city lie in the distance illuminating the clouds. But Fleeson knew there were no cities nearby. *The strangest thing,* he thought to himself, *is that those clouds look like a beautiful woman with an angry face. And what's that strange bronze glowing just behind her?*

At that moment, lightning struck again. There were three bolts. The second one destroyed the ships last backup computer system and power supply. The lights went out. The instrument lighting vanished. The air conditioning, which had been heating the cabin, stopped humming, but the most dreadful change of all was the dead silence. The constantly vibrating throb of the big Diesels in the lower hull had stopped. As the ship's momentum alone, carried it forward and the left turn continued, ADRIANNA began to roll in those following sixty-foot seas. "She won't roll like that for long," said Dudely with awe in his voice. "The wind has stopped. The old timers call this a Rapanui Storm. Just look at that sky."

Chapter 16: The Pinnacle

Johnny's sleep was troubled. In the morning, he felt that he'd barely had any sleep at all. It took until after the noon meal for him to feel that he had finally awakened from his dreams and the visions of the night before. Working among the plants on the terraces, helped him clear his mind of the troubling images he had seen in his sleep and meditations, but just before the noon meal there was another incident which added to his stress and fear.

Johnny and those working with him were on their way up the hill toward the main building and the refectory to eat when Johnny suddenly felt unsteady on his feet. He paused, then continued up the path. It happened again. *I guess I should have taken a walk before I went to bed last night. I'd have slept better. I obviously needed to have slept better. I can't even walk right today.* Then he heard the comments around him and a loud exclamation.

"Tremors!" someone called out.

"Look at the volcano," someone else shouted.

Johnny looked. Smoke was rising from the mouth of the eastern peak. *Tremors?* He thought. *So, that's what an earthquake feels like. I wonder if there's any danger. I don't think that mountain was smoking before.* Then he noticed that the western peak was smoking as well. *What's she up to?*

Caleb walked by and as he did so he slapped Johnny on the back and said, "No point in being afraid of it. If we die, we die. No one has ever left the island. Every time any one has ever tried, we get a bronze cloud cover overhead and all ocean currents turn toward here."

"What about the SEA TROLLOP, the boat Tarek and I came in. He said it didn't stop because it didn't rely on any electronics. I bet it will still start," said Johnny.

"It might," interjected Lee Moy, who was coming up from behind them. "But even if it did start, it's not big enough to take more than four or five of us safely and it's doubtful that it has enough remaining fuel to make it to Easter Island. We have a few other boats, but their fuel is too old to be useful."

"Then if that thing really starts to erupt, we're trapped," said Johnny, fearfully. "Aren't we?"

"I think we can handle it," said Lee Moy. "I'll alert the meditation teams."

Lucias, Cardac and a few others appeared from within the building. As they exited the main porch, they began looking toward the mountain, talking among themselves. Johnny stayed to hear what was being said. Cardac seemed the most perturbed by the tremors and smoking mountain, his eyes bulging a little more than usual. Lucias, more the academician, appeared concerned but not overly alarmed. Caleb and Lee Moy joined them.

"I mean," Cardac was speaking with animation as Johnny came within earshot. "If that thing blows up it could take the whole bloody island. There'd be nothing left but the tidal waves."

"I don't think it's going to blow up," said Lucias in calming tones. "If you look at it you can see there's no apparent swelling, no sign of a lava flow, yet. In our history this has happened two other times and each time after our teams focused on it in meditation, it stopped smoking and calmed down again."

"Look at that, will ya.'" Said Cardac. "The western mountain's smoking too. Has that ever happened before that anybody knows of?"

Johnny looked toward the western peak. There was smoke still coming from both peaks, sure enough. The distortion caused by the shimmering barrier gave it an impressionist appearance, like an animated, Claude Monet or a Renoir painting.

"We have no record of both volcanoes coming to the point of emitting smoke at the same time," Lee Moy replied. "This just makes a more interesting problem for us to address. And besides that, I suspect that the entity of the western side of the island wants an eruption about as much as we do. I think it will stop."

Lucias looked round at the group, finding Johnny, he smiled, and said, "I think it may be a good idea for you to go back over there and see if you can make peace with her."

She'll kill me if I go back," said Johnny with a chuckle. Then sobering, he said, "She really might, if she can."

"Or she might be relieved to learn that you aren't still angry with her," said Lee Moy. "Your reaction to her attack probably felt as much like a slap from you as her attack on you felt like it. You might be surprised, but I believe she might be glad to see you. Besides, that may have been just what she needed to make her stop attacking you. Didn't you say every time you've gone to see her that she attacked you in the same way?"

"Yes," said Johnny. "She has done that."

"She sounds like a petulant teenager who lashes out at those she cares for but only when she's sure she can do no real harm." Lee Moy considered for a moment, then added, "Didn't you say that yesterday was the first time you reacted badly when she attacked you?"

"It was," answered Johnny. "She took me by surprise. It wasn't what I was expecting."

C3 &0

The hike to Inanna's compound went surprisingly fast. *As a trip becomes familiar,* Johnny thought, *it seems to grow shorter.* Climbing the cold lava flow this time was more frightening, somehow, than it had seemed before. He found himself trying to feel any difference in the temperature of the rock, as though he thought the new lava would follow possible vents that may be inside this old flow.

When he could catch a glimpse of it between the tall palms, he would watch to see if the volcano had increased or decreased the volume of its smoke output. *I can't really tell,* he concluded each time. *Every time I see it, it's from a different angle than before. One thing I don't want to see, is sparks flying out of that thing, either one of them or the beginning of new lava flows down its side. But it would be worst of all if the mountain starts to swell. That would indicate internal pressure that could blow just like Mount St. Helens did a few years ago. I bet there'll be a real light show tonight, if it keeps up.*

With that thought, he turned off of the beach and headed onto the path leading up the side of the mountain and eventually to Inanna's lands. The forest was unusually quiet. No birds or insects were making the least sound. The only disturbance to the serene silence was the breeze moving through the trees and the sounds of his footsteps on the path.

When he emerged from the forest at the northwest end of Inanna's compound, he was surprised to see no one there. Those who worked in Inanna's fields were gone. No one was lounging in front of the guest cottages where Chip Evans and his wife Joyce were staying. As he walked toward the entrance to the ballroom, he observed the remains of the afternoon's work. There were cut branches and the remains of bark peeled from them strewn everywhere. As Johnny drew closer to the main building, he noticed something else that was new, and understood the mess of twigs, cut branches and stripped bark he had seen on the grounds. Stacked against the wall on either side of the entrance to the ballroom were hundreds of primitive wooden spears with seashell heads lashed to the wood with thin vines. *She's either going to have all her people spear fishing or she's going to start a war,* thought Johnny.

A shiver ran down his spine at the thought of who Inanna might have in mind for the enemy in this war he envisioned. *What's she going to do, march the islander gardeners after us at the eastern end of the island? All she has to do is push that volcano a little more and we'll be just as gone and with a lot less blood shed by her own people.* He dismissed the thought that she was going to try to march on them. Then he remembered the visions he had the night before in his meditation. The possibilities represented by the many spears and knives were exactly what he had seen and with Inanna in the lead, blasting away with her blue lightning.

The one thing in the visions that was out of place for this scenario was the fact that the Essene brotherhood would not bear arms against her or anyone else, except in quiet meditation and prayer. That one thing did not fit the visions where men were fighting each other. *What if they held a war,* he thought, *and no one came? That's what Inanna will have if she attacks us, if she's able to get past our barriers. But that might not be so hard. After all, I can pass the barrier as easily as if it weren't there. She probably can too and with as many of her people as she sees fit to bring with her. Maybe there is going to be a small war, and it will be over very quickly.*

Still he heard no sounds produced by humans and saw no one. Inside the ballroom, it was the same. No one was there. There were the remains of an unfinished dinner distributed to the many tables but not eaten. There was the blue throne but there was no common table beside it, set up for the people Inanna imagined were her friends. Johnny walked slowly through the room, listening for the least sound of another person. Still, there was no one. He picked up a piece of fruit from one of the tables and munched on it as he approached the dais and climbed the three steps to its elevated level.

The lighting in the room was provided with torches and what rays of the setting sun were able to make it through the open ballroom doors and the few windows. Dim as it was inside the ballroom without Inanna to brighten things up, there was enough light for him to more closely examine the notch, he had seen cut in the throne of Lapis Lazuli. He searched briefly then found it. He pulled out his amulet given him by Belili what seemed to him so long ago.

Well, look at this, he thought to himself. *Isn't this amazing? It's a perfect fit.*

The fit looked snug enough that he decided not to slide it in for fear that he might not be able to get it back out again. Instead, he put the chain back around his neck and stood up. Looking around again he saw a figure seated in the alcove beside the front door. It was watching him in silence. He froze for an instant before recognizing the figure of Belili, the old woman. In relief, he sat down on the throne of Lapis Lazuli. Before he could leap to his feet, he was surrounded with the energy of the stone and the power imparted to it from constant use by Inanna. He could feel the energy entering him almost as intensely as when Inanna struck out at him with her lightning. This was a more constant charge than the sudden blast and it seemed to soak into him more fully. Finally, he felt that the energy had equalized. He remained seated, feeling the comfort of the stone and appreciating the skill of the craftsman who carved it.

Belili was approaching him in the dimness of the ballroom. He could only see her shadow moving through the room. He knew it was her because of her form and shape. As she drew nearer the lines of her face became more visible, the lace dress and veil, the black shoes, the thin lipped smile. The brilliant energy in her eyes smiled at his discomfiture. She took a seat at one of the front tables below the dais. "Do you find that chair comfortable, DeMuzzi?"

"Very," he answered. "I would think a stone chair would be cool to the touch. This one is not."

"Don't be surprised," Belili replied. "It is the throne of Inanna. If she found you in it, she would be very angry. But I am sure she can feel you in it and is very angry without actually catching you."

Johnny quickly rose from the blue throne. With a quick look at it behind him, he moved off of the dais and took a seat across from Belili. "So tell me something, Leelee. How did you get off of the island to meet me at the airport in Santiago? I have a few other questions too, if you don't mind."

Belili's smile broadened slightly. "She needs you, you know. You have been good for her. Enlil was very wise."

"Enlil?" Johnny asked. "You mentioned that name before. As we speak, more and more questions pop into my head. There's so much, I don't understand about what's happening on this island. I think you could explain it to me if you wanted to. Will you?"

Belili gave him a wry look, folded her arms and began gently rocking on her bench. "I do not know Enlil's plan," she said. "His reckoning is far greater than mine. I could tell you what I do know but you are not ready to accept it, to believe what I could tell you. You are not ready."

"Then just tell me. Who is Inanna?" Johnny pressed.

"Inanna," answered the old woman. "She certainly is beautiful is she not? I could see. I know you think so."

"Yes, beautiful, but what is she? Who is she? People can't do what she can do. Tell me. Please."

"She is not as old as the Elohim, the birth goddesses. Her time began soon after. Her mother and father liked to make their home on the moon, so men called them 'moon gods.' Men called us gods then, but now man would know that we are not. That is in fact where her name comes from. In the old tongues, just as in the tongues of the local native peoples, Ina and Nanna refer to the Moon."

"There have never been homes on the moon," replied Johnny. "We only just got there a few decades ago. How do expect me to believe..."

Belili cut him off with, "NEVER is a long time, young man. NEVER is a very long time, indeed. Never say 'never.' Now, Inanna needs you. Come with me and I will show you where she has gone.

ᚳ ᚹ

The Pinnacle

Inanna was seated on the top of the cliff overlooking the sea to the northwest. It was the same place, where Chip and Joyce first saw her, when they cleared the reef with their ketch, MOON DAUGHTER. Chip recognized the spot, though he had not seen it before from this perspective. Inanna's presence overlooking the bay and the gathering ring of the bronze clouds beyond the reef told him of its significance.

"She causes this, I think," he whispered to Smithson seated next to him.

Smithson gave him a frightened look with his finger to his lips.

"What is she saying?" Chip could hear Inanna's voice at low breath, but not what she was saying. *It's as though she's in some kind of trance or something.* All had taken seats on the ground in what appeared to be an impromptu amphitheater of sorts, cut into the hillside. The spot where Inanna was seated facing the sea was the highest point with the rest of the gathering on descending levels behind her. The islanders with Chip and his companions were seated in a semi-circle arrangement, *Like a half moon,* Chip thought. *How appropriate.*

Chip had been surprised that after spending most of the day cutting spears and other weapons, that Inanna would instruct them to leave these weapons behind to follow her to the pinnacle. Obediently Chip, Joyce and the others stacked their primitive weapons on the porch of the ballroom and followed her into the forest along the path leading to the pinnacle. The islanders did the same, except that Chip, Smithson and Big Al had kept their roughly made sea shell knives wrapped in a piece of palm leaf, hidden under their shirts. At a nod from Big Al, they began to inch closer to the woman in the purple sarong who was intently watching the horizon to the northwest.

The cloud cover over the sea darkened with its odd, bronze coloration. The swirling pattern so familiar to Chip and Joyce had begun and a breeze off the sea followed the curvature of the land down from the point where Inanna sat, carrying with it the smells of the salt water. Joyce noticed Chip's movement and about the same time, she noticed that of the other two. She shot Chip a warning glance and when Chip met her eye, she shook her head in a stern "Don't do this."

She knows I have to, thought Chip. *We can't spend the rest of our lives in bondage to this crazy woman, or what ever she is. We're slaves. She drinks our energy like it's air for her; like breathing. She kills anyone who she catches trying to escape. That poor DeMuzzi she brought for us to meet is probably dead. I never saw her so angry as she was last night. Jorge is probably dead, too.*

Chip glanced back at the volcano. They had been concerned when they saw it smoking that morning, but Inanna indicated no interest. Now in the gathering darkness, he could see its red orange fire reflected off the clouds, but so far, there was no visible lava flow. *That's all we need,* he thought. *If that thing starts erupting, there is no way for us to escape. Well, there are all kinds of volcanoes. Some erupt quietly, pouring lava down one or two flows for centuries without really bothering anyone, then there is the Mount St. Helens type that explodes with a big enough bang to wipe out half a state. I wonder what kind this one is going to turn out to be.*

Smithson was the farthest back from Inanna. Chip and Al stopped moving forward to wait for him. They had made enough progress that if Inanna turned around she would be able to clearly see that they were no longer seated with the rest of the group but slowly approaching her from behind. Chip wondered if she did see them, if she would know that they had murder in mind.

I bet there's another boat out there somewhere, Chip mused. *There's probably a fishing boat or another yacht like ours. She's going to dash someone else's boat on the reef and trap them here. We have to stop this at all costs.*

They had discussed it among themselves several times and agreed before dinner that since they now have weapons, this would be as good a time as any. Smithson had caught up. It was Big Al's turn to slide forward a little bit. Al took his turn. Then it was Chip's turn. Then Smithson's.

These little toy seashell knives are very sharp but they don't have the weight or balance for throwing, thought Chip, remembering his Marine survival training. *If I had my old knife, I could easily nail her from here.* Then he reminded himself, *don't stare at her back. Keep your eyes averted. Any living thing can feel the approach of death if the stalker stares intently at it.* He had warned the others but Big Al didn't believe him. "How many times in your life have you turned around to meet the eyes of someone watching you?" Chip had asked him. "Even you can feel it when someone's watching you. If you and I can do that, Inanna certainly can."

"That's a bunch a' damn hogwash," Al had replied. "I stalked many a' critter that never knew what hit 'em."

Now was the acid test. If Inanna could feel the intensity of what they had planned, there was no way they could succeed. He glanced at Al to see if he was keeping his eyes averted, watching only with the peripheral vision. *Thank heaven,* he thought. *Al isn't taking any chances.*

Chip could feel a change in the air. Jimmy and Al could feel it too, Chip could tell because of their sudden expression change. *What's different?* He tried to sense it with his eyes closed. Then he realized that the difference was not the presence of something new, but the lack of something old. Inanna had stopped chanting. She seemed now to be listening, head cocked slightly. Chip closed his eyes and added some fervor to his chanting, joining his voice with those of the islanders, and listening to the voices of Al Johns and James Smithson beside him. He could hear Joyce, Rosemary and Teri behind them, now by about six feet, with a hundred or more Polynesian people behind and all around them. Inanna was still ten feet away, more or less and still above them on the rock. Chip was too frightened to keep his eyes completely closed.

Inanna silently arose to a standing position, still gazing out to sea. So slowly as to be almost imperceptible, she turned to face them. Her gaze felt like the heat of the sun on Chip's face. Her anger was somehow indirect, but very present. He could feel her voice inside his head so distinctly that he almost confused it with his own thoughts. "How could you be so foolish?" she thundered in his mind. The blue bolt formed in her hands and from her eyes, forming one bolt that encompassed all three of them. "Can't you see I'm busy? If I stop now, I may lose them."

The three men collapsed on the ground where they had been sitting.

Not quite conscious thought Chip, *but not quite unconscious either.* He could see their wives start to move forward but stop themselves with the paralysis of fear. He could see the gathering anger in Joyce's eyes, the fury in Teri's, the terror in Rosemary's.

Then he could feel Inanna's voice ringing in his mind again saying, "Don't make me hurt anyone else. I can. You know. And I don't care if I do. There are many in sight I can use to replace you now."

What does she mean by that, Chip thought. *Maybe there's a caravan of boats sailing together. We have to stop her.* He tried to get up, but found that he could barely move, much less get to his feet. The chanting was increasing in volume. *The islanders must have seen what she did to us and they're trying to add some strength to their worship so she won't get mad again. What kind of monster is this woman? This Inanna.*

Six of the Polynesians, as though on order from Inanna, approached them. Two helped Chip to his feet and began half carrying him, helped him back down the path toward the palace compound. Two more half lifted Big Al and two more took Smithson. Together they headed down the path through the forest. *Does she have a pet alligator somewhere and they're going to feed us to it?* Chip wondered. *I haven't seen any alligators. Maybe it's a crocodile or a something worse.*

CƷ ⅋Ɔ

In the distance, Johnny could hear the sounds of voices, chanting. Belili had left him as soon as she was sure he was on the right path. Both volcanoes were still smoking in the distance, but now it was the eastern mountain distorted in his view by the shimmering barrier. The reflection of the mountains' inner fires off the clouds lighted his way toward the pinnacle as much as his own glowing from the energy he picked up by sitting on the blue throne. *What's she up to now,* he thought as he trudged up the steep path. *Is she playing church again? Why didn't she do it in the dining room like she did when I was here before? Is this some special occasion?*

He could hear them coming before he saw them. There was grunting and heavy breathing accompanied by low moans, as though of pain. He stopped to listen more carefully. The forest sounds had not returned. The effect was as eerie to him as the sparks jumping from his fingers. *This sparking thing is too much. I'm going to have to stay off of that chair of hers. How does this work, anyway?* Then he saw them. There were six islanders half carrying Smithson, Al and Chip. *What happened now?*

Instead of continuing up the path to Inanna, Johnny followed Chip and the others back to the ballroom where the islanders sat them at one of the tables and began encouraging them to eat. None of them could speak English but from their gestures it was plain to Johnny they were trying to help the injured men. Johnny had tried to ask what had happened but all three of the men were still too stunned to be able to talk. After eating a little, the color began to return to their cheeks. Al was the first to speak.

"We best not try that again.'" The other two nodded in agreement, their mouths full.

"Try what again?" asked Johnny, but before they could reply, the doors to the main entrance opened and Inanna entered, alone. Her hair was wind blown and her purple sarong had stains of green as though she had brushed against some bushes along the path in her hurry to return. He could see she was angry. *So, what else is new?* He thought.

"You," she snapped. "How dare you come back here!"

She raised her hands as though to blast him with another bolt of lightning but Johnny raised one hand, allowing a couple of sparks to leap from his fingers and said simply, "I wouldn't do that again if I were you. You might hurt yourself. How about a hug instead?"

"You were sitting on my throne," she stated as though she felt personally violated.

"It's quite comfortable, actually. I can see why you prefer it. Where can I get one like it?" he asked. "What about the hug?"

"Go back to your cloistered sleepers," she said as though distracted. "I have work to do," and she disappeared again into the night.

Chapter 17: The ADRIANNA

"Where are the women?" asked Johnny. Al, Chip and Smithson were seated at the long tables below the dais eating slowly. The islanders had refreshed some of the torches. The blue throne glowed in the background. *If I'm not mistaken,* thought Johnny, *that thing is getting a little brighter.* To test his theory, he climbed the dais and again sat down on the throne. He knew instantly it was a mistake because the remaining Polynesians who had stayed behind to tend to Chip and the others immediately began chanting.

"Mawkee. Mawkee."

Chip started chuckling, joined shortly by Al and Smithson. "You're apparently the only one who ever faced her down and survived," said Chip.

"Mawkee's the name of the head bird god," said Al. "It's a wonder they ain't callin' you Hurrikahn the storm god 'er something."

"Wrong ocean," said Chip. "Hurrikahn is the storm god from the Caribbean. I don't know what they call him in these parts."

"Maybe we oughta' start callin' him Mawkee instead a'... What'd you say yer name was?" asked Al.

"DeMuzzi," answered Johnny.

"How 'bout raise yer hand 'er somethin,'" said Al. "See if y'all can make them stop that racket."

Johnny could feel that the energy in the blue throne was indeed gathering more power. It was augmenting what he had already soaked up from it, like water seeking its own level, but he was the receptacle the energy was filling. *How in the world does this work?* He wondered.

She's out there soaking up this energy somehow and it seems to get stored here. Is this like a battery? He raised his hand as though in blessing and the Polynesians stopped chanting. Then he noticed that the Lapis Lazuli obelisk hanging around his neck was feeling warm. He pulled it out from below the neckline on his shirt to look at it and discovered that it was glowing with the same color and intensity as the throne. *So, I guess the throne is her battery. The amulet is my battery. I guess she's more powerful because she has a bigger battery.* He smiled to himself and was unable to resist the thought. *I wonder how long they can keep going.*

"We thought you were dead," said Chip. "Do you happen to know what happened to Jorge? He disappeared the last time you were here and at about the same time as you disappeared. Did he escape to the monastery with you?"

"Yes," said Johnny. "He's at the monastery now. She shot a last bolt at us just as we approached the barrier, but she missed. He's as safe as can be expected on this island. I about half expected to find you there too, when I got back. Why didn't you escape too?"

"She caught up to us," volunteered Smithson. "We were trying to get away. She was furious with you. We've never seen her so angry. What did you do to her?"

"Oh, we had a little quarrel," smiled Johnny. "She's not used to men who talk back."

"I think she's not used to havin' a man around at all," said Big Al. "Just slaves. She can't seem to hurt y'all, but she can hurt us plenty. I'd thank ya' ta' not piss her off like that again. We coulda' got hurt."

"If you're able to come and go as you please," said Chip, "You should go and not come back. She's a lot more dangerous than you may realize."

"Maybe I should go now," said Johnny "and take you three with me."

"Not without the women folk," said Big Al.

"I don't think I could walk that far tonight anyway after she blasted us again," added Smithson.

"That's right," said Chip. "We'll wait till our wives can join us. Maybe tomorrow or the next day, after we've rested a little."

"From the looks of those stacks of spears, I think you may be headed to the eastern side of the island anyway in another day or two," Johnny commented.

"We was wonderin' about that," said Big Al. "I'm kinda' gittin' the idea that she's thinkin' a' stormin' the monastery with us an' them islanders as soldiers. Them spears ain't fer fishin,' I don't think."

"What's she doing now?" asked Johnny.

"We don't know fer sure," answered Al. "She got another one a' them ole Rapanui Storms brewin' out over the ocean. We think she's tryin' ta' catch her another boat or two. We tried ta' slip up on her but..."

"You can see how that worked out," muttered Chip.

"I thought she was going to kill us outright," added Smithson.

"Listen, DeMuzzi," said Chip. "She has some sort of hypnotic power that she can exercise over just about anyone she wants, including us, and probably including you. You should get out of here as fast as your legs can carry you while you can still walk on your own. Look at us. We can barely move."

"That's really hard to imagine," said Johnny. "I know she's not like other women I've known but to think of her as having abilities like that..." *Well she is very remarkable,* he thought. *Her aura is immense, not to mention powerful.* He was remembering how the energy of the barrier struck out at him and how he was able to change its color and form. *I'm denying she has hypnotic powers and at the same time suspecting that, her personal energy caused those volcanoes to become active. They've seen more than I have. Maybe they're right.* "Assuming you're right, how could this be? She seems like an ordinary woman, most of the time."

"She's the damned islanders damned moon goddess, Heena," said Big Al. "That's who the hell she is. I never believed in stuff like that, and I wouldn't now if I hadn't a' seen her in action my own self. An' I don't know who the hell you are neither, but I wouldn't be a bit damn surprised ta' find out you're the damned head bird god MawkeeMawkee, 'er what ever the hell they been callin' y'all."

"Al," said Smithson. "He's just a man like us."

"Man hell," said Big Al. "I seen her back off when he raised his hand just now. Didn't y'all see the sparks jump from his fingers?"

"If he is MawkeeMawkee," said Chip, "He can fry us as quickly as Inanna. Don't you think you'd better be a little more respectful?"

"Calm down, gentlemen," said Johnny. "I am not a god. I am not like Inanna. I am just a man." *I am Hjet,* he reminded himself. *I am the divider between good and evil. I have been sent here by the brotherhood to polarize this evil, find the good in it, discarding the negative. I am to be Binah to her Chocmah, Yang to her Yin. But am I enough?*

"What's all that racket goin' on outside?" interjected Big Al, turning to look toward the doors.

"Sounds like the islanders are arguing about something," said Smithson.

Johnny rose from the throne of Lapis Lazuli, descended from the dais and approached the doors to look outside. Before he reached the doors, they burst open and about a dozen of the islanders, all men, came through the door, still arguing. The six who had helped the men return from the pinnacle were among them. They kept repeating the words 'Mawkee Mawkee,' while the others frowned in response replying with what was obviously a negative in their own tongues.

The most frightening thing in the aspect of their appearance was the presence of the spears. Each man had one of the newly made weapons and they were all leveled in one direction, toward Johnny. With surprising agility, they surrounded him in seconds. Johnny waited. When they had finished encircling him, one stepped slightly forward and said in halting English, "Heena say - MawkeeMawkee stay off throne."

The man was obviously terrified of Johnny. He was sweating, eyes bulging, swaying from one foot the other as if expecting an attack. All of them appeared frightened. The six who had been inside when Johnny was sitting on the throne held back, not wanting to be part of this affront to the god. The man who spoke seemed on the verge of falling to his knees when Johnny smiled. Very slowly, he raised one hand, still charged with the energy from the throne. Slowly he formed it into a fist with his index finger raised, pointing straight up. He allowed one spark to leap from his finger, then he slowly lowered it to point at the man who had spoken to him.

As one, they all fled back out through the doors, the way they had come and vanished into the night talking animatedly among themselves. Johnny listened for a few minutes as their voices faded in the distance, until all he could hear was a far away rumbling, apparently coming from the volcanoes.

The night was still too quiet, almost spooky, but Johnny left the ballroom and started back toward the forest to retrace his steps in search of Inanna. Chip and the others had told him that she was on the pinnacle overlooking the sea to the northwest not much farther than where he had found them earlier. The climb was gradual. The path paralleled the sea on his left with the mountain rising to his right. He had not gone far when he could see Inanna's blue glow in the distance. He continued along the path until he found her seated on the point of the pinnacle facing the sea. It was only then that he recognized the bronze glow of the clouds to the northwest.

A large gathering of the islanders sat quietly behind her. He noticed Joyce, Teri and Rosemary in the front of the group. They looked at him with obvious questions in their eyes. He tried to indicate reassurance that their men were all right with a wave and a nod but felt he had failed to communicate it. Rather than disturb Inanna's focus with background talking - and risk another confrontation - he quietly turned toward her. The purple of her sarong was hard to see in the absence of daylight. Her long black hair hung straight down her back stirred only slightly by the wind coming from the sea. In the background, light from the volcano reflecting from the clouds glistened in her hair. The bronze clouds to the northwest swirled angrily into the distance.

How is she going to receive me? The last thing she said to me after ordering me to stay off her throne was to go home. Is she going to hit me with the blue bolt again? I won't be surprised by it this time. But I don't think she'll do that. The last time it backfired on her. I don't know how since I had the amulet off - if that's even what protected me before. Maybe I was protected because I was so charged up with her energy, like I am now.

Johnny took a step toward her. She gave no sign that she knew he was there, so he took another step. She still gave no sign that she recognized his presence. So, he walked right up to her, sat down on the ground beside her.

귕   쟌

Seaman First Class Kenneth Fleeson was at the ADRIANNA's taffrail. Sullenly he stared at the sea behind the boat where he had stood many times in the past during his time off duty. The immense wake put out by the ship under way at twenty-five knots was as hypnotic as watching the water flow over the Niagara Falls. The vast volume of liquid moving in a smooth flow all in one direction holds the eye and mesmerizes the thoughts if only briefly, until one pulls away from the vision. The wake of the ADRIANNA at full speed was just such a spectacle. Unlike the big falls, the ship's wake flowed straight back, lifting into graceful arches forming waves like the sea's own rollers.   But not tonight. The cruise ship ADRIANNA lay in the water like a bloated whale, drifting aimlessly, out of touch with the world under a dimly lighted sky filled with madly swirling clouds. Fleeson watched the water, not the sky, trying to see down into its depths. Far out at sea, the ocean water is usually clear as water from a crystal clean, rocky mountain spring, but the fish are bigger. *The old man called this a Rapanui Storm,* thought Fleeson. *What does he know about it? Nothin.' Who does he know whose ever been in one of these? Nobody. How in hell did he know the wind would stop. He said it would and it did.* Fleeson began walking. He rounded the starboard quarter and headed forward toward the bridge, several hundred feet ahead and three decks up. His Navy Blue windbreaker was hanging open in front since there was no identifiable wind and the air temperature was close to seventy degrees Fahrenheit. The windbreaker was a habit more than a necessity to him.

Tonight it represented the comfort of routine. Little else had been routine since the engines quit.

As he passed by the first of the two on board swimming pools, he noticed there were quite a few passengers lounging on deck. The aft pool bartender had a full house, lighted with candles and lanterns. *No wonder,* he thought to himself. *With the power off, it's too hot below for anyone to want to be inside their cabins. The dining rooms are also too hot and stuffy. There's no refrigeration, so the food isn't going to be keeping very well. At least they can have cold drinks, till the ice is all gone, then there'll be no more scotch on the rocks, 'cause there won't be anymore rocks. - except on the ocean floor and we don't want to see any of those rocks. Now. Do we?*

Much to Fleeson's amusement, the auxiliary Diesel engines used as backups to run the pumps were working perfectly - *no electronics,* he mused. *At least we aren't going to sink. It's too bad the big Diesels have to rely on all those wires and microchips. If we kept to the old ways, we wouldn't be having this problem. Diesels don't need electronics. It's just some geek visionary type in the home office trying to save a few gallons of fuel. Sure the computer controlled Diesels are more efficient, but they sure have their problems, otherwise. They're going to save the company a few gallons of juice but it's going to cost them this ship if we can't jury rig some power somehow.*

Light from the rising moon revealed that the bronze tint to the sky remained. *I wish we could see the moon instead of just the light,* Fleeson thought. Back on the bridge, Blunt was off duty but still hanging out. Fleeson's replacement for the night shift was sitting dogmatically at the helm. *What for?* Fleeson thought when he saw him. *It'd take a hydraulic jack to move the rudder without the ship's power.* "How ya' doin' Spoon?" Fleeson said to him after nodding to Blunt. Jack Spooner was about twenty-two and in training. He was six feet, a hundred fifty pounds, dark hair and eyes, a quiet sort of man. *He looks more intelligent than anybody has a right to be,* Fleeson had thought on first meeting him, but Fleeson liked him in spite of himself.

"I'm doin,' Ken. What I'd like to know is where we're bound for on this nice coppery kind of evening. Have you ever seen clouds like this before?"

"Nope. I've never even heard of clouds like this before, except in Pittsburgh when the coke plants were still running. But I have a feeling, that bronze color overhead is not caused by some nearby steel mill. I wish it was."

"The old man's out on the bow with that ornamental sextant he always keeps on his desk trying to get a shot at the sun or the moon, or anything," said Spooner. "He's pretty frustrated with the clouds. He can't see any thing to get a bearing from."

"Tell me Spoon," said Fleeson. "You still have that battery operated hand held GPS set in your cabin? Maybe he can get a bearing from that?"

Spooner looked up with a frustrated expression and said, "It's useless. The batteries are dead."

Blunt, who had been listening to the conversation as he watched the captain on the forward deck playing with his sextant said at the same time as Fleeson, "Spoon. We have a ship's store that sells batteries."

Blunt continued. "Go get your GPS, then go down to the ship's store and get some batteries. Charge them to the company account and tell the clerk I'll sign for them myself."

"As warm as it is below decks, you might have to go find the store clerk. I doubt that the store's open. You'll need a flashlight too. There are no lights below the decks these days," Fleeson added.

Spooner returned in about half an hour with his GPS in one hand and a small bag from the ship's store in the other. Captain Dudely had been informed about the coming of the hand held Global Positioning System. He was waiting when Spooner arrived. "I wish you'd mentioned that you had one of these things a little earlier," Dudely said to Spooner. Coulda' saved me a lot of trouble. You know how to work it?"

"Yes sir," said Spooner, popping the back off the device to insert the new batteries. "It works the same way as the ship's GPS, sir. From here, we ought to be able to hit about five satellites. The device triangulates our position, heading and speed. These little hand-held units don't last very long though. They eat up the batteries pretty quick. I got some back up batteries, just in case."

Spooner began feeding his machine the new batteries while the Captain paced. Blunt took up his position by the starboard hatch and Fleeson lounged just outside on the deck, with the door open, keeping track of events inside. "I've never before been in one of these weather effects," Dudely was rambling, his most recent Camel burning short. "I've heard about them before. I even saw one once from the air on the way to take a new command in Australia, but I've never been in one."

"What do you know about them sir?" Blunt asked. Fleeson noticed the gravy stain was still evident on his right trouser leg.

"No one knows much about it. It never happens anywhere but in this part of the world so no one has paid much attention to it. The fishermen out of Chile and Easter Island call it a Rapanui Storm, Rapanui being the natives' name for Easter Island. They say no one has ever come back from one to tell about it. I can't see why though. The weather's calm enough. It's not like the Bermuda Triangle where the ship drifts away with all crew and passengers vanished. They find boats like that north of the Bahamas sometimes. Around here, when this happens, everything disappears, all crewmembers, boat and passengers, never to be seen or heard of again.

"Captain Cook was the first to report the phenomenon but he didn't see it first hand. The natives warned him about it. There have been some whaleboats and fishermen lost in the area, but I've not read any official reports of them being lost in this kind of thing. It's all rumor and innuendo, word of mouth stuff from other seamen."

"It's ready, sir," said Spooner of the GPS.

"Good," said Dudely, snubbing out his cigarette. "I'd like a report as soon as possible on our position, speed and direction of drift."

"I'll get a more accurate reading if we can step outside, sir," Spooner said.

"By all means," said Dudely.

On the fore deck in front of the wheel house, Spooner hunched over his GPS, a small tan colored plastic device looking like a transistor radio, no bigger than a large hand held business calculator.

"Currents at sea are a funny thing," said Dudely. "They're like huge rivers so vast that the flow can't be distinguished except by instruments. That the ship's pointing northeast doesn't mean we're going in that direction."

"According to the chart," said Blunt, "the predominant currents in this area are northwesterly."

"If they're northwesterly today," said Dudely, "We're headed back toward Fiji, but I just have a feeling something's different today. Other boats lost in these storms haven't washed up in Fiji, or anywhere else that anybody knows of."

"According to this," said Spooner of his GPS, "we're drifting southeast at a speed of about fifteen knots."

"There you have it," said Dudely. "Who would ever think that a boat this size could be drifting sideways at that high a rate of speed. And here's another strange thing about this weather phenomenon. Take a look at the sky in the direction we're traveling, dead ahead, so to speak"

They all turned their eyes toward the starboard sky. "My Gawd. What the..." muttered Blunt.

Spooner stared dumbly at the bronze sky, backlighted by the moon, "It's just a cloud formation. You guys aren't looking for omens in the clouds are you? I mean geez."

"Cloud formations change constantly," said Dudely. "That's been there for hours."

Fleeson watched the face of Inanna staring down at them from high above and far away. Her large eyes seemed intent and very focused. The expression was serene, benign. *Like the innocent, mindless malevolence of a shark or a rattlesnake,* thought Fleeson with a shudder. "It's just clouds," he said coldly.

Chapter 18: The Husband

The rumbling of the volcanoes was becoming more frightening to Johnny. The western peak was glowing brighter than before. *It looks bigger than it did, somehow. Can a mountain swell?* He wondered. *The eastern peak looks bigger too. Well, they said Mount St. Helena swelled up before it exploded, why not this one? Or these two! I hope I'm just imagining this!*

He turned back toward the sea, pushing the thought of the volcanoes out of his mind as much as possible. There was a half moon overhead but the sky to the west and the north was tinted bronze. *Does Inanna really cause that? How is that possible?* He could feel her next to him. Her energy was almost pulsating in its strength.

He turned to watch her profile against the night sky. She was like a painting, impossibly beautiful. Her hair shimmered in the light from the mountains, its light mixing with that of the moon. The breeze in her face off the ocean lifted her hair slightly behind her and ruffled her sarong. Her face was gently lifted toward the sky as though listening to some music only she could hear.

Johnny closed his eyes again, hesitating to join in her meditation. *If I do,* he thought, *what kind of visions will I get this time? Wars? Battles? Passion? Meditating with her in mind can be dangerous.* The rumbling from the mountains was distracting, introducing thoughts he didn't like, couldn't hold back. *If they actually do blow up, we could all be killed. But there's no escape. We can't leave the island. If we did manage to get off on some small boat or other, we'd be swamped by the tidal waves set off by any explosion, and then what? Swim back to the island, if it's even still here afterward, if it's not overflowing with molten lava. Can't swim to Easter Island. Even if the boat doesn't get swamped, we could drift for weeks before sighting land or being found. No ships come down this way. There's no point in thinking about it. If it happens, it happens.*

He finally began to calm down, entering the meditative state, and the visions started. He found himself drifting in the bronze colored sky, next to Inanna. The sea was far below. It made sense to him to seem to be drifting in the sky since their perch was on a high pinnacle overlooking the sea. In a sense, they actually were high in the sky. But had the clouds come lower or had the pinnacle gotten higher?

Clouds were swirling around him forming all manner of amazing shapes. Some looked like Inanna. Some looked like images of other people, people he didn't know. Then he saw it. Lying on the flat sea, there was a large yacht with Jorge and Alphonso, Al and Teri and the Smithsons on board. *This can't be,* he thought. *Those people are already on the island... and Alphonso is dead.* Then he realized he was seeing the past. *How did I know that was Alphonso? Well it must be him.* The vision faded and suddenly far below, he could see a sailing ketch with two people on board. *Chip and Joyce, of course,* he mused. He tried to focus his mind a little closer to the ketch and found himself next to Chip looking up into the clouds with the incredible image of Inanna staring back. Frightened for a moment, he pulled himself away from the image and was again floating in the sky with the bronze clouds swirling around him and Inanna at his side.

Far below he could see a large ship, a passenger liner drifting sideways toward him. *So that's what she's doing,* he thought. *She showed me the capture of the other two vessels and now she's trying to capture a full sized ocean liner! Why does she want so many people here on the island? How will she be able to feed them? What possible use could they be to her?* Then in his mind's eye he could see the Polynesians worshiping the Moon goddess, Heena. He could see Inanna's uplifted face soaking up the praises and adoration as though she were absorbing nourishment. He refocused on the ship. There were many people lining the rails, watching the sea and the sky, fearfully.

There were several uniformed people on the bow in front of the wheelhouse studying an instrument and intermittently glancing and pointing at the sky. He could almost hear their voices, feel the fear and uncertainty they were experiencing. He sensed people below the decks, out of sight, working on the ship's engines, trying to improvise a solution to some problem that he couldn't quite see.

The ocean around the ship was the same as in the other visions, around the other boats. *It's so calm without so much as a ripple from the wind, yet I can feel a wind and there's a current in the sea. It's a strong current, carrying them where? Here, of course. She's bringing them here. But why?* Then the image returned to his mind of the islanders, worshiping the Moon goddess. *Oh yes. She thinks she's going to make them worship her.* He came out of his meditation with a start, feeling anger. *There can no longer be any doubt that Inanna is the source of the evil our people have been struggling with for so long. It has to be her. But wait. Maybe she's a victim of it herself - can't resist it and does these things because of its influence?* He began looking around himself, trying to discern the presence of some other intelligence, some other perverting source causing Inanna to be its instrument. *She can't possibly be that evil!*

The feel of her energy next to him was disconcerting. Her glowing had increased and her focus seemed to have deepened. "You know, you're making a big mistake," he said to her. She either didn't hear him or she was ignoring him. The rumbling of the volcano behind them seemed to have grown slightly in volume. Johnny glanced at it, noticing a thin stream of lava coming down one side of the western peak. "For one thing," he continued, "you really need to be focused on that volcano. If you have the power to do anything about it at all, now is the time. It looks like it just might be preparing for a big display that none of us might survive."

Inanna continued to ignore him, face lifted to the sky, the wind stirring her hair. "Inanna," Johnny raised his voice to get her attention. "Come out of it. Wake up."

"I'm busy," she replied in a low, distracted tone. "Go away."

"I said you're making a big mistake," said Johnny. "You think you're going to capture that ocean liner and have a thousand or more people here to worship you. You're making a big mistake."

Inanna's brow furrowed enough that Johnny knew she could hear him. "There is a new kind of people on the Earth today, not like those primitives you have around here who chant 'Heena, Heena' every time you walk by. Don't you know that, yet? It won't work."

"I don't see why not," she replied without opening her eyes. "The others are quite serviceable."

"But the ones you've captured lately don't worship you. Do they? No. You have to spend more energy making them comply with your demands than they produce for you. Am I right?"

"They'll come around," she said. "They just need to see some more spectacles and they'll be on their knees with the rest of the crowd. You'll see."

"And if you're wrong?" he asked. "If you're wrong you could have a full fledged revolt on your hands. Are you equipped to handle an organized assault? There must be a thousand people on that boat. Can you handle that many?"

"There are one thousand three hundred forty three people. Yes. I can handle them," she said.

"To what end?" he asked sarcastically. "Even if you do manage to get all these people singing your evening hymn, why are you doing this? How can you in good conscience steal the lives of all these people? How can you even live with yourself after stealing the lives of the few you already have here? Why are you doing this?"

Inanna lowered her face and opened her eyes. Johnny could see that she was growing impatient. She turned to look at him and said, "With the people I already have, I lack the power to leave the island. With more worshipers, I will be able to rule a wider area."

Johnny was as surprised that she had answered so civilly as he was by the answer she gave him. *So, she does gather power from the worshipers. What kind of being is this who can do that?* "So it's about power, then?" he asked.

"Yes," she answered him. "It's about power."

"Why is power so important?" he asked. "Look at what you have here. What about peace of mind? What about love? Those things are more important than power. And you can't have peace of mind or any kind of peace in your life, while you're trampling on people. Peace of mind begins with self respect and self acceptance, and respect for the humanity of others."

"Power is everything," she said simply. "I don't need to accept myself. I am what I am. It is for others to accept me, as you have. Peace of mind is absolute power."

"I accepted Inanna, a woman, not Inanna some sort of freak goddess image. Be the woman. Forget about this power obsession. It's meaningless. It has no purpose. Let those people on that ship go their own way."

"Few who have spoken so harshly to me have survived it," Inanna snapped. "How do you dare to talk to me this way?"

"Should friends not be open and honest with one another? Would you have me conceal my thoughts from you as so many of the others do? Do you expect me to become just another slave? I am not a slave."

"You speak of peace of mind," she said. "There was a time. I suppose the peace I felt then is what you speak of. Power is exhilarating. It became more important to me than that simple happiness of my childhood.

"You say I'm trampling on the lives of these people," she continued. "They are a slave race. They serve no purpose, except to work in my gardens and carry out my wars. Their purpose is to die in my service."

Johnny was stunned with the callousness of her statement. *If ego were food, you would never need to eat,* he thought. "Don't you know that every living thing, the least snail or fiddler crab on the beach has as much right to its life and freedom as you have. You are just another life form, nothing more, nothing less." He hadn't meant to raise his voice again, but he was carried away with the momentum of the argument. "You live among many other life forms. You should find a way to peacefully exist side by side with them, instead of using all others for your own selfish needs and desires."

Inanna was growing angry. "Go away DeMuzzi. Can't you see I am busy? Go to the palace and wait for me. Sleep there. I'll join you soon."

In frustration, Johnny rose from his seat beside Inanna and headed back down the path toward the palace complex. *So how does the fence, Hjet, get between Inanna's good side and her evil side - her domineering side? How can I get her to see that what she's doing to the people around her is an abomination?*

The night remained quiet except for the sounds from the volcano. No night birds cheered the darkness. When he arrived back at the gardens, no one was in sight. He could see in the distance that the ballroom was dimly lighted. *There must be someone in there tending to the torches, waiting for Inanna to come back,* he thought.

Nearby he heard voices chanting Mawkee, Mawkee. The sounds drew his attention to half a dozen Polynesians kneeling, facing him, on the porch to the ballroom. *I wish they would stop that,* he thought. *Can't they see I'm nothing more than they are, just a man.* As he continued toward the buildings, the chanting gathered momentum and volume. *Strange,* he thought as he climbed the few steps to the ballroom porch. *When I passed them, they didn't turn to keep facing me.*

Without another thought, he entered the large room, slightly aware that he contained much of the energy he had soaked up when sitting on the throne of Lapis Lazuli. *Maybe that's why they're chanting at me like that. I'm probably still glowing a little bit, something like Inanna does.* He continued into the room, taking a seat at one of the tables. Al, Chip and Smithson were gone, *probably to their quarters,* he thought. He took a piece of untouched fruit and began munching on it. Something feels different in here. Is it a smell in the air? A change of temperature? The energy feels different somehow.

Still munching the piece of fruit he climbed the dais and seated himself again on the blue throne. The energy was as powerful as ever. He could feel it flowing into him. *I don't care if she gets angry about this,* he thought. *What will she do about it? Besides this feels kind of good. It's raw power.* Then the sobering thoughts began to flow. *Power corrupts. Look at what it has done to Inanna. That must be the source of the evil affecting her. It's the corrupting influence of power. Power just wants more power, endlessly. It's an addiction, like cocaine. It's a perversion of the soul, an influence that over rides every other instinct, every other impulse and urge. THIS is what drives her. It has to be the answer. I must go back and tell the others.*

He dropped the remainder of the fruit he had been eating, feeling guilty for eating an extra meal and rose to his feet with the intention of leaving. The chanting outside had grown louder, as though more voices had joined the chorus. The sounds of Mawkee, Mawkee were now mixed with Heena, Heena. *What is going on?* He wondered. *There seems to be some sort of light outside. I wonder if Inanna is back already.* He walked to the main entrance, stepped outside, and froze in stunned amazement and dismay.

It seemed that all the islanders had returned from the pinnacle where they had been waiting with Inanna. Chip, Joyce and their friends were outside at their lawn chairs and table. The spears and other weapons were still stacked by the ballroom door and the volcano was still rumbling in the background. Inanna had indeed returned. She was standing at the foot of the pier at the other end of the grounds with her back to him, gazing out to sea, and she was glowing a bright magenta. Inanna was in full form, nearly twelve feet tall. Beside her stood an even taller male figure clothed in what Johnny had to admit to himself looked a bit like a toga. This new companion was also glowing, but his color was green.

When Johnny finished reacting, he walked over to Chip and their group. "So who's the new guy?" he asked. "The Jolly Green Giant? What's going on?"

Big Al was the first to respond. "I don't know for sure who he is, but one thing I can say for sure is that she calls him DuMuzzi and I think y'all best make yourself as scarce as you can."

"Take a good look at that ole boy," said Teri. "He looks like you, De-Muzzi - spittin' image. I think she thinks he's y'all."

Johnny stepped back into the shadows, toward the door of Chip and Joyce's quarters. "I can't get to the path without them seeing me," he said softly. "I don't think I can find my way through the building to the other exit without help. I think I'll just stay out of sight here till they go inside." *How many of them are there?* Johnny asked himself. *Lee Moy said in the mythology of ancient Sumer that DuMuzzi was the husband of Inanna. He said that DuMuzzi comes to her in the spring. This is spring. Maybe she does think he's me, that I am her husband. But she knows I'm from the other side of the island. How could she make such a mistake? Good grief. How could I? Look at the size of that guy and if he has the power that she has, there could be some real trouble brewing. With the two of them working together, they can probably handle the people on that ocean liner without any problem.*

He watched the two at the foot of the pier, holding hands, like lovers, watching the moon setting. They looked like any two people, anywhere, except for their clothing and for the fact that their sizes dwarfed the pier and those islanders who were nearby chanting their mantras of "Heena, Heena," and "Mawkee, Mawkee." As Johnny watched, the two kissed. Turning toward the ballroom, they began to walk slowly through the garden area toward the building complex. As they drew nearer, Johnny stepped out of sight into the room behind him and waited for them to pass inside. When they were gone, Chip whispered through the door to let him know, but he still waited, hoping to give them a chance to move completely through the large dining area and toward Inanna's private rooms. Still, the chanting continued.

Most of the worshipers followed the two inside the ballroom and out of sight. As soon as they were gone, Johnny headed for the path at the other end of the grounds. His trip back to the monastery seemed to pass in moments. He was relieved to see that the new lava flow had not yet reached the sea, blocking his path back to his brothers. Climbing the terraces, back on the eastern side of the island, he was dismayed to see that the shimmering barrier had turned green and was pressing closer than ever before, but that wasn't the least of the surprises in store for him.

He paused on the top terrace, before entering the porch, aware that the energy he had soaked up from Inanna's throne was still with him. He slowly entered a meditative state and focused his energy on the shimmering barrier, now encompassing both peaks. When he felt that he was ready, he released the stored up energy he had from Inanna's throne, in an attempt to change the energy in the aura encompassing the large area. He could feel the sudden release of the power. As he released it, he opened his eyes to watch the change, but instead of a change, he saw a face appear at the edge of the barrier, glaring down at him. It was his own face. In shocked realization of what he had just done, he dived for the cover of the porch just in time to miss the blast of green energy shooting from the barrier to the spot where he had been standing.

Due to the late hour of the night, no one was outside to see what had just happened, but the clap of thunder which accompanied the green bolt was loud enough to rouse more than a few. Among them were Lee Moy and Cardac, both looking concerned and worried. When they saw him they hurried up to him and with a number of others surrounded him with expressions of concern and something that surprised and disappointed Johnny. It was suspicion.

"Look who is back with the change of the energy," said one. "He's no doubt the cause of it."

"We were nearly overwhelmed, just a few minutes ago," said another. "I was monitoring the meditation. It was incredible."

"We thought it was all over this afternoon," said yet another. "There's a new Rapanui Storm started to the northwest. It's the most powerful one we've seen since we've been here."

"All these changes did start when you arrived," said Cardac matter-of-factly. "What do you have to say for yourself, DeMuzzi?"

I don't know why you guys are getting so alarmed," said Johnny. "I haven't done anything wrong." Then after a short pause he said, "Well, I did eat too much. There was so much fruit over there."

"What else did you do? What did you do that upset the balance?" asked Cardac.

"Balance?" asked Johnny. "Look at those volcanoes and tell me there's balance. If they keep growing like that, we won't have to worry about Inanna anymore. Nothing will be here, including her."

"The volcanoes didn't become active till you got here," said Lee Moy thoughtfully. "Something has evidently upset some sort of balance, but I don't think DeMuzzi has what it takes to set a volcano to erupting. Do you?" He addressed the question to the group in general.

"He's been up to something over there. He's the only one of us who ever went there who has come back in one piece," answered one of the men.

"Or come back to us in any pieces at all, for that matter," added another. "The brothers who ventured to the western end of the island have never been heard of again. How is it that you alone can come and go as you please?"

"It would appear," said Johnny thoughtfully, "That I have some sort of protection, or at least I had some protection. I don't know about what's up now. The Jolly Green Giant has arrived and I fled for my life."

"Jolly green what?" asked Lucias who had just arrived on the scene.

"Well, there's this giant green guy who showed up this evening," said Johnny. "I'm serious. He glows green and he looks just like me except that he's huge."

"The aura did change to a greenish tone," said Lee Moy. "This could be the reason. Did you manage to get his name?"

"The others said she called him DuMuzzi. It sounds like my name but it's a little different," answered Johnny. "He just snuggled up to her like they were old lovers or something like that."

"Well it is spring," said Lee Moy. "Perhaps your little flirtation has brought on the jealous husband?"

"Maybe," answered Johnny. "I think she may have thought me to be him. That could be the reason she was so friendly to me at first."

"At first?!!" several blurted at once. "You can still come and go as you please. How did you get away if the jealous husband is on hand? Why didn't he kill you?"

"Well," said Johnny. "I think he just tried to do that. Did you see the bolt of green lightning I just dodged?"

"I did see a green flash," said Cardac, but I didn't see what it was."

"He just missed me," said Johnny emphatically. "I barely anticipated his move in time and ducked under the porch roof here."

The rumbling of the volcano appeared to be increasing in tempo, but there was a strange nuance to it, a rhythm it had lacked before. Johnny stepped out from under the porch roof to look up at the nearest one, but ducked back just in time again. Another green bolt narrowly missed him. The thudding was growing louder.

Lucias called for silence. "I was in meditation when DeMuzzi came back to us just now. In my meditation, I was in communication with the ascended brotherhood who instructed me to confine DeMuzzi to his cell. Although this is not consistent with the practices of our order, I agreed with their reasons and in obedience to their request I must insist that DeMuzzi go to his cell now and remain there until he is summoned."

"I'll stand watch to make sure he stays there," said one of the brothers, one Jacob. "We don't want him running back and forth like he's been doing."

"I'll stand the morning watch," added another. "I agree with Brother Jacob. There'll be others from the present meditation shift who will volunteer their spare time for the afternoon watch."

"So am I going to be a prisoner then?" asked Johnny in stunned amazement.

The thudding was growing louder. Suddenly a huge green figure came out of the forest at the bottom of the path to the sea, the earth vibrating with his footsteps. It was the creature Johnny had seen with Inanna, but Inanna was not present. "Where is the imposter?" it thundered. "Bring him before me."

Those gathered with Johnny fled inside, crowding the corridors leading toward the meadow in the rear of the complex. The flight was in silence, as though every one feared that the creature pursuing them would be able to follow by the sound of voices.

As the flow of the crowding brotherhood carried Johnny right past his own cell, he dropped off to remain there. *Better to be here and in meditation, than fleeing like a rabbit before the hounds,* he thought. *Besides, if Inanna can't hurt me maybe he can't either.*

The thudding of DuMuzzi's footsteps grew louder then stopped. The sound was replaced by that of falling rocks and shattering wood. *My God! I guess he's too big to come inside so he's tearing the building down. I wonder how far he'll come before he gives up.* The sound of crushing rocks came closer as Johnny waited. Then it stopped suddenly.

Chapter 19: Inanna Giveth and Inanna Taketh Away; Blessed Be the Name of Inanna

First light stirred Johnny's sleep. The sun was approaching but on this morning, there was no ceremony opening the day. The silence was as disconcerting as DuMuzzi's attempt the night before to tear the building down to find him. *What's outside?* The thought forced his eyes open. *Where is he?* Through the window of his cell, he could see that the terrace itself had not been disturbed. Looking to the left, he shuddered. Most of the face of the building complex had been torn off exposing the rooms the outer walls once sheltered. As he surveyed the damage of the night before, a new awareness gradually settled into his mind, that no one was in sight. The gardeners who would normally be approaching their daily tasks were not there. No one was meditating on the porch. Then he heard footsteps approaching from the corridor.

Johnny drew away from the window, stepping back into the shadows of his cell to wait and listen. He could tell that the feet making the sounds he heard were wearing sandals. He breathed a sigh of relief, then thought, *but I don't know what DuMuzzi was wearing on his feet. It couldn't be him. He's too big to be walking down our corridors. He'd barely fit under Inanna's tall ceilings.* The sounds drew nearer. Finally they paused just outside of Johnny's cell and a figure appeared in his doorway. It was Cardac.

"He's here," Cardac said to unseen others.

Then Tarek appeared, looking shaken and tired. Behind him were Lee Moy and Lucias. Lee Moy was the only one of them who appeared to have not completely lost his composure. He was wearing a full robe with a hood pulled over his head like a monk. "He's right outside, you know," said Lee Moy in a whisper. "He failed to find you last night so he's waiting you out. We must keep our voices down."

"Come," said Lucias. "We need to get to a safer place than this. He might hear us through that window or worse yet, peek in the window and see us. Come."

Johnny followed the group through the winding corridors enlarged from lava vents. The island had many such tunnels and caves. These had been made good use of in the construction of the monastery, but where they led, Johnny had no idea. His sense was that they were going deeper and deeper into the mountain.

"What's the volcano doing?" Johnny asked. "If it's still building toward an eruption, couldn't these vents be filled with lava again?" He realized he had not heard any rumbling yet this morning, but that meant nothing to him.

"It's still smoking from both peaks," answered Tarek. "But the lava flow that started last night seems to have stopped. Some of the brothers say they think the mountain is showing some swelling. If that's the case, there's the danger of a major explosion, but we have no where to flee to, so if it blows, we'll all be killed in any case. There's no point in worrying about that with the eminent threat of the giant at our door."

"He seems to have calmed down a bit from last night, "Lucias volunteered. "But that's no guarantee, that he won't become enraged again as soon as he sees you. What happened over there?"

As they walked, Johnny explained what he knew of the situation from the other side of the island, how he met DuMuzzi and the subsequent events. They had arrived at an interior cell fitted out with a cot, a chair, a low table and a dim torch. There was no window and only one entrance. The walls were cut from the native volcanic rock. Lucias sat down on the cot while the others took seats on the mat covered stone floor. "This is a dismal cell," Johnny remarked.

"Dismal it is," said Cardac. "This is where you are going to have to stay for the time being. What's left of the fraternity is fearful that you have been converted to the other side and that you are a clear and present danger to us. In fact, as soon as we can get enough men and materials together, we intend to wall you in here for the time being, until you've had a chance to clear your mind and settle in as one of us."

I'm going to be a prisoner? thought Johnny. "Since when does the fraternity imprison its brothers?" asked Johnny. "Isn't this a bit extreme?"

Lucias sighed deeply and answered in a troubled tone. "You have no idea what happened here last night, do you? You dropped into your cell and went to sleep, didn't you? How you could sleep with all the noise and devastation is another question altogether."

"I didn't sleep until things quieted down," answered Johnny. "I went into meditation. There didn't seem to be much point in trying to flee. There's no way I could out run that guy. Hiding seemed to be the most sensible option."

"I wish the others had done the same," said Lucias.

"Nearly half of our people are now imprisoned on the western side of the island," said Cardac. "Many who were not taken were killed and horribly. Have you seen how those creatures kill?"

"No, but I've heard about it," Johnny answered.

"There is barely anything left but the dried, withered shell," said Lee Moy thoughtfully. "And as he did it, it seemed that he drew sustenance from the victim, as though he took the life force to himself. You know," Lee Moy continued. "This is much along the lines of our own philosophy in which we believe it is the life within the food which nourishes us, rather than the minerals, carbohydrates, proteins et cetera. So we eat only living food; fresh vegetables, uncooked nuts, sprouts and so forth, only in this case, they take the life force directly from other creatures, other animals, not just plants."

"An interesting theory," said Lucias. "For the present, knowing that doesn't help us. We know that we are food to them. That tells us that we had best avoid them at all costs."

"But they can feed without killing," said Johnny. He then explained the song of worship he had seen the islanders sing to Inanna several times and her reaction.

"All this sounds ludicrous to me," said Cardac. "No creature can nourish itself from worship of such a nature."

"It may not be so far fetched as it sounds," said Lee Moy. "We know that love is a form of nourishment. People who live in a loving environment live much longer than those who do not. Even our own species benefits from this type of nourishment. The worship offered by the primitive islanders is a form of love given willingly and it may well be nourishing to Inanna and her kind, but what of this forceful stealing of a life? How could that be nourishing? It would seem more likely to poison the thief."

"Maybe that's why we sense the presence of Inanna as evil," said Johnny. "She has taken some lives in this way herself, according to the people I met over there."

"Can these creatures be reasoned with?" asked Lucias.

"Trying to reason with them," said Cardac, "seems like the sheep trying to reason with the meat seller who has sold the sheep's flesh. Would the meat seller listen to the pleas of the sheep? I think not."

"There are those among even our own species," said Lee Moy, "who object to taking the lives of animals for food, saying that the animals have the same right to life as do we. If our own species can make that leap of logic, perhaps this other intelligent species who seems superior to us in some ways can also make that leap."

"But how do we get them to do that?" demanded Cardac. "I think it's time to beat our plowshares into swords and plan to defend ourselves."

"That would be impossible," said Johnny. "Inanna can kill with a gesture. Apparently her new friend can too. I think we need to just avoid them."

"We can't do that, just now, unfortunately," said Lucias. "They have taken many of our people. We need to rescue them if that's possible. In the mean time, this DuMuzzi is still at our gates waiting for you to appear."

"Maybe I should face him," said Johnny. "Running and hiding has only got a lot of people killed and harmed. Maybe if I turn myself over to him, he'll let the others go."

"I think it's unlikely," said Lucias. "I think it's more likely that the result of your facing him would be your death."

"Inanna has tried to kill me several times," said Johnny, "without success. I may be able to survive his attacks too, unless he wants to get physical and actually kill me in some conventional way. I think I can probably withstand his energy. Let me try."

"It is better for the time being," said Lucias, "that you remain here. Meditate. Try to find your center. Just for a few days, while we study the matter. Cardac will remain for now and make sure you stay in this cell."

"As you wish," said Johnny. "Has Inanna's aura filled our side of the island or is the barrier still between the two peeks? I didn't get a chance to take a look at it this morning."

"The aura covers the entire island," said Lee Moy. "We have been completely overrun. This has happened before. We will eventually be able to take back our territory but the cost of doing so has been high in the past and will no doubt be again."

"If you look carefully, you can see the tint of green over everything," said Tarek. "It's not the usual blue, red or magenta we've been seeing in the barrier. It looks like his color - green. Where did he come from anyway? He hasn't been there all along has he?"

"I haven't seen him before last night," answered Johnny. "I don't know where he came from. He was just suddenly there."

"The myth says that DuMuzzi comes to rescue Inanna from the underworld in the spring," said Lee Moy. "Apparently that is exactly what he has done."

"If that's so," asked Lucias. "Where was he last spring and the spring before that? This is the first we've seen of this green aura since I've been on the island and that's been quite a few years."

"True, true," said Lee Moy. "I'm certainly no expert in the mythology of Sumer, but I could offer this question in answer. When exactly is their spring? We don't know where they're from. All we know for sure is that they are not human in any sense of the word with which we are familiar."

"Oh great," said Johnny. "Now you're talking about little green men."

"No," said Lee Moy, seriously. "We are talking about very big green men."

CB ƎO

Chip was stretched out on his sleeping mat under a light blanket with Joyce lying beside him. He still felt quite weak from Inanna's attack of the night before. It was first light. He had heard no unusual sounds after DuMuzzi left in pursuit of his miniature look-alike, De-Muzzi, the monk from the eastern end of the island. *What a bizarre situation,* he thought. *Had Inanna really confused the one with the other? How could she have done that? I mean, it's not as though there aren't some major differences.*

Joyce could see that he had awakened and brought him a cup of hot tea Teri Johns had been brewing. Sitting up and sipping his tea, he could see through the open door and window of their sleeping quarters. The Polynesian gardeners were hard at work in their fields again, and this time, instead of making spears and knives out of seashells, they were actually tending to the crops. There had been some rain during the night. Everything was still wet out of doors.

"Where is Inanna?" Chip asked Joyce. "And where is the new guy?"

"When I went for the tea," she said, "I saw Inanna on the pier staring out to sea. There's a new spec on the horizon. It looks like she's capturing another boat."

"You'd think she'd had about enough of that. The last ones she captured haven't been exactly cooperative, now have they."

"I suppose you mean us," Joyce replied. "If you and the others don't stop challenging her like you did last night, you're going to get yourselves killed. "Just cooperate with her. She doesn't ask for much."

"Not much," said Chip. "She wants us to pretend we think she's some sort of god and she wants us to worship her like a god. She's nuts. I mean - I've never been particularly religious, but I believe in God and she is not Him. Neither is the other one. I can't give her what she wants."

"You're putting it mildly," chuckled Joyce. "Teri and Al are Southern Baptists. I won't repeat what they said about her. I don't think they're going to cooperate with her either. Neither are the Smithsons. They're Anglicans."

"Sounds like she needs to capture some more Polynesians. She seems to fit right into their old religion. They even have traditional names for her and her new boyfriend."

A disturbance outside drew Joyce and Chip to the window. In the distance at the edge of the forest, Chip could see a line of strangers emerging at spear point, each with one or two Polynesian guards. "Who do you suppose they are?" asked Joyce.

Chip watched in silence, for a moment as more and more people came into view. Some were dressed in monks' robes, while others were in blue jeans and other types of work clothes. Most of them were bearded. All of them looked wild eyed and unhappy. "It looks like Inanna raided the monastery," said Chip. "I don't know where else they could have gotten all those guys. I don't think the new boat Inanna has coming in has arrived yet, so I don't think they're coming from there. Besides, some of them actually look like monks. Do you see DeMuzzi with them?"

"No," said Joyce. "As mad as the Jolly Green Giant was last night, I doubt that our DeMuzzi is still alive."

"I think he probably is," said Chip. "He struck me as being pretty resourceful."

"I think you're right," said Joyce. "I don't think Inanna would let her new friend kill her pet, either. She treats him like a pet. Don't you think?"

"Good way to put it," said Chip with a chuckle. "I wonder what Inanna's planning to do with all those new guys."

"I'm sure," said Joyce, "that she plans the same thing for them that she planned for us. She thinks she has a whole new set of worshippers."

"She may be in for another rude awakening," said Chip. "I don't think she'll be able to convert those monks so easily as she did the islanders."

"In that case," said Joyce, "I guess we'll have to be digging a number of graves later today."

"Maybe not, if we can get to them in time and explain the situation. They can probably pay lip service to her like we do until something turns up to get us out of here."

"I'm beginning to appreciate how the Jews felt during the Spanish Renaissance," said Joyce. "If we don't pay convincing enough lip service we could get fried like Alphonso. At least she doesn't burn us at the stake like the Spanish would have done."

"Don't give her any ideas," said Chip. "Before you know it she'll have those Polynesians building a wrack she can use for torture."

The captives from the monastery were being lined up at the foot of the pier, waiting for Inanna to turn her attention away from the sea for long enough to tell the islanders what she wanted done. Finally, she turned and looked at each one of them, slowly in turn. Then without a word, she walked past them toward the main building. The islanders followed her, leading their captives in tow. When she reached the porch to the ballroom, she climbed the few steps and turned to face them again. The islanders lined up the prisoners at the foot of the steps.

"There must be twenty five or thirty of them," said Chip.

"All ages," added Joyce.

Inanna was now close enough that when she raised her voice for the prisoners to be able to all hear her, Chip and Joyce could also hear. "Kneel to me," they heard her say.

None of them did. Inanna repeated her command, but the men stood around staring at her in amazement without comprehending their danger. One of the men began reciting the twenty-third Psalm and after the first few words, the rest of them joined in. It was an act of defiance worthy of Daniel in the Lion's Den. But they weren't as protected as Daniel. Inanna flew into a rage, exploded to her twelve-foot tall image of power and struck the man down who had started the Psalm. Her bolt of blue lightning was blinding in its intensity even in the full light of day. The man dropped like a rock, instantly withered.

Another man started singing at the top of his voice. It was the hymn by Martin Luther and in German. "Ein feste Burg ist unser Gott, ein gute Wehr und Waffen." The look in the man's eyes was pure, confident defiance. Several others joined in at the top of their voices, looking Inanna straight in the eye. "Er hilft uns frei aus aller Not, die uns jetzt hat befroffen." The words and tune were so stirring that if Chip had known the hymn in German he would have joined them and almost did so in English but Joyce stopped him. Inanna was growing in fury, tempered only by astonishment at their bravado. "Der alt boese Feind, mit Ernst ers jetzt meint..."

Inanna couldn't contain herself another moment. With another blinding flash of blue light, twelve more men dropped dead and the singing stopped. The islanders had dropped to their knees and were chanting, "Heena, Heena." The gardeners who had been working among the crops had also stopped working and joined in the chanting. The remaining dozen men from the monastery, seated themselves on the ground, not in kneeling positions, but cross legged, palms up and began their own silent meditation. Within moments, Chip could see a protective bubble form around them, shimmering with blue light. Inanna watched in amazement as these few monks who remained alive continued to defy her.

Chip watched in horror as she raised her hands, expecting to see the remaining twelve men fried to a crisp as were the others. The bodies of the dead men were lying where they fell, scattered among those meditating. Just as Chip thought she was about to unleash her horrors on the remaining men, as one, they uttered a most ancient name for the One God, "Om." Chip could feel the resonance of their voices vibrating in his own chest. As they uttered this one syllable, Inanna drew back for a moment, then in anger strode right down into their midst and started kicking them over. Once their concentration was broken, she continued with her bolts of blue lightning until not one of them remained animate.

Chip and Joyce were frozen in horror watching this wholesale slaughter of their fellow human beings. Then something happened which totally amazed them even beyond the stunned disbelief they felt at watching this scene of death. Inanna sat down on the top step, dropped her face into her hands and began sobbing, angrily. Gradually her sobbing subsided and she began to glare at the corpses of the men she had just slain. Then she arose with resolve in her eyes and approached them. Stopping at the nearest of the dead men, she raised her arms, aiming her palms at him. Light, bright enough to be seen in the dazzling sunlight emanated from them.

Chip and Joyce watched in amazement as the withered corpse began to change. Before their very eyes, the skin smoothed and finally the eyes regained the appearance of animation. The man then struggled to sit up, rubbing his eyes. When he did this, Inanna moved on to the next closest man. When she had re-animated all of them, she turned toward the path to the beach and disappeared into the forest, head down and sullen.

03 80

Johnny's stay in his new cell was growing as tedious as any imprisonment. *I can't meditate all the time,* he thought. *It's too dark in here to do any reading, if there was even anything to read. My guards haven't been all that good at conversation; those few that can speak English. Every kind of person is here it seems. There are Europeans, Africans, Middle Easterners, men from every country, just about. Thank God most of them can speak English.* He exercised out of boredom. Pushups. Sit-ups. Anything to get his mind off of the confinement. Finally, Lucias came back to talk with him. He looked like he hadn't slept or changed clothes in days.

"How long have I been in here?" Johnny asked before Lucias could say a word to him.

"A little over three days," answered Lucias.

"Don't you think this is a little excessive? I'm really not enjoying this experience at all," Johnny stated.

"You're going to enjoy what I have to tell you even less," said Lucias, grimly.

"Now what?" asked Johnny.

"The brotherhood has decided to keep you here indefinitely."

"You're kidding," said Johnny. "How can they do that? I'd rather take my chances trying to swim back to Easter Island than sit here much longer."

"The brothers feel that you're the cause of the problems we've had here in the last few days and they're afraid to turn you loose. They think you'll go back to the other side and bring more hell and mayhem on us than before. I argued in your favor as did Lee Moy and several others, but you know the majority rules among us."

"I haven't done anything wrong," said Johnny vehemently. "I don't deserve to be imprisoned in this cave."

"No one deserves to imprisoned in a cave," said Lucias. "I think they'll relent if you can become accustomed to a meditative life style and quit going over there."

"I have to go over there," said Johnny. "That's the reason I'm on Arrata. I have to try to reason with her."

"It's not just her anymore," said Lucias. "The other person is there now. I believe you called him DuMuzzi? Because of his presence, many of our people have been captured. We believe them to be dead."

"How many?" asked Johnny.

"Twenty eight were killed the first night he showed up here. He captured a little over two dozen more with the help of those islanders and they were shepherded off to the western side of the island. I doubt we'll ever learn of their fate. We don't know yet exactly how many of our brothers are missing, but it seems to be in the neighborhood of about sixty."

"You're saying I'm responsible for sixty deaths?" Asked Johnny.

"Are you beginning to understand why the remaining brothers want to keep you locked up?"

"I guess so," answered Johnny.

Chapter 20: Innuendoes

Solitude can be either healing or damaging for the psyche, thought Johnny. *It's my choice. I can either focus on the good or on the negative of this confinement. If I focus on the negative, I could completely lose my mind, eventually. On the other hand, if I focus on healing and spiritual growth, it could result in my ascension and ultimate freedom. It's all a matter of how I want to interpret this experience. It's all a matter of my attitude toward the experience and toward myself.*

He could hear renewed sounds from deep inside the earth, the volcano. If he listened very carefully, he thought he could even feel the vibrations of the earth as the rumbling took place. *Are there shifting plates down there?* He tried to spiritually project himself inside the mountain to try to see what was going on. *As if I'd understand it if I could see it,* he thought. After waking, he noticed fresh dust on the floor of the cell. *I wonder if this ceiling is going to cave in on me.*

Cardac was back at the door to the cell, but he wasn't interested in talking. His daily meal was delivered by Tarek, the next day by Caleb. Today, Cardac brought it himself. It consisted of sprouted beans, nuts and several leafy vegetables. *What I wouldn't give for some Kentucky Fried Chicken right now!* He thought. Then, *Wow. Where did that thought come from? I haven't eaten the flesh of another creature in, - how long? Seven years? It must be the boredom of sitting in here. Sensual deprivation can be very clarifying. Do I really want to eat some KFC? YES,* he answered himself. *Okay, while I'm dreaming, how about some filet mignon? YES, or a prime rib, two inches thick, with a baked potato and tossed salad with blue cheese dressing no less. And why not a nice cold beer as well? And while I'm dreaming, how about some nice company to go along with it?*

That thought sobered him up suddenly because the image of Inanna seated beside him on the pinnacle came instantly to mind. *What a beautiful woman she is. What ever else she is, she's that. How I wanted to touch her hair that night. My hand seemed to have a life of its own and I had to struggle to hold it back. God, the contour of her face seemed to reach out to me begging for a kiss, a touch, a caress. When we first met, the feel of her skin nearly drove me wild, and the sense of vulnerability about her made me want to hold her, protect her, love her.*

Okay! Get a hold of yourself, boy. You've left all that behind. There will be no more women for you and certainly no Inanna. She belongs to the Jolly Green Giant - DuMuzzi. He could kill me with the frown across his brow, and would have if he had found me the other night. There will be no Inanna for me. No woman. No love.

He found himself sinking again and caught his attitude change remembering the litany he had written on his heart for this experience. *If I focus on healing and on spiritual growth, this solitude could result in my ascension and ultimate freedom. It's all a matter of how I want to interpret this experience. It's a matter of my attitude toward the experience and toward myself. I need to forget about those things of the flesh that I left behind when I joined the Fraternity and became a Nazareian, of Ha Agudoss.*

The elevated volume of the rumbling in the ground seemed to answer his attitude adjustment. He seated himself comfortably on the cot, closed his eyes and allowed himself to sink into meditation. The first image that came to his mind was the sight of Inanna seated next to him on the Pinnacle, silhouetted against the sky. He allowed the vision to remain; loving it, giving it the pent up emotion of seven years, admiring the magic of the feelings it inspired in him. In his mind's eye, the face of Inanna turned toward him with her eyes open, wide and dark. Her lips turned slightly toward a smile then they surprised him by opening. "Where are you?" she asked.

The question was disconcerting for Johnny. The contrast of his stark captivity in a stone hole in the mountainside with Inanna's luxurious lips and haunting eyes broke his concentration. The mental image of his cell, dim torch and cot flashed through his mind before he could stop it. *Oh my God. Have I just told her where I am?* He thought. *Now what's going to happen? Will she tell the green guy? I need to focus away from her as much as possible. I keep forgetting she can tune in to me when I think about her.*

He closed his eyes again, trying to sink back into meditation, this time deliberately calling to consciousness the image of a seagull floating through a blue sky, a Lapis Lazuli sky, wheeling and turning through his mind, higher and higher, then suddenly to the sea's surface catching a fish. The bird climbed again, circling. Was there a school of fish below that it was stalking? If it climbed high enough, would the fish not see his return? Then without warning, the seagull folded its wings and dived again, spreading them out again just before it struck the surface. It skimmed the waves, grabbed another small fish and began the climb, again.

As the gull wheeled through the cloudless heavens, the sky began to change color, subtly at first, then more quickly. It changed from lazure to bronze. Johnny didn't notice the change until the blue had completely vanished. *Hey, he thought. This is my meditation. No Rapanui Storms in my meditation.* In his mind's eye, he changed the color of the sky back to blue. Pushing the thoughts of Inanna out of his mind, again, he focused on the imaginary seagull wheeling in the sky, but the blue deepened again and gradually turned back to the metallic color. Before he realized what had happened, he saw Inanna's eyes peering down at him from the swirling clouds of the bronze sky and again heard her voice. This time it was more demanding, more urgent.

"Where are you, Profligate?"

He snapped out of meditation to again find himself in the dimly lighted stone cell with Cardac dozing at the door. *Why can't I meditate without my thoughts turning to Inanna? Does she have such a hold on me that I can't get her out of my mind? I don't think I could be in love with such a dangerous woman. But then, isn't it danger that draws us as men? I don't think so. She isn't even a real woman, but my oh my, how I do tend to return to her in my heart.*

The rumbling of the earth had a new quality, a new timbre somehow. Johnny cocked his head to listen to it. It was more like a crashing than a rumbling sound. It seemed distant enough, but there seemed to be a new urgency in the air. Johnny sat back on his cot waiting. *What's going to happen? What's happening?*

One of the brothers came running down the corridor. Cardac had already been awakened by the new sounds so he was not surprised when Broesseus appeared, out of breath. He was still wearing the same sleeveless wool jerkin as when Johnny had seen him before in the meeting room.

"The witch has over-run us again," he said heavily. "She's smashing what's left of the building, looking for DeMuzzi. I think if we don't hand him over she's going to kill all of us till she finds him."

Cardac shot a disgusted look in Johnny's direction. Rising from his seat, he said, "Come on lover boy. It's time for you to play sacrificial lamb."

Johnny was on his feet when Broesseus showed up. After hearing what the man had to say, Johnny was at the door and ready to go. *Where are you?* He could still hear Inanna's voice in his mind. *Where are you?*

Broesseus hurried him through the labyrinth of corridors with Cardac close behind. They seemed darker than before. As that thought occurred to him, he realized that there were no torches lighted in the tunnels this time. *Is it day or night?* He wondered. *How long have I been penned up in that hole? Is it Inanna or the green man who's smashing things - looking for me?*

He felt at his throat to make sure the obelisk of Lapis Lazuli was still present, still hanging around his neck. *If this is what protected me before, I need to make sure it's still there,* he thought. *But what protected me when I took it off to show it to her? As soon as I had it off, she struck me with the lightning bolts she likes to throw around. Geez. She's like the old stories of Zeus casting lightning bolts.* Then his thoughts stopped in shock at what he had just told himself. *Zeus? The King of the Greek Pantheon - the head god, son of Chronos - Time. Lightning bolts were supposed to be his favorite weapon. Of course, that's just mythology - or is it? Inanna's favorite weapon is a lightning bolt too - blue ones, like her throne. I can't deny that Inanna's lightning bolts are real. No mythology there. How does she do it? When I've been with her, lightning bolts jump off of me too!! Well, more like sparks than bolts, but I'm a human. I'm not like her. I can't soak up the juice like she can.*

It appeared to be late afternoon. The sky was as blue as in his vision of it. They had arrived at what had once been the main entrance to the building complex. It was gone. The buildings on the top terrace had been mostly leveled. The roof over the patio was shattered and lying in pieces all over the terrace. The room above it was gone, broken blocks of stone scattered everywhere. And there stood Inanna, all twelve feet of her, raging for all she was worth, casting bolt after bolt of her blue lightning at the building and with each strike, more stones would shatter and fall.

"Inanna," Johnny called out, but she didn't hear him at first. Just then, Johnny saw Cardac appear from within the remaining caves. *What's that he's carrying!* thought Johnny. *Oh no! It's a rifle.* Before Johnny could cry out, Cardac brought the weapon to his shoulder and fired. The sound of the shot echoed through the corridors with a deafening roar. Johnny whirled around to see if Inanna was hit, then back toward Cardac. "Cardac!" yelled Johnny. "No." But as he uttered the word, he saw the bolt of blue lightning strike Cardac full in the chest and as he watched, Cardac instantly shriveled up like a dandelion in a bonfire. Johnny whirled back to see if Inanna was injured. It would seem that Cardac had missed his shot.

"Inanna!" Johnny called out again. This time she saw him. "Stop. Please stop!" he called to her. As soon as Inanna saw Johnny, she shrunk back to normal human size and began walking toward him, picking her way over the rubble she and DuMuzzi had left behind. Johnny looked around to see if there were any more bodies lying around, besides Cardac.

"You have got to stop killing people. What is wrong with you!? You're like a lion among sheep, killing for the pleasure of it! Why can't you understand that you don't have the right to kill ANYTHING." Johnny realized he was yelling and stopped himself.

"He tried to hurt me," said Inanna simply. "Now be quiet and come with me." She took his hand and began to lead him toward the path to the beach. Her touch was hesitant and the look in her eye revealed fear of rejection.

"Alright," said Johnny. "Let's go."

"Before we leave, "said Inanna, "I have a small chore to do for you." Slowly she picked her way through the rubble to the body of Cardac. With one bolt of her blue lightning, she struck Cardac's rifle, which, to Johnny's shock, melted. Its wood stock burst into flame. Then she raised both palms toward his shriveled body and focused her light on his corpse. Johnny watched in stunned disbelief as Cardac's body came back to life. As Cardac struggled to sit up, Inanna returned to Johnny and said, "Please, come with me?"

Fearfully, he glanced toward the mountain. Both volcanoes were still smoking, *a little more than before,* he thought. *So, not only can she rip the life right out of a man with her bolts, she can also give the life back to him.* The words of another myth leaped into his mind, *"Don't be so fast to take away what you cannot give back."* Looking over his shoulder at the monastery, he saw Lucias and Lee Moy leaning over Cardac, helping him to his feet. Then he turned his eyes toward the path to the beach. "Where is your new friend?" Johnny asked, a bit breathless in his astonishment. "He seemed quite interested in tearing me limb from limb not too long ago."

"He is gone. I sent him home," said Inanna.

"Who was he?" asked Johnny. "Where did he come from?"

"A long time ago, he was to be my husband. Is name is DuMuzzi, like yours. He comes to me sometimes to try to see if I am ready to come home and marry him. I always say no. This time I have a reason and my reason made him angry."

"Where is home?" Johnny asked.

"I don't know how to tell you," she answered. "It's away from here, quite far actually. NO," she added with hostility. "This is my home. Arrata is my home. Once it was a great land, but the ocean keeps getting deeper or the land keeps sinking. I don't know which. Now all that remains is this island with its two volcanoes. Once it was known as Mount Mashu. Now it is just Arrata."

Mount Mashu of the twin peaks, thought Johnny. *So, that's the real name for those two mountains. One mountain actually, with two volcanic vents.* "How long has it been since they erupted?" asked Johnny.

"A long, long time," she answered. "In fact, the last time they erupted was before I came to Arrata, to Mount Mashu. I don't think they will erupt even now. They are only stirred by my passion for you." She stopped and turned to face him. The intensity in her eyes was actually startling, as was the intensity of the sudden arousal it stirred in him. They had reached the bottom of the path and were about to enter the forest leg of the journey to the beach.

He reached for her and pulling her closer, kissed her, full on the lips. She kissed him back, briefly and pulled away. "First," she said, "I have a secret to share with you. Follow me."

Inanna strode off through the forest, down the path to the beach. When she reached the sand, she waited for him to catch up, then hand in hand they strolled toward the west. "What's your secret?" asked Johnny.

"You will see," she smiled up at him.

The fiddler crab Johnny had playfully named Innuendo jumped out of a clump of sand and darted toward the water. When Inanna and Johnny stopped instead of giving chase, the crab stopped and watched them, waving one larger claw up and down, its mandibles working from side to side. "Odd little creatures. Aren't they?" Inanna remarked.

"I've seen that one so many times," said Johnny, "that I've come to think of him as a friend. I named him Innuendo because he implies the human situation to me. He fiercely demands his freedom and independence, flaunts his huge claw in facing hopeless challenges rather than admitting inferiority and upon being approached dives into the nearest hole, preferring peace and security to battle with such fruitless odds. He's food to countless birds and fish. If I manage to pick him up, he'll pinch me hard enough to draw blood. When I drop him again, he will flee to a safe distance and again challenge me. Better to challenge than admit cowardice. Better to hide than die. All he really wants in life is enough to eat and the chance to make babies, but his personality is complex. He feels compelled to make the challenge. He is an innuendo of the human condition, in my opinion."

"But he is only a crab," said Inanna. "He doesn't matter."

"He matters," said Johnny, "because he challenges me to think about him. He has the wisdom to teach me about myself and he is only a crab. If a crab can be so valuable to my mind and my growth, what about the value of other human beings? You must stop hurting people, Inanna."

"I only hurt people when they make me angry. They shouldn't make me angry."

"Do you get angry because they challenge you and you kill them before they have a chance to dive into their holes? Like the crab, all humans want is enough to eat and the chance to make babies. Humans are more complicated than crabs, but not profoundly so. They like to compete concerning the size and nature of their holes. The crabs do too."

Inanna began laughing. "You make it sound so simple. I suppose before long you'll be telling me I am like the crab also."

"If the shoe fits..." Johnny chuckled.

Inanna continued down the beach with Johnny in tow. She watched in amusement, as he laboriously climbed over the frozen lava flow. She then floated over it like a bird. They continued until they reached a shallow slough which apparently filled when the tide came in, carrying sea water to some low lying area farther inland. Inanna turned and followed the slough into the undergrowth with Johnny close behind.

"What's in here?" Johnny asked.

"You will see," she repeated with a smile.

After winding around through the forest, they came upon a small salt marsh, much longer than it was wide. Grayish marsh grass adorned its banks with blades tough enough to weave. Broad leaf succulents lined the banks where the salt water didn't reach. Beyond the broad leaf plants rose stately palms. There were oyster beds present, emerging above the high water mark in the deeper parts of the marsh. Tiny crabs scurried into their holes as Johnny's shadow passed over them. A large white crane or egret lifted off with a squawk as they rounded a bend in the main channel. The water was very shallow.

"It gets much deeper when the tide is in," said Inanna. "Just now it's perfect. We can wade to the pool without getting more than our feet and ankles wet."

As they made their way farther inland, Johnny noticed the foliage changing in its type and color. The marsh grass was still present but only in the lowest places where the salt water was able to feed it every time the tide came in. Finally, they came to a wide pool. At the far end was a low water fall where a spring-fed brook worked its way down the mountain side finding its entry to the sea through this pond and finally down through the slough Johnny had just traversed. There was a sandy bank at the north side of the pond. Inanna made her way to it signaling him to follow and once there, took a seat in the sand.

"Isn't this a beautiful place?" she asked him.

"It feels almost magical," he answered, taking a seat in the sand beside her.

"It is magic, in a way," she said. "The water from Mount Mashu has very special qualities. One can drink it if he wishes. Here, where it mixes with the water from the sea, it is neither fresh nor salty, but a mixture."

"Brackish, we call it," said Johnny.

"That's the word. Yes. This is the secret, I promised to share with you. In this pool, where the special water from Mount Mashu mixes with water from the sea lives a plant that enhances youth and long life. The ancients called it the Tree of Everlasting Life, but of course we know that nothing lives forever, not even the gods."

"Are you telling me that this is the Garden of Eden?" asked Johnny.

"Oh. No," she answered. "That was between the four rivers, quite far from here, actually. I had some transplanted in my own domain so that I could enjoy it if I wished. And so that I could offer it to special humans who particularly pleased me. Think of it as a gift of the gods." With that, she stood up, dropped her sarong in the sand and dived naked into the water, disappearing from view. A moment later she reappeared on the surface and swam back to him with something green in one hand.

I wish she would quit doing that, he thought to himself of her nakedness. *It's very disconcerting. I'm a young man, for heaven's sake.* Before he could say anything, she was seated beside him again in the sand, still naked. She held leaves from some underwater plant in her hand, and was offering them to him. He took them and looked at her quizzically.

"Eat them," she said with a smile.

"What will it do to me?" he asked hesitantly.

"It will make you live for a very long time," she answered. "It will slow your aging. If you eat this, you will live as long as me."

"I'd like to think about it," said Johnny. "I'm not so sure I want to live longer than my allotted life span."

"But the lives of humans are so short," she insisted. "If you eat this you could live almost as long as me."

Is this another temptation - like her nudity? Johnny wondered. *What must I trade for it? What if I do eat it and live longer. What does she want from me?*

"You could live thousands of years," she said. "Wouldn't you want that?"

"I need to think about it," repeated Johnny. "I don't know if I want to live that long. Let's go. Please get dressed." *How can I tell this fabulous woman to get dressed? Well, first of all, she's not really a woman. Maybe I should put my vows first. I am supposed to be celibate - a monk, a brother of the Fraternity. I need to rise above this. Can I? A long life is not a bad thing. To have a beautiful woman is also not a bad thing. But she's not a woman, at least not like any I've known.* "If you want to," he added with a smile, putting the rich bundle of leaves in his pocket.

Chapter 21: Flight

The palace grounds were very different to Johnny. It had been a day of constant amazement. The experiences of his sudden release from his cell inside the mountain, the slaying and resuscitation of Cardac had left him in a state comparable to shock. He was stunned, suspending disbelief; unsure that he should rely on his own senses to verify the reality of what he had himself witnessed that day. But the surprises were not over.

Inanna's palace grounds were a hubbub of confusion. When he emerged from the forest hand in hand with the goddess, the first thing he saw was the ADRIANNA riding at Anchor just beyond the reef. She was white, trimmed in a shade of blue slightly darker than that of the sea on a clear day. Her three smokestacks were not emitting any sign of activity from the engines. Her decks were clear of humans but littered with luggage and lounge debris - overturned deck chairs, life jackets, coils of rope and one life boat resting belly up just abaft of the port beam. His survey of her length was short lived because he was distracted by the sounds of many voices from the direction of the palace, and none of the voices were saying, "Heena."

She captured the ship, was his first horrified thought. *But they don't seem to be worshiping her,* was his second. He scanned the area looking for Chip and Joyce, the Smithsons, Big Al and his wife. The people were gathered in clusters. The crew was easily identifiable by their uniforms. They were standing around mostly on the south side of the complex of buildings, some looking toward the forest as though contemplating escape. Others were studying the well-tended fields.

Inanna's Polynesians, most of them naked to the waist, were gathered on the porch to the ballroom as though ready at a moment's notice to flee inside. Then he noticed the passengers scattered all over the grounds in small groups, trying not to tread on the cultivated areas. Johnny stopped in horror as Inanna dropped his hand and morphed to her full twelve feet.

The islanders on and around the porch to the ballroom, fell to their knees and began chanting, "Heena. Heena." The crowd from the ship all turned, first to stare at the chanting Polynesians, then followed the eyes of the worshipers to the glowing goddess who had just emerged from the forest. "Mawkee Mawkee," some of them began and the chant became "Heena, Heena, Mawkee Mawkee. Heena Heena, Mawkee Mawkee." Johnny stepped back toward the path to the beach but paused to watch the scene unfold. The people from the ship had stopped talking with each other. All of them watched wide eyed and open mouthed in disbelief as Inanna, the Love goddess of Shinar, daughter of Nanna and Ningal, strolled toward her palace of Arrata soaking up the praises of her worshipers while Mount Mashu smoldered and rumbled in the distance.

When Inanna had reached about half way to the palace entrance, Johnny began following her through the morass of human cargo from the ADRIANNA. Although he was in their midst, none saw him because every eye, including Johnny's was on the beautiful Moon goddess, Heena, Inanna as she strolled toward her palace. When she reached the first of the steps to the porch the music began. The words of the ancient hymn echoed over the grounds, otherwise totally silent.

A Flame burns for Inanna.
May she bless those who love her with fertility.
With Fertility may she bless those who love her.
Oh Queen of all power.
Oh Queen of bright burning light,
Triumphant woman clothed in brilliance,
Beloved in heaven and earth.
Chosen to wear the grand adornments
Crowned with goodness, rightfully.
In your hands are the seven fixed powers.
The Fundamental Forces are in your grasp.
Guardian of the cosmos, the universe.
You bind the elements with your hands.
Press the powers to your breast.
You kill the evil, which poisons the land,

The Storm god you subdue.
You cause bread to spring from the earth.
You are Inanna, supreme over heaven and earth.

The clear tones and sweet voice of the singer stopped and in a moment was replaced by the chant of the islanders, until Inanna raised her hands for silence. *Oh my God*, thought Johnny. *What's going to happen now?*

Almost in answer to his question a huge puff of smoke arose from the western volcano followed a few seconds later by a resounding
<< *boom* >>
of the explosion. Johnny could feel the accompanying vibration of the earth under his feet and waited in horror to see what was going to happen next. What did happen both relaxed and added to his fears.

The islanders stopped chanting. After a few seconds of silence, he heard Inanna's voice as though from a public address system turned up to its full volume. She was now on the top step of the porch facing the crowd and the sea. He had never seen her glow so brightly. Her sarong shimmered in brilliant blue. The flower from her hair was lying on the porch and her hair blew freely with the breeze off the ocean. Her height seemed to increase so that she barely fit under the roof of the porch. "I am Inanna," she announced in a tone of authority.

"And you are my chosen people," she continued. "I have selected you from all the peoples of the Earth to enter my domain and worship me. I will be your god and you will be my people."

"Like hell I will," came an angry retort from the crowd. A woman in her sixties stepped forward with a tall, gray haired man trying to hold her back by the arm. "I don't know what the hell you are, but you ain't no goddamned god, I can tell you that..."

Before the woman could continue, she found herself on her knees in the dirt. The half-strangled words, "Heena, Heena," were coming from her lips. Her husband who was trying to help her back to her feet was Inanna's next victim. He too fell to his knees and began the chant.

Without a second thought, Johnny started toward the porch at a run, calling out, "Inanna. Inanna! Stop! What are you doing? Are you going to kill them all?" Just then, he noticed Chip and Joyce standing in front of their small room with the rest of their party. The alarmed look on their faces stopped him. But, much to his surprise, Inanna had also stopped her attack on Mrs. Hodges and was staring at him in anger. All fell silent again expecting to see this DeMuzzi fried on the spot. Instead, she shocked everyone by turning on her heel and disappearing inside the ballroom.

It was now that Johnny saw the monks who had been slain by Inanna, then raised from the dead. They were congregated near the ship's crew on the south side of the compound. The air was once again filled with voices. The islanders had begun their chanting, this time with "Mawkee Mawkee, Mawkee Mawkee." The ship's passengers, it seemed all began talking at once and the crew had turned to each other discussing something earnestly at low tones. Only the monks remained silent. Johnny headed in their direction with Chip trying to intercept him.

The rumbling of the mountain in the background, as desperately urgent a danger as any other currently presenting itself, was drowned out of Johnny's attention by his relief at seeing his brothers alive. His first thought was to speak with them, to reassure himself that they were all right, but Chip got to him first.

"I need to talk to you," said Chip breathlessly. "The captain of the ship is at our quarters. Come," and taking Johnny by the arm, half dragging him, he set off back toward the compound. "You have no idea what's been going on here. Where the hell have you been? You wouldn't believe it," he continued without waiting for an answer from Johnny. "She fried those monks. We've seen her do stuff like that before but this time, she brought them back to life. I've never seen anything like it. She's far more powerful than we ever imagined. And she acts confused. We haven't seen that before either."

"How do you mean, 'confused?'" asked Johnny.

"Well, she tried to force them to worship her. They refused. She fried them with that blue lightning bolt she uses. Then she sat down on the top step over there and sobbed like a child. If I didn't know any better, I'd think she felt guilty about it. Then she went over to them. They were lying on the ground like fallen trees- dead wood - and she revived them. It was incredible. We all saw it."

"She actually killed them then brought them back to life?" Amazing," said Johnny in disbelief. *Chip must be losing it,* he thought. *But then I saw her do the same thing with Cardac. What is she?* "How are the people from that ship taking their new captivity?" he finished.

"Their captain and some of the officers are with us. Inanna doesn't know it but they left some crew aboard to improvise repairs to the engines so they can run without their computers. If Inanna finds out there'll be hell to pay but if they get it running, maybe she can be distracted enough that we can all get away. Maybe when she's playing with you down on the beach or something like that."

Johnny's look of displeasure silenced Chip as they neared the rest of Chip's party. Captain Dudely had an extra carton of Camels in the sea bag he brought with him from the ship. "Damned glad I brought 'em, too," Johnny heard him remark as he and Chip arrived. "No telling how long we're going to be here."

After the introductions, Johnny excused himself and headed for the ballroom to find Inanna. The room was empty. The throne of Lapis Lazuli glowed faintly in the dim light. All else was silent. The natives stopped chanting when he disappeared into the building. In the silence, he thought he could hear voices coming from the chambers behind the ballroom. He followed the sounds and paused in the corridor when he could clearly hear Inanna's voice.

I wonder if she knows about the men who stayed on the ship to fix the engines. Johnny wondered to himself. *She probably doesn't. But how could they have hidden that from her. She seems to - just know things like that.*

"It seems that people aren't anything like they used to be," he could hear Inanna saying to someone. "There were more than a thousand people on that boat and they act like I'm a science fiction plot or something. Don't they believe in the gods any more?"

"Of course they do, Darling," it was Belili's voice. "They just don't believe in our kind of god anymore. It's why the others left. The Lulus are too hard to control. It's better that we live among our own kind. I think you're beginning to see this finally."

"I can subdue them, yet," retorted Inanna.

"Why did you restore the monks?" asked Belili. "Are you beginning to feel some sort of misplaced fondness for your food?" The sarcasm was evident.

"DeMuzzi has taught me new meaning for an old word," Inanna stated simply. "It's not really a new meaning, but because of him I have a new understanding of it. It troubles me."

"And the word is?" Belili's impatience came through clearly in her voice.

"It's 'compassion.'"

"Inanna feels compassion?" snarled Belili. "There is a new thing under the sun. Could it be that you are finally growing up? You certainly have taken a long time to sow your wild oats. What brings you to this new understanding of a word you never before believed in?"

"It doesn't matter," snapped Inanna. "I will subdue these people or kill them. It makes no difference. I will have their energy either way. Then I will be able to leave this island and take power from the rest of this planet's peoples."

"So much for compassion," muttered Belili. "Are you discovering some inner turmoil, a conflict of some sort? If you kill them, you won't be able to renew their energy and draw on it again. A onetime harvest will leave you hungry. If you can subdue them without killing them you can draw on their energy again in the future. Think about it."

"You're right of course," said Inanna. "But I don't think I can subdue this group without killing them and killing has become distasteful to me."

"Now there's a thought," chortled Belili. "Killing Lulus has become distasteful? Why? They are only Lulus. They serve no other purpose than to serve us. Isn't that what you have always said?"

"I will kill them only if I have to," was the last thing Johnny heard Inanna say before he withdrew. The rumbling of the volcano was making itself clearer moment by moment. He was afraid the building would collapse.

Should I warn Inanna and Belili? They should leave too. They could be killed if this building caves in. Can they be killed?

Outside he was as surprised about what he found, as he had been when he and Inanna returned to the compound from the beach. The lifeboats that were lined up on the beach and tied to the pier were full of people and strung out across the ocean between Inanna's grounds and the ship. The brothers from the monastery had appeared with Lucias, Lee Moy and Cardac among them, looking very tense. Even the islanders were glancing apprehensively at the volcanoes. Johnny followed their looks and discovered that the mountains had both swelled visibly. Their once narrow peaks were now rounded. Both peaks were emitting large volumes of smoke and the western peak revealed a clear lava flow down the north bank.

Lucias and Lee Moy tried to approach him, but Johnny was earnestly looking for Captain Dudely, Chip and the others. Finally, he found them in one of the lifeboats, almost too distant to be recognizable. Finally, Lucias got to him by the pier.

The monks, who had been revived, now referring to themselves humorously as "born again" caught up with Lucias and the others at about the same time. The confusion was overwhelming with the newly arrived Essenes trying to understand what happened and what was happening. "Where is Inanna?" asked Lucias.

"Who are all these people?" Cardac wanted to know.

"The barrier dropped," Lee Moy managed to insert, "and we rushed over here to see if we could help..."

"...As well as to escape that crazy volcano," Cardac added. "But it looks worse now than it did before. I think it's going to blow."

The first of the lifeboats had reached the ship, were unloaded and were heading back for another load of people. "Even the islanders are lining up for a ride to the ship," Johnny remarked in surprise.

"Why is that a surprise?" asked Lucias. "We had no idea there were so many people over here."

"They always seemed to worship her willingly," Johnny answered. "Now they seem as eager to leave as the rest of us."

"It would seem that they know about volcanoes," answered Lee Moy.

Just then, Johnny noticed Tarek among the newly arrived brothers. "Let's get on one of those boats," he suggested to him. "We'll be ship mates once more."

"What about Inanna?" asked one of the ship's crew who had just walked up. It was Fleeson, who had remained ashore to oversee the loading of passengers into the lifeboats. If she comes out of that building and catches us trying to leave, there could be hell to pay."

"If she comes out before we get away, I'll stop her," said Johnny. With that he left the group by the pier and began walking toward the ballroom entrance. *The silence is amazing,* he thought to himself. *With the throngs of people moving around, there's hardly a sound. I guess everyone's afraid Inanna will hear and come out and stop them. That's a valid fear.* He was still close enough to the pier that he could easily see the twin peaks. Suddenly he saw an enormous cloud of black smoke interspersed with fire erupting from the eastern peak, the one closest to the monastery. Several seconds later he could feel the ground underneath his feet vibrating radically and very shortly after that, he heard the explosion. It was deafening.

If they don't hurry they may not get off the island in time, he thought worriedly glancing over his shoulder. There were still enough people to fill a dozen, or more lifeboats. Most of the boats on their first trip had unloaded at the ship and were headed back with several heading toward the ship for their second trip. Johnny stopped when he arrived at the door to the ballroom. Then he went inside, climbed the dais and seated himself on the throne of Lapis Lazuli, with his back toward where he knew Inanna would appear. The earth was still rumbling. *After shocks,* the words inserted themselves on his consciousness. *Or is it really afterthoughts of this once great land Inanna described to me.*

He could feel the power of the Lapis Lazuli flowing into him as never before. He relaxed into the sensation with the ease of a habitual meditator. He didn't know how long he had been sitting there when he heard Inanna's voice behind him.

"I told you not to sit in my throne," she said softly. "Why are you there?"

"Because when I sit here," replied Johnny, "I can feel your energy. It makes me think you are close to me. I'm in love with you Inanna. Did you know?" He still faced the door to the ballroom. He did not turn to look at her.

"You are food to me, Profligate. You are a Lulu like the others. Why shouldn't I kill you where you sit?"

Johnny was not afraid of her. She had tried to kill him several times before and failed. Why would she succeed now. "Because you are also in love, in your own way. Is it not true?" *If I can just keep her inside here with me for another hour, everyone should have made it to the ship by then. I have to keep her inside so she won't see them escaping.*

She circled the throne to face him. She was human sized this time, instead of the twelve foot tall goddess, she represented herself to be to the others. "Don't be ridiculous, Profligate. How could a goddess fall in love with a Lulu, a mere human? What kind of weaknesses do you think my kind has?" With that, she came closer and sat in his lap on the throne, curling up close to him, snuggling her nose into his throat.

He wrapped his arms around her and held her warmth against him. With his face in her long flowing hair he whispered, "I don't know, my lovely goddess. Maybe it's because I am like the crab on the beach with one claw larger than the other, challenging you to think. Maybe it's because I don't fear you enough to not challenge your power?" He kissed her just under the ear, lingering to experience the full sensation. Maybe it's because you can sense the passion I feel for you? Why are you in love with me, my goddess?"

"I think it's the way we met, that first time in the water. I've wanted you ever since. But you are so maddening - a monk. How could a monk fall in love? Oh yes, you are a Profligate. I almost forgo...." He silenced her with a kiss.

"You shouldn't interrupt me like that, Profligate. I may forget you are a mortal. I don't think you could survive making love to me."

"I don't know if I can survive not making love to you, Inanna," he replied.

She uncurled from his lap and stepped off the throne back to the dais. "If you don't hurry, you will miss the last boat back to the ship. They have forgotten about you," she told him.

"You knew," he said weakly.

"Of course I knew," she answered. "I am a goddess. I can be misled. I can be fooled for a short time, but if I reach for the knowledge, I always find it ... John." She uttered the last word, his real name with mock contempt. "So run for your hole, little crab. Make babies." With that, she turned her back and began walking toward the interior corridors, audibly sobbing. "I just may change my mind and kill all of them anyway, so you better hurry and leave."

"B-b-but, what will happen to you if the mountain explodes?

Shouldn't you come too?"

She was gone.

From the ballroom porch Johnny could see the last of the boats approaching the ship. He sprinted for the beach to find one last boat loading its last two passengers. He knew neither of them. There were two seamen from the ADRIANNA, who frantically rowed the boat toward the breach in the reef. None of the passengers spoke. He could see in the distance that two of the ship's three stacks were smoking. They got the engines running, he thought with relief. He looked back at the mountains in the dying light of the late afternoon. Fortunately the wind was from the west so the smoke from the erupting eastern peak and its prolific lava flow was carried to sea and away from them. Otherwise, we'd be choking on the ash. *We need to get out of here as quickly as possible.*

In the gathering distance, he could still see the entrance to Inanna's ballroom. Belili was standing under its roof watching, as the last boat, this one containing Johnny Lewis, reached the ADRIANNA. He assumed it was Belili by the black clothing and the light, gray hair. As he watched, Inanna appeared behind her, glowing blue in the dim light, then they both disappeared inside.

Chapter 22: Metamorphosis

The taffrail of the ADRIANNA was not as elaborately finished as Johnny thought it would be on a luxury liner. He stood on the top deck in the extreme stern of the ship watching the ship's wake and Arrata shrinking in the distance. *Why is she letting us slip away like this? There hasn't been a peep out of her. Oh. I'm going to miss her.*

The ship was limping toward Rapanui on one engine. The taffrail was a simple, white painted, metal railing standing between Johnny and the roiling wake far below. Over the sound of the engine, he could still hear the rumbling of the twin peaks of Mount Mashu. The smoke from the volcanoes was thicker than ever and the lava flow was heaviest on the eastern side of the island. *The monastery's probably been completely consumed by now,* he thought. *We couldn't go back even if we wanted to.*

He studied the smoke rising off of the mountain. *I wonder if she's watching. I'm sure she can see us.* Something tapped him on the shoulder and he startled violently. Turning, he saw it was Chip. "Sorry about that. I didn't mean to surprise you. I hunted all over for you," he said. "Come on down to the main dining room. They're throwing a party. They got the oven going and what food is still good, they say has to be eaten or tossed by the time we get to Easter Island."

Johnny turned back to watch the smoke from the Volcanoes. "I can't believe she's letting us go so easily," he said to Chip.

"Maybe she knows something about that mountain that she didn't tell us," he replied. "I'm surprised she didn't come with us. Look at how both peaks are swelled. It could blow at any moment. I'm glad we're out of there."

"What will she do if it blows?" wondered Johnny half under his breath. "She could be killed. I'd hate for that to happen."

"There are worse things to worry about," said Chip. "For example, if either peak blows, the other one will probably explode too. If the explosion is a violent one, and it very well may be, we're only about two or three miles away. Even a ship the size of this one could be swamped by the tidal wave that follows."

Johnny was still watching the smoke. "Does it appear to you that the sky is bluer above the island - above the smoke I mean?"

"It's your imagination," said Chip. "The sun's going down. It's getting dark. It's normal for the eastern sky to look a little darker this time of day." He paused, watching Johnny. Then he said softly, "She's not up there, my friend. She's not there."

Johnny didn't answer. He was lost in his own thoughts, wondering, *What happened on this island? Who is Inanna? Who is Belili? I mean, really. What power did she wield and why did the fraternity find her such a threat way out here on this remote island in the South Pacific? Why did they send Hjet, the fence, and as Hjet, what did I do?* Now as he watched the southeastern horizon grow darker in the glow of twilight he thought he could see her eyes watching him, watching the ship from high in the sky, but there was no bronze glow. *Chip's right. It's my imagination.* He raised his right hand to his throat to feel for the obelisk. *Yes, it's still there. At least this is real.*

Suddenly he startled again at the sound of the clearing of someone's throat. He turned sharply and was doubly startled to see an old woman completely dressed in black lace. She wore a black lace shawl over her head, which didn't quite conceal her snowy white hair. Although the shadows were growing deeper with the failing of light, he could see the brilliance of her laughing blue eyes and feel the warmth of the smile which she wore. "Belili," he said in surprise. "I thought we left you on the island with Inanna. I'm glad you're safe with us."

"You're more startled and fearful than glad," Belili chuckled. "You're worried that Inanna is with me and at the same time you are afraid that she is not." The old woman laughed. "You saw her watching us and choose to think it was your imagination. You humans amuse us. You have the power of vision and creation yet you refuse to believe in it and call it imagination. Someday your race will learn how to use this ability."

"So it really is her? She really is watching us? I can feel her."

"Of course. She finally understands and has made some hard decisions. She watches over your voyage to safety."

"What about the volcanoes? How will she survive it? Where will she go?" worried Johnny.

"Inanna is finally no longer a child," said Belili in a tone which told Johnny she meant far more than what she had just said. "She is in no danger, and she has made some remarkable decisions. I am here to ask you to return the obelisk of Lapis Lazuli I gave you. You will no longer need it. I trust that it has served you well?"

"I thought I'd like to keep it for a souvenir," Johnny replied reluctantly.

"Some souvenir," muttered Belili, "a piece of the very throne of Inanna. "Do you know who Inanna is? I think not. Please give it to me."

With a deep sigh, Johnny reached up to his throat and lifted the neckpiece over his head. "Thank you Belili." He handed it to her saying, "You were a friend unasked for in a strange land. Thank you."

"Only by accident," chortled the old woman. "Only by accident." She tucked the obelisk into a pocket inside her shawl and said, "And now may the blessings of Anu, Enlil and EA be with you always as will the love of Inanna." With that Belili morphed into the owl image that Johnny had seen before and hopped onto the taffrail. With a squawk she flew off into the night.

He watched until the shadow of the bird vanished into the darkness. Even after he could no longer see it, he stared into the night trying to see the twin peaks. The moon began to rise and as it did the sight took Johnny's breath for a moment. The twin peaks were clearly visible in the distance, only partly obscured by the smoke of the volcanoes. In the moon's light he could see their silhouette and for the first time realized that they perfectly described the shape of a new moon. "Heena," he gasped almost involuntarily. He watched for a few more minutes until the moon itself passed behind a cloud and the image of the twin peaks disappeared.

Johnny was almost to the entrance to the main dining room on the upper deck when it happened. At first, he didn't understand what had caused it. He thought it was lightning and paused only a few seconds to glance at the sky thinking, *certainly was a strange colored flash for lightning.* He didn't put it together until there was a second flash a few seconds later. He realized at the same time as he saw a crewmember headed down from the wheelhouse at top speed. *My God! The mountains have exploded! Now what's going to happen? We couldn't be over five miles away.*

Several more crewmembers were headed aft at top speed shouting at each other... something about a sea anchor. Johnny turned into the entrance to the dining salon and stopped with a gasp. Then he began to back up again toward the port rail. Inside the salon, he could see Chip, Joyce and the others watching him and laughing. He stopped backing and stared at the woman in front of him. They had almost collided.

"Inanna? Is that you? I thought you were on the island?"

The woman was wearing cut-off jeans and a print tee shirt sporting a picture of Chris Smither and his blue guitar. Except for a much shorter hairstyle, she looked exactly like the goddess. She too had stopped short when she saw Johnny's reaction and after a moment of surprise, started laughing. "Wow. I've seen guys look before, but your reaction gets an Oscar. Who are you anyway?" she wanted to know, laughing. "I'm Anna from Skokie - not who you think. I know they said I look like her but I'm just a schoolteacher. Honest. I teach fourth grade."

Just then, several crewmembers burst through the doorway out of breath. One of them had a bullhorn and announced, "May I have your attention please."

All conversation in the dining salon quieted. "Both Volcanoes have just exploded. We are expecting a substantial tidal wave at any moment. Please gather at the stern of the cabin and lie down on the deck. The crew is placing sea anchors to hold the stern down in case the wave is taller than we are. Please remain calm. This danger will pass in a few minutes." With that, the crewmember with the bullhorn left and the other remained to help the passengers get ready for the wave.

Johnny was still face to face with Anna. "Let's hang onto something, shall we?" he said to her.

"I'm with you brother," she replied. "How about this thing?" she said indicating an upright steel pole evidently supporting the ceiling of the cabin.

"Looks good to me," he replied. "We better do it quick." With that, they embraced with the pole between them. Some of the other passengers were doing the same, hanging onto the ceiling supports, door jams and other fixtures at the sides of the room. Many had lain down on the deck as instructed by the crew, with their feet planted as firmly as possible toward the bow of the ship.

She feels like Inanna, Johnny thought quietly. *She smells like Inanna, too, like flowers.* "Are you sure you're not a goddess?" He said to her as matter-of-factly as he could muster.

"I told you I'm Anna from Skokie and I teach fourth grade. It's true, really. I am only a woman, not a god, but thank you for thinking that."

The tidal wave didn't seem all that violent, at first. The stern of the ship gradually rose till the deck was at an angle of almost fifteen degrees. Then the wave broke over the ship. It had not towered over the ship, but broke at almost the same height as the top level. Ocean water came racing down the exterior decks from the stern. Some washed into the dining salon until, briefly, it was almost waist deep, then receded leaving everyone soaked to the skin. There were a few bruises and scrapes, but other than that, everyone came through it unharmed.

Concerned for the island, Johnny headed for the exit to the dining area and once outside, turned toward the stern to try to see if anything of the island was still there. "Hey wait for me!" he heard Anna call out behind him. He did wait "You don't think I'm going to turn loose of a man who thinks I'm a goddess do you?" she laughed once she caught up to him. Together they made their way back to the taffrail.

Both of them strained their eyes into the southeast trying to see anything other than the sea. Only water reflecting the moon's light was visible. There was no sign of the island. "That we can't see it doesn't mean it's not there," he said. "It could be that we're just out of sight by now."

"I think we're not that far away. Those mountains should be visible if there's anything left of them," she said with some distraction. "Ya' know, I'm hungry. I have some salad," she said pulling a plastic bowl out of a voluminous purse. "But I don't have any greens. The lettuce and stuff was all spoiled 'cause the boat lost its refrigerators when the power went down. But I have a couple of tomatoes, some turnips and green onions. Want some?"

Who is this woman offering me live food, he thought. "Sure. I'll share. Thanks. I might even have some greens of my own here in my pocket. *Thanks to Inanna,* he added in his mind. *This couldn't be what she said it was. It's a myth.*

Reaching into his pocket he pulled out the leafy green water plants, he had placed there that afternoon. "Ooo that looks good," said Anna. "Sort of like Romaine but darker. What's it called?"

"It's a gift of the gods," he replied with a smile.

"Thanks for sharing, profligate." she smiled up at him.

About the Author

Robert G. Makin found his life paths growing up on Laurel Mountain. There he became friends with Elves and Flying Squirrels, did spelunking at Wild Cat Rocks and listened at the feet of his grandfathers to the stories of the Railroad, the Steel Mills and the Old Country. Bits and pieces of Old German and ancient Scottish Gaelic still creep into his conversation from those days gone by. A degree in Fanciful Literature from Indiana University of Pennsylvania fueled his drive to learn more about Elven History and their social structure. He sought fulfillment at Lancaster Theological Seminary of the United Church of Christ where he discovered Essenism, some of the precursors of Biblical History and the stories told to Abraham as Abraham sat at the feet of his grandfathers. They were stories of Nanna, Ningur, Inanna, Ya and Enlil, at the birth of Human Kind. Makin found that there is no history quite like oral history, nor quite as honest. Some truths have been politically incorrect for millennia and forbidden from written histories. Some truths have been corrected and updated to fit what's popular. Makin has found them hidden in Social Artifacts and takes pleasure in their unraveling and revelation.

Makin earned his bread for many years by selling opinions. Today he spends his time, sharing his love for and the history of St. Augustine, Florida with visitors from all over the world who come to hear his tales. In StrathNaver Legends, Makin expresses the exuberant mysticism of the unknown, the what-if's, the maybe's and the things that very well may have been, like friendships with Flying Squirrels and Elves.

Other Books by
Robert G. Makin

Available at Amazon, Barnes & Noble and other book sellers

Strathnaver Legends

The heart of a quiet, peaceful village, ripped open by the remorseless vitriol of a sadistic predator drives kith and kin on a hunt for the hunter. Falling in with unknown races and cultures, they are forced to overcome prejudice and distrust in their drive for a common interest, to live in freedom from terror.

Aleister Through The Looking Glass

This is a children's book written for children over the age of 30. Starving-Writer Aleister Smiley takes a job returning unread manuscripts and depositing reading fees. He shortly finds himself whisked into Never Ever Land where he can Never Ever be published. Provinces of Never Ever Land parody the plight of the writer in this new age of formula loving editors, agents and publishers.

Return to Masada

The historic Battle of Masada has become a symbol of freedom, hope and courage to die, if necessary, for one's principles. Makin delivers a new version of this famous "David and Goliath" struggle of the Jewish people against the Roman Army.